# THE TRIGGER EPISODE

# THE TRIGGER EPISODE

## TOM STRAW

CARROLL & GRAF PUBLISHERS
NEW YORK

THE TRIGGER EPISODE

Carroll & Graf Publishers
An Imprint of Avalon Publishing Group Inc.
245 West 17th Street
11th Floor
New York, NY 10011

AVALON
publishing group incorporated

First Carroll & Graf edition 2007

ISBN-13: 978-0-78671-878-8
ISBN-10: 0-7867-1878-1

9 8 7 6 5 4 3 2 1

Interior Design by Maria Fernandez

Printed in the United States of America
Distributed by Publishers Group West

For Jennifer
It's such a lovely ride.

# ACKNOWLEDGMENTS

My loving and supportive family: Kelly, Andrew, Chris, and Parker; Betty Ann and Andrew Dzelzitis; and my mother, Peggy Straw, who always believed

Sloan Harris, my agent, respected and admired on a daily basis

Will Balliett, my publisher and editor, with whom I made a friend and a book

Nancy Josephson for her early belief

David Hume Kennerly for his generous time, anecdotes, and technical assistance

Mitch Semel for the introduction to Mr. Kennerly

Rick Richter for his kindness and advice

Ken Levine for opening the door to TV writing

Bill Cosby for making me glad I stayed in

Early readers Bruce Marr, John and Miranda Dunne Parry, Clyde Phillips, Tom Reeder, Bob Tzudiker and Noni White, and Gene Wilder

Walter & Donald for the swell tunes

And finally… All the wonderful libraries which provided carrels and quiet corners for a writer on the go: The British Library, London; The Boston Public Library, Copley Square; The Rose Reading Room of the New York Public Library; The New York Public Library for the Performing Arts; The New York Society Library; The James Blackstone Memorial Library, Branford; The Westport Public Library; The Wilton Public Library; and The Mark Twain Public Library, Redding

*Something ineradicable still remained, as the unfrocked priest or the repentant murderer, even though unfrocked at the heart and reformed at the heart carries forever about him like a catalyst the indelible effluvium of the old condition.*

—William Faulkner

*You can straighten a worm, but the crook is in him and only waiting.*

—Mark Twain

# THE TRIGGER EPISODE

# CHAPTER ONE

I was in the shrubs outside a gated street in Toluca Lake pretending to hang a Med-fly trap from a Japanese maple. Being a celebrity shooter is a lot like being homeless. You have to look like you belong or you attract attention, which often means a police escort. Amateurs and losers stand around like camera-slung vultures. I scrawled non-sense numbers on my clipboard and studied my homemade trap as if the field pack on my shoulder contained specimens instead of a Nikon. As if I were the pest inspector instead of the pest. As if I weren't waiting for my Get.

I call it my Get, but it's the shot everybody was gunning for after the infamous press conference when Tim Dash threw his microphone at the reporter who dared to ask about the affair. Two schools: One that says the star was protective of her because she's pregnant; the other says he was pissed because his movie was supposed to edge out the new Tom Cruise but barely struggled into second place. Like I cared. I just wanted the score. Nobody else had been able to grab a picture of the happy couple together. I was going to capture them in the same frame and put myself back on the covers.

Just past noon the Valley Response rent-a-cop slowed as he passed. Worry started to chip at me that my tipster fucked up and I'd blown a hundred bucks I couldn't afford to crap away on bogus information. Maybe Top Ten Tim and his leading lady weren't going to hunker down at the screenwriter's house after all.

My cell phone vibrated. I took a half-step into the brush and scoped the caller ID as if I didn't know. As if he expected me to answer. As if I wouldn't pay up if I had it.

The sounds of the Universal tour rolled down the hill about a half mile away. Pyrotechnic blasts. Jurassic roars. The usual. I tried to calm myself with the elegance of my setup. I liked the idea of the gate shot. Gate unmanned, so it's a keypad. The mark has to pull up, stop, and punch the code. Even if he has a clicker, there's gate swing. I had spent the morning clocking entries. In the time it took to execute the fastest opening I could practically set up portable light stands and reflectors. But all I needed was my two-shot. One Get to clear the boards. I could answer my phone again without feeling the nest of bees in my gut. Maybe stop looking over my shoulder. I could go back to my house for the first time in a week.

Motor. I thrust my hand in my bag and fisted the Nikon. A pool maintenance truck rolled up. I acted busy. Motorbikes ying-yinged in the near distance. The pool pickup idled. No keypad, no call. The kid driver popped the hood to look at his engine. Shit. I started calculating that wrinkle, Plan B-ing the situation in a hurry, my heart nudging my chest.

Tires took the corner a little fast. A blue Beemer SUV on a mission. The X5 pulled up behind the pool guy. Tim Dash at the wheel, Kendra Lee Shearing, his married, pregnant costar riding shotgun. I hadn't cleared my camera from my bag, but I heard Tim call, "Duck!" as he palmed her head down out of sight. The star kicked it in reverse, and that's when I saw the pool kid with his camera. A pro-model Canon.

Tim Dash slammed the brakes as a custom-tricked Honda pulled up to box him from behind. Two shooters got out and flanked the X5.

One of them, the driver, was lanky and sleepy-eyed, with a black ponytail down to his belt and a Musketeers goatee. "Shit," I said. It was the goddam Canuck.

I read the same expletive on Tim Dash's lips. He threw the BMW in gear, jacked the wheel, and climbed the driveway curb onto the grass median, coming right at me, chewing up sod. I stepped from the bushes to get out of his way, and when he saw me, he fuck-swore and said my name. He slammed it in reverse again and fishtailed into the street. He tried to U-turn, but two motorbikes zipped up to block him.

Then Tim Dash, who had taken the Secret Service driving course when he played the first lady's bodyguard in *Lay Down This Life*, sped up the street, streaking twin clouds of blue tire smoke—in reverse. The Canuck ran back to his car, pointing and hollering to the others. Engines thundered off up the block; I stood there, feeling like my pocket was just picked.

I could draw the schematic of the hunt. The motorbikes were nimble and would overtake him before he made the freeway. They'd cut him off and zigzag to slow him until the Honda and the pickup could catch up, and he'd get Lohanned at a stop light. If he could get out of the winding Toluca Lake residential streets, Dash might stand a chance.

Valley Spring Lane would be his only hope for wide-open speed, and as that came to me I remembered how I had self-accessed the celebrity tournament at Lakeside last year by sneaking in the greenskeeper's gate not far from where I stood. I started toward it at a walk, and when I spotted my old hideout, the drainage ditch, I quickened to a jog. The narrow concrete ditch formed a bowl-shaped path that ran between eucalyptus trees and the golf course fence and connected to the next block, Valley Spring.

The blast of car horns broke me into an all-out sprint. Engines roared, coming fast. Fifty yards to go. Maybe too late. I poured it on. Quads burning. Almost there. Tires squealed. I broke through overgrowth blocking the end of the spillway and scared an old lady walking her toy poodle. No breath for a "sorry." The X5 was coming. And fast. I made the curb, a blink from my op. Too much motion. The SUV was speeding; I was shaking. I went back to 'Nam, how I shot those napalm runs so many years ago. Sucked in a big breath and held so I wouldn't pant. Elbows tight to my ribs. Pivoted with the car as it passed. Soft finger. Squeezed it off easy. All dipped quiet for that glorious millisecond.

Tim Dash roared off toward Riverside Drive, and after a three-count came the motorbikes, the muscle Honda, and the pool truck in hot pursuit. As always, I had the instinct to follow. An automatic spasm like the one you get when you're falling asleep and make that false stumble. As always, I didn't. Risky enough to chase after an A-list type A. But why put his pregnant passenger at risk, not to mention bystander pedestrians? Besides, I had my two-shot. I had my Get.

But if I knew the Canuck, he and his pit bulls would grab a shot, too. I had to move fast and file first. The notion of losing this score to that fucking Canadian released all the fear juice into my brain, crowding out caution. I started rolling through stop signs and driving with my horn, desperate to find a HotSpot to upload the shot, quick.

I didn't dare go home, but my WiFi accounts at Starbucks and Borders were all dead because of the damned credit cards. And screw the public library. This wasn't the day to pace around waiting for my turn on the web behind some prepube gamer. Jared. Jared had broadband at Java Mouse, and he owed me for those stills I shot for his brochure. But a glimpse of caution peeked through. Hadn't I spent most of the week avoiding my usual haunts? I cruised Ventura Boulevard, drove by the Mouse anyway to check it out. Afternoon empty. What the hell. I parked around the corner behind Art's Deli so my Xterra wouldn't be in plain sight.

In the Java Mouse I booted up to e-mail from an editor pal on one of the major tabs. I'd sold him hundreds of shots over the years, but he was rejecting my submission of event security disarming Mo'Torious at the music awards. He said my photo had the usual high quality storytelling, but the one he bought from the Canadian, "however contrived or coerced, had more excitement. Sorry about this, Hardwick, it's new policy here. It's all about cover wars and who owns the story. . . . Keep sending. . . ." blah, blah.

As I FireWired my camera to my laptop, I reflected on how it was all different since Diana in that Paris tunnel. Rather than chilling the shark-pack shooters, it emboldened them like some naughty thrill rush. They tasted blood and they liked it. Now it was an aggressive team sport. And it isn't just the Canuck. It's all the brazen cowboys who force events instead of documenting them. If my Mo'Torious shot wouldn't clear the editorial high bar, I knew what would. And when Tim Dash and Kendra Lee Shearing popped on my screen— together in the front seat—with the action-blurred background, I rode the exhilaration spike I'd felt with my first sale, the life changer. I smiled to myself. This round goes to Hardwick.

Then the bottom fell out of my stomach.

Through the front window there he was, leaning against his car. Rudy Newgate, arms crossed, looking right at me. And he'd brought muscle. I didn't know the other guy, but knew the type. Rudy finds them on Venice Beach. Iron pumpers, keeping up their prison rips, willing to do odd jobs for cash.

I pretended I didn't see them and sauntered to Jared at the counter with my coffee cup.

"Watch my stuff for me till I get back, OK?"

He asked me a question, but the alley door closed behind me before he finished it.

I started for my car, but there was another bodybuilder waiting at it. Like Rudy bought the salt and pepper shaker set. He didn't see me, and I pressed against the wall. In seconds Rudy and his pal would come through the door, or flank me at the other end of the alley. Sure enough, I heard gutter splash and Rudy's car nosed into view.

The dumpsters beside me were padlocked into a chain-link pen with enough shade to hide in and at least buy some time. A shitty choice but all I had. I kept close to the wall and climbed over and in. Found barely enough cranny to wedge between the two trash bins, then lifted my feet just as the car stopped beside the cage.

"Anything?" said Rudy.

The other voice approached from my car. "If he came out, it wasn't past me."

The coffee shop door opened. "He's not in there. I checked the can."

They talked about whether I had ducked into Art's or the toy store, but those alley doors were locked. Then, whether I had climbed the roof. Too high, they all agreed.

"What about in here?"

Rudy. Somebody rattled chain link. My mouth went dry.

"Locked, Mr. Newgate."

Then a crushing silence. The kind that follows a finger put to someone's lips and all the loose talk stops. Footsteps. The car trunk opened. Metal clanged metal, and then more steps. I peeked, betting what I would see. Bolt snips, the kind they use at public storage units and gyms. They snipped through the padlock like it was a breadstick. When the lock hit the pavement, I squeezed back in my cubby, in full recognition of the futility. Two sets of hands clawed me out of there and threw me on the ground at the feet of my banker.

Rudy squatted down on the balls of his feet to meet my face and lifted his sunglasses onto his brow.

"Collection day, Hardwick."

He held out his palm. Theatrical. Like if he was going to do this, he was going to have his fun.

"I'm working on it."

As soon as I said it, he slapped me with the palm. I smacked him right back, knocking those fucking sunglasses off his face.

I paid for that. One of the thugs threw a kick into my ribs. The other pinned my arms back and my cheek bit asphalt while they held me there. From my sideways view, I made out Rudy's sockless loafers crossing off to get the sunglasses and coming back.

"That's a first, gotta tell you that."

"You didn't have to hit me."

"Yeah? You calling the shots here?"

"We could talk about this."

"Want to talk?" He took a step back and the goons stood me up. "Start talking." He leaned on his fender, striking a heard-it-all-before pose. Probably because he had.

"I know I'm late with the payment."

"A week late. That can be fatal."

"Some income I expected didn't pan out." I tried to hold some sort of high road here. Not like some lowlife, whining. "I honor my debts. My word means something, Rudy, you know that."

This was getting nowhere and I could see it all over him.

"Everybody wants to be good for it. How are you going to pony up all of a sudden?"

"I just scored a picture. A big payday. I'd be selling it now if you hadn't. . . ." I let it trail. Beneath it all, he was a businessman and I could see his wheels turning. Keep it concrete. Talk specifics, not hopes. "It's big."

"How big?"

"Enough to bring me current. Just like that."

"How soon?"

This was good. A shift in mode.

I started to calculate the editorial review period, the price haggles, the lag for the funds to clear, the chance I might even sell to *People* or *Entertainment Weekly* for a bump. Rudy began to fidget so I just took a flier.

"This time next week."

Rudy pondered. "Tell you what. This time next week."

"Great."

"Double the vig."

"Hey, come on."

"I can't let you off light. Everybody'd pull this shit, and then where'd I be?"

"Double is crazy. Your fucking interest is what's got me so under."

"Hold him," said Rudy to the others. "Put him right here."

He stepped aside. I tried to make a break, but his two men had me clamped and they pinned me across the hood of his car. It was hot and I struggled to lift my face off the burn.

"Get his arm back. Come on, idiot, get it fucking back and hold it."

They twisted my right arm behind me. Something gristly in my shoulder crunched. I swore, but didn't cry out. I wouldn't give him that.

"Now give me those snips and hold his finger."

"Hey, no, don't." I balled my fist tight. "Jesus, no."

"Come on, asshole, get it open." They whacked my wrist with the flat of the tool and when I flinched they pried my forefinger out. "There, that one. Keep it out. Yeah, like that." The scissor jaws of the bolt cutter pinched between the knuckle and the bone.

"OK, I get it. I'll pay the vig. Rudy, come on, you don't have to do this."

"I think I do."

"I said I'd pay."

"You disrespected me. You broke my glasses."

"I'll buy new ones." I felt the snips bite skin. Felt a wicked cold run inside me. "Hey, if you cut that finger off I can't work. How much money will you be out if I can't snap off a shot?"

Rudy's pressure on the snips held. Would it be quick? The worst of it was the waiting. Bracing for the chomp. Then he released.

# CHAPTER TWO

"Get him off my car."

They yanked me upright. Rudy slipped his sunglasses in my shirt pocket.

"These are Persols. Next week with the money." He tossed the bolt cutter on the passenger seat and took the wheel. "Remember the kid at Santa Anita?"

"Yeah," said one of the thugs.

"Same deal." And then he drove off.

They worked me, but just enough to hurt. It's not like TV where guys duke it out for ten minutes. One or two well-placed punches do the job. When they finished, they left me in one of the dumpsters, aching and twisted. I gave them time to go before I tried to rise up and, as I waited, I found a kind of sleep. I hovered above myself, floating, looking down at my pretzeled body half-submerged in deli trash. *The worst is over* drifted by and I grabbed that. Clung to the good thoughts. Meddy's face on the river that night. Me in a tux, with my beard and long hair, accepting my first Pulitzer. Meddy's face framed by tea candles in Georgetown. The candles blurred. My head was heavy and my vision was thick. I needed to rest my eyes. Just for a minute, that's all.

My cell phone brought me back. I had to reach down through some rather funky trash to snag it off my belt. The effort killed my shoulder. I didn't bother with caller ID. I wanted a voice. Any voice.

"Hardwick?"

"Yeah?"

He sounded familiar, but I wasn't sharp enough to dig it out.

"Monte Arnett. I've been leaving you messages since Friday."

"I know."

Rudy wasn't the only one I was ducking. Although I had a different reason not to speak to Monte Arnett or anybody else at Hobby Horse Productions.

"Might be a courtesy to return the call." Irritated, but reining it in.

"Well, see, Monte, my lawyer advises against me talking to anybody I'm in litigation with. You could go through him. You sure as hell know who he is."

"Look, I don't want us off on the wrong foot—"

"I'm not the one whose TV studio is trying to sue my nuts off for making a living."

Tough talk from a guy in a dumpster. Glad he couldn't see me.

"Let me cut through that. What if it were possible we dropped our suit?"

"How possible?"

"Depends."

"On?"

"Elliot Pratt wants to meet with you."

"Why don't we set this up through my lawyer. That's what I pay him for."

"No." A little quick on the draw with that no. Why the edge? "This is just us. You, me, and the boss. The lawyers will fuck this up. Can you be here today?"

"Today? I don't know about today."

"Hardwick, it's about an opportunity. Give us five minutes, and if you're not interested in what we have to say, then walk away."

"And the lawsuit?"

"Show up and we discuss it." He worked that pause, knew I was sniffing bait. "Say, four-thirty?"

"All right. Four-thirty."

"Cool. I don't have to ask if you know the way to the studio."

He laughed a smoker's laugh and hung up.

My first visit home in a week I had just enough time for a shower and a change. The spot on my sternum where I took the lesson punch was blotching into the satellite view of Katrina. Maybe I'd have felt like I got off easy if it weren't for the quick reject of my Tim Dash coup. The Canuck not only beat me to file, he had sequence art of Dash ripping a biker's helmet off, then pegging it at the other shooter, all with Kendra Lee framed in the passenger window behind him. So much for my big score.

I descended the hills into Hollywood in the Xterra that had put me in hock to Rudy. Common sense should have kept me away from that fringe character. But someone torched my Trail Blazer, the one with the lapsed insurance. Stupid, but that's one of the corners you cut when all the tipster payouts you have to make nowadays just to be competitive strip you clean. And try to make any living in LA without a car, especially in my line. So you take the cash when it's offered, and next thing you know, you're sleeping in that damn car, afraid of your own bed. The truly shitty irony is that celebrity shots are worth more than ever. But if the shark packers don't make you crazy enough, there's all the citizen shooters—the mom-'n-pop-arazzi—with their pocket digitals and cell phone cameras crowding the market with their lucky Gets.

Enough of that. I cranked *Deacon Blues* on my iPod for a mood shift. As I cut through the bungalowed neighborhoods near Las Palmas to avoid getting black lung behind another double-decker tour bus, I chewed on how I've spent my adult life alternately trying to avoid becoming and hoping to become a faded hipster from some Steely Dan song, arguably a no-lose aspiration.

I found a meter across from the studio and crossed to the gate. A security guard spread himself wide to block my way.

"Where do you think you're going, asshole?"

"I have a four-thirty at Hobby Horse."

"Bullshit. Move along."

He took a step to me, but without contact, the way baseball managers posture to umpires. Backup arrived. Two golf carts, three guards. All deployed while the carts were still rolling. I wondered if they practiced that. One of them took over the guard shack. The two others flanked me.

"Off this property. Now, shutterfuck."

"I have an appointment, dickweed."

Sergeant Olson bunched my shirt in his paw and walked me backwards. Pain ripped through my shoulder. It would have been simpler to step away, call Monte, and let him deal with this. But simpler eludes my nature when the wolf tilts back to howl.

I sidestepped, and Olson's momentum sent him stumbling. He landed on the pavement, scraping all fours. The biggest guard threw a choke hold on me. I used his bear hug for support and lifted both feet to kick his partner ass-down in a planter. Olson grabbed a leg and hollered to the gatekeeper, who was clearing a news van off the lot. He joined the party along with planter boy. I resisted fiercely against all four of them until my eye caught the passenger riding shotgun in the news van nosing out the driveway.

I stopped struggling completely. The blood left my arms and legs. Was it her?

My God, it was. Meddy, leaning forward, looking across her driver at the sidewalk scuffle. Guards and some nut. Then she reacted when she saw I was the nut.

I wanted to call out. I wanted to explain everything to her. Not this, but everything. Everything that kept me up nights. But the van was gone.

# CHAPTER THREE

"Hey! Let him go! Hey!" Rubber squealed and the guards turned at once and released me. Monte Arnett stalked over from his golf cart. "Help him up." Two guards pulled me to my feet. "What the hell is this, Claude?"

"Well, Mr. Arnett, this fellow is a permanent eighty-six from the lot."

"He has an appointment with me. Don't you check drive-ons?"

Olson registered a look of confusion, of wires not sparking the right terminals. The other three guards looked at each other, then at their shoes.

"If you want, I'll fire him," said Monte as I sat beside him in the cart.

"No. It's not my first welcoming party, won't be the last."

He popped the accelerator and I winced.

"Sorry. Had the governor taken off this puppy. Against the rules, but, hey." He Groucho-flicked his eyebrows at me, including me in his little larceny. "When they need the Mont-ster on the set, I'm blowin' the fawkin' doors off, you know?" Then he added, "Did they just fuck up your shoulder? We have a studio doctor if you need anything."

I turned to study him. Monte was one of those guys who said "anything" as if it carried global weight. Coming from him, it sounded like it could mean anything from a second opinion to an unlimited supply of morphine.

"No, I'm good."

Empire Studios is a small lot as they go. Hobby Horse is the largest tenant, with long-term leases on two sound stages and over half the production offices and ancillary facilities like dressing rooms, makeup, wardrobe, and construction. For that, Monte Arnett rides ungoverned, where he wants, as fast as he wants, his business-modified NHL mullet flapping, holding the fate of security guards in his meaty hands.

We zipped past Stage 2, where Hobby Horse taped its phenomenally successful sitcom, *Thanks for Sharing*. The elephant doors of the hulking beige hangar were painted with the show logo in tall letters above a billboard-sized mural of its star, Bonnie Quinn, looking skyward, one arm draped on a telescope, the other hand on her hip, in her trademark pose of sassy defiance. Her face was as big as an Encino garage door.

"Thar she blows," I said.

Monte ignored her image looming over us.

"Yup. Stage 2. Biggest on the lot."

"Is that to fit her ego, or the crypt for all the writers she's had fired?"

Silence. What was that about? Not only did the whole town know about Bonnie's outrageously difficult personality, the nation did. On any given week there was a story about her latest antics splashed on the cover of a tabloid or leading the teasers on *Entertainment Tonight* or *Access Hollywood*. With her foul mouth, drug abuse, drinking, sexual wildness, violent temper, and public verbal abuse of cast and crew, she carried the torch of the over-the-top sitcom diva into the new millennium, eclipsing Roseanne, Brett Butler, and Cybill, who never even came close. So the tone from Monte struck me as strange, loaded with avoidance.

The door handles of the Hobby Horse executive offices were a single brass hobby horse, split down the middle on either side of twin tinted glass panes. Monte cupped a hand under the rocker and opened one side to let me in. Notably, the first time a studio employee at any level knowingly allowed me in a door, let alone held it for me.

"He's still in a screening," said the assistant in the library-quiet upstairs suite. She had a serious air and *cum laude* grooming. Attractive, yes, but no dummies allowed on Elliot Pratt's outer perimeter. "But go in. He'll be wrapping up soon."

As I followed Monte into Elliot Pratt's office with my requisite free bottled water, I surrendered to the butterfly in my stomach. Had I really seen Meddy in that van? How many times before had I seen her only to discover with a turn of her head in the produce section of Gelson's, or an adjustment of her bangs in a Lexus on Coldwater, that it wasn't Meddy after all? Of course it was her. There was eye contact. Recognition. But what did I see in those eyes besides surprise? Any chance it was forgiveness?

"So, you decided to show."

Elliot Pratt carried a lidless banker's box filled with DVDs and scripts, which he tossed with a clatter beside his desk on the way over to me. He shook my hand with one of those shakes that pushes you away about an inch.

"Guess you could say there was an incentive," I said.

"He wants us to drop the suit," said Monte.

"Bullshit. You offered to drop it. I'm still ready to fight it and win it." Contentious of me, but fuck 'em. Whatever the junk sculpture my life has become since my *wunderkind* days of the war and the White House, the one thing I cling to is my inner compass. The needle always points moral north. Some ground I'm just not made to give. It gets me in a lot of trouble, but some trouble's worth having.

Monte started to retort, but Elliot jumped in.

"You're right. I authorized Monte to suggest that offer, so let's agree the lawsuit is off and have our meeting." Elliot gestured to the love seat while he took the rocker. "We have bigger fish to fry here."

Monte bristled and looked uncomfortable in the wing chair. His gut buttons were spread, giving me unwanted navelage. Monte Arnett was the only person I knew who could make a Nat Nast bowling shirt actually look like a bowling shirt.

"Sorry if I'm still pissed off. Those shots of yours killed our paramedics pilot, you know."

"I didn't tell your male lead to wear a Klan robe to a spring break party on a public beach. Besides, looks like you survived." I scoped out the antique furniture, the pale yellow walls with sage wainscoting. And the bookcases lined with gilded first editions beneath framed original maps. "This what independent production buys you?"

"You know what they say," said Elliot. "A sure way to make a small fortune in independent production is to start with a large one."

The executive producer rocked back and forth, smiling, bygones forgotten, let's be friends. I had heard about Elliot's charm. Kennedy charisma was the phrase everyone liked. When *People* did its Hollywood Power Elite issue, they boldfaced his profile with "Camelot on the Backlot." That's just the sort of bloated PR I'm always looking to blast out of the water, but I could see where it came from. He was blond and '80s rock star-tousled instead of dark and wavy, but the Boston accent, the athletic carriage, and the air of relaxed privilege made for a first impression if not of Camelot then of a more evolved species of TV producer.

Yet, there is something about a forty-year-old man draping tennis sweaters over his shoulders that says artifice. The Jack Kennedy rocker suddenly seemed a pose. I decided to remain resolutely uncharmed by Elliot Pratt as he rocked and smiled.

"I think this is your meeting," I said.

"Bonnie Quinn is missing and I want you to find her." Elliot paused and let that pause hang, and when he was sure I had absorbed it and that he owned the conversation, he said, "I know this is a bombshell. You must have a lot of questions."

"What bombshell? I mean, she's gone AWOL before, right? Is she using again? Off on a lost weekend?"

Elliot spoke evenly, sounding very Hyannis Jack.

"Let me say one thing very clearly. I have no firsthand knowledge of any drug use by Bonnie Quinn. She was put in a facility once by her manager for a medical condition. She assures me that is all taken care of."

"No elephant in this living room," I said. They just stared. "If you're worried, why not call the police?"

Elliot shook his head. "That's a nonstarter. This is too delicate to let outside the circle. The circle being the three of us in this room. And her manager."

Monte crossed his legs, flashing some halibut calf. "You go to the cops with this and, next thing, the Channel 5 helicopter's circling, news vans are camped outside, and the gate's knee-deep in paparazzi scum."

"No offense," I said. "Next question: Why me?"

"Because you found her before."

"Twice," added Monte.

Elliot rose to pace. "Know what this week is? The end of Season Four."

I nodded. "Critical mass for syndication. A hundred episodes."

"Wrong. Ninety-nine. Episode One Hundred was supposed to be this week. I should be at a run-through right now. But we can't shoot the episode without our beloved star, and she is—who the hell knows where this time?"

"Lots of shows go into syndication on less. What's one episode?"

"It's contractual. This episode triggers all the big numbers. It's cash, it's financing commitments, bonuses, back-end points. But, you see, with all she has cost me on this show—and not just heartburn, I mean actual costs—in reshoots and shut downs and lawsuits and perks and demands ... Well, I'm not going to open my books here, but the deficit I have to cover personally on each episode has me upside down."

As Elliot laid out his money woes, all I could think of were my own. It was like that *Far Side* cartoon where the man talks at great length to his dog, and all the dog hears is its name. The *"Blah-blah, Ginger"* part for me was my cold sweat over Rudy's next move.

Elliot sat heavily, as if another year had left him. "It's as simple as this: If we get Episode One Hundred in the can, I am the ramblin' gamblin' wonder boy who rode the wild pony and it paid off. If we don't, I've actually lost money on this series. I am one episode shy of make-break, and I cannot get there unless I find my God damned star." Elliot leaned close and whispered, "Will you help me?"

I gave it a decent pause so as not to appear rude. "Sorry."

"We'd pay you," Elliot said, and, for a blip, I wondered how much. But to raise the question would steer me down a road I wanted off of. I didn't have to ask, though. He named a figure. "Monte says that was your rate for your biggest picture this year."

I nodded. "Close enough. But, see, I'm not a bounty hunter. I take pictures."

"Simple as that," said Elliot.

"Simple as that," I said.

"Don't you hunt for people so you can take their picture?"

"That's different."

"How so?"

"It's an ethical thing." Monte scoffed and Elliot gave him a reproving look and I continued. "I've always been a journalist. There's a line for me between capturing a picture and, well ... a person. Or working for a company I may end up covering."

"And what's the problem with that?"

"Conflict of interest. How do I know you aren't just finding a way to spiff me so I'll back off a little. Or hesitate next time I'm at a beach bar on spring break."

"Are you really that cynical?"

"I'm that experienced. I know how things work, Elliot. I've seen how things work. That's why I hold a line."

"And how big is that line?"

I didn't hesitate. "Big. And clear."

Monte must have taken some cue because he unbuckled his briefcase and tossed an envelope onto the coffee table in front of me. I didn't need to open it. I'd seen enough movies to know what it was.

"Is it this big?" he said.

I tried not to stare, but I knew they saw through me. That envelope must have held my top Get, times three. Maybe four.

"Tell me something, Hardwick," said Elliot. "When was it you sold your last picture?" When I didn't answer, he added a ball-squeeze. "Monte tells me things aren't going so well as they used to. Must be a big adjustment after being the king."

I hated them for playing me like that as much as I hated myself for not walking out. But I felt immobilized by the tug. How could I not after the week I'd just had? After the alley that day? Knowing another collection day was coming, and it was double?

"This is Tuesday. Find her in time for a Monday table read and that envelope's yours."

It was fat. It was the end of my worries. No. Fuck these guys. I slid my feet under me, got ready to stand up and just go. Then Elliot told me how much was in it. My mouth tasted of chalk, same as it had between the dumpsters when Rudy rattled the cage.

"So, do we have a deal?" Elliot asked.

# CHAPTER FOUR

Ten minutes later I hopped out of Monte's golf cart at the Cahuenga gate. When I asked for an advance for expenses, he eyed me but peeled off new bills from his pocket clip. When I reached, he held them back.

"One more thing. Bonnie Quinn's a walking basket case. When you find her, call me. I bring her in, got it? And if for some reason she talks to you, don't believe everything she tells you."

I took his money and said, "I never believe everything anybody tells me."

Follow the drugs. That's how I found Bonnie Quinn every time before, and I was gonna dance with who brung me. Elliot Pratt and Monte Arnett could parade before me with a Bible in one hand and Old Glory in the other, riding piggyback on Supreme Court justices, and I would still scoff when they said they weren't aware of her drug use. Of course, that's not precisely what Elliot had said. He said he had no firsthand knowledge of it. A dripping-with-denial denial, no doubt parsed by his legal dream team and buffed to a high gloss in the public relations boiler room.

• • •

Come on. We're talking the same Bonnie Quinn they sent on an image-cleansing PR visit to a nursing home, which Monte had to cut short when they discovered Bonnie dearest was swiping painkillers from the elderly right off the med cart. But I could care less about the expedient denial of Elliot Pratt. I was going to do the job he hired me for by staking out her drug source, the makeup artist on his own sitcom.

Brick Tennant was not a drug dealer. Oh, maybe in the eyes of the law he was. But Brick was really more of a drug fetcher. He lacked the courage and the brains to be much of a public enemy. What he could do was party and kiss ass. He did both better than he did makeup, but those two talents are the ones that kept him employed and in the graces of Bonnie Quinn while he powdered her nose.

"That's him there, second floor window," I told Pinkman.

The old man beside me raised his binoculars and snorted at the sight of the slightly built Jamaican with bleached dreadlocks dancing alone in his Boy's Town apartment.

"Looks like a damn Q-tip with ants in his pants."

"We don't judge, Pinkman. We follow, right?

In his day, Pinkman was the top celebrity candid shooter in Hollywood. He ran with my dad and did his best to keep him off bar stools. You could look at him now and be transported back to the days when. The fedora hat, the brown suit and tie. Except now the suit looked big enough to be somebody else's, and you could fit two fingers between his shirt collar and his neck.

"And if, by any chance, you see Bonnie Quinn, blow this guy off and lock onto her. Just don't get too close."

"Like I'd ever get close to that beast. I was there the night she totaled Dellroy's Trans Am. Dell wasn't even shooting. Just cooling his heels outside the Improv, and she plows her Boxster into the broadside of his car, right where he was leaning. Missed him by less than a foot. Witch."

He hocked something and spit out the car window.

Although following the drugs was my best shot, with only five days to find her, I had to cover multiple bases. Pinkman was as old school as they come, but I knew if I put him on a mark I could split off and never give it a thought.

"Just stay on him till I get back tomorrow morning. No contact, just tail. You know the drill."

"Hey, Hardwick. I invented the fucking drill."

Waiting again. This time in Larchmont, a neighborhood not far from Paramount and wealthy enough to be called an enclave. Bonnie Quinn's manager was late, even by LA standards, so I camped curbside at the diva's house trying to blow off the disrespect.

I called Cheryl, my lawyer's receptionist, and canceled yet another dinner date. Not the most inspiring sign for our relationship that it didn't bother me that it didn't bother Cheryl.

All my numbers for Meddy were dead. The UEN switchboard sent me to voice mail at her home desk in the New York newsroom. After the beep, I almost said I was just thinking of her that day because, the fact was, I did. A lot. I mentioned I saw her while I was being subdued, small world, ha-ha, left the number of my cell phone, then plugged it into the cigarette adapter, thinking fat chance she'd call.

So many years since Nashua. Even more since the last gasp of Vietnam when she and I first made love floating on the Mekong.

The day had been a blaze of carnage after the Montagnarde guide for the platoon we were embedded with walked us into a buzz saw. Half an eternity after the ambush, Meddy and I sat dazed in the back of a crippled chopper, a couple of twenty-year-old kids with mud and human tissue caked to our clothes. We sat glassy-eyed and mute with too much to mourn and what we could manage to forget was on film in my camera case. I shouted to her that she was bleeding and when I didn't think she could hear me I pointed at my own eyebrow to indicate hers, but she just turned to stare out the hatch at the river below.

The first engine shudder almost dropped the Huey into the drink. The skid on my side dug up spray but the pilot made a heroic save and struggled us twenty feet aloft. He called back that we were too heavy and had to ditch our gear. Meddy opened her pack to save the mashed pages of her reporter's notebook, then flung the rest, including her portable typewriter, out the hatch. My case of lenses and a spare camera body was heavy and replaceable. I gave it a toss. The helicopter lurched again and we sank below tree level. The pilot shouted over his shoulder for me to lose the other case, too. Meddy got animated and slid forward to plead with him. That case held all my film from five days in-country. I bargained the case could go, but to let me gather the film out of it. Before I could pop the seal he was pointing his sidearm at me.

"No time. I'm not dying for your lousy pictures."

I moved to the hatch with my case and smiled to Meddy. "Everyone's a critic." And then I jumped.

Even at low altitude, smacking water felt like the hits I used to take from defensive tackles in JV ball. The impact tore the case right out of my hand. When I broke the surface it was bobbing on the lazy current. I backstroked toward it so I could catch a look at her and wave that I was OK. She stared back at me from the hatch under a plume of brutal smoke. I figured she thought I was crazy. Then I saw her jump after me. And that night, drifting on a sampan I bought—with a wad of wet bills—from a Viet fisherman, we clung to each other under the distant flashes of a sputtering war, making ourselves tiny on the planet and invisible to our fears.

Headlights filled my mirrors on the quiet street in Larchmont. I got out to say hello but Rhonda York was already talking.

"I'm missing a showcase at the Laugh Factory for this circle jerk."

What sort of person signs on to manage a nightmare celebrity like Bonnie Quinn? It was my night to find out. In the dark alcove at the front door, Rhonda held a busy ring of keys up to the spill from the streetlights.

"Besides, you're wasting your time here," she said. "You think we're going to open the door and find sitting her in a corner, sucking her thumb?"

"You're right," I said. "Why don't we just put a dish of cocaine out and throw a net over her when she finds it?"

I turned my Mini Mag-Lite on the keys.

Rhonda's black leather suit creaked as she walked me wordlessly through the house, snapping on lights in every room. And every room was the same as the one before: the living room, the dining room, bedrooms, kitchen, maid's room, the walk-in closets, the loft over-looking the swamp water pool.

All of the rooms were empty.

The glare of naked bulbs in the grand deco house made the void surreal. A hotel out of season. Two stories, eleven rooms, and the only furnishings were a couple of folding chairs, a card table piled with back issues of *Sky & Telescope* and *Night Sky Observer*, and a futon on the cigarette-burned carpet below a pair of jeans, a bra, and a sweat-shirt crammed onto a bookshelf.

Not one towel in the master bath. Just a roll of Bounty and some mouthwash. The bottom of the Roman tub was lined with dated issues of *Scientific American*, plus half a dozen tabloids. One of my own cover shots of Russell Crowe from two years back looked up at me from where it had likely been tossed from the crapper. The medicine cabinet was bare except for an empty prescription vial with no label and a rusty box cutter blade with a few white crumbs on it.

The kitchen told me the most. A fridge full of hairy fruit and shriv-eled KFC. Trash can dead beyond odor.

Her manager was waiting for me out front with her arms folded like a real estate agent showing a place built on toxic landfill instead of a seven-figure home in Larchmont.

"You about done?"

"Any contact at all? Anything?"

"Bonnie didn't call, Bonnie hasn't called. Bonnie's fucking using cash so I can't trace her credit cards. Bonnie pulls this shit, and worse. It's part of her Bonnie charm. You should know that. You seem to know every move she fucking makes."

"Rhonda? In case you missed it, I'm trying to find your goddam client."

"Then do. I told you this was bullshit. We bought this place for tax advantage with the second season pick-up. Bonnie only flopped here occasionally. Mostly she either crashes in her dressing room at the studio or just sleeps with whoever." She shrugged and her tailored leathers groaned like a cop's belt. "You gotta know Bonnie."

At the sidewalk, I looked back at the hollow, abandoned house, dark as a missing tooth, surrounded by bright homes with lives being lived, children getting baths, love being made, arguments being had, jokes being told. I think I did know her.

# CHAPTER FIVE

Reno is an easy hour by jet from Burbank capped by a carnival ride landing of air pockets and sideslip. Amid the usual passenger gasps and falling personal items, I surveyed the flickering casino city at night and thought about gambling and my work. Not just luck or risk or winning or losing, but the common sense principles you follow to stay in the game. Like not showing all your cards. There was one card I had kept face down for years.

The log cabin was rustic and simple. A by-the-week rental snugged in the pines on the mountainside straddling Reno and Tahoe. I had found Bonnie Quinn there before. In the summer before her second season, she was holding out for a new contract. She made a deal to rehearse in good faith for the premiere episode while negotiations took place. But the mercurial star of TV's number one sitcom blew good faith out her ass.

Bonnie pulled a no-show and hid out up here in the woods off the Mt. Rose Highway. Monte and his posse spent days playing a futile game of Find the Diva. Elliot Pratt blinked, caving to all her demands. She was both maligned and respected for playing the brink. Except I knew the real reason she was up there, and it wasn't to play hardball with business affairs.

Bonnie Quinn had come to this mountain to meet secretly with her illegitimate daughter, the teenage girl she had given up for adoption at birth.

And from all I had observed and heard, it went miserably. Arguments on the driveway in the pines. Arguments in big hats and oversized sunglasses on King's Beach down at the lake. Arguments at night. Breakfast dishes got thrown, the girl shot gravel out the driveway behind her Jetta, and Bonnie spent the week with the drapes drawn, alone except for the visits from Brick and his magic bag.

When Bonnie flew back to LA and her fat new contract, I decided to sit on the pictures and the getaway cabin. Something in me couldn't see the good in revealing either one.

Three years later, as I looked down from my old hiding spot at a van whose color eluded me, the cabin was dark. Of course I snooped the windows, but how much can a guy learn through closed curtains? This was going to be a stakeout. There is so much waiting in this job that I never go anywhere without something to read. Something good is better than just plain something, and with a shielded mini light, I reclined my seat and waded into *Life on the Mississippi* by the self-made rascal with the pen warmed up in hell.

When I rejoined him, Sam Clemens, now famous as Mark Twain, was back on a Mississippi riverboat, standing at the back of the pilot house. The author was traveling incognito to better observe the watch, unable to speak the very name he had taken from his apprenticeship on those same waters without the noisy brute of celebrity crowding the deck.

At dawn I woke up to Chinese music blaring through the woods. Scattering blue jays flew across my lens as a dozen Asian men and women filed out of the cabin and assembled on the lawn. When they began a slow-motion meditation exercise to the warbling tune, I thought of another aspect of gambling: odds. They were pretty good that unless Bonnie Quinn had run off with the Falun Gong, I needed to keep looking.

Pinkman was not a friend of technology. His cellular hello always had a slightly suspicious edge to it. I called to tell him I was back after following a dead end. He had spent the night in his Le Baron across the street from Brick's apartment.

"Q-Tip never left his place," he said. "Plenty of boy toys coming over, though."

I offered to let him go home and get some bed sleep, but he said he had plenty of hours left, and we both knew that since his wife died Pinkman was never in a hurry to go home, so I didn't push it.

Monte Arnett was eating a bagel at his desk when I walked in holding up the tabloid I'd snagged at the airport: "Bonnie the Brat Benched." The cover art was our girl frown-to-frown with Elliot Pratt. A clue this might be a composite: She was in wardrobe; Elliot was in a tennis outfit.

"The writing's almost as good as the picture." I recited, "'This time it's not her fault! A stinkeroo script and not Queen Quinn's antics have shut down production of the mighty UEN giggler *Thanks for Sharing*. Show topper Elliot Pratt couldn't be reached, but insiders say he was 'livid' and wanted to 'fire all the writers.'"

I folded the tabloid. "Insiders?"

Monte laughed up a wad of masticated bagel that flew somewhere.

"Oh, look at you, Mr. Journalist Purity. We have to cover with something. It's bullshit, but it's better bullshit than a page one that says we can't find her again, right?"

He found the soggy bagel wad stuck to his pencil cup and ate it.

"Why aren't you busy finding our lady?"

"I am. Show me Bonnie Quinn's dressing room."

"No pictures in here," said Monte outside her door. I nodded and took a step to enter, but he blocked me. "The cameras stay outside."

I hooked my gear bag on the outside doorknob, wondering what the big deal was until I followed him in.

Bonnie Quinn's dressing room looked like the Manson family had taken a studio apartment for a weekend and decided to stay. It was two small rooms of delinquent destruction and serial vandalism.

The walls hollered. Every surface was a full body tattoo of obscenity, poetry, song lyrics, jokes, limericks, names, political slogans, and crude homilies. An assault of graffiti shot out in all colors, all sizes, and all media: spray paint, markers, ballpoint, pencil, even lipstick. The writing came from one hand, albeit reflecting various stages of sobriety or sanity or both. Instead of the sharp spikes and balloon figures of urban taggers, these were the legible rounds of The Palmer Method, which only served to make it more disturbing, as if Sister Mary Margaret had been slipped a tab of acid instead of the communion wafer.

Where words failed, illustrations wove between the slogans and slanders. Her drawings showed impressive craft and imagination, not to mention a sense of angry depravity generally reserved for avant-garde radical presses and X-rated comic books. Above the sofa, anatomically correct Looney Tunes characters performed all manner of sex with world figures from Gandhi to Nixon. Adorning the space above the bedroom door, a study of Thomas Jefferson with his breeches down around his ankles made a Feifferesque morph over six panels to George Jefferson with his pants down around his ankles. Her caption read, "Six Degrees of Fornication."

Monte perched on a bar stool, studying me for reaction.

"This is so weird," I said. "I have a room done exactly like this."

"Hey. This is what I have to deal with on a daily basis. You get to go away after you find her."

Veins of fractured glass splayed out across the entire surface of the makeup mirror from an upper corner where something had been thrown. The dark stain above it on the wall could have been from recent coffee or old wine. The etching across the top of the mirror instructed: "Do not make me glamorous," and concluded on the bottom with: "I am the American Single Mom."

Indeed, quite the role model. It was all there but the soccer minivan.

"Tell me again, Monte. Tell me about the drugs."

I could see him behind me, a broken reflection in the shards of the mirror.

"We told you. We have no firsthand knowledge of any drug use by her."

"They say she gets a lot of oral surgery just for the painkillers. They say she gets a tooth pulled, then finesses multiple doctors to write prescriptions at multiple pharmacies to score enough Vicodin or Percocet or whatever. When that runs out she finds another dentist and gets something else yanked or stitched."

"So they say."

"How can she function with all this in her? What does your studio doctor say?"

"Nothing," said the production manager. "Dr. Pizzarelli's a joke. Carmen does insurance physicals, period. 'You're breathing? You're beating? You're cleared. Get to work.' Old Pizzy hasn't had a regular practice since, like, the Korean War."

"Doesn't it work the other way, too?"

"What other way?"

"How much does it cost you to shut down production for a week?"

"None of your business."

I knew the number and said it.

"If she's not capable of performing because of . . . " I gestured to the lunacy of the dressing room. ". . . whatever, couldn't your house doctor shut things down for medical reasons and kick in your insurance to cover your losses?"

"Sure. And it has happened. Flu. Food poisoning. Laryngitis . . ."

"Not for drugs?"

"Never for drugs." Monte grew restless and moved to the door like he remembered he needed to be somewhere else. "I'll be outside when you've finished playing looky-loo."

The instant the door slammed I whipped the Canon Elph out of my pocket and began shooting every inch of the place.

# CHAPTER SIX

Sometimes I worry that years of this work have dulled my ability to be shocked, but after ten minutes in Bonnie Quinn's dressing room-cum-residence I am at least certain I have retained the capacity to be unsettled. The feeling lingered as I took my shift tailing Brick Tennant through West Hollywood that afternoon. He was an easy mark in his top-down Beetle, loungey-loosey in his seat, cruising the sidewalk café action. Getting plenty of attention himself, this slender mahogany man with the ropy white dreads dancing on the tie-dye muscle shirt. It all told me I was wheel-spinning.

When he was on a mission for Bonnie, Brick was tense: back straight, chin over the steering wheel, drawn tight. This Brick, the cool breeze Brick, had time to kill, which meant Bonnie Quinn was not a factor in his day.

While he ate a salad in the window at Hugo's, I parked at the Mobil and downloaded the dressing room shots to my laptop. One by one, I examined forty snaps.

When I shoot, I don't edit. I hose the scene. Whatever instinct is accessible to me that day may help me compose, frame, choose, but I just kick into machine mode. Document it, don't make love to it. I take my time later. On my ThinkPad, I study; shift from the experience to the examination. It's the best clue shopping you can do absent stumbling on the lucky hotel matchbook with a room number written inside.

The books surprised me. Books in every photo: a pillar of Dickens and Tolstoy supporting a pile of dirty underwear; Yeats, Faulkner, and Stegner tossed on the CD player; the Seamus Heaney *Beowulf* bedside; Joyce, Donleavy, Hemingway, and Faulkner on a shelf next to a plastic soap bottle that looked an awful lot like a bong. Some were trade paper, but most I recognized as the first editions I drooled over in the rare book shops near the Beverly Center.

I scrolled to a shot of the vanity where an 1897 first edition first issue of *Following the Equator* acted as the most expensive coaster ever for a can of Bud Light.

Scrolling, scrolling. A pile of *National Geographics* under the TV. Beneath the telescope and tripod Sagan's *Cosmos* and some back issues of *Astronomy Monthly*.

Candles everywhere. Pillars, votives, thin tapers, and erotics of anatomically gifted male sex, without which no American Single Mom's home would be complete.

I shuttled to my bedroom shots. The walls were not the only surfaces with, ahem, art. The impression of a nude female had been applied to the ceiling above the bed as if naked skin had been painted and pressed upward onto the plaster like a wet stamp. I could guess whose impression it was, and speculate that it must have been some party.

Various angles of the wall at the foot of the bed, and a striking three-foot patch of pure black. In the center, a spare design dabbed with an artist's brush: a grouping of white dots and a smear of white paint that looked like a fishing fly. Or a tuft of lint. Arresting, but I couldn't make sense of what it was. Click to zoom. No help. What the hell was this painting? Dominoes? Some occult symbol? A bunch of dots and lint?

Pinkman showed up at midnight outside Brick's to relieve me. Here was a guy about to spend eight hours doing crosswords in his car, but he arrived in a pressed tan big-suit from yesteryear, a fresh shave, and two slaps of Old Spice.

"Your starlet's not in there, you know," Pinkman said. He blew little ripples across his Thermos coffee, tested it with a slurp, and continued, "I got thinking, wouldn't it be a pisser if we were following this freak and the whole time she was right there in his place, sucking on a hookah? So when Bricky Boy led you off today, I snooped it."

"You peeped the windows? What did you do, Pinkman, scale balconies to the second floor?"

"Screw that. I walked the whole apartment. Picked the lock and walked it, closets and all. Now we know she's not in there."

I wagged the naughty finger. "That's B&E, you know."

"Hey, I quit doing balconies when I turned seventy."

The marine layer put a gray lid on the Westside, dampening the night and eating the tops off the Century City skyline. I flipped the wipers once to blade off the dew so I could keep tabs on Brick, who was across Santa Monica Boulevard at his gym. While I watched his exercise class move in ridiculously unified cadence, clumps of worry rose in me about finding Bonnie Quinn on time. I batted them right down because worry doesn't find people.

I won't slog through all my dead-end moves, but trust me, I spent the day jamming it. I worked my phone, I worked my ass. My undercover contacts at the rehab centers came up negative; ditto my hotel, car rental, and airline sources. I got zip from oral surgeons, pharmacists, and old stagehands Bonnie fucked and fired. She wasn't at her normal hideouts, wasn't using her cell phone, ATM, or credit cards, so forget an electronic trail. And her drug source was spending his days in open air markets and step aerobics classes instead of muling for her, which meant she either had an ample stash, found a new source, cold turkeyed, or was dead. Now there was a happy bit of conjecture to spice up the Monday table reading.

As Brick sweated to the oldies, I performed a ritual check of the evening gossip shows on my relic of a WatchMan. I started with *Rough Cut*, which lacked the polish of *ET* and *Insider* but had hungry reporters with roller derby ethics. If anyone was going to catch wind of Bonnie Quinn's disappearance it would be these punks.

True to form, their opener was a blood-on-the-sidewalk story about a runaway cheerleader stomped to death in a stage rush at some metalpalooza. Shock, dismay, body bags. Then, actual news: a video bite of Otis Grove, the Jacksonville-based media tycoon, at his press conference announcing his purchase of UEN, the United Entertainment Network. Big. You'd think the first African American to own a major TV network would be the top story, but this was *Rough Cut*. Maybe if Mr. Grove had surrounded himself with body bags instead of his wife, children, and grandkids he would have made the lead. "This is not about a business transaction. Nor is it about the dream of a man who began his working life five miles from here as a laborer in a pulp mill," he said. "This is about families who are weary of the television sewer. I make this announcement in the circle of my own family as a statement of purpose and to greet the new day in quality network broadcasting."

Back to the *Rough Cut* investigative team for a piece on celebrity penile implants.

My cell phone vibed. I hoped for Meddy. Instead, I got an urgent, "Hold for Monte Arnett," then some distinctly un-urgent Lite-FM. Usually, I hang up when self-important executives do that to me, but the pace of my investigation dictated a little goodwill, so I mellowed to the soft hits of the eighties and nineties and watched TV on mute.

Monte finally clicked on, sparing me the rest of Rod Stewart's heretical version of "So Far Away."

"I'm at The Palm," he shouted over a waterfall roar of restaurant noise. "A little working dinner."

Monte. A mere two blocks away from the supermarket parking lot where I was having my own Hollywood working dinner with Paul Newman and his Salted Pretzel Rounds.

On my portable TV, Bonnie Quinn stepped onto the fire escape of her apartment and peered up through her telescope. Eight o'clock. *Thanks for Sharing* was on the air.

"Hey, Monte, are you right with your Maker? Are you ready to produce quality sitcom for the Lord's own broadcaster?"

"Otis Grove? Shit, not a problem. It's a great day for the network."

Mr. Company Line covered the phone again, and I heard Elliot mumble around a thirty-dollar appetizer before Monte came back on.

"Listen, the reason for the call. El was hoping for an update going into the weekend."

The squeeze. But how could I blame him? It was Friday night, his balls were on the block, and after three fruitless days, he was fighting panic. I knew the feeling, felt my own deadline dread. The "just checking" calls from Rudy had already started.

On TV Bonnie Quinn took her eye from the telescope and spoke to the sky, which was somewhere above the camera. It was a long speech. I was muted, but she looked pissed. Her character looked pissed most of the time. Outraged at the insanity of today's world. Although the network press release filed the teeth of that animal down to "Urban comedy about a plucky single mom whose ne'er-do-well husband stows away on a NASA mission to Mars, leaving her to deal with the earthly responsibilities he has escaped."

Every episode began and ended with these telescope talks. Early reviews lauded them as clever, feminist op-ed pieces wrapped in comedy. To me, they were more like stream of consciousness rants you could hear at any strip mall bar before last call.

"You still there?"

"Uh, yeah. I was just watching your star on TV. The show that's paying for your dinner is on the air, you know."

"Seen enough of that train wreck. I had to piece her whole perf together in editing," he said. "With all the jump cuts, the audience is going to think it has epilepsy. I hate those fucking telescope talks."

"Why don't you just drop them?"

"Because the fucking Quinn of comedy says it links her passion for astronomy to her character. I tried cutting them once, and she stayed home that day."

"Let me guess, tooth problems?"

"Asshole." And then, enough dancing. "So. Am I having a table reading Monday or not?"

I swallowed. Felt my skin flush. "I'm working it. This is a process."

"That didn't sound like a yes."

"Back it off, Monte. I said I'd find her and I will."

Monte went back to his expensed shellfish, and I went back to *Thanks for Sharing,* which was a lot of Bonnie chewing out easy-target HMO bureaucrats who wouldn't approve a second eye test for her TV son. It was supposed to pass as *vox populi*, but barely achieved warmed-over *Mr. Smith Goes to Washington*. It wasn't even plucky.

At the end of the episode, when she stepped up to her telescope to talk to the husband up there in the heavens who left her with all these problems, I deemed myself sufficiently harangued and hit the off switch. I reached for my paperback of *Mississippi* but stopped myself. Popped the TV back on. To Bonnie Quinn. And her telescope. Just like . . . what? I booted the laptop and reviewed my shots of her dressing room. Found the telescope. And Carl Sagan's *Cosmos*. And all her astronomy magazines.

I pressed my speed dial.

"Pinkman. I need you to cover Brick while I go chase my tail some more."

While I waited for him to show, I looked at my laptop screen again. And that funny black patch on her bedroom wall with all the weird dots painted on it.

# CHAPTER SEVEN

Ray Ortiz didn't get out much. He was always reachable at home or office, he was always in the middle of work, and he was always willing to drop everything for a cup of coffee and some conversation with a real live human from Out There. Out There was where Ray Ortiz seldom went. Ray Ortiz was too busy solving the mysteries of matter versus anti-matter, black holes, and light pulses in other galaxies bent by unseen but calculable forces. He was not so swift at street directions, though, and I beat him to the Starbucks on Colorado even though I had to drive from West Hollywood to Pasadena, where he lived.

Over my coffee and his jumbo blended frozen mocha something with a dome of whipped cream, I feigned interest in the departmental politics at Cal Tech. For twenty interminable minutes my face beamed endless fascination as he droned on about rivalry with Stanford and spat on the names of grant-hungry academics as if I had read their shamelessly derivative papers.

When he paused to squeegee the inside of his cup with a fragment of cookie, I took out my ThinkPad. Ray laughed bits of oatmeal and raisin down his shirtfront. Ten more minutes on why I should go Apple. He brought himself up short when I turned the screen his way. A pleasant sort of agony squeezed his forehead as he stared at the image. I had seen chess masters survey a board that way, and his reaction was all I needed to feel the claws come out of my chest for the first time that day.

I watched him in silence and imagined something like the chirps and whistles of R2-D2 playing in Ray's head. At last, his brow eased and a sly crease dimpled his cheeks.

"Hale-Bopp, 1997," he said. "Not bad. Who's the artist?"

"Wrong question." I waited for his eyes to meet mine. "Where's the artist?"

Ray Ortiz looked back at her painting of the white dots on the black field with the tail of the Hale-Bopp comet shining the beam of God's flashlight back from heaven. He didn't take his Bobby Fischer eyes off the screen. He just said, "Got some time to come to campus?"

"Dude," I said.

The help was generous but it came at a price. Like enduring his all-night harangue about Stanford's inferiority to Cal Tech in the arena of particle acceleration application, interspersed with *Simpsons* episodes synopses while he crunched Bonnie Quinn's Hale-Bopp mural through the department mainframe for a geographic point-of-view match.

"You've got some most excellent markers here, sir. Your artist's POV was facing the eastern horizon, and the comet . . . see here?" Ray tapped the monitor with the wet end of his chewed ballpoint. "That bad boy's adjacent to the constellation Sagitta. And look above. See this string of pearls? Awesome. That's an asterism named the Coathanger in Vulpecula. The comet tail in the painting is short, three degrees long, but that's because it was rendered from the naked eye. Binoculars would have made it six degrees long. . . ."

He went on and on, but I came out at noon the next day with more than a headache. Ray couldn't give me the address, but he did come up with the zip code. I held a map of the Sonoran Desert with a five square-mile grid marking off where her painting was sketched on February 9, 1997. It didn't tell me Bonnie Quinn was there back then, or if she was there now but, stacked against a night of watching Brick sip *doppio* espressos in West Hollywood, it was the better shot.

Two hours of desert driving past Palm Springs and the Salton Sea, I spotted the town through mirage-bent miles of sand and cactus. The low-rise motels and strip malls of Borrego Springs looked like dice and Chiclets strewn across a barren valley floor. The hope of finding her there was tethered to a slender thread, but all my experience tracking taught me that when people violate their habits, you track their passions instead.

I hadn't given up following the drugs. Hell, they were her habit and her passion, right? Although I had no clue where she would score the illicits locally, Monte's poker-faced response to her oral surgery pre-scription scam made the local pharmacies a juicy square-one.

The good and the bad news about sifting leads in a town whose population would fit into a high school football stadium and still leave room for the marching band is that the choices are few. Three pharmacies served the good citizens of Borrego Springs, and one of them was in a medical complex that was closed on Saturdays and Sundays. That left me with a chain drug store in the main strip mall and a home-grown place that looked like it had been there since the stage coaches rattled down the Butterfield Overland Route out of the San Felipes.

It was Saturday after five, and both were closed. The Spring Inn looked like it would do for a night, so I booked a room and cruised Palm Canyon Drive all evening, showing her picture at the short list of motor hotels, gas stations, and convenience stores. Everybody said she looked like that sassy woman on TV; nobody had seen her in person. Late night, I hit the cocktail lounges and the Morongo Tribe casino. No joy.

Sunday at noon I presented myself at the chain drugstore as Ms. Quinn's personal assistant who was sent to pick up a prescription. A cheerful Native American woman searched the database and came up with no record of any Quinns using that store or the nearest sister stores in Brawley, Indio, or Julian. Bonnie either knew better than to mess with big chains or knew exactly how to mess with them using aliases and whatever other desperate resourcefulness a drug life brings. Or, I was wasting my time less than twenty-four hours from the table read. I thanked the pharmacist for her help and stepped out of the coolness and the Captain & Tennille muzak into the baking glare.

When I announced myself at Roadrunner Drug as Bonnie's personal assistant, the pair of Western Swing geezers behind the counter gave me The Stare and a pimply stock boy on the toy aisle stopped feathering dust off unsold Power Rangers. The old man crossed his arms across his lab coat, looked to the old woman in the Dale Evans hairdo who stood behind the register, then back to me.

"We don't do any third-party transactions," he said. "Kyle, you get back to your dusting, this is no concern of yours."

The teenager in the apron got the cheap toys swaying on their spindles but kept watch of me through a green pyramid of sunburn gels. The pharmacist softened his voice but not his tone as he addressed me.

"Prescription painkillers are carefully regulated pharmaceuticals, young man. I don't know how it is up in Los Angeles or Hollywood, but I have an idea. We don't tolerate any funny business here. Never have, never will."

Bingo. No more calls, please, we have a winner. He went right to painkillers even though I had never mentioned them.

"Painkillers . . . You think I'm here for her painkillers?" I laughed. "No way. Ms. Quinn gave me a list of stuff she wants delivered. All over-the-counter, I assure you."

I opened my notebook to an old page of travel expenses and pretended to refer to it while I inventoried the sad shelves of the little store.

"Let's see—Woolite for her hand wash." I stacked three bottles next to the register and continued. "Mouthwash. Four of those. Bath beads, a dozen Neutrogena face creams with the SPF-15, a Timex sports watch—Chocolates. Do you have the big Whitman's Sampler? The pounder?"

"Brach's," said the Dale Evans lady at the register. I thought she had something in her throat until she said, "We only carry Brach's."

"Perfect. I need ten of each."

"Kyle, what are you doing? Help the man."

I could have tailed Kyle on foot. He took Palm Canyon at a crawl, one hand on the wheel and the other slapping his wood laminate car door to the beat of some white gangsta rap that guaranteed him a Miracle Ear by the time he reached the age he never thought about reaching. At a stop sign, I pulled up beside him and held up a twenty.

# CHAPTER EIGHT

The travel trailer sat on the sandy floor of a place my GPS called Hellhole Canyon. PR reason enough to keep its location secret. According to my topo map, her acre cove of virgin desert was the last parcel on the western skirt of Borrego Springs. Go any farther and you hit the protected wilds of Anza-Borrego State Park and the forbidding ascent of San Ysidro Mountain. If she wanted solitude, this bought it.

My man Sam got it right in *Roughing It* when he called the arid West a waveless ocean stricken dead and turned to ashes. There's something about the desert that taps a spring of gloom in me. It isn't just the remoteness, the horizon-to-horizon of seeming nothingness that dwarfs everything but your conscience. It's stumbling upon signs of life gone to litter and engulfed by the petrified sea. You see an old wood shack, once somebody's fresh start, now caved-in and bullet pocked by vandals goofy for targets. Or drive by one of those road-side shrines of handmade white crosses, often painted with a first name and a date and "so young." I have stopped at these shrines and wondered about the neat stacks of coins left beneath the artificial flowers, until I stacked a few of my own and moved on, never soon enough.

My melancholy grew as the mountains gave the sun an early set and the desert cove below me turned all Ansel Adams. The camper became a grey box on bone colored sand. Leafless smoke trees, waxy green the hour before, rose up like silver ghosts. Chollas became milky trolls. The deeper the mountains dropped into shadow, the more they revealed their chalky injuries—white crumblings where the sun's power caused mere granite to split and peel.

I pulled on my jacket and opened a couple of the Brach's bags from the carton. Dinner. When I got to the Peanut Butter Meltaways, I saw light. I wrapped my hand around the Nikon FE my father had given me; ran my thumb on the pebbly black rubber sheath on its body; felt the little nick in the metal on the bottom which was once sharp enough to snag skin but had worn smooth in the years since a rapper's bodyguard slapped it to a Vegas sidewalk; found my initials etched in block letters beside the shutter release, right where my dad had put them so I would feel them there as I rested my finger before and after each picture, to make sure, he had said, that I was putting my name on every shot. I used my long lens as a scope and trained it down on the window, where a faint cuff of amber seeped under the shade at one end of the trailer. A gas generator droned somewhere. Probably blocked by the car.

I checked my cellular for signal again. Still no bars. I tapped the stub of antenna against my lips and dismissed driving to town to phone Monte. How bush league would it be for me to call in the Marines only to startle an old prospector or some meth chemist? I needed a sighting.

I needed to wait.

I needed patience.

As they often do on a stakeout, my thoughts drifted to Meddy. I resolved if she returned my call I would ask her to dinner. I placed her in flattering light. Maybe at the Peninsula. Or else Ivy at the Shore for sunset and Billie Holliday instead of candles and Yo-Yo Ma. I framed her on the patio, surrounded by couples who looked like they belonged together and had endured things. I tried to organize her face into something like gladness, pushing aside my burnished memory of her pain and judgment and anger and, at last, detachment as she set me adrift under copper oxide lamps in the HoJo's parking lot in Nashua for what I had done.

Patience.

A soundless jet left a pink contrail miles overhead. The bats were out, flitting from cliffs and wild palms to feed on night bugs. And somewhere Rudy Newgate was lining up a couple of WWF rejects for the day after tomorrow, expecting money and sunglasses.

Could Bonnie Quinn be in there, just a hundred yards down the sheer of the canyon? Was she a day sleeper behind blackout drapes, rising to prowl with the kangaroo rats and scorpions? Or was she passed out in a chair, sleeping off some Belushi Special, unable to master the disposable lighter at this stage of the fun? Or maybe she was face-down on the bathroom floor, a dry floater, the cops called them, when the bodies were ballooned up like cows waiting on the forklift.

Fuck patience.

The aluminum skin of the camper gave my ear hints of the day's warmth when I pressed it there to listen. But the stupid generator damped any sound I could pick up inside the Hellhole trailer.

I circled around to the packed dirt drive under half a moon and a canopy of stars bright enough to cast my shadow. There was an Audi there, a TT that was new, but only technically. Its color was a multiple choice guess hidden under a film of desert and neglect. One of the rear fenders had been creased enough to buckle the trunk and mangle the tail light. Who had she played demolition derby with in her Boxster? Dellroy Means. I wondered who she backed into with this car, and felt the hood. Cold.

I tiptoed to the door. Professional reflex: I leaned forward and sniffed for the sour death. Before I drew a full inhale the door flew open and all I saw was gun.

"The fuck you doing?" she shouted.

She must have switched off the lights because there was no face. Just a hand waving a revolver in my eyes, close enough to see hollow points nested in their silos.

I eased back and whispered "Whoa," the way you'd soothe a spooked horse.

She stepped out of the darkness, an entrance into starlight. Well, I had my sighting. Bonnie Quinn was holding a gun on me. Her eyes flashed wild, wary. The 9mm looked heavy in her hand. She waved and dipped it unsteadily. Then she thrust it into my face again. A jerky, you-tawkin'-to-me move. I put both hands in front of me. Like that would help. Ask any coroner about defense wounds to palms.

"I asked you what you're doing." The flat, South Boston accent was hoarse from adrenaline. "Trying to catch me sleeping? That what you were sent to do? Come at night and put one here?" She jerked the muzzle to her temple, then put it back on me just as fast. "Is that why they sent you, to cap me in my bed?"

"No."

I eased backward. I felt safer with Rudy's pros.

"Hands."

"Here they are. I don't have a gun. See?"

"What's that?" Pointing at my belt. "That there."

"It's a camera."

"A camera?" Her voice lower, still raspy.

"Yeah." That didn't seem like enough. "I'm a photographer."

She fired. Planted one in the dirt in front of me.

I jumped back and yelled, "Hey!" and caught some sand on my tongue.

"Don't hey me, motherfucker, this is my house."

She shot twice more. Two more in the dirt. Two more dragon snorts in the dark. Slapback echoes bounced off rock. I measured the distance from me to her. Thought about rushing her instead of taking one in the spine on the run or in the chest standing there like a dumb fuck. All in a blink, still hearing the reverberations roll up Hellhole, I measured my odds and decided on the rush. Then she stopped shooting and started laughing. I felt no safer. It was an asylum qualifier if I ever heard one. A raspy, buccaneer's laugh, cruel and wounding and over the top.

"Fuck," she said, and finally wheezed in some air. "It's you. It's the asshole."

I went back to measuring distances and counting bullets. Bonnie didn't seem to know what to do. She looked at me and then at her gun, then over her shoulder to the open door of the dark trailer, then back to me.

"Over here. Sit down."

She gestured to some Wal-Mart patio chairs beside her.

"How about the gun?"

She fired it. Sky shot this time.

"Yup, still working." She barked out her buccaneer's laugh again.

I slipped my digital camera off my belt and strobed her. When the flash blinded Bonnie, I slapped my palm around the cylinder to jam the revolver and yanked it free.

"Shit," she said and made a sloppy lunge at me, but I was behind her by then, and she stumbled into the patio chair. "Motherfuck."

Just one wild swing of her arm, another air ball, and Bonnie Quinn was down for this round. She began to weep, rubbing her eyes either from the afterflash, the sting of her tears, or both, then sat heavily on the ground. She drew her knees up to her chest, buried her face in them, and sobbed.

Unmoved by the theatrics, I sat in one of the cheap plastic chairs.

She looked up. "You got your fucking picture, why don't you get out of here?"

"I'm not here for your picture."

She sniffed hard and shut off the tears. "Then I was right."

"About what?"

"I am not afraid, you know." She sat Pilates tall and put her shoulders back. "You've got the gun. Go ahead. I've prepared myself."

I extracted the remaining bullets and casings from the cylinder and flung them into the night.

"Then, what?"

"They want you back."

The actress softly rocked her head, processing data. "Monte?"

"Elliot and Monte. You're wanted on the set, Ms. Quinn."

"They sent you here?"

She struggled to her feet and looked at her open door again and the darkness in there, then turned back to me, staying put, but wanting to run somewhere, anywhere. "They know about this place?"

She turned a panic circle and surveyed the cliffs as if instead of warring Apaches they would be rimmed by TV executives. A dog's whimper caught in her throat.

"You have to tell me. It's important. Do they know about this place?"

"Not yet." I palmed my cell phone to check for signal.

"No." Bonnie Quinn dropped to her knees before me. "Please?" She chased my eyes, beseeching. "Please," she whispered. And again, "Please?"

"They're waiting to hear from me."

"Fuck them."

"They need you at the table reading tomorrow."

"Fuck. Them."

"I'm supposed to let Monte come get you. That's my deal."

"They can't know about this place. They can't. Please? A favor for me?"

"You shot at me."

"I thought you were here to kill me."

"I showed you I was unarmed. That's when you shot at me."

"I did not shoot at you. I shot near you. Look, I am licensed and police qualified to carry that firearm. If I wanted to shoot you, asshole, you'd be coyote meat about now. You got a cigarette?"

"No."

"Oo." She slapped her forehead. "Got it, yay. And it's win-win. I'll just go back on my own. Don't snicker at me like that, I mean it, I will."

"Sure you will."

"I will." She grabbed the arms of my chair and shook. "You've already got me. Bam. I have been bagged by the mighty hunter and now I am at your mercy."

She draped her hands atop her head, POW-style. The actress.

"But do you have to break my spirit by blowing this place? Isn't it debasing enough that I have to slink back to do their bidding without the additional degradation of having them know about this?"

She rose and pounded the side of the trailer, making it rock on its supports of stacked cinderblock. Even as trailer trash, Bonnie Quinn was an overachiever.

"This is all I have. This is the only place I can go. The only place nobody knows about. This is sacred ground to me. Do I have to watch it sullied by Monte Arnett trotting his ass around here in his Italian driving shoes, claiming one more thing of mine that I do not wish to give up?"

Tears plopped on my knees. Bonnie Quinn made no attempt to swipe them from her eyes but knelt there at my feet.

"For a signature on a production contract I have made a Faustian bargain and sealed my doom, I know that. Just like the servants who cook their meals and the maids who brush their rusty piss stains off their toilets and the illegals who hose their garbage cans, I am just another hireling to do their drudgery."

"You get six figures an episode to put on a play once a week."

"Don't!" She slapped both hands on the plastic arms of my chair. "Do not presume to lecture me. I came here to take stock of my life after the relentless piecing off of my human dignity and immortal soul. For years I have been a willing agent of my own spiritual demise at the hands of those dickless goons. And if—if—I manage to survive, which I am not sure I deserve to do, but if I live, I beg you—beg you—please, please, please do not torch the one shred of myself I have left to cling to in the dark hours of my soul." She paused. "I will allow you drive me back to LA yourself, but please do not send for them or tell anyone about this place." Her eyes were not six inches from mine: black dimes, unblinking, waiting. "Is there enough humanity in you to do that for me?"

The high opera didn't sway me, but I did review the practicals. Elliot's priority was to get her to the table reading. Yes, Monte instructed me to let him bring her in from the cold, but I blew that by getting doorstepped. Plus, no cellular service. I couldn't exactly leave to call him, and I was not up for false imprisonment charges by restraining her. Like I would, anyway. Which raised the next red flag. What if she got violent? Recently, an audience member, some bewildered fan from Iowa, coughed during a scene and now owned a Cadillac after America's Soccer Mom climbed the rail and bitch slapped his John Deere cap off. No, I didn't want to rumble with this tenement Southie, and since, for the moment, I had the consent of the governed, I chose the safer path. Besides, at this point, I just wanted my money so I could get my life back.

"OK," I said.

"God fucking bless you." She rose, lurching to the next thought. "Oh, hey. Will you just wait out here while I finish up inside? You caught me in the middle of something." I gave her a wary look. "Ten minutes, tops."

"Tops."

"Put 'er there." I reached to shake but she grabbed my hand in both of hers and massaged it on her chest. "Here ya go, you get some of this." I pulled away, and she smiled. "How'd you like that? Just a little treat for being a good boy to Aunt Bonnie."

One word: Ew.

By rote she drew her T-shirt up over her head, exposing her naked breasts, pallid and implanted, which I could already verify from the feel. Then she rolled back to lie on the sand and raised her pelvis to unfasten her cutoffs.

". . . I don't think so."

"You sure? Get it while it's hot, cowboy."

"I'm good, thanks."

I picked up the T-shirt and tossed it over her chest where she lay. It had a picture of the Tasmanian Devil on it. Perfect, I thought. Looney Tunes.

# CHAPTER NINE

I f I had to go on a cross-country road trip with Bonnie Quinn, one of us would be dead by Phoenix. Some people pinball through their lives, spinning and twisting, fueled by their whims. Bonnie was rocket fueled with no apparent guidance system. She couldn't land on a radio station and stay there. My presets were LA, so she spent the hour out of Borrego Springs to Coachella bouncing around the local signals, twanging along with Hank Snow's *I've Been Everywhere*, shouting out *amens* and *testify, brothers* to a microphone-eating black preacher, and improvising bawdy translation to a tribal broadcast, setting back the concept of diversity to the days of Italian Injuns on *F-Troop*.

"How come you're not laughing at this shit? This is my A material. The folks in Vegas mortgage their houses to come see me do this."

"Just concentrating on my driving."

"You're sulking. You're sittin' sorry you didn't dive into the thank-you poon, aren't you?"

My personal comedienne fluttered back to the radio and was off on a chunk about KNX Traffic and Weather Together Every Ten Minutes.

"It's fucking midnight Sunday. They want to perform a service this time of night, they ought to broadcast domestic violence every ten minutes." She lapsed into matter-of-fact traffic reporter. "Uh, Bob, we've got two bleeders and a black eye at Van Nuys and Oxnard. And on Century Boulevard in Inglewood, use the right lane to avoid a laid-off construction worker with a piece of rebar. Says he's going to cave in his old lady's teeth with it when he gets—Oo, pull off here, pull off."

She grabbed the steering wheel, but I held it.

"Hey. What the hell are you doing?"

"Sorr-ree." She turned and knelt, looking over the back of her seat like she was seven. "I want an In-N-Out. You like In-N-Out?"

"Love In-N-Out."

"That's what a hamburger's all about," she sang from their jingle. I checked the mirror and saw the sign shrinking behind us at the Bob Hope Drive exit.

"I gotta eat something now."

I weighed the prospect of another riff on bleeders and black eyes.

"We'll stop at the next off-ramp," I said. "I could use some food, too."

No, what I could have really used was about four inches of duct tape.

When I woke Monte up and told him he could green light his table reading, I had to hold the phone away for the whoop he let out. Bonnie heard it across the laminated table from me.

"Hot damn, bet that's the loudest scream they've heard in Brentwood on a Sunday night since OJ—'allegedly'," she added with that derisive laugh, then stuffed a bundle of fries in her mouth.

Monte soured. Turned on a dime. "Is she fucking there? With you?"

"Yes."

"Shit, Hardwick, I gave you clear instructions not to deal with her. Jesus H. Christ. Where are you?"

"On the road. Making a little pit stop."

"Where?"

No idle chitchat. A demand. I had visions of tough guys who owed Monte favors rolling out of the sack, deploying on my ass.

"Some roadside place," was all I said, sounding casual enough.

"Where did you find her?"

I looked at Bonnie, lid off her burger, frowning at the cheese, who knows, but listening just the same.

"It doesn't matter where."

"What? Who the hell are you working for?"

Bonnie couldn't miss his shout and took the phone from me.

"Hey, Mont-ster, this yo bitch." She laughed and picked off a glob of paint or Wite-Out from her dirty fingers. "Listen, I'm coming in and that's all you need to know, you needle-dicked weasel."

A trucker at the counter swiveled to stare. Bonnie lit into him.

"Hey, Willie Nelson, shouldn't you be out drilling air holes for the wetbacks in the rear of your truck instead of surfing my private call?"

She went back to Monte without missing a beat.

"You still there? Of course you are. You're probably taping this to play for Elliot. Listen, Mont-ster, wanna make yourself useful? Have whatever turd sandwich you're calling this week's script in my dressing room before the reading so I can figure out what writers to fire. Meanwhile, I am bored listening to your breathing and you can fuck off and die."

She slid the phone across the table.

"Thanks for not throwing me in," she said.

I poured syrup and ate my cold pancakes.

"You just roll along, don't you? I mean you don't seem freaked by a strong woman. Do you like strong women?"

"I like smart women. Strong sort of comes along with that."

She nodded to some internal dialogue and said, "How'd you find me, anyway?"

"Trade secret."

"You give it up, or I ride off with Willie Nelson. And trust me, he'd take the poontang, if I offered."

I gave her the *TV Guide* logline of how I connected her wall painting of Hale-Bopp to the place it was painted.

"Hot damn, you're a smart one, aren't you. That's different." She kept staring. Thoughtful. "Look at you, so damn mellow. I want to put a mirror under your nose, see if you're breathing. Nothing gets to you, does it?"

I kept eating, wishing I hadn't pulled off the I-10. We'd be coming down into Redlands about then. That much closer to wrapping up this clusterfuck.

Bonnie swept her arm across the table and wiped everything onto the floor in a sixteen square tile clatter of plastic, stainless, and road food. The little window to the kitchen filled with two faces under white paper caps. A tiny old man appeared rolling his bucket rig to the clean the floor. Bonnie slammed the table with the flat of her hand and leaned at me.

"Do not invalidate me with your indifference."

The little man U-turned back inside the swinging door. I wanted to join him.

"I may be cargo to you, but I am a person. A scared person without much time left." She gave her eyebrows an important lift and stared at me under black arches. "I believe I am going to be dead soon."

Why didn't I just let Monte come get her? I tried to fathom what sort of worm bucket of a mind I was dealing with. A drama queen in denial? Clinical paranoia? Pharmadramatics? A cry for help? Or a combo plate of the above? How do you respond to a statement like that? I led with my strong suit, ignorance.

"I don't follow."

"Nobody does."

She made a weak gesture, a flourish with both hands, indicating

Bonnie Quinn, the whole damn package, then slouched back in her chair.

"You know why I came along with you tonight? Why I let you take me back?" She didn't wait for an answer. "Galena Forest. Don't pretend you don't remember. Reno? Just before second season? You staked out me and my daughter up at my cabin off Mt. Rose."

I shifted a little.

"Hey, it's OK, Hardwick, I know it was you. I saw you."

"I've got to reevaluate my stealth. I was supposed to be a mountain hemlock."

"I saw you from the cabin my last day there." Her eyes cleared. For the first time they looked lucid, penetrating. "But you sat on the pictures."

My visuals spooled. Bonnie Quinn's illegitimate daughter blasting out of the driveway after days and nights of shouting and tears and recriminations and heartbreak.

"You ate the story."

"There was no story," I said. "And the pictures were bad."

"Bullshit. I know what you saw. And I know what you did for me. And what you could have done."

"Whatever you want to believe."

"So. I took this ride with you tonight 'cause I knew I'd be safe. At least for now."

By the time I merged onto the Interstate, Bonnie Quinn was turning pages in my copy of *Life on the Mississippi*.

"Mark Twain, huh? You into Mark Twain?"

Thank God, a subject change. "Oh, yeah, big time."

"This book was pure fucking commerce."

Shit. Why did I leave that out for her to violate with her greasy fingers? And double-shit, why did I set myself up so she could yank the rug right out from under me? Let it go, Hardwick. Shut up and drive.

"Are you going to tell me this is good?"

Let it go, bro, let it go.

"Glorified travelogue the *Sunday Times* wouldn't waste the ink on today." She flipped pages and I could hear some of them rip. "All he did was take a big, steamy dump and publish it to bail his egotistical butt out of bankruptcy."

I wondered what would happen if I drove into a bridge support at this speed. Not head-on, mind you, just her half of the car. My teeth were locked, my knuckles were vise grips on the steering wheel, and adrenaline was streaming chunks of murder fantasies to all the volatile parts of me. My fault. I'd bought in. Two more hours left with this noxious payload. I could endure that. All I had to do was not engage.

"You don't know what the hell you're talking about." Screw it. That felt very, very good.

"Oh, my. Is that a rise? You're actually going to talk to me?"

"*Following the Equator* was his bankruptcy book. Maybe if you had actually read it instead of using it as a coaster, you'd know that."

"You mean it was his bankrupt book. Bigger piece of shit than this."

She tossed my paperback over her shoulder and into the back.

"The man crafted the form for the American novel. Not every page can be as lofty as *Thanks for Sharing*." This was starting to be fun.

"Oh, I see. You're into content."

"Yeah, if you mean reading a good story."

"Beginning, middle, end?"

"Helps."

"Big surprise, a content man."

I checked my side mirror to change lanes and heard something like M & Ms rattle in her hand. I turned back as she popped something, practiced and casual. Jack Nicholson eating bar peanuts in *The Shining*. Not such a random parallel, on reflection. Whatever she ate, it must have been in her cutoffs. She had no purse. No nothing. In fact, when she came out of her trailer, she just locked the padlock and left the generator to run itself dry.

"You read Faulkner?"

"Some."

"Bullshit. You tried to read Faulkner and he was too true."

"I tried to read Faulkner and he was too . . . What am I saying?"

"That you probably move your lips when you read. You're so hung up on the words, the fucking words, your Twain-dulled expectations of content." Disdain, like a fart in front of the parson. "You can keep your damn Huck Sawyers. The best river writing ever committed to paper was those losers trying to float Mama's casket across that water in *As I Lay Dying*, fuck me. But you don't get it, I can see that on your face."

"Oh, I got it. I'm just not into rereading every other page because I can't follow what's happening or who's talking."

"Because your reading habits have inbred you to the level of Appalachian drooler. Strindberg got it. He took his famous panoptic photo of the night sky without a camera. He exposed the stars on a plate facing the heavens so he could see it all at once."

I calculated time and distance and goosed the gas pedal five MPH.

"Ach!" She flailed the dashboard like bongos. "You just don't get it. Look, the genius of William Faulkner—as opposed to the gee-whiz hackwork of a Mark Twain—was that he was able to fuse the content with the container."

She was slurring and speed-talking now and I saw her labor to slow herself down from whatever was releasing into her bloodstream the way some drunks drive too slowly. "I'll repeat it for you, because I want you to memorize it. Faulkner's art was to make the container itself the content. Can you get that? No, of course not. But you will. You'll need to. God damn, hear me. You must see what Faulkner saw. The content is the container."

With that Bonnie Quinn shut down for the rest of the drive. She turned away and curled in a ball on her seat, facing sideways to the slow lane. Every once in a while I caught her reflection on the passenger window and saw her eyes, open and blank. Staring, but unseeing. Like waiting for the coroner to come close them. That was the drugs, I guessed. Or maybe it was all her death talk creeping into my head like intruders in a dream.

If Monte Arnett was still pissed at me it was clenched behind a piano key smile when I put it in park outside Stage 2 with Bonnie Quinn riding shotgun. Of course, the grin was for his prodigal star. Me, I got a cursory, "Got it from here, man."

I also got a thick envelope.

Bonnie saw it change hands and mock-cried, "My name not be Toby. My name Kunta Kinte."

It was as half-hearted as it was distasteful and wouldn't spark one cellular video upload to TMZ from The Laugh Factory. At 3:30 in the morning, stoned to numbness, I guess you just don't give up the A material.

No good-bye. No thanks. No can I split the gas? Just a view of their backs on their way up the Astro-Turf runner leading to her dressing room. She gave a lost look over her shoulder and I thought I saw her take a step to say something to me when Monte guided her inside with one of his gentle bear arms. Then the door closed and I stood there feeling finished, but incomplete. Or maybe just diminished.

# CHAPTER TEN

**B**ig glow on Sunset. Somebody's night shoot. I pulled up beside the half dozen paparazzi outside the yellow tape, a pigeon cluster strutting like roosters.

"That's how you get the great shots, fellas. Stand close together behind a cop." Dellroy Means laughed and toasted me with his coffee. Chuck Rank, the kid standing off alone, flipped me off.

I first noticed Chuck when he was a gawky high school pest who started showing up premiere nights in Westwood with an erection and a shoplifted Polaroid to shoot starlets for his bathroom wall. Since then his gear had improved, but little else. He dropped out to "work the job," and still lived in a two-bedroom apartment with his bickering mother and about a dozen cats.

Chuck approached my window, pinching at one of the swollen amber pimples on his cheekbones. He gestured with his camera. "There's a Desperate Housewife in there."

I looked behind the barrier and nodded, then said, "Hey, Chuck, I saw you hanging out at the Farmer's Market the other day."

"Yeah?"

"With the Canuck."

"Armantrout. So? What about it?"

"Watch out for him," I said. "You don't want to be falling in with him."

"Why, because of the competition? Because he's been scoring all the Gets?"

"Because he uses young guys like you. He's bad news." I wanted to tell him about Fagan, but if *Oliver Twist* ever made Chuck's summer reading list, it never got home. "I'd steer clear."

"Like I need your advice."

"Fine, I'm just trying to keep you out of trouble."

"Yeah, big tip from the big has-been." Then Chuck leaned his face in my car window close enough to smell the breath. "Loozah!" He made an L on his forehead with his thumb and finger and inched closer. "Loozah!"

I didn't think about it, I just backhanded him. We were both stunned. He put his hand over his nose and blood ran down his wrist toward his elbow.

"Fuck you, Hardwick. Just fuck you." Then he hiked up Sunset to his car.

"Nice going," said Dellroy Means. "You just chased off my ride."

I watched Chuck drive off past us, listened to his parting "Loozah!" then turned back to Dellroy.

"Pinkman told me about your fender bender down at the Improv."

"My insurance payment was late. Now I'm shagging rides off Chuck Asswipe. How sad is that?"

"Then rent."

As soon as I said it I remembered Pinkman also told me Dellroy was struggling. The CPA who'd seen enough of his cubicle and just walked out the door one day last year with a camera and a 'tude was this close to losing his house. I could relate.

"Yeah, been thinking about that. Renting."

He lowered his eyes. I thought of the fat envelope in my glove compartment and the slack I just bought.

"Listen, Dell," I thumbed my BlackBerry e-mails. "*London Look* is all over me to grab some naughty royal. He's due in on a private jet at Van Nuys about noon with a Russian figure skater he's inducting to the mile high club. It's not huge, but you want it?"

"Oh, hey, man, thanks. But I couldn't."

"OK, first off, I'd grab it myself, but it's been one hellacious week. All I want to do is go home and crash. Second, what the hell is the matter with you?"

"Nothing. I'm just—"

"—You're just losing your ass. This isn't the goddam CPA office, Dellroy. You want to make some money at this job, you've got to learn to clang some brass between your legs." I held out the BlackBerry screen. "Now do you want the Get or not?"

Turning onto Laurel Canyon, I was so done for the night. Or, in this case, morning. Guilt simmered over smacking Chuck Rank. I rolled down all my windows to deep-sniff the chaparral as I ascended the hills, and I wondered why I lost it like that. It all felt bad and mingled with the toxic residue I wore from the Bonnie Quinn job and what it took out of me to take it in the first place. But that envelope saved my hide. Combined with some recycled Angelina Jolie candids I sold to a German tabloid, it was enough for me to make good with Rudy a day early. Maybe bank some goodwill for next week if the Gets didn't pan out. A deer bolted into my brights from the scrub oak guarding my driveway and almost won a free makeover at the taxidermist. It scrambled for purchase on the pavement and disappeared into the thicket leading to the canyon below Mulholland. After I recovered, I smiled a little, glad to live in what passes for nature in this town.

I doused my headlights and drove slowly past the main house so I wouldn't wake up the old woman. But I could see the blue flicker of Turner Classic Movies against her lace sheers on the second floor master suite. By the time I pulled around to my guest cottage at the back of the property, her flashlight was already bobbing across the half acre lawn, sending shimmers off the koi pond between our houses.

"Home from the wars, Mr. Hardwick?"

Her rich voice cut through the night, bold and grand, full of piercing enunciation and amused privilege. When she emerged from the arbor of wisteria onto my small brick patio, the motion sensitive flood kicked on, bathing her in light. The lady hadn't stepped in front of a camera since David Niven cut in on Dirk Bogarde to waltz with her in *Mutineer's Dowry*, but if anybody knew how to make an entrance, it was Amanda St. Hillaire.

"Now tell me, where was it this time? San Francisco? Rome? Monte Carlo?"

"Borrego Springs."

She gave a mild shake of her head. I hitched a thumb east.

"Out past the Salton Sea. Between Palm Springs and the Mexican border."

Her eyes sketched a picture of disappointment. "Well, then. It is a professional's duty, is it not? Go wherever one must. It was fruitful, at least?"

"Oh, yes."

"Good for you, Mr. Hardwick, good for you."

Singing her words. Everything's luscious.

"Is that heavy, Amanda? Would you like me to take that?"

I gave a side nod to the saber in her right hand.

"Nonsense. I hardly knew I was holding it." She lifted the old sword. "There've been some tough looking men coming around your door recently. One even peeked into your back window."

"That's all done now. Don't worry about them."

"Oh, I'm not worried, trust me. Not with this."

She air-carved a figure-eight before letting it clang to a rest on my Adirondack chair.

"You've still got the moves, Miss St. Hillaire."

"I taught Mr. Niven how to riposte on our last picture, you know."

I knew. Knew from every single time she told me. My nostrils flared in yawn concealment, and I leaned my ass against my car.

"*Pride of the Legion?*" I asked, knowing otherwise.

"No, that was with Randolph Scott. I was just watching Randy on my Turner channel. Elegant, even as a cowboy, that man. Oh, look at you, I'm keeping you from your bed, Mr. Hardwick." The old woman gathered her heavy bathrobe about her and took up her saber. "I could bring you a late breakfast, if you'd like."

"Thank you, but not this time. Can I walk you back to your house?"

"You sleep," she said, then disappeared through the arbor with a wave of her saber.

I stood at my cottage door until her bobbing light reached the big house and I heard the porch door close and bolt.

The dream featured Meddy. As usual. But it was a jumble. A casket beached in sand. Bonnie Quinn's desert dump. Meddy hears a ringing phone and walks to the dark open door of the trailer. My warnings choke off in dead air. Meddy laughs, says it'll be fine in there, and when she turns back, has on the Tasmanian Devil shirt. If I could only get that phone for her she'd stay out of there, but I have those dream-dead legs and so she goes in anyway, swallowed by the dark, and the damn phone keeps ringing and ringing right through my dream until I haul myself up the ladder out of my sleep and find my phone and croak out a hello.

"It's me."

Pitch black in my bedroom, thanks to drapes. Blue digits say 9:08 AM.

"Monte?"

"Get down here. Just get down here now."

Click.

# CHAPTER ELEVEN

"**B**onnie Quinn refuses" to work. She won't come out of her dressing room to the table reading. Unless—"

He hung it there to pull my attention.

"Unless?"

"—Unless you work the week as the stillsman."

I laughed. Had to. The cosmic absurdity of me working as a member of the crew was too hilarious to sit on. Monte waited me out. Glowering. No doubt wondering if he just reached out and choked me if my eyes would bug like those pink rubber Obie dolls.

"This is your fucking fuck-up, Hardwick. I told you not to deal with her."

"I got doorstepped, for chrissakes. I had to play it on the bounce."

The intercom double-purred and Monte snapped it up.

"OK, put him on." He swiveled his ergonomic chair and forced cheerfulness up from his socks. "Brucie, you dog, coming to the reading, I hear." Then nodding, "Yeah well, we have a few notes, too. We should be starting in like five minutes."

While Mr. Good News spread sunshine, I rose to look out his second floor balcony. From his strategic view of this corner of

Empire Studios I counted three mini meetings on the lot below. The *Thanks for Sharing* supporting cast formed a circle in the parking area beside the stage. Deane Tacksdale, her bachelor neighbor, ranted and threw pissed-off gestures. Outside the Writers Bungalow a guy I recognized from one of the old NBC Thursday Night Must-Sees pitched a Nerf baseball to the other writers, who were using rolled scripts as bats. At the third cluster, a pair of junior network executives shuffled feet beside a seriously big and black Mercedes. Inside, a UEN Comedy VP crooked his cell phone to his ear and listened to Monte's bullshit. When the veep of laughs hung up, I turned from the window. Monte set his phone down and I shook his hand.

"Thanks anyway, but pass-adena."

He followed me downstairs and caught up with me on the outside steps.

"Come on, Hardwick. You owe me."

"For what?"

"I got the lawsuit dropped."

"You did yourself a favor with that."

"I set you up with your gig. You had a sweet payday."

"And you got your star back. And, frankly? I've seen enough of the creep show, thanks. Movin' on to the next tent."

Elliot Pratt stepped out of the air conditioning with a script and a pencil.

"El, can you believe he's just going to leave?" said Monte. "And he hasn't heard our offer."

For a man with so much at stake, Elliot Pratt showed great ease. He silently took my measure, then nodded slightly.

"It's the ethical thing again, right? Your . . . line?"

Even as he recognized my issue, his little hitch, that tiny hesitation, demeaned it. Power games.

"Elliot, it's a conflict of interest for me. I'm not a house man, I'm a bring down the house man."

The executive put a soft touch on my shoulder.

"Would you do me one favor? Hear me out? Give me a fighting chance?"

His bald technique might be effective with sycophants and stooges but, I'm sorry, charm just isn't a strong enough disinfectant. It deodorizes, but it doesn't kill germs where they live.

"I looked the other way last time. I don't think I can go there again."

"What if I offered you a matching envelope?"

Fuck, this again. No. I needed to say *no*. But I had just dodged a bullet with the last envelope, and in a week the next payment was due. And one more after that. And look at how things had been going. And hadn't I already crossed this line, so what was one more week? Shit. This was scooping out my soul from the inside. I broke off eye contact and looked down at the scab line etched on my knuckle where Rudy had held the bolt cutters, when the doors of the UEN van parked up the alley opened and the news crew filed onstage. One of them was Meddy.

"What's all that?" I said.

Meddy lingered in the elephant door, busy with her crew, not looking out, not seeing me. Not hearing my pulse.

"That's Meredith Benson," said Monte.

Elliot added, "She's going to be with us all week for an on-set exclusive on Episode One Hundred."

# CHAPTER TWELVE

**H**obby Horse Productions was so elated to have me join the crew for the table reading that they hid me away, high in the unlit nosebleed section of the empty audience bleachers. Monte said it would be less disruptive to tuck me into the shadows and let the cast and crew get used to me in tiny doses later. I wondered if I could take a nap. Not likely with the goosey chatter going on below.

I hosed the stage through my 10:1 zoom. Everyone sat in red canvas chairs around four tables jigsawed together to form a jumbo oblong. The big table filled the apron between the bleachers and the standing sets of Bonnie's TV living room and kitchen, which waited in half-light, shrouded in dust sheeting. Production staff filled rows behind Monte, who sat at one end of the conference table. He faced Bonnie's empty chair at the opposite head, which was flanked by the regular cast. I snapped off that picture worth a thousand words. The writers ringed Monte; there were a dozen of them, two for every cast member. I wanted to pose all twelve for The Last Supper. Maybe at the wrap party.

A roar of laughter erupted from the craft services coffee urn. I panned to Elliot charming the network VP while the junior managers laughed along, twin bobble head dolls fulfilling ancient roles in the executive food chain. My interest in them vaporized as they passed Meddy. Diligent, prepared Meddy. She scribbled notes while her crew shot B-roll footage to cover edits and talking heads for her report. I zoomed close enough to see the Y-shaped scar in her eyebrow, wishing she'd look up from her journalist-cut steno book and see me. I held the shot of her, studying her until my hand started to shake.

The stage manager appeared and held up a finger to Monte to signal Number-One, coming in. A hush a lot like dread fell. Brick slid by the stage manager and conga danced to a seat with the crew. The head writer took out a Hemingway Montblanc fountain pen, drew three neat lines under his name on the script cover, put it away and grabbed a pencil from the cup. The script supervisor kissed the crucifix on her necklace. A metal push bar squeaked and a heavy door slammed into the wall behind the sets. Then a voice leaped over the false walls, piercing the suspended rigging of chain and pipe. Her voice:

"Where is he? Where the hell is he?"

The Hobby Horse PR flak approached Meddy and whispered briefly in her ear. Meddy nodded and touched the elbow of her camera operator, who angled his lens to the floor and killed his twitching red light.

"I said, 'Where is he?'" called Bonnie Quinn, loud and Southie, like from a project balcony, as she rounded the plywood wall of her make-believe Astoria, Queens, apartment.

She breezed past the stage manager, demanding again and again to know where he was. It never occurred to me that the he was me until she looked in the high seats and thrust a stiff arm my way.

"There he is!"

Hiding in the dark, I felt like a spot was on me. Bonnie Quinn toed out her cigarette, hoisted herself up over the rail of the bleachers and mounted the steps to my perch.

"Nobody fucks with him," she said. Pointing at me. "This man is here at my request, got it? Fuck with Hardwick and you deal with me."

Below lay a canyon of up-craned necks. At the sound of my name, Meddy rose up to look. Her mouth dropped before she turned away and sat. Monte's head was in his hands. So much for that less disruptive strategy of tiny doses.

The star quit the bleachers for the head of the table and flouted the fire code with another cigarette. No one else smoked. Ryan, the director, who stood at a little rolling podium, opened the cover of his script and recited, "*Thanks for Sharing*, Number 425." He looked up and smiled, "Episode 100." Flaccid applause surfaced and died.

"Let's go," said Bonnie. "There's a perfectly good hard-on going to waste in my dressing room."

"*Bonnie Smells a Rat*," the director continued. "Fade In: Exterior: Fire Escape, Night. Bonnie takes her eye from the telescope and addresses Petey."

Bonnie reached for an apple in the basket in front of her, chomped off a bite and mumbled her dialogue around the mouthful.

"'Hey, spaceman, how's life up there tonight in zero gravity? Zero gravity. Hey, isn't that the theme for Paris Hilton's class reunion?'"

The writers laughed. Bonnie clawed the page out of her script and balled it.

"Glad you liked it, you hacks, 'cause it's the last time you'll hear it. If you're into shopworn references so much, why don't you exhume some hippie jokes while you're at it? I could put on that Beatle wig Bob Hope used to wear on his Chrysler specials."

She lobbed the discarded page on the floor. Awkward silence. Monte stepped to the rolling podium, flipped the director's script to the next scene and tapped the page.

"Scene Two!" said the director. "'Interior: Bonnie's Kitchen, Morning. Little Jimmy enters, dressed for school.'"

"'Morning, Mom.'"

It startled me to see the young boy. He wasn't at the table but off to the side with a social worker and a slob who was surely his father.

"'You haven't seen my rat have you?'"

From the director, "'Bonnie takes a potholder and lifts a lid on the stove.'"

"'Mm-no. Although check your oatmeal. I swear I saw one of the big lumps move. For a while, anyway.'"

The network laughed, Elliot laughed, and quickly everyone else chimed in. Sanction for the first joke and the ice breaker for the script about her eleven year-old underachiever losing his pet rat the same day Bonnie invites her boss over for dinner. You can imagine.

As the reading continued, I trained my lens back on Meddy and felt fully rationalized about taking this gig. See? It wasn't just the money. But what was she doing there? Meddy didn't do entertainment puff. She was UEN's senior reporter. Hard news, lots of good investigative stuff. But a sitcom feature? I zoomed close and her face fused with the vintage version that had burned itself into my long-term memory of the night we parted in the HoJo's parking lot in Nashua. Of how her tears reflected copper light from buzzing lamps. Of how we talked to each other, taking stands.

"Are you asking me just to forget what happened?"

"We can't forget it," I said finally. "Can't undo it, either."

"Would you? Undo it, I mean?"

"It doesn't matter. It's done."

"It matters to me," she said.

"To hear me say I wouldn't take that picture, is that what you want to hear?"

"I want to hear the truth."

She left me alone with my duffel, two feet on the ice, watching her take her seat on the press bus beside my empty one. Feeling my chest in a vise as the Greyhound crunched away across the parking lot into the night as I waited there in the cold until the last sound of the diesel blended with the air and was gone.

At Fade Out, thunderous applause startled me back. The UEN exec rose, shouting "Brava!" to the writer, Karen somebody, who had recently signed a deal to develop a comedy pilot for him. Big mistake. He lauded the writer first and the tide turned. Cheers died. Lightning bolts shot from Bonnie Quinn's eyes at the author.

Meddy got another visit from media relations. She nodded and left the stage with her crew. Curious, Meddy playing ball like that.

Bonnie Quinn snagged the craft services trash barrel and circulated it around the table.

"Give it up," she said. "Come on, right in here." Crew members hesitated, then tossed their scripts into the trash. Next she targeted the writers. "Come on, you frauds, get 'em in here before they get all stinky."

The apostles gut checked each other then looked to Karen, the writer, who held a brave look of indignation despite a quivering chin. Monte whispered something to her. She squeezed her eyes tightly, then tossed her own script into the can. Her colleagues followed suit with half-hearted lobs.

"Better," said America's Single Mom. "I'd rather be skull fucked by Jessie Helms than perform that little wet dream."

Chairs scraped back. The social worker hustled Jimmy, the TV son, to the exit. His father lagged to rescue his bagel, then waddled after.

Bonnie called out to the stage dad, "Aw, lighten up, Earl. It's not like the little shit doesn't know what a wet dream is."

Monte stood and sang out, "Thanks everybody. We'll call this a stage wrap for today. Cast, released till ten tomorrow for rehearsal of new pages. Keys and department heads, in my office after network notes. Thank you."

The stage didn't empty, it evacuated. Bonnie rocketed off with Brick. The cast abandoned scripts on the table, knowing better than to take them home to learn those lines. The writers huddled into a chain gang behind Elliot, Monte, and the network, off to a post mortem on the good script that crashed and burned into Mt. Vicodin. It all had the feel of a drill everyone knew. I didn't have to guess if they had done this before. Perhaps ninety-nine times.

Neglected, forgotten, and, thankfully, ignored, I took the bleacher steps in twos to get outside. The late morning sunlight fried my eyes as I pushed past the stagehands playing Hacky Sack and scanned the alley. The news van was still there, but when I jogged over for a look it was empty. I stepped back as a tractor rumbled by, pulling a flatbed of greens and the folded walls of a schoolroom set. When it cleared, I spotted her crossing the executive parking lot.

"Meddy."

She didn't stop but she did look around for me and then wave. I only made it halfway across the parking area, though, when she called back, "Maybe later, OK?" She pointed to her camera crew, which was shooting video of Elliot outside the production office. She waved again and quickened her pace to join them and then followed the parade inside the Hobby Horse offices.

I sat on a bench to sort out whether I was chasing delusion. Up in Monte's window across the way, light from her minicam fell on the writers as they slouched back against the glass in various poses of resignation. Elliot Pratt walked along the picket fence of his battle-weary staff, gesturing to his open script. I saw an op for a nice candid and fished out my Nikon.

"Photography is not permitted on the lot, sir."

I turned behind me where a gym rat in a polo shirt and aviators relaxed at the wheel of Monte's golf cart.

"Kind of pulls the pins from under the old job description," I said. "I've been hired to do stills for Hobby Horse."

"If you'll get in, sir, I'll give you a ride to your gate."

# CHAPTER THIRTEEN

"So you got me a babysitter," I said to Monte the next day on the set while I sealed my film camera into a soundproof housing. Across the stage, my minder sat on a bar stool, arms crossed, heels looped on the bottom rung, all the picture of a Bowflex ad.

"I just want this week to go smooth, is all. Now that I've got the wolf in the henhouse, can you blame me if I want to watch the eggs?"

I didn't care enough to blame him. In fact, here's how much I cared: I almost didn't bother to load a memory card. This was just a mime show. For whatever her divanatrix reasons, Bonnie Quinn needed to see me holding a camera on her set. So I looked the part and held a camera.

"I don't see the UEN crew here today," I said. "Meddy still working this?"

"She's covering Elliot at a network meeting off the lot." He studied me, a control freak scouting for unforecast gales. "Meddy? Not Meredith? You know her?"

What do you tell him? That she was going to be my wife? Once. Share that with the Mont-ster?

"We have a sort of history," I said, a toss off. "Years ago."

"Places, please," called the stage manager.

And the parade commenced. The director wheeled his rolling podium to the fire escape set followed by the script supervisor and Zack, the head writer, who skateboarded his lectern ahead of the cameras and microphone booms, which were dollying to their marks.

Monte became my tour guide.

"Normally we'd be rehearsing today without cameras. You know, let the actors experiment, let Ryan work with them to find little moments without technical distraction. But I'm compressing the week to shoot this puppy Thursday night instead of Friday. So Ryan's blocking his shots as we rehearse."

"Cutting a day of rehearsal?"

"Network wants early delivery for sweeps."

"Right. It has nothing to do with cutting production costs."

He must have remembered I wasn't on some career day field trip.

"Fawkin'-A it does. You think I got where I am by spending money?"

Bonnie Quinn squeezed between us.

"No, you got where you are by parking your nose up Elliot Pratt's ass cheeks." Monte glowered at the stage manager whose shrug told the obvious story. She'd slipped through his net. "Hello, Monte," Bonnie continued. "No hello for me this morning?"

He responded immediately, in sing-song ritual, "Good morning, Ms. Quinn."

"Good morning, Mr. Arnett," she sang back. Then, "Good morning everybody." She beamed at them as they answered in chorus by rote. "If I seem like I am in a particularly good mood this morning, class, it's because of this."

She held up the rewrite the way models on *Price is Right* coo over The San Francisco Treat. I burned off a shot, what the hell.

"Where are my writers? Where is my wonderful, wonderful writing staff?" They baby-stepped in from the shadows. "Come on out," she coaxed, "Momma's not gonna whip ya."

Their eyes were all puffed beyond weary as if they had driven the freeway without a windshield.

"I have no idea how late you wrote last night, but you have worked a miracle."

"Four-thirty this morning," reported a story editor, who took a quick elbow from the Must-See-TV veteran.

"Well, hot damn." The star knelt before them and bowed low, fanning them with outstretched arms. "I am humbled and honored to perform what you have crafted for me." While her head was down— her nose practically touching the floor—Monte winked behind her to an old man in a bow tie and a navy blazer dusted with scales of eczema or dandruff or both. Dr. Carmen Pizzarelli, aka Dr. Pizzy, aka Dr. Feelgood, was on the case. Considering her manic praise, I was sure something more than a new script got delivered to Bonnie that morning. I didn't see Brick, so I was laying Vegas odds Dr. Pizzy helped her with a nagging pain. Not my deal. I just held my camera.

"This is excellent writing," she went on. "Funny, textured, and honest to our characters. And I say that not as a ninth grade dropout. . . ."

Ever the standup, Bonnie paused for the laugh, before she continued.

"I say that as autodidact. By the way, that means self-educated for those of you who don't know because you stayed in school. And now, this is just my small token of gratitude, appreciation, and, above all, awe at a job well done by my amazing writers. Thank you!"

Her manager, Rhonda York, strode in leading a procession of studio gophers bearing massive bouquets of long-stemmed roses. The baker's dozen bouquets, twenty-four perfect roses in each, were delivered into the wary arms of the staff. Some smiled, one said thanks, and all but a few held the buds in front of their mouths to mask the bullshits and fucks.

"Now let's go to work," Bonnie called.

"You go girl," answered Monte without a lick of shame.

Apologies to the Russian, but an unhappy set is unhappy in many ways. However, on a mood-driven set it is always the same, as the crew constantly forms itself around the shifting insanity of the alpha dog. And even though each member of the extended family adjusts and copes in a unique way, that doesn't mean the bullying and slights are not profoundly felt. They cut deeply. On my way to the fire escape set, I passed a garbage barrel filled with roses in cellophane. It was the same one that ate their scripts the day before. If nothing else, these writers knew poetry.

Bonnie took her mark beside the telescope and said, "Ryan?"

Ryan, the director, paused to trace a gentle finger on the school photo of his daughter taped to his podium before he said, "Yes, love?"

"What do you need to rehearse? Four cameras, two booms, one actress and a telescope—none of which is moving."

"I hear you."

"Stevie Wonder could block this scene."

"Stevie Wonder, yes, ha, very good."

At least she wasn't into shopworn references or anything.

"Ryan? Then we're moving on?"

"Actually, Bon-Bon."

"Yes?"

"I'm good for my blocking. I was thinking more of you."

"I'm good. I stand here and read it. Hell-o?"

Bonnie left her mark to get a bottled water over at the craft services fridge.

The head writer tugged Ryan's sleeve and whispered, "We were, you know, sort of hoping we could hear the, ah, words."

"We're good for the scene, Zack," said the director.

"What's happening?" called Bonnie from across the stage.

Zack looked back to his writing staff and they fed him nods of encouragement. "We were up all night," he said, "And we deserve to hear what we've written."

"Deserve? You deserve?" Bonnie strode to the stage door. "I'll be in my dressing room. Call me when you're ready to move on."

"Ryan?" said Monte. "Moving on?"

One of the writers whispered something to Zack, who spoke from behind his wood laminate rolling podium as if it were the latest in blast shield technology.

"It's going to be a long week without any new rewrites from us, Monte."

Monte cursed to himself, looked at the writing staff, shoulder-to-shoulder, and said, "Hang on. Let me talk to her."

He crossed off, snagged Dr. Pizzy by the elbow, and led the old man backstage.

A full half hour later, the two men returned, followed by Bonnie Quinn, who took her mark next to the telescope. Her face had a flatter affect, as if it had lost some of its animation. Her brow was low, an awning. She ground her teeth.

"Zachary wants to hear the words." One look told me what Zachary really wanted was to light the fuse on the ass rocket and ride it out of here. "'Kay-fine. Hear them you shall."

The director waited for Bonnie to open her script, touched the photo of his daughter once more, then called *action*.

And Bonnie Quinn began to read the teaser monologue. Secret nods and low-fives passed among the writers, who could say that on the landmark episode of this hellish series they had finally leveraged some respect. It was a short celebration. To the disbelief of a stage family that thought it had seen it all came something new.

As Bonnie stood there holding the script in her left hand, she snaked her right hand down the waistband of her sweats. I thought it was an itch. Really, I did. I have seen enough people without social boundaries—especially celebrities—that I gave her the dubious benefit of that doubt. But as she continued to recite the monologue, the rubbing continued. Eyes averted, eyes returned. Gaping in disbelief while her hand moved under the gray fleece.

Then her moans began, and Bonnie's hand moved faster. Her hips began to thrust in cheesy, porn rhythm. Between clauses of her speech, her moans became whelps. A door opened sidestage. Jimmy, the TV son entered from the studio classroom, flanked by his father and the social worker who actually said, "Oh!"

Both adults spun the boy back through the door as Bonnie brought it to a crescendo yelp. And she was done. The whole thing couldn't have lasted much more than a minute, but it lived in that slow motion realm where horrors elapse on eternity's timetable.

"Well," she said to the frozen writing staff, "Hope you liked it, Zack. I figured as long as you were jerking yourself off, I might as well, too. See ya tomorrow." She tossed her script on the director's podium, then leaned to look at the photo. "Nice," she said. "What's that, your kid's DUI mug shot?"

When she was gone, there was a beat of church silence, Monte usurped the director and called the day a wrap. As the stage cleared, he and Dr. Pizzy fell into hushed conversation near me. My instinct was to listen in. Instead, I turned my back. Just busied myself packing my gear. Chalked one more hash mark on the prison wall.

"Congratulations." Zack and some of the writers encircled me. "You lasted two days. You qualify for the party."

"Party?"

"At the Sheraton Universal. Whenever it comes—the night she buys it, I mean. Cocktails, hors d'oeuvres, and cocktails. Did I mention cocktails?" Zack didn't like my reaction. "Hey, come on, man, you don't think it's gonna happen? Sooner or later she's gonna OD, or she'll wrap her car around a power pole, or she'll forget Mister Electricity says you can't actually take a blow dryer in the shower, something. And the standing deal is, wherever we all are when we hear about it or read it, take a plane, take a car, walk, sprint, or crawl to the Sheraton U that night." Zack toasted an imaginary glass. "And then, it's par-tay!"

The elephant door was shut, and I had to leave through the stage exit. There's a vestibule about the size of a cargo elevator that forms a sound lock between the set and the outside, and when I pushed my door open and stepped in someone else entered the opposite door. Meddy. Meddy alone.

We both came up short. Startled and breath-caught.

"Hi," I said. The conversationalist.

"Hi."

After we went through the hug-or-shake ritual of exes, landing on a platonic hug of minimum duration, I told her, "You missed rehearsal. In fact, so did Bonnie."

Meddy laughed.

"So I heard. Hope you got pictures. On second thought, maybe I don't." She laughed again. Nervous. "I got your voice mail. Sorry, but I've been . . ."

"Sure, I know. Kind of a different beat for you, isn't it, Hollyweird?"

"Yeah, it is. But there's a method to this madness I can't discuss. Not yet."

Silence in the sound lock.

"Listen, Meddy. As long as we've crossed paths, maybe we could sit down for a coffee later. Or something."

"Do you really think it's smart? We both have jobs to do here and, all right, I confess. I have been avoiding you. There are just too many live wires. The emotions are still raw for me."

"Me, too. But since you seem to be all hung up on this 'thing' about 'professional decorum'"—We both chuckled.—"how about after we wrap?"

# CHAPTER FOURTEEN

I fell in next to Rhonda's noisy leather ensemble but stopped her at the garbage can of roses, now out beside the dumpster.

"Why don't you donate them to a hospital?" I said. "A lot of money to rot in the trash."

She shrugged.

"All the same to us. I got so tired of sending so many apology bouquets for Bonnie that two years ago I just said screw it and bought her a flower shop. Don't keep her waiting talking to me. You know the way."

I was just about to knock when Bonnie opened the door.

"Hey there, handsome. Come on in and kick."

Everything was exactly as before, which is to say eligible for a federal superfund cleanup.

"Pardon the mess. I caught the butler humming the pool boy so I fired 'em both, ha."

She swatted a greasy chicken bucket off the couch.

"There," she said.

I sat among the crumbs of secret herbs and spices. She toed a couple of malt liquor cans aside and sat on the floor at my feet, a re-creation of our desert tableau. I prayed she would keep her top on this time. She pulled her knees to her chest and rocked, studying me.

"What happened to you?" she asked.

"I got here as soon as I could."

"What. Happened. To. You."

Probing eyes bored into me. No embarrassment, only license in them. She leaned forward, staring an unbroken beam. And then, like the rudimentary acting exercise of repeating the same line over and over with different shadings, she asked more simply, "What happened to you?"

And I saw her change when she saw the change in me. That I could not hide from her meaning: that she had found me out and reduced everything to the single essential of my private pain. She was the naïve toddler asking the man in the wheelchair why his legs don't work. But not so naïve. Because her question was kindred at the root. The way survivors talk about the fire. Or drunks about the bottle.

When I didn't answer, she broke off and lit up a cigarette, only to X-ray me again. "Why did you do it?" Just curious. No judgment. "The picture, I mean. Why did you take the picture?"

The Picture. She knew.

If Bonnie Quinn was so nuts, how could she do this to me? Turn a call to her dressing room into a surprise customs inspection of my life's baggage. I started to rise.

"Please wait. Please? I have a reason for asking. It's important."

I sat.

"Let me help you along. You step out of the war hot as they come. Pulitzers. *Rolling Stone* assignments. Monte says they optioned your life story for a movie."

"This is Hollywood. They option everybody's life story for a movie. Doesn't mean they'll make it."

"They wanted Harrison Ford to play you. Or Michael Douglas."

"Only younger."

"And then they pulled the plug."

Because I took The Picture.

"Because you took the picture."

We had gone from routing through my baggage to full cavity search. Why didn't I just go? Hard to explain. How do you explain the magnetism of madness that draws you into its dance? Like all the fights I couldn't walk away from, her morbid fascination engaged me. Lashed to me the mast.

"Did you invite me in here just to mess with my head?"

"No. I just need to know. Didn't you know the shit rain would fall on you?" I nodded without realizing it. "Didn't you have a clue all the doors would slam hard and lock you outside?"

"An inkling."

I saw myself back on the day I took it. One click of the shutter release that pulled the trigger on everything in my life. Such a picture today would be nothing, barely raise an eyebrow. It might not even sell. No, it would sell. And it would make news just like it did then, which was my undoing in what polite folks call mainstream journalism. My picture made news instead of recording it. Even that's not so bad. Making news with a picture is held as a worthy goal in some circles, and the shooter is celebrated instead of vilified. My Vietnam shots made news and earned me Pulitzers because they did just that. They may have even saved a few lives, shortening the lunacy over there by showing it for what it was. But that was then. It was a different kind of news and a different sort of picture.

Even I know that.

But I took the picture that damned me for the same reason I took the others that drew praise. I even used the same camera.

Hudson Landry, a flag draped congressman who rose to power on family values and law and order platitudes, had unchallenged power in his subcommittee's purview over drug smuggling. My own news-magazine cover shots of him in a DEA flak vest, kicking down doors in Cartagena with the local militia, put him on the party short list of presidential prospects.

A buddy of mine, a deep-cover cowboy who had graduated from spook work in 'Nam to undercover federal agent, told me off the record that Hudson Landry was kicking down third world doors by day and taking drug cartel bribes by night to steer legislation, budgets, and attention the other way. The problem was, he said, nobody could prove it. Meanwhile, drugs flowed, doors got kicked for show, and tracking polls picked up the blip of a political rising star.

The cynic in me was prepared to accept that as the grand tradition of politics through history—until my DEA pal got killed in a very suspicious ambush outside Bogotá.

Demagogues eventually do themselves in. How many times have you seen that? Greed makes them careless, or they piss off an old ally who goes Deep Throat on them, or their tainted money buys them a private jet that noses into the waters off Grand Cayman. But in the swelter of Arlington National Cemetery, watching my friend eulogized as a hero by the same congressman who was the houseman for the thugs who killed him, I decided that *eventually* was not soon enough for Hudson Landry to take his fall.

The congressman was in Boston gearing up for the New Hampshire primary. He and his wife were booked into the Four Seasons. But Landry was at a lesser hotel up Boylston, enjoying a tryst with a cartel-provided hooker. I was having a Sam Adams in the bar downstairs. When I signaled for my bill, the black vinyl folder arrived with a slip of paper inside. Suite 1604 was all it said.

The hallway was deserted. Suite 1604 was unlocked thanks to a Landry for President brochure strategically wedged between the jamb and the latch. I listened at the door over the thud of my pulse. Then I did something unusual for me. I hesitated. Thought about what I knew I would find in there and held, recognizing the deed I contemplated for what it was. And I nearly walked away. Until I looked again at the wedge of brochure sticking out the door. Half a picture, but I knew the shot because I had taken it in Cartagena of "No-Knock" Landry kicking cartel booty. I crossed the threshold and was in.

My picture created a firestorm. Landry was shamed out of the race and his seat. But I flamed out along with him. When I entered Suite 1604, I crossed an ethical line. Whatever folks want to believe, the press has standards. Real journalists don't do bedrooms. Not now, and especially not then. I had avenged my friend and become a pariah. One picture, and my career as a mainstream photojournalist was over.

Bonnie Quinn let her cigarette smoke drift out in a curl.

"You had it all. But you took the picture that fucked the dog, and all I want to know is, why? Why did you take the picture?"

It didn't take me long to reply. I'd only had about half my life to think it over. "Because he had it coming."

My answer made her blink. Then a toothy grin opened up, and she wrapped her arms around herself, hugging something invisible and yummy as she rocked back and forth.

"My man," she said, but to herself. "He's here. I knew it, I knew it, I knew it." She stopped swaying and said, "I had my cards read last night. The tarot? They said my angel on tarnished wings has arrived."

"Very flattering, but if you're looking for a hero, I'm not your guy."

"It is you. I knew it in the desert that night. My fears sent me away, but you found me because I was not hiding, I was lost. And now I am found. You are the only reason I am here. Why do you think I squeezed Monte to have you on the set? And the cards, the tarot, bore it all out. Don't look away from me. What? What are you thinking? Come on, you can tell your Bonnie."

I was thinking that my Bonnie had just shifted a big load onto me out of nowhere. "I'm just a photographer," I said.

"Yet you remain blind to what's before you. Imagine the sum of all the anguishes in your life. That's what I am living." She shook her head and took a deep drag. A blue-gray exhale enshrouded her. "The fact of my life is that it ends with this episode."

OK. Check, please.

"If you're saying what I think you are, the help you need isn't the kind I can give you. But you should get it. Do you know someone?"

"I will tolerate your patronizing bullshit as uninformed. You would not placate me if you knew the truth—which you will know if circumstances warrant." She amused herself with that and repeated, "Circumstances . . ." Then she looked up at me. "Ask yourself this. If I was going to off myself, why would I run away to the desert and come to my door with a loaded gun?"

The answer I came up with was etched on the walls, smeared on her mirror, and lodged down the Alice rabbit holes of her pupils. But instead of confronting her, I did what everyone else did. I mean playing along as little as I had to. In the game, but not enough to get my uniform dirty.

"If you think you're in some sort of danger—"

"Fuck the police."

"What about security, then? Doesn't Hobby Horse supply you with somebody?"

"You mean Sleepy? Last month I tied his shoe laces together and yelled lunch. Saddest part was watching him pick at those elbow scabs and still not know who did it."

"Hire your own. What about Gavin de Becker, or—?"

"Balls. That's how I know it's you, Hardwick. You act like you have nothing to lose even when you have everything to lose." She pulled herself up by the arm of the couch with a grunt. "So now that I've got use of your non-risk-averse balls for a couple days, who knows, maybe I can grab hold of your puny imagination, too."

She went into the bathroom and I waited, wondering if we were done until I heard a telltale sound. I stood and saw her through the crack of the bathroom door, stooped over, mincing something on the countertop. I almost walked in. Almost took her wrist and told her to get her butt back to the desert. Instead, I left. My official babysitter was waiting outside her door and whisked me to the gate.

# CHAPTER FIFTEEN

The next morning, when I cleared security at Empire Studios, I gave my Bowflex nanny a Starbucks. The gesture took him aback but it was my third day of enforced supervision, therefore, a relationship.

"Stage is that way," I said when he swung a turn.

"Monte wants us to chill in his office a bit." He zipped into a space at the Hobby Horse building and said, "There's no debate here."

My minder kicked back to ESPN on the Hi-Def with his free Americano while I paced. Man, I hate feeling caged. I tried to relax by telling myself they'd bought me for the week so a little Sports Center on their nickel wouldn't kill me.

Turned out the show from Monte Arnett's window was better. In the executive lot below, a white stretch pulled up, followed by the UEN News van. Meddy and her crew hustled around to the limo, and when they were set and rolling, the door opened and I knew why I was sequestered.

Otis Grove, the new owner of UEN, slid his tall frame out of the car. He buttoned his suit coat, then extended his hand to help his wife out. I hadn't paid much attention to her at his TV press conference but she was radiant. Remember Lena Horne and you're close.

She laced her fingers through her husband's, and when Elliot Pratt arrived to lead the newly-minted media titan to the set of his network's top-rated sitcom, the Groves walked hand in hand.

Monte brought up the rear, and when the VIP group entered Stage 2, he turned back and saw me watching from his balcony. He knew I wanted in there as bad as he wanted me out. Maybe I could talk Meddy into letting me screen her video of the encounter between the champion of values television and his satanic diva.

But, as the stage door closed, I looked at Bonnie Quinn's parking spot. It was empty.

"What's the deal with Bonnie?" I said to Meddy after the white limo had left. "Is the Quinn of Comedy pulling a power play, or is Mr. Grove simply not an appreciator of onstage masturbation?"

Meddy laughed and plucked some grapes from the craft services spread to go with her paper plate of cheddar cubes.

"Neither," she said. "Elliot didn't want fireworks to spoil the tour, so he had Monte arrange a late set call for her."

Was it me, or did I not like the way she said Elliot? Definitely me.

"By the way, I never got a chance to hear you officially shoot down my invitation."

She sucked in her upper lip. "Yeah, you caught me little off guard yesterday."

"And I've been thinking about what you said about mixing work and was thinking, maybe, after we're all done. Grab a quick coffee, or . . . you know."

"Why don't we make it dinner?"

I accidentally ejected the fresh battery I had just put in my camera.

"Tomorrow night after the show wraps," Meddy continued. "Do you know Arabesque on Melrose?"

I did. I knew it as Napa fare with quiet charm. Soft pinks, votives, perfect. I snapped the battery back in.

"That would be fine, sure."

Her crew joined us, and she saddled up.

"Tomorrow night, then."

"You're not staying for rehearsal?" I gestured to the stand-in wearing a cardboard sign around her neck that said BONNIE. "And you call yourself a journalist."

"Much as I'd love to, I'm meeting Elliot." There it was again. Not quite intimacy, but— "He's casting a pilot off the lot. Know who's actually reading for him? Kimberly Duggan."

Meddy primped her hair melodramatically and left.

After the lunch break, still no Bonnie. Rehearsal resumed with the stand-in, a poor, upgraded extra who gave each line of dialogue Emmy effort, which only added a comically pathetic quality to her dinner theater acting. But with their words unexpectedly heard, the writers punctuated her dialogue with over-the-top laughs. The fun ground to a halt as the scene ended and the Bonnie who needed no sign slow-clapped from the front row of the bleachers.

"Beautiful, Tina, just beautiful."

The stand-in gave a demure smile.

"It did my ol' Irish heart good to sit back and watch you and Deane and Gramps play the scene as written so I could see how absolutely donkey-fucked this series would be if I left it to you and you and you to pull the rabbit out of the hat every week. Now, Tina, we've got two choices: Either you get your high school pageant pudenda off my goddam set, or I burn my SAG card on *Larry King Live*."

Tina made a brave exit, but leaned on a PA for support at the door. Bonnie descended the bleacher steps and passed through the crew, which had assumed its collective posture of wished invisibility. Behind the downcast eyes, I imagined mortgages being calculated, tuitions being weighed against unemployment bennies, and days to retirement being counted. I'll bet there was more than one silent scream.

A whoosh of corduroy and some panting. Monte arrived Mont-ster quick. Someone had beamed up the bat signal over Gotham: Trouble on the set.

Bonnie vacuumed back a prolific slurp of nasal drip and forearmed her nostrils. "Tell me, what is this so-called scene supposed to be about?"

Zack, the head writer moved a toe onto the set.

"This scene is about your TV family coming together to help you in your crisis."

"Crisis?!" Bonnie clawed tissue from Brick's belt pack and blew something analysis-ready into its folds. "What crisis? My idiot kid lost his rat. In real life, how many nutty neighbors and senile grampas turn an apartment upside down like a Marx Brothers movie looking for a rat?"

The Tony-Emmy-celebrated grampa stepped up.

"If I may? My character is not senile. I play Grampa as a step behind in a fast-paced world."

"Hey, I'll bet the Jesus freak lapped that shit right up on his visit this morning." She squinted and found Monte standing/hiding behind me. "Too bad I missed the Otis Grove grand tour. What did you all kiss? Ring, ass, what?"

Monte distracted her with the work.

"Bon, do you have another way to go? Something better?"

Bonnie hiked her crotch. "Fawkin'-A, coach." She turned to Multiple-Tony-Emmy. "Gramps, what's your entrance line?"

The actor licked an arthritis-crooked finger and flipped to the page.

"I am eating as I enter, and—"

"Just the line. Jesus."

"I say, 'Do these raisins taste gamey to you?'"

Bonnie laughed, "Great, great fucking line." She tapped pencil on the script super's podium. "I'll say that."

"But that's my only line in the scene."

"Then it looks like you get to sit out tomorrow night and practice being a step behind in a fast-paced world." Bonnie riffled pages in the super's three-ring. "In fact, I don't think we need any of these other yahoos in this. My audience is not sitting home wondering why that pruny old souse isn't in this scene. They want what's real. And the real of this scene is how do we deal with my moron son after I lost his rat."

"'We?' So we're back in?" asked Deane, the next door bachelor.

"Are you even listening? This is a two-person scene. Me and the little snot, working together to find his rat."

Deane threw his script down. Monte got his head bobbing.

"Ryan?"

"Loving this," agreed the director, also spring-loaded.

I noticed, in spite of his grin, that he picked at the shred of Scotch tape on his podium where the photo of his daughter had been. In QuinnWorld everything personal you exposed became a target.

Bonnie held out two arms, forming a papal frame of the writing staff.

"Cancel your lives tonight and write me a scene that's real. Mother and son. Quest for rodent. Mother fearing discovery by the bugger that she lost it. Boy aiming to show self-worth by finding the rat he thinks he lost first. Big. Very big. Forget jokes. Eighty-six the plot moves. Truth only. Content is container, container is content. Only connect. Passion, prose, yadda yadda. Dismissed."

The diva clomped off with Brick. Monte vanished out the opposite door. As the writing staff shitcanned its scripts, I said to Zack, "Productive day."

"Now you know why we've been through fifty-two writers in four years."

# CHAPTER SIXTEEN

O f the many benefits of exercise, fitness is secondary. For me, mind
and spirit get a boost you can't just call a side effect. I first learned
that in tenth grade when the dean suggested I might get in fewer fist-
fights if I worked out my righteous indignations on the gridiron
instead of the lunch court. These days, I air it out running. Which is,
of course, why I am the quintessence of serenity. Cleansing sweat and
the whole endorphin miracle transform my runs into transcendentals
afoot. I get answers to questions I never asked. Sometimes that's even
a good thing.

Mulholland Drive is tricky. There's not much shoulder, and blind
curves force you to listen as well as look, otherwise you're flying
Stephen King Airlines into the ditch. But on a clear late afternoon,
the Valley gives up majestic views, and better yet, for long stretches,
you're surrounded by nature despite the urban zip code. I struggled
with the climb up Laurel Canyon on legs that hadn't run since the
dumpster. At the crest, I opened up into my 10K pace along the flat
spine of the mountain. At the overlook just past Coldwater Canyon,
something in me pulled the plug. My spirit shut down.

Sitting on the weather-scabbed Parks and Rec bench, feeling anything but serene, I listened to my heart. Not its beats, its message.

Some damn escape run. All it did was put the stink right under my nose. And it was my stink. I was the one who had crossed the line. I was the one who joined the dysfunction team for ready cash. And no blind eye I turned could stop the looting of my soul.

As my pulse leveled and my breathing settled, a breeze out of the east rustled the scrub oak and manzanita in the ravine below. Swirling grit from a rising, late season Santa Ana peppered my eyes and dried the sweat to salt on my skin. I blinked and sat staring at the rising twinkle of city lights against the Valley floor and the empurpled Santa Susanna range twenty miles distant.

The next sunrise would bring tape day. Then it would all be over. A two-edger, though, because it was also my last chance to rescue what was left of me by doing what I should do. What I would have done a year ago without blinking.

The sun disappeared and the sky greened before it blackened. I grew chilled at first, then warmed by the desert winds fanning the city clean. The air had cleared. I embraced the decision that called out to be made and jogged home to call Elliot Pratt, already feeling a little lighter on my feet.

Headlights swept the canyon wall on the curve near Houdini's brooding old house. I stepped onto the shoulder as the car passed. Brake lights. It backed up even with me. Rudy Newgate at the wheel.

"I was just at your place." It looked like he was alone. I couldn't make out any hulks in the dark.

"Went for a run." I raised my arms from my sides to frame the shorts and T-shirt. "You could have called."

"Like you'd pick up." Had to give him that.

"Next payment's not till Friday. There some problem, Rudy?"

"No, no." Another car rounded the bend. He stayed put and made it squeeze by. "You showed me something, coming up with the payment like that." I waited him out. Shivered a little in my damp shirt. "I was thinking, good customer like you, things tight, you could use an extension." Clever fuck. Trying to keep the hooks in me. Spread the payments, increase his vig.

"Thanks the same. I'll stick to the schedule."

"Huh. I usually don't get that. You sure?"

"Anything changes, I know where to find you."

"Likewise," he said and drove off.

"Good morning. Go right in, he's expecting you," said Elliot's assistant.

He and Monte were waiting for me in the conversation pit when I walked in. Elliot rose and pumped my hand. Monte looked ridiculous in his show-day suit. Something about a mullet doesn't work with Armani unless you're on the Maple Leafs.

"When you called last night, you said it was important," Elliot began, as soon as we sat.

"I need to talk about where we are here. There's my situation to discuss, but first off, there's your star. She needs help. I mean immediately."

"Bonnie does have her demons," Elliot said, rocking easy.

"I think it's more than a few demons. You do, too." It felt good to bring it. It felt like me. "You even hid her from Otis Grove yesterday."

"Call it good management. Look, Hardwick, whatever's happening with her, none of it's new," he quoted from his Statesman's Phrasebook. "It predates our involvement with her."

"Really?"

Elliot looked at me evenly. "Yes, really."

"Let me ask you this, then. If Bob Woodward were to write *Wired-2* and instead of Belushi he investigated Bonnie, how would you guys come out?"

"Elliot, you don't need this from him," said Monte.

"No, I'll answer. And I'll take it a step beyond giving her a livelihood through all her"—He searched for the defensible quotes.—"'medical troubles.' I would come out as the boss who puts up with emotional and financial exposure because I owe it to this crew. Sixty-five people I care about deeply and personally who rely on me to keep this running or they're out of work. The bottom line for me? I do it for this little family of ours."

"Tell you what, El. Name six members of your little family right now." His forehead smoothed. "OK, then. Just four. I'll take first names, nicknames, even."

He pondered a beat, then said, "Let's move off this, it's getting us nowhere. You said you wanted to discuss your situation?"

"It's all sort of tied together."

"I figured on this."

"You did?"

"There's a shelf life, a threshold for people working around her."

I relaxed. This would be easier than I thought. Maybe they wouldn't even make me give it all back.

"That's why we want you to have this," he said. Monte placed a gift box on the coffee table. "A little something to ease the pain of the week. Go ahead, open it."

I hesitated, then lifted the lid.

"You like it?" asked Monte. "The newest Leica. Props says it's not even in the stores yet."

"Read the card," said Elliot.

It was under the camera. All it said was *Thank you*. There was five thousand in cash tucked inside.

"It's a little bonus," Elliot said with a smile.

I tried not to run the numbers, but couldn't help myself. That little bonus, along with that week's envelope, would cancel the whole Rudy debt.

"An acknowledgment of your commitment."

The whole fucking nut. I'd be free of the creep. No more calls. No more visits to my house.

"That word means something to both of us, right?"

Then I reflected on my run the night before, and of my resolve. I put the money and the camera back in the box, closed the lid, and stood. Elliot and Monte stared up at me. The room swooned like a vertigo tilt.

"Thank you," I said, then I picked up the box and left for the stage, feeling like the cock had just crowed the third time.

# CHAPTER SEVENTEEN

The day's rehearsal was perfunctory at best. The star mumbled her dialogue, rubbed her gums with her middle finger a lot, and frowned studiously while flipping pages with Evelyn Wood speed. Or, perhaps, just speed. She barked at Zack to have his "monkeys with keyboards" come up with alts for jokes, mainly the scene buttons.

Meddy arrived as the audience loaded in, and just the sight of her made me shed the grim weight I was carrying and feel airborne, weightless. I wanted to tell her that, but they're not the sort of words you put to music in front of a news crew with rolling cameras.

As the mediocre stand-up comic warmed the three hundred guests in the bleachers with Viagra jokes and threadbare Michael Jackson sex references, I figured I might as well work, too. I shot candids of the ensemble while they waited sidestage for Bonnie to arrive from makeup. I didn't capture a lot of smiles. Shoulders stiffened in a wave emanating from backstage, and I knew it before the stage manager gave the sign to Monte and said, "Number-One, coming in."

With her entourage of hair, makeup, and wardrobe cutting a human V in front of her, Bonnie Quinn strode out of the forest of cameras and booms past her supporting cast with no more acknowledgment than a busboy gets for crumbing the tablecloth. She pushed by them in a game-day strut. Makeup artistry had morphed her from sallow day sleeper with olive eye sockets to a more telegenic if lifeworn version of her *TV Guide* cover. She looked like someone who would be OK once she had her coffee.

"Look at you, darlin'," Monte cooed.

"So I pass muster, boss?"

Bonnie poked a finger in a dimpled cheek and turned a pirouette. Monte sang a short catcall, which the actress loved. Then a storm gathered on her face, and she stalked over to Deane Tacksdale as he joined the ensemble sidestage.

"And what town have you been working in that lets you think you can fucking come onto a set after the star? This some needle-dick power play, making me wait?"

"Climb down off my ass. I was in wardrobe. I had a spot on my collar." He turned to me and added, "Blood from trying to cut my throat."

I could smell scotch and Altoids.

Bonnie grinned, and I thought he'd disarmed her.

"Monte?" she said. "I'm cutting shithead from intros. He can wait backstage."

Monte turned to the stage manager.

"Tell the warm-up Deane's in the penalty box, then let's roll with the damn intros."

"Ho-ho-hold on. I just need one second." Bonnie rushed over to me. "Lose the damn camera for one minute, willya? Shit, man."

When I did she took a package from Brick, a thick manila envelope. She pressed it into my hands and held both of hers on mine, squeezing tightly.

"This is a gift for you."

I hefted it and, for a split second, I pictured bars of cocaine wrapped in cellophane. I drew the big envelope to me.

"Thanks, but you didn't have to—"

"No!" She squeezed harder on my hands, and I could feel bubble wrap around whatever was inside. "Do not open it yet. And definitely not here. And don't trust this with anyone else, not even for one second. Understand?"

I broke off to survey the cast, crew, Monte—all drinking in this little psychodrama.

"Look at me, Hardwick. You are the only person in the world I can trust with this. Hold it close. Keep it safe."

She leaned close. I thought—or feared—she was about to kiss me, but she spoke low in my ear, "Be my hero. Guard the truth."

She whirled to the stage manager.

"Let's lay this fucker down, Cliffie."

At which he signaled for intros, the lights came up full, and the warm-up led the house chant for "Bon-nee, Bon-nee, Bon-nee . . ."

When I picked up my camera and juggled her gift, my minder appeared with an open hand. I almost gave it to him, but winked a cheery *I got it* and stuffed it into my bag, mildly curious but mainly annoyed at the prospect of shouldering the weight.

Most people would never go to a TV show if they knew they were in for a minimum of three hours of captivity. That's a lot of cheek time to watch the same scene shot over and over for camera coverage, performances, or joke punches. That's why they have stand-up comics, hand out candy, and screen the audience for weapons. It is common for a quarter of an audience to leave near the end of a taping when the need for escape outruns the social compact. That night, Bonnie Quinn lost half her fans in twenty minutes, a record for any sitcom stage not experiencing an open fire or a bomb threat.

The trouble started with the breakfast scene. The bell rang for silence. *Action* was called. Bonnie stood at the stove, stirring prop oatmeal. Little Jimmy, eleven years of innocence, bounded in and asked, "Mom, you haven't seen my rat, have you?"

Bonnie lifted her lid for, "No, but check your oatmeal. Now that you mention it, I did see one of the big lumps move."

A nice opening laugh for the line that survived the table reading, and then trouble. Trouble in the kitchen. Bonnie stepped off her mark and crossed over to the child actor. Bewilderment from the camera operators. The director's shouts bled through headsets, calling for zone coverage instead of following the shot list. Bonnie waited, staring down at the young boy until her camera settled into its shot.

When the tally light came on she said, "Looks like you've got a lump moving in the front of your shorts, too, tiger."

It had all the rhythms and timing of a joke, so a few of the audience members laughed on reflex—until the split second they processed what they had just heard and the laughter decayed into gasps, and then, the death knell of comedy, into conversation among themselves.

"Cut!" called the stage manager. "Cut."

The stage bell rang twice.

Bonnie whirled, eyes flashing.

"Why are we cutting? Who said to cut? Fuck."

In the glass booth up behind the audience, Monte rose from his leather chair, took a long pull off a styrofoam cup, started to go, thought better, and brought the cup with him, descending to the stage.

Little Jimmy's father harrumphed on the sidelines, his chubby face purple with the rage of the powerless. When Monte lumbered down the last creaking stair to the floor, the stage dad tried to intercept him before he could reach Bonnie. But Bonnie charged over and wedged herself in front of Monte, shouting at Jimmy's father, even though she was nose-to-nose. Bobby Knight would blush.

"What do you think you're doing, you fucking parasite? Yeah, parasite. You leech your goddam living off that snot-nosed cash cow and guess what? He's gonna be finished as soon as he sprouts his first curly, and you know it. Then you're going to have to find some other way to pay for that Tarzana ranch with the pool because his cute little pudgy face ain't gonna be so goddam cute anymore, and he sure doesn't have the acting chops to Ron Howard his way around that, so maybe you'll have to start tricking his freckled ass on Santa Monica Boulevard if you haven't tried that out already, you sweaty fuck. Shut up, I'm not done. Every day I let that talentless piece of shit on my stage is another day you don't have to pay your own way, Earl. And just to show you who fills the jock around here, the kid's off this week's episode."

Then she grabbed Monte's styrofoam cup and threw it on the dad, cubes and all. "Hit the showers, motherfucker."

The stage became a wax museum. Still figures, lifelike, but not breathing. I could have shot them time lapse with no blur. Cast, crew, audience, Monte, Earl, Meddy, and her crew—everyone froze, defining the word dumbstruck. Only Bonnie showed life, panting from effort, joy, or both. The silence hung there for a timeless interval, the space between the tire squeal and the crash. Then Monte calmly strode to the warm-up and reached up. The comic handed down the microphone to him.

"Ladies and Gentlemen, apparently we've had a slight technical problem with one of our cameras," Monte said with a Disneyland guide's lilt. "Please bear with us while we make the repair."

The warm-up took a break and was replaced by a Michael McDonald CD, an improvement in my view. Meddy and her crew were packing up when I found her. "You're bailing?" I cared less about her puff piece and more about our plans.

"I think we've got all the Bonnie we can use."

"We're on for later, right? Arabesque?"

"Sure. If you're still up for it. After this, I mean."

"For the woman who followed me out of the hatch of a smoking helicopter? I think I'll be equal to the rigors of dinner."

She said they served late and to call when we wrapped. I began to worry how late was late when the stop-down lasted over an hour for a backstage summit.

They decided to broom the audience, toss the script, and block and shoot the rest of the episode in small pieces. It would be a one-woman show. Bonnie Quinn's tour de force as a mother in search of a lost rat. No script. No audience. No costars. Just a burned out, drugged up, bipolar actress and an empty set. Thank God, at least she was an autodidact.

The first crisis came immediately when Bonnie refused to wear her sweater. She ditched it, only to reveal the tattoo of a marijuana plant on her shoulder that UEN standards and practices would not permit. The obvious solution was just to have her wear the sweater, but obvious solutions root themselves in deep thicket on *Thanks for Sharing*. Bonnie said it made her ass look big.

"The tattoo's only a temp anyway," she said, "It's an appliqué."

Brick and his assistant swooped in with cotton balls and rubbing alcohol.

"I can't stand one fucking needle, do you think I'd want some Hell's Angels reject with HIV jackhammering my arm with his electric prick machine?"

"Copy that," said the stage manager, watching me review shots on my LCD. "Our Gramps is diabetic. Injects his insulin one day in front of her, and she faints right there. Topples like the damn statue of Lenin."

Tattoo crisis averted, Bonnie Quinn reconceived the episode to take place all in one set, the living room. Amid the ugly quiet and tense residue of four years, she improvised ten minutes of Wile E. Coyote retreads, devising traps out of found objects to ambush the rodent. She constructed a snare out of an inverted Tupperware bowl propped up by a carrot stick. She performed a series of one-sided phone calls: first to pet stores, futilely seeking an identical replacement rat; then to a fictitious neighbor who owned a cat that Bonnie wanted to borrow "just to do some light sniffing."

It was all improvisation, which meant dialogue in search of a scene in search of a point in search of a joke in search of a punch line. She did more searching than finding, and took hours to do it. If *Thanks for Sharing* had not yet had its jump-the-shark episode, I was betting this would be the one.

I gave up taking pictures at all simply because the toll showed too much on her. The bruisy bags under her eyes pushed obstinately through the foundation. And, most prominently, her jaw slid into a chin-jutting underbite. Watching Bonnie Quinn's face do a slow mudslide I figured I was witnessing the parade of the muscle relaxants.

"Still speeding," said the stage manager without irony.

Bonnie sniffed back and said, "I want to talk to the rat."

Unsure looks passed around the company.

Bonnie faced up to the fishpole microphone and said, "Ryan?"

Over the studio address came the director's cheery, "Still here, Bon-Bon."

"I want one camera. Take down the lights. I am going to talk to the rat."

The set dimmed to summer stock *Our Town*. Cameras repo'd.

Bonnie sat on the floor, back against a bookcase, closed her eyes again, either gathering thoughts or watching some private animation fantasy, who knew? Then she opened her eyes and began.

"You're here, I know it. Yes, I do. Think you're pretty cagey, huh? Well, I guess that is the whole issue, ain't it? Felt a little caged up, I'll bet. Was a nice ol' home at first, wasn't it? Clean pine shavings, fresh water, a little dish for that crap you like to eat. You know it's hamster mix and you're a rat? Just wondering about that. Whatever. Lots of love and attention when you first got here, right? You were out of that cage more than you were in it, what with all the people wanting to hold you and pet you and stroke you and see if you could swim in the bathtub. Sorry about that. My bad. But you grew fast and that cage got pretty small for you. And the pettings and the holdings and the strokings sort of fell off the more everyone got used to you, I know.

"I'm thinking about you, rat man, and I'm not thinking about why you broke out, I'm thinking, now that you've been out and know what it's like, how will you ever survive back inside there? I'm also thinking I know what you're thinking and you're wrong. You think you are hiding, but you are not. Because what you are hiding from is not inside that cage, but outside, too. We are not out of our cages. It only looks that way."

Bonnie Quinn folded herself at the waist and lowered her head to her knees. A long, still beat as she waited in silence like that.

"You can cut now," she muttered.

The stage manager gently announced a cut and Bonnie raised up, smearing wetness off her cheeks.

"Beautiful," said Monte as if Mass had ended. Then he whispered to the editor beside me, "Jesus fucking Christ, what are we going to do with this piece of dog shit?"

The director called a wrap and a small army of caterers pushed in carts of rolled cold cuts and plastic champagne flutes. Decoration commandos deployed helium balloon bouquets. Rhonda York loudly orchestrated the placement of floral centerpieces. I didn't recognize the recycled roses from the table reading and felt a little disappointed in a way I am not proud of. It would have made a good story.

I approached Monte, who was fishing for beer out of a galvanized metal tub of ice.

"Seems more like a surprise party," I said.

He took a long pull off the bottle and cleared foam off his mouth with the back of his hand.

"Hey, surprise is the only way to get anybody to come."

Judging from the cast and crew clinking plastic glasses and mirthlessly peeling labels off longnecks, I'd say he knew his people.

"It's sort of a get-your-paycheck-at-the-end-of-the-party party. By the way, you can come by tomorrow, I'll have your envelope."

"I don't see Elliot anywhere."

"Elliot had another commitment tonight."

Monte tipped up his amber bottle and I studied him around the flat bottom where a drip formed.

"Kind of a slap, isn't it? The executive producer pulling a no-show for the centennial wrap party. Bad enough it's on the stage instead of Chaya, or maybe Patina. But Elliot's not even here? That's cold."

"I'm sure he'd be deeply touched by your concern."

Then he turned and gave me the wide of his back. I was off his radar, just like that. I grabbed my gear and made for the door. No way I'd miss Meddy for this.

"No, no, no, don't go, you can't go," said Bonnie.

She seized both my hands again. Annoying enough the first time.

"Rhonda, cake! Cake now, goddammit!"

Rhonda York rounded up caterers.

"At least stay for my cake, Hardwick, please?"

When the cake was presented, nobody had bothered with a hundred candles. Or any candles. "Thanks for Sharing" was scrolled in the frosting above the numerals 100. The captives sang "For she's a jolly good Bonnie" with half a beer's enthusiasm, which seemed OK to Bonnie, who had a head start on them all since breakfast. She uncoupled from me and ran to the cake, weeping. Elliot Pratt was not there, nobody from UEN was there, but as long as I was, I figured I could spare two minutes as a crowd filler, and planted myself near the exit.

"Check out the cake, Dad."

Little Jimmy and his stage dad, Earl, were also at the door but still there. Contractually, I assumed.

"I dunno, Jimbo. Could be almond or something. And you know what almond does to you with that nut allergy."

He turned to me.

"How do you like that, the kid's allergic to nuts and look who he's working with."

"How long has your son been on the show?" I asked.

"Just this year."

"Then you knew her rep before you signed him up?"

"Hey, asshole, I don't like what you're saying."

"Probably not," I said.

Rhythmic clapping and hoots. Bonnie started chugging Cristal from the bottle. The crew clapped and clapped and the star chugged and chugged in a sad enactment of the college drinking game. Froth erupted around the corners of her mouth and dribbled down the front of her T-shirt. She plucked the wetness of the shirt away, then grew serious. Her jaw worked back and forth. Vicodin mudslide.

"I want to say something."

The stage fell silent.

"You people are the only family I've got. And I know sometimes— all right, lots of times—I can be a pain in the ass. But I want to let you all know that I not only deeply appreciate all you have done for me, but I am going to show you how much."

She grabbed the hem of her T-shirt and ripped it over her head. Before the first gasps she lasso twirled it up high, sending her naked breasts shaking.

I turned, expecting to see Little Jimmy's dad hustling his son away. Instead, father and son stood frozen in wide-eyed gawks. Bonnie spotted the boy and channeled Judy Holliday.

"Omigosh, there's a minor present. I better cover these up!"

And she did, by plunging her breasts into the cake, each one pressed firmly into a zero of the "100." The group let out rebel yells in response to some other move she made. I don't know what the move was because I was in the alley walking to my car when I heard it.

# CHAPTER EIGHTEEN

"**R**ight this way. Ms. Benson is already seated."

The hostess led me past the late diners to a cluster of potted palms at the French doors giving onto the patio. Meddy sat bathed in ginger-pink light, smiling up at me over a half glass of chardonnay. Her hand was light and cool and I wanted to believe it lingered on mine after I kissed her cheek.

"So glad we could do this," I said.

Meddy nodded. Desert wind swirled through the patio doors. The candle sputtered and the flame bent into the clear liquid wax. I cupped a hand around it to keep it burning. When the gust slackened I moved it to a sheltered place.

"Santa Anas are up," she said. "Big brushfires out near Agoura and in San Dimas. Can you smell them?"

The dry air tasted scorched. I leaned forward to get more of whatever Meddy was wearing.

When the waiter came I ordered a bottle of the Cakebread she was drinking. Meddy sidestepped a toast, but it was enough for me to touch glasses over a quiet table with her.

"You missed a great photo op. Bonnie, topless at her wrap party. Yee-haw."

"I can live without that."

"Apparently so can Elliot Pratt. The guy pulls a no-show, can you believe it?"

I noted her change of expression when I slammed him but pressed on.

"Bonnie Quinn, Elliot Pratt, Monte Arnett . . . the network, the security goons, the manager, the writers . . . the whole thing had me feeling like a gopher for the scum council."

She laughed.

"I'm serious. There aren't enough showers I can take or runs I can run to get it off me."

"Well, cut Elliot a bit of slack. He had something come up."

My gut took a churn again. Meddy ran her fingers through her auburn hair and I watched her triceps pull taut from her swimmer's shoulder. I caught the fall of her gray pearls across the round of her breasts and then I saw she was looking at me.

"You do know this is not a date, don't you?"

She mustn't have liked what she read in my hesitation and said, "Why don't we order?" from somewhere behind her menu.

Meddy got the cold soup and the seared rare tuna burger they only serve at lunch. But Chef was only too happy to accommodate the dining whims of Meredith Benson of UEN's *First Team*. Chef even came to the table to tell her so. My strip steak did not turn any toques, but then, I can live with that as long as it's done the way I order it.

"I was hoping to talk about our relationship," I said when we were alone.

"We need to."

"But here's the thing, Meddy. I don't just want to talk about it. I want to see if we still have one."

Who was more shocked, Meddy or I, going for broke like that? Her face tightened and the candle reflected the growing swell of tears rimming her eyes.

"I know I'm pressing, but I'm finally with you for the first time in too long and I can't let this pass."

She held up an arresting palm and swallowed hard.

"Do you really believe, after all that happened, after what you did and, forgive me, but what you have now become, that we can just pick up where we left off?"

"No."

"Then what can you possibly be talking about?"

"Change. Forgiveness. Healing."

One tear finally welled over the dam and fell to her cheek.

"Why are you doing this, Hardwick? We're done."

"Then why did you see me?"

"To . . . I don't know, find some closure, I guess."

She touched her eyes with a corner of her napkin and drew a composing breath. "No, I don't guess. That's exactly what I was hoping for. Closure."

"Because it doesn't feel over to you, either?"

"No. I mean yes, but not that way, I mean."

She took another deep breath, which shuddered a little on the intake, but she was regaining herself.

"Look. Sometimes lines get crossed and we can't cross back over. As much as we want to, we just can't."

"I can't untake the picture."

"Get it through your head, it wasn't the picture."

She poured herself more wine and topped mine, even though I had barely touched it.

"Then, what?"

"You knew what you were doing. You did it anyway and acted like the consequences didn't bother you."

"I wasn't acting."

"You ruined his marriage."

"He ruined his marriage. I only took a picture of him doing it." I sipped some wine. "He was dirty. He needed to be stopped."

"See, this is where I get nuts. You make it sound like you performed a public service. You violated a code."

"Which code is that?"

"The journalistic code."

"To follow a stronger one."

"Your moral code?" She sighed and wagged her head.

"Well . . . yes. It was a moral decision."

"It was thoroughly immoral." She pursed her lips, made an internal leap. "OK, can I say this to you and not have you feel attacked?"

"I'm not sure. I'll give it a try."

"I think Bonnie Quinn clicked with you because you are so alike. You're both working out your anger for a living. There. I said it."

"All right. Look at me, not feeling attacked."

"Very evolved."

"And you're feeling safe?"

"Quite."

"Can I tell you, then, that you are so fucking wrong?"

"And you are so fucking blind. Hardwick, look what became of you."

"Working for the tabloids?"

"It's not *working* for the tabloids. It's *why* the tabloids."

"I have a standard. I record the truth in pictures."

"But you don't just record. You go for retribution. The two-fisted loner dishing out his own brand of justice. It's like road rage with a camera instead of a gun. Be honest with me. When was the last time you took a picture that wasn't a payback?"

I should say that right about there this started feeling like less of a date.

"Meddy, what I do doesn't come out of anger."

She cocked an eyebrow.

"All right, the Congressman Landry tryst shot, maybe. But for me this is still journalism without the relationship deals or compromises. It always falls to an outsider to do this. It has to. Somebody has to care enough not to care."

"But a paparazzo."

"OK, first of all, what was I supposed to do? The mainstream cut me loose. Right? Second, call me a paparazzo, but I'm an independent shooter, plain and simple. Even in the jungle I wasn't one to lap up the official briefings. Neither were you. I shot what was outside the frame and you wrote about it. We were mavericks then and still are now. My turf's just different. I used to cover war and politics but now media's the big beat, so I cover that."

"By doing what, taking pictures of celebrities with their pants around their ankles?"

"Only if it's news. Tara Reid? Who cares. Ralph Reed? Get my camera."

Her soup came. She ignored it.

"Meddy, listen to me. We were going to buy rings. What we had was big."

"It wasn't easy for me, either. But we move on with our lives."

"Where is yours now?"

She broke off and watched traffic out on Melrose without focus.

"I'm in what you might call a state of flux right now."

"Meaning?"

She smiled a private smile and left it at, "I've been happier."

"I'm alone, too."

"Oh, I didn't say I was alone." A pause, and then, "You're not seeing anyone?"

"Nothing you'd call steady. A couple of almosts over the years."

"But you haven't joined the monastery."

"No, ma'am. I'm just too irresistible to go behind those walls. And those robes make me itch. Do I reveal too much?" I waited out her laugh before I continued. "The truth is, every woman I have ever been with since you has only made me think of you." Any trace of her laugh faded as she watched me with a fixed gaze.

"And the relationships ultimately die in comparison. I still wake up some mornings and wish your pillow had a dent in it. Or that I could hear you in the shower singing bad Anita Baker."

"What do you mean bad?"

"Hell, I even miss our fights."

"Liar."

"You see? I miss that. Tell me you don't miss that."

She reflected a long time. "Hardwick," she began, but before she got a word out there was a commotion across the restaurant.

"Who the hell let him in here?" a man shouted.

I parted the fronds of the potted palm beside our table for a better look and saw Tim Dash chewing out the hostess.

"Are you going to get the manager, or is that too big a job for you?"

Meddy was too evolved to part her plants and asked me what was going on.

"Pissed off actor coming this way."

I smoothed the air yoga style to let her know I would be cool.

The restaurant fell to the sort of quiet you get when the ground shakes and everyone pauses to ascertain if it's a passing bus or an earthquake. All eyes were on the star, who laced through tables as if going up for his Golden Globe. When Tim Dash stalked up and stood over me, all he said was, "Out." I ignored him and held Meddy's gaze, trying to reassure her with my air of calm. More footsteps. The manager arrived.

"The asshole goes. Now."

I didn't look up, but I believe he was indicating me.

"I don't want to breathe the same air as this prick." He poked me. "And my lawyer's filing papers over that chase in Toluca Lake. You could have killed somebody."

"I wasn't part of that."

"Bullshit you weren't. You were standing right in front of me."

"I wasn't with them. I didn't chase you."

"I should have driven right over you. Paparazzi roadkill—Boom!"

He punctuated it with a slam to my back that pushed me against the table. Meddy's wine landed in her lap. I bolted up and clawed Tim's shirtfront with one hand and his belt buckle with the other, looped a calf behind the crook of his knee to trash his balance, and launched him through the open French doors. He landed hard on the patio.

Meddy rose and took a step back. "Hardwick," she called, either as warning or its cousin admonition, I couldn't tell. Tim Dash sprang through the window at me with a fury. The force of his tackle sent us both onto the tabletop, and we crashed onto the floor in a heap. I hauled myself up and cleared my hands for some fist work, but Dash stayed down. He curled into a ball and moaned.

"Tim? Just stay as you are," said the manager. "Lisa, call for the paramedics."

"Cedars, not Queen of Angels," moaned Tim. "They know me at Cedars." Then he curled up tight. "Fuck, I think you broke my collarbone. Fuck," moaned the actor.

The handcuffs pinched my skin when he squeeze-locked them.

"Hey?"

"Shut it," said the cop.

He up-slapped the back of my head and spun me, arms behind my back, to face him. Then he kicked my feet wide apart and tipped me backward by the fingertips against the trunk of his bronze Crown Victoria.

"He moves, introduce him to Officer Baton," he said to the uniform.

He left me straining backwards at a forty-five degree angle and strode to the valet stand, shrugging in his silk blazer so it would drape clean and cover his service piece.

Over at valet he made quiet talk with the miraculously recovered Tim Dash and his entourage. I heard derisive laughter and saw their hard looks come my way. Tim shook the plainclothes cop's hand.

"Thanks, Lieutenant, this is a solid. I owe ya." Movie cop dialog.

Meddy watched from the restaurant door, hugging herself as if against some cold. Then the lieutenant came back. He hauled me upright by the shirt and tossed me hard into the back seat of the Crown Vic. His sharp toe to my ass brought more yucks from the Dash party. The cop tore off fast onto Melrose. He turned the next corner into the dark residential street and lurched to a stop. Popped my door, hauled me out, and stood me up to face him.

"Getting sick of saving your ass, Hardwick."

"That why you tried to circumcise me with those cuffs? Jeez."

He turned me gently and unlocked my wrists.

"Man's an actor. Did you want him to see it was an act?"

"Don't bullshit me."

"OK. I may have been venting some sideways aggression."

"Do it on somebody else."

He grinned.

"Don't need to now."

He snapped his cuffs onto his Sam Brown while I examined my wrists in the headlight.

"Rub some dirt on it. That bitty welt's nothing compared to what I told Tim Dash I'd be doing to you about now."

"Promise a little street justice, did you, Loot?"

"Enough to keep him from filing on your ugly butt. Probably saved you a lawsuit, too."

"Well, then we're almost even."

Loot's eyelids settled to half mast. No doubt reliving his first week on the LAPD Celebrity Unit. How he had lost track of the rock star with all the death threats he was babysitting for the Grammys and how I found her for him and never told.

"I say we got even a long time ago. How long you going to hold this over my head?"

"As long as it keeps working, I have no complaints."

Meddy's car eased up behind us. Loot shrugged.

"Had to tell her where you'd be. Couldn't leave a wussy with a sore wrist to walk home sniffling on a dark night."

He was still laughing when he drove off.

Meddy didn't bother to get out. She lowered her window and said, "We never should have done this. I only did it because I felt boxed and thought, get it over with."

"I was cool till he knocked the wine all over you."

"Yes. You were a model of reason over righteousness. You have changed."

Crickets and wind. I could smell distant smoke.

"Know what's funny? I chose a nice restaurant because I thought it would keep things from getting volatile."

Her lower lip quivered and she bit it.

"Here. I got your car keys from valet. The others are gone now."

She handed them over, then turned away quickly and chunked the transmission. Such a warm, dry night, but as she drove away I felt like I was right back in Nashua, standing on the ice.

After the fourth ring my phone kicked over to voice mail. I thought about getting up, but my head didn't want to leave the pillow. I had not slept. Just repeating a night I had had so many nights before, just waiting on the dawn. My pager sounded. It was Loot's number. I hauled myself up and pressed his speed dial.

The lieutenant didn't even say hello. I just heard police scanners in the background and then his voice.

"Listen up, this is going to break real fast. It hasn't been out on the air yet, so I'm giving you the jump."

"Hey, I appreciate the call, always do. But I'm sort of done for the night."

"Up to you, H-man, but I thought you'd especially want the exclusive."

"OK, what?"

"Your lady is dead."

I stood. "Lady? What lady?"

"Bonnie Quinn. Looks like she can join Belushi in comedy heaven after all. Hardwick? Hardwick, you there?"

# CHAPTER NINETEEN

"Sorry, this is a restricted area."

This again. Christ, sometimes I think I hear that for a living.

Loot spied me over the shoulder of one of the three detectives he was huddled with under the garage light. They all wore latex gloves. He left the driveway and came over to the black and white that was blocking the Larchmont street in front of Bonnie Quinn's house.

"He's here for me."

"No problem Loot," said the uniform. "Just that we were told to keep it sealed."

"He's here for me."

Quieter this time. Heavy with loaded patience. The uniform stood aside and I fell in beside the lieutenant, who walked me across the lawn without a word. His colleagues on the driveway pivoted to give me a once-over, which Loot must have deflected with some gesture or look I never saw, and they went back to their conference.

"How'd she go?"

"OD, knock me over with a feather. Just the early-early, though. Medical examiner needs to confirm. You know the ME dance."

A parked van had its back doors yawning, waiting for the gurney when they were done in the house.

"Listen, Hardwick, this went out on the TAC frequency a couple minutes ago, so you've got about ninety seconds to do your little number before I have to push you behind the yellow plastic, right?" When I nodded, he said, "Side gate. Follow your nose to the light." He left me for his buddies, but over the shoulder repeated, "Ninety seconds, in and out."

As soon as he joined the others, they moved in a group up the front walk.

I lifted the U-ring at the service gate. It was still dark but a spill of bright light from a window illuminated the stepping-stone path between the house and the trash barrels. It was intense light. Investigation-grade light. DOA light. I stayed on the dark side of the cut it made so I could look in at the Bonnie Quinn death scene without showing myself.

The window gave into her TV room, the same one I toured with her manager the week before. Two techs from the medical examiner's squatted near the wet bar. Loot and the other detectives arrived in the doorway. They exchanged brief comments followed by a startling burst of laughter, muffled by the window. The female ME shook her head and gave one of the cops the finger as she chuckled. More laughter, and two of the cops broke off to survey the rest of the house, leaving one, plus Loot. The female tech beckoned them to the marble countertop to inspect an array of drug paraphernalia. With their backs to me and attention drawn away, I inched closer to the window and then felt my throat draw up tightly.

Bonnie Quinn's body sat on the floor opposite me, leaning back against the empty bookcase. It struck me as her same pose on the set just eight hours prior when she slurred through her feeble improv.

*And, scene*, as they say at the end of a sketch.

One leg stuck straight out in front of her, while the other tipped to the side as if she had drawn one knee up to her chest and it fell over. Her torso tilted to one side, but a shoulder was wedged against the bookcase which kept her upright. Her eyes hung fixed under half-open lids like a bad candid from a cocktail party. Her chin was thrust low toward her chest, beyond the Vicodin mudslide. She was a Madame Toussaud's of herself, in character even in death, wasted and scowling at the world she departed in a room of rootless squalor.

Loot shot his cuff and looked at his watch but did not turn to me. He didn't have to and knew it. I drew my camera from my bag. There was ample source light, thanks to the crime scene techs. I checked the flash defeat and raised it to my face. Focused. Held her in frame. A couple of bottle green flies landed on her lips. One went in her mouth, the other up her nose. The image blurred. The frame floated. I braced my elbows against my ribs, drew a deep breath for stability, and reframed. But I slid my finger off the shutter release. Felt the etching of my initials on the cold metal. I blew out my air and lowered the camera. And stared at the first picture in my life I just couldn't take.

In less than ten minutes the street zoo hit full tilt. It was feed time to the East Coast morning shows, and the dozens of snorkels and dishes reaching up from the jam of news vans transformed the neighborhood into an antenna farm. Radio and print reporters filing from cell phones created a monkey house of chatter. I counted seven helicopters holding geosynchronous pieces of sky. Shooters from the *Times, Daily News,* weekly magazines, and wires all gained important turf ahead of the stringers and, especially, the paparazzi, who had gotten there first, but lacked the LAPD respect. No matter, the tabloids would do it their way, with long lenses, computer enhancement, and pilfered ghoul shots. Regardless of credential hierarchy, nobody was fooling anybody else that morning. The moment wasn't about journalism. It was all about The Gurney Roll and deadline sweat. "What the hell are they doing in there?" was the recurring lament from every crew at every van. Bring on the gurney. Roll the meat under the sheet. For the national breakfast shows this was hot oatmeal with a cinnamon stick. Breaking News, Live.

Meddy did her stand-up report to *Sunrise America*, the UEN embarrassment that trailed *Today*, *GMA*, and even the CBS morning laugher. I slid over to watch her on the monitor in the UEN van, where she shared a split screen with trench-browed cohosts in their Times Square studios. I heard Meddy's words through a hash of my own brain noise. . . . LAPD public information officer says body found by her manager about four AM . . . probable OD . . . no evidence of foul play . . . last seen leaving the wrap party burning rubber in her Porsche, top down. *Hers or the car's*, I wondered.

My cell vibrated and I stepped away so I wouldn't distract Meddy, as if that could ever happen while she was working.

"Hello?"

No answer. Just a lot of background noise like a wrong number from a car wash. I gave it one more hello.

"Hardwick, it's Elliot Pratt."

His voice was weak. Low and sober, almost lost in the whoosh.

"I can hardly hear you, Elliot."

"Sorry, I'm in the canyon, coming in from Malibu. Listen, I'm calling because I figured you'd be there and LAPD isn't telling me shit about this. You *are* there, right?"

"Yeah, but I don't know how much I can tell you. You do know she's dead, don't you?"

His news radio voxed up to fill the silence.

"Elliot?"

"Yes, yes. I know she's— That much is all over the air. Anybody say how? I mean, it's obvious what she did, but is there a specific?"

This time I paused. "Not sure what you mean, Elliot. Specific what?"

"I don't know. My star is dead and I'm just trying to get some God damned details, some information, and it's so frustrating to be here and not where I could get a handle on all this before the press jams microphones in my face."

"From here there's not much more to know, Elliot. I mean, she's dead. They're still in there doing forensics. I think you're about as close to this as I am right now."

My lie of omission floated Bonnie's corpse through my brain. The sneering death mask, the fly in her nostril.

"Yeah, I suppose . . ." Long pause. Audible sigh. "You know, it's weird, man. Not a day passed in the last four years that I didn't expect this shoe to drop. But now that it has? I'm thinking of what you said yesterday. About Belushi and *Wired-2*."

"Really?"

"Oh, I'm good with the law, I know that. It's just . . . I'll always wonder if maybe I couldn't have done more. I mean, it is a life, after all, isn't it?"

"It was," I corrected, then let one launch. "And, if you want honesty, here it is: You could have done more."

Either he hadn't heard me, or the it's-all-about-me segment of our conversation was complete.

"I'll be at the studio in thirty minutes. Call me if you hear anything. Right away, OK?"

"Sure."

"And Hardwick. You haven't seen Monte have you?" Yet another odd question.

"No." I scanned the crowd. "He's got a phone, too, doesn't he?"

"Ah, I didn't hear that. You're starting to break up. If you can still hear me, call if you see him or hear anything, thanks."

And Elliot Pratt disconnected.

The crowd of reporters tightened at the barrier for the big roll. Journalistic courtesy gave way to NBA-level body checks as the pack condensed for lead footage and the above-the-fold front page art. The ritual ride of the celebrity corpse. Feet first in a zippered pouch atop aluminum tubing and shopping cart wheels, choreographed to the tune of self-wind motors and clean-toned voice-overs of the respectfully detached and the appropriately solemn. Good gig for golf announcers, come to think of it. The money shot came as the Ziploc corpse rolled by her newest Porsche, past the DVA FRM HL vanity plate. Nobody missed that one. The fusillade of shutter clicks reminded me of hail hitting the lid of a trash bin.

"I can't believe she's dead." Meddy, later, standing on the curb behind me. "Can you?"

Was I going to tell her about Bonnie's paranoid ramblings and doom talk? No. I let it go at, "Hasn't sunk in."

She pulled the IFB from her ear and handed it to the audio tech. "I mean, there she was yesterday, her crazy Bonnie self, and now this. Gone. It must feel weird, even to—"

"Even to me?"

"Don't read too much into that. I just know how you detach."

She indicated her crew, milling in the van.

"I have to leave."

She took a step away but held there. Something nagging her.

"You didn't take any pictures. I watched you during the rollout and your cameras were hanging."

"It was a gurney roll. The Addams Family version of working the velvet rope at a premiere. Why bother if every drone with a camera is getting the same snaps?"

"But you always shoot coverage. You never leave it to somebody else."

She looked at me, trying to look into me.

"Why didn't you take a picture?"

"Like I said, it's not my story if everyone can tell it."

I unslung my cameras.

"Listen, I think we got sabotaged last night. Any chance we could resume our conversation this evening? I promise not to beat up any actors."

"I think we'd just end up doing another lap around the same track. Let's not do that."

I spent the drive home in a funk over Bonnie Quinn's short and tortured life. I had seen tragic cases flash and crash before. Some of their passings saddened me, others were mere facts. Meddy pegged it: my famous ability to detach. But not this time. And damned if I knew why.

I didn't even like Bonnie Quinn. How could you? In her maelstrom of wickedness there was a core of black unhappiness that revealed how little she seemed to like even herself. The quiet eye of Hurricane Bonnie was a vacuum of the soul. It made me wonder if her overdose was a suicide. Or to hope that it was. Because the accident of one too many pills only added to the pathetic equation of her life of unfulfillable self-regulation. She had squandered her days either dosing herself with drugs to dull the pain or dosing everyone around with ingenious misery as her way to find kinship in suffering. Even hell is no fun alone.

And these were my happier thoughts.

The caller ID said Hobby Horse Prods.

"Hey, I got a message you called." Monte Arnett. "Relax, you'll still get your envelope."

"Damn well better. But I wasn't calling about that. Elliot was looking for you."

"Yeah? Did he whistle or just snap his fingers?"

"Work out your deal with Elliot any way you want. Just giving you a heads up."

"So you want your fucking money?"

"Stupid fucking question. But I know it's not your best day."

"Aren't you the Boy Scout."

It sounded like a meeting walked into his office. He covered the phone and came back.

"I gotta deal with something. Come tonight, and I'll have your envelope."

"Come where?"

"The Sheraton Universal. Zack told you about the party, right?"

"He was serious?"

"You'll see."

"I don't think so."

"If you want your money, be there. Eight o'clock. Don't wear anything you don't want stained."

He was laughing when he hung up. The Mont-ster, indeed.

# CHAPTER TWENTY

The awkwardness of talking money around the death of Bonnie Quinn kept me from voicing a very practical concern. Rudy Newgate was expecting his payment at noon. His flea-sized heart was not going to miss a beat for a dead actress, but I called to get ahead of the trouble. Voice mail. A big part of me was glad not to talk to him. I left a message to assure him of payment first thing next morning, testing that goodwill.

I self-parked at the Sheraton Universal. Not from economy but experience. This would be a surgical strike and I didn't want to get stuck in a half-hour wait at valet behind losers in turquoise satin leaving some low-end wedding reception, clutching gaudy center-pieces and stolen cocktails. Instead, I trailed slow-moving German tourists parading lobster sunburns down the parking structure stairwell.

I found the digitized events board and scanned it for the Bonnie Quinn wake. There was a marketing seminar that reeked of pyramid scheme in the West Ballroom. Numismatics in the New Age promised geek sexual fantasies in the Lanai Suite. Two wedding receptions—thank God for self-park—something called a Champions of Sales Awards for an acronym company, which could have been either failing aerospace or failing tech sector. The bottom listing was for the Roof Garden. All it said was Survivors Support Group. Which was plenty.

The elevator doors opened on the twenty-first floor to thunka-thunking megabass and drunken whoops. The shocker was not how many people packed their sweaty bodies into the place, it was the level of unabashed celebration. I don't know what I had expected to find. I don't know . . . bittersweet introspection, perhaps. This was a balls-out frat party. The tone-setter was the handmade poster with Bonnie Quinn's publicity head shot plastered on Margaret Hamilton's shoulders with the colorful proclamation, "Ding-Dong, the Witch Is Dead!" That was about as bittersweet as it got.

There was a reception table with adhesive name tags and goldfish bowls brimming with tic tacs and Altoids. But the bowls were labeled Vicodin and Percocet. Say what you will about the diva, at least she inspired her colleagues.

The room was a crush of humanity fired up by repressed anger and no-kidding cocktails. I blinked when I thought I saw Bonnie Quinn upending a can of malt liquor in the far corner. But after the synapses did their job I recognized JT, one of the writers, in drag, sporting a Bonnie wig and one of her office outfits from wardrobe.

"OK, who wants to cop a feel of Good 'n' Plenty here?" he shouted, lifting his blouse. "Come on now, don't be shy. Get 'em while they're hot."

"Hey, pull your shirt down, pervert," called Deane Tacksdale, Bonnie's TV neighbor. "At least have the self-restraint to wait till there's a minor here to corrupt!" Gang laughter ensued.

Somebody called out "Fuckin'-A," and I looked around the room half expecting to see Borat filming his next movie. It was Monte Arnett.

"You're not drinking, what's wrong with you?" he said after I pushed my way over to him.

"I'm good. I'll just take my envelope and go."

"Hang out for a while. You can't tell me this offends someone like you."

Before I could respond he went back to the bar for a refill.

"Oh, don't be such a tight ass," said a withered guy beside me I didn't recognize. "Why'd you even come if you're gonna wear that face? What the hell do you think this is, a wake?"

Whoever he was, he staggered on, holding onto his fellow party-goers like hand rails. Zack filled his place beside me and toasted me with his schooner of margarita.

"Who's the scarecrow?"

"Ron Steiner. My predecessor. Head writer-show runner for season one. Most of season one, anyway. After Bonnie gave him herpes, his wife left him, along with her inherited case, took the kids back to Shaker Heights, and Ron disappeared himself into the Topper Motel on Ventura for three weeks without bothering to call in. His agent found him there sitting on the bathroom floor. Poor fuck came out looking like Howard Hughes at the end. Fingernails like yay, beard like this . . . Developed a twitch."

I looked at the ex-show runner, emaciated and holding his drink with two hands. "What's he been doing since?"

"Waiting for this day."

Clearly not the only one. I tried to peg a reference for the spirit of the occasion. The closest I could conjure was Eastern Europe when the Soviet Union posted its going out of business sign. Bonnie was the Berlin Wall and everyone wanted a swing of the hammer.

Two grips showed up and hoisted something above their heads with chalky hands and scuffed knuckles. A chant of "Bon-nee, Bon-nee" swept the room. I squeezed forward and saw what they were holding up. Her star from Hollywood Boulevard.

Not everybody joined the chant. Brick sat hunched over a frozen daiquiri in a brooders corner staked out by hair and makeup. As if he sensed my gaze, he torqued my way and stared. He remained fixed on me, disdainful and angry, the way people always look when they make their decision about me. These looks rarely impact my sleep rhythms. Finally, he turned down to study his bar napkin. Behind him on one of the many big screen TVs, a video loop of Bonnie Quinn's busted scenes and on-camera rants played unwatched but still part of the celebration. Reduced to wallpaper, she could now be ignored.

I looked for Monte again but he was lost in the crowd somewhere.

Zack climbed up on a table and called, "Ladies and Gentlemen, many life-affirming traditions have developed over time among the little family we like to call *Thanks for Sharing.*"

"Yeah, like pagan sacrifice!" somebody shouted.

"I am speaking, of course, of the vaunted tradition of—Shit Theater!"

Cheers and whoops filled the room and somehow the crowd grew.

"Our *Thanks for Shitting* players will be Stan Finkel and JT O'Toole."

One of the staff writers carrying a script and a heavy black garbage bag stepped up onto the table. JT, still in his Bonnie Quinn drag, also climbed up to calls of "Bon-nee, Bon-nee, Bon-nee."

Zack hopped down and stood beside me.

"You're gonna love this, man," he said taking a hit off a found bottle of beer. "We did this every show night in the writer's room. A little guerilla theater to blow off steam."

"Please tell me that bag isn't what I think it is."

"Not to worry. We call it Shit Theater, but it's not real shit. It's prop doody. Finkel & O'Toole brew it up on show day for our make-believe Bonnie to crap on that week's script. Watch. It's so wrong."

Whatever foxhole demons were being exorcised by this rite, they were not mine, and I wanted to be anywhere else right then. I cornered Monte for the envelope and forced my way shoulder-first through the crowd. Another chorus of "Whoa!" did not slow me or even turn my head. Outside the fake wake I waited for the elevator, wearing the dirty-guilty diminishment that had cloaked me since my first encounter with Bonnie Quinn just the week before. I wondered when it would shed. Or if it would. I got on and pressed Lobby, but when the doors began to close, a hand reached in and bounced them open. Brick Tennant slid into the opening and stood staring daggers at me.

"You on or off, chief?" I said.

The door wanted to close, but he found the electric eye and bounced it open again, then held it open with his bony hand. When it fought him, he braced his pipe cleaner arm against the black rubber to keep it open.

"She's dead because of you, mon. I want that you know that, you. She's dead and it's on you."

The whites of his eyes were bloodshot parchment, glassy enough to have been placed there by a taxidermist, and swollen from a day of tears. I gave him a prudent once-over for weaponry. His fishnet tee was tight to his skin, revealing nothing more than bare midriff and a stud in his belly button. Nothing in his belt.

I let myself return to his stare and said, "Look, party's over for me. I pushed the embossed L on the panel again. "Mind?"

"She only came back because of you. She called you her hero—her hero—and you abandoned her, Hardwick."

The elevator warning buzzer bit into his accusation, putting hair on his words. The door bounced against his shoulder once more. He stepped into the car and it closed behind him. As the car descended he turned and pressed every button.

"Christ, how old are you, thirteen?"

I leaned back against the rear of the elevator, resigned to a score of openings and closings on the way down. Resigned to be this whisper of a man's captive audience.

"That woman, she relied on you, Hardwick."

Tears made slow rolls down his sunken cheeks. White strings of spittle connected his upper lip to his lower. I could smell rum.

"You make a promise and now my lady is dead now, gone. How does that sit with a man such as you?"

"I know you and Bonnie must have been close—"

"No. Do not minimize this, don't. Do not wrap this up in the neat little package to let you sleep, no. That is so . . . disrespectful."

Some of his bleached dreads stuck to his cheek. The door behind him opened and closed again, admitting or letting off the invisible. Spirits? Demons, maybe.

"I'm not dismissing her, Brick."

His face registered mild surprise that I knew his name.

"But I'm late to this circus. If she eats a handful of beans too many, how can I possibly feel responsible?"

"Because you let them kill her."

Here it comes, I thought. I could have predicted it would start. The speculation. The conspiracy theories. But I had imagined them seeping from the folds of a Florida tattler or beaming from the grave-yard shift of a Nevada coffee-pot AM station.

"Don't do that," he shouted. "Damn you, mon, you do not roll your eyes at me when I tell you this."

He squeezed his temples as if wringing the wet from his eyes. Then, with a sudden air of calm, drew his nose in the air with regal disdain.

"My lady, she was murdered." Coolly. Measured. "This I know."

The doors continued to open and close crazily behind him.

"If you know something, you had better tell the police. They see it as an OD. The only question is whether it was accidental or . . . or if she'd had enough of all this. It happens. She wouldn't be the first."

"The police, they do not know. The police, they do not want to know. They are bored now after their OJs and their Bobby Blakes. They look the other way because the trials are costly and it always makes them look bad in some way. And the city, the city has lost its thirst for the sensational murder."

"That'll be the day," I said as the door finally opened at the lobby.

I took a step toward the opening and, for a nanosecond, Brick moved as if to block my exit. That would have been a mistake and he quickly concluded the same thing. I brushed past him with no thought of looking back, but he called my name with a tone that stopped me. It was a plea.

"Mr. Hardwick?" he said. And when I stopped, "Don't question me, then. There's proof."

I told him Loot's name. "Give it to him. If you have it."

"But you have it."

Right. I should call the police and report her paranoid chin music.

"Yes, mon. Walk away. Just like you did when she was alive." He pushed another button, and as the elevator door began to close, he said to me, "After she bet her life on your trust."

The doors met like the curtain of the first act and the makeup artist rose upwards to the Wake of the Century. I hurried across my level of the parking garage, chirped the remote, and opened the back door of my Xterra. The shoulder bag was on the floor where I had left it after the wrap party the night before. I pulled out the thick envelope Bonnie Quinn had given me and saw my name calligraphied across its face.

# CHAPTER TWENTY-ONE

**E**xactly what had she said to me when she made the presentation? Dire words of a drama queen. How I was the only person in the world she could trust with it. Something about being her hero, guarding the truth, and, especially, that I should "hold it close and keep it safe." Nice job, Hardwick. I sat in the driver's seat and slit the seal with my key.

To my mild disappointment it turned out to be neither a stash of narcotics nor a cellophane-wrapped block of hundreds. It was a book. *A Fable*, by William Faulkner. This book was what she wanted me to put in the equivalent of Fort Knox?

I held it under the dome light. It was a nice first edition, at least. Not mint, but what collectors would call VG/NF, very good to near fine condition. The bipolar Ms. Quinn was known to give extravagant gifts, and, forgive me, I flipped the cover to see if the Nobel laureate had left an autograph. There was an inscription, but not in Faulkner's hand—unless he used sepia ink, sweeping flourishes, and knew my name. Under the title and author, it said:

To Hardwick—
A Fable reveals fact when content is container.

Be smarter like your damn Tom Sawyer at the fence.

Seek the truth. Go there.

BQ

Excellent. A posthumous American lit lesson from the high school dropout. I slipped it back in the envelope, tossed it on the back seat, and started the car.

Twenty minutes later, brush fire ashes from another area code drifted through my headlights like flurries. When I parked in my driveway I looked up through the high altitude smoke at a smudge moon of tarnished copper. The cinders laid a thin coat on the ground that could have been snow in that light. Why was it so dark? My porch light was off, even though it was on a sensor. At the little window beside the front door a curtain billowed out through broken glass.

Impressions fired in rapid succession. The dark cottage. No sound within. Footprint streaks in the ash . . . Think, wasn't there a car parked on the shoulder down the hill?

A hoarse stage whisper rolled out from under the trees.

"Mr. Hardwick, is that you?"

I turned to the silhouette of Amanda St. Hillaire parting strands of the willow. I signaled in vain for her to stay back, my gesture lost in the darkness.

"I heard glass breaking and I—"

The cottage door flew open and a massive body shot out, head down, a bull out of a chute in Pamplona. He was beefy, thick. But when he cut left off the path to avoid me it was a sharp, easy move. I chased after him and he cut another turn, but when he looked back to measure my advance, he clipped Amanda. They hit the driveway with a clang of heavy metal. Amanda's sword. The big man was up again, gymnastic quick. I threw a running tackle on him, but it was like striking a telephone pole. I hurt my sore shoulder and he didn't go down. He clamped iron skillet hands on both my arms, slammed me against the side of my car, and sprinted yards away by the time I bounced off and hit the ground. I used the side mirror to hoist myself up as he reached the splash of light from Amanda's front porch. When he glanced back to assure himself of his lead, I believe I actually saw a smile—or most likely, a smirk—under the shadow of his low brow before he pointed his block head to the street and buffalo trotted into the night.

The paramedic drew her hand away. "Does that sting?" she asked.

"Yes, of course it does, dear," said Amanda. "But it's killing germs, so let it pour."

The old actress thrust her eyebrow upward with resolute defiance. The EMT soaked a fresh cotton ball with hydrogen peroxide and finished cleaning the cut. When that was done, Loot instructed the two female uniforms to walk Miss St. Hillaire back to her house. One of the cops offered to carry the sword. Amanda yanked it back.

"This stays in my possession. And if that brute returns, he shall taste steel for not knowing how to respect a lady."

She clanged Excalibur on my door jamb on her way out. Always make an exit.

"That thing weighs more than she does," said Loot after they were gone.

I said I wouldn't bet against her in a fair fight, and he agreed.

"Anything missing, that you can tell?"

"Hard to know. He wasn't carrying anything, so I'm sure I interrupted the party." The man had completely trashed my darkroom. In my Luddite's transition to full-digital, the darkroom was slowly becoming more of a storage closet. Glossy paper stock, rolls of film, negatives and CD-ROMs littered the floor. The living room was a partial. Just the bookcases and the videos were tossed.

"Haven't had a B&E around this part of the hills for a long time. TV set like that, Hardwick, you should start using that alarm system."

The plainclothesman knelt next to the TV and sighted an eye along the side of the picture tube.

"What is this, a flat-screen?"

Of course, I wasn't thinking burglary. The invasion reeked of my loan officer, Rudy. His style, his brand of thug, his way to remind me that goodwill only stretched so far. But I didn't share my poor choice of lenders with Loot. I wouldn't even have called the police. Amanda did that when she heard the glass break before I even got there.

After forensics wrapped up and left, Loot took some folded sheets of paper from his suit pocket and slapped them on my chest.

"Prelim from the ME on Bonnie Quinn. This didn't come from me, understand?" I nodded and Loot gave me the highlights. "Definite OD, duh."

"Vicodin, OxyContin?"

"Valium and Demerol, by injection."

"Not heroin?"

"Do I look like I'm making this up?"

"Touchy."

"Anyway, she had pot and Vicodin and some other narcotics in her system—quite a fun zone in there, even polyurethane residue, so she must have been a sniffer, too. But the injection is how she bought it. And what's with the face?"

"Doesn't go. Bonnie Quinn had a thing about needles. Couldn't even get a tattoo or watch her costar get his insulin shot. And that's how she cashes out?"

"Hardwick, you crack me up. I know lots of people afraid of heights. Guess how they kill themselves." He whistled the sound of a bomb dropping. "Lady didn't like needles? Not a problem anymore, now, is it?"

Loot slid the report in his breast pocket and gave the suit a pat. When he offered a few extra black and white patrols the rest of the week, I told him I'd be fine.

"Not worried about you, Hard man. I don't want that Norma Desmond you got next door slicing and dicing the bad guys."

I didn't wait for Rudy to find me. The Jacob's ladder of anger over the violation of my home and what happened to Amanda put me on his tail from his house first thing the next morning. I followed him to a Korean facial place on Pico, watched him settle in under the steamy towel through the storefront, and then paid a call.

I shooed the beautician away and leaned next to his ear.

"This is how easy it is to get to you, Rudy."

He started and bolted up, whipping off the towel.

"What the fuck is this?"

"Emancipation day." I tossed the cash in his lap. "Paid in full. We're done. You don't talk to me again, you don't even think about me. Got it?"

"Are you threatening me?"

"Come to my house again, you'd better kill me, because you're going to be my bitch."

"What the fuck are you talking about?"

"You crossed the line last night when you sent the Hawaiian."

"I didn't send any Hawaiian. You said you'd come through. I knew you were good for it. Didn't I tell you the other night you were a good customer?"

"Somebody paid me a visit."

"Hey, asshole, if I were going to pay you a visit, would you wonder who?"

Jump ball. In a facial spa, no less. Now what? Probably wasn't Rudy. And once I climbed off my rage and thought it through, even if it was, what real threat could I make against this guy, anyway? Play that out and see where it goes.

So I just walked out. When I reached the door, he said if I needed another loan to call. Nice to know I didn't spoil a good relationship.

Monday morning I went to Bonnie Quinn's funeral. A weekend of partying wasn't very long to put one together, but then, it wasn't much of a service. The preacher was an old priest from her girlhood parish in Boston. Father William not only would have easily won the homecoming blanket for most distance traveled but also for most effort. Nobody else broke a sweat on this do. Notably absent from the Forest Lawn hillside were Elliot Pratt, a no-show, same as the wrap party; Monte Arnett, not in attendance; brass from UEN, zippo, except for a low-level manager who must have lost a card cut. Costar Deane Tacksdale was there in the same clothes he had on Friday night at the fake wake. I could only wonder if JT would show up in his Bonnie drag. Not to worry. No writers came. This was not exactly the Sinatra send-off. Meddy's crew was there without Meddy. Pinkman, Dellroy and even Chuck Rank made it. I watched him trade a knuckle-five with the Canuck. It looked like the press outnumbered the mourners. Now *there* was a loose term for the two dozen stragglers who chatted freely during the old padre's words. As Father William stood over the coffin ringed by a schemeless cluster of flowers my own attention swam a lap to wonder if her manager had bought Bonnie Quinn's memorial blooms from her own flower shop. I was certain she had and even appreciated the elegance of the deal. Fish gotta swim. I nodded to Rhonda York, who sat sweating in the ten AM Burbank bake in long-cut black leathers.

The priest choked up over his long ago memory of "this splendid, lively girl from the projects, one of God's creations making her First Holy Communion in her white veil and lace. So sweet a Bonnie, so innocent."

"And later that night, she blew the Celtics bench," whispered Deane Tacksdale. He and the crew guy behind me slapped low fives.

The white-haired priest either did not hear, or pretended not to, and continued. "Bonnie Quinn's legacy could have been one of triumph over her life station: the girl who went from the mean streets to the Walk of Fame."

Until two grips with bloody fingers stole her star from Hollywood Boulevard. "But tragedy and pain stalked her to the highest levels of material success. The pain in her life was not so much a price of success as a companion to it, from her brave battle with drugs to the shocking loss of her illegitimate daughter to suicide.

"A few years ago, when I reached out to comfort her after the death of her beloved Shannon, I asked Bonnie, 'Is there anything I can do to ease the suffering that has visited you?' She said, 'No, Father William, the hand is dealt. We all suffer as part of the package. Lucky me, I get to do mine in the back of a limo.'"

"Along with doing half the coke in West Hollywood," said Tacksdale, not bothering to whisper this time.

"Hey, shut your trap," someone shouted.

It was the priest. The hole of silence that ensued filled up with shutters and auto-winders from the shooting gallery. Deane Tacksdale gripped the back of my metal chair and rose on imbalanced feet to challenge the priest.

"Sit down, mon," said Brick.

"With all due respect, your holiness, this is a load of horseshit."

"Quiet, you drunk," the old man gave back. A boxing scar stood white across his nose as his face colored. "Why did you come here if not to pay your respects?"

"Why am I here? Why am I here? I'm here for the same reason everyone else is here. To make sure they lock that box and use enough fucking dirt."

No silence this time, but cheers and whoops. Blame Jerry Springer.

"That is blasphemy," said the priest. "I pray for your soul."

Tacksdale climbed over the crew guy between him and the aisle and wove up front to shake a finger at the holy man.

"No, Father, I'll tell you what is fucking blasphemy." He turned a little Joe Cocker turn to address the gathering. "Blasphemy is when some street ho makes the promise of an ensemble role on a show so you give up your own pilot commitments only to find yourself locked in hell's outhouse with Satan's niece."

A chant from the back, "Deane, Deane, Deane . . ."

"And while you watch your pilot chances wither and die, your lawyers try to free you and come back with 'Ironclad, baby, ironclad.' And then your wife splits because now you hate everything, but you got three kids to put through college so you keep at it, but sainted Bonnie knows she has you by the onions and squeezes every day." The actor smiled to the priest. "But you are right about one thing, Father. I do need to pay proper respects."

And then, Deane Tacksdale, costar of *Thanks for Sharing* and one-time *People* magazine star of the future, unzipped his fly and arced a long, sunlit leak onto Bonnie Quinn's casket.

During the shoving match, Brick stood to sing *Everybody is a Star*, lending an even more absurd quality to the proceedings. If nothing else, it stopped the fight. There were a few tears, but mostly I detected giggles hidden behind those hankies. That's what happens. When melodrama meets kitsch you get bathos.

Yet, even with the karaoke-reggae taint, when he sang the part about falling stars not stopping until they're in the ground, I stared at the casket and the dirt and heard her call me her hero. Instead, I may have delivered her to her death. Whether it was murder or suicide or one of her home chemistry experiments gone bad, I had a twisting ache that I had escorted her from her safe place to the danger zone.

And that responsibility invested me right there in finding out what really happened to Bonnie Quinn. My culpability was that I didn't take her seriously. But how was I supposed to know the difference between a real alarm and a drugged-out bipolar crying wolf?

I caught up with Brick on the grassy slope on his way to the parking lot. Ahead of us, the Canuck and the other shark packers surrounded the actors, lenses in faces, on their way to their cars. Brick picked up his pace.

"Stay away, mon."

"I just want to ask you about something you said in the elevator the other night."

"Go. Go 'way. Can you see I am not talking with you?"

He said it loudly, as if it was for someone else to hear.

"Just one question. What did you mean when you said I had proof?"

He looked around at the others filing out, but nobody in particular, then came back to me with a voice again too loud.

"Hardwick-mon, I have nothing to say to you, so go away from me. Away, shoo." He jogged ahead on the worn path, his bleached dreads flouncing.

# CHAPTER TWENTY-TWO

If you work long enough around Hollywood you stunt your capacity to be shocked but not to be amused. At noon the day of Bonnie Quinn's burial, Elliot Pratt held a news conference on the steps of his production offices at Empire Studios. It was later clipped on *ET*, *E!*, *Rough Cut,* and *Insider,* but the UEN station in LA carried it in their *LunchTime Live!* news hour. With his curls wafting in the breeze, Elliot began.

"I am proud to announce that an exciting challenge has been presented to me. One which I gladly and humbly accept. Otis Grove, chairman and chief executive officer of UEN, has named Hobby Horse Productions as the in-house production entity for his recently acquired network."

I set the armful of CD-ROM cases down on my coffee table and cranked the volume, lest I couldn't hear Elliot over my laughter.

"Since deregulation of syndication years ago, an economic cornerstone of any network is its capacity to produce programming. It was for Mr. Grove the obvious missing component in UEN when he purchased it. I am keenly aware that many options were open to Mr. Grove, including building his own UEN Productions from the ground up. But, as he said when he made this exciting overture, Hobby Horse is not only up and running with the infrastructure of a turnkey entity, it has limitless headroom if powered by UEN resources."

As Elliot ran on about television's new day, blah-blah, I looked at my watch and figured all of fifty-six minutes had passed since the first trowel of dirt had hit the lid of Bonnie Quinn's coffin. Granted, life goes on—there I was tidying up after my Hawaiian burglary—but, come on, I wasn't on the tube doing PR the very day my star took her curtain call at Forest Lawn. And, oh yes, at least I attended her funeral even though she hadn't made me a demibillionaire.

"Questions? . . . Barry?" Elliot pointed over a cluster of microphones.

"What about fit?"

I knew the voice, a reporter from one of the trades.

"We've seen, for instance, after the AOL-Time Warner merger, that there was a significant clash of corporate cultures. Given your background in Hollywood, and Otis Grove's strong faith-based approach, is there a concern about synergy?"

"Did I mention my baptism is this afternoon?"

Shock laughter from the reporters. That Elliot. This guy could run as a Democrat in Orange County and get nominated by the Birchers.

"Look," he said after the laughs settled, "first of all, you're not giving Otis Grove his due as a man. Otis is an exemplary model of someone who doesn't just talk the talk, but walks the walk. And as his steps led him into this business, you'd be wise to look at his path through his paper mills, to packaging, to his newspapers, to his radio stations, and to his charitable foundations. He has strongly held beliefs which guide his course, but do not impose themselves on content or on those he works with. And don't forget, Otis and I have history. He was my mentor when I was a know-it-all at the Harvard School of Business twenty years ago. And you know? He's done pretty well since."

More laughter. Paging Dr. Soundbite.

I refiled my vandalized books and videos while Elliot answered more questions. Yes, Hobby Horse would keep its name. Yes, they would relocate to new office space at the UEN complex. Yes, Hobby Horse would explore all forms of programming, not just sitcom. In fact, they were already developing a syndicated daytime talk strip, to be hosted by UEN's senior journalist, Meredith Benson. I stopped cleaning and sat down. When Elliot called her "franchise talent," Meddy stepped up briefly and waved and I got a scoffer's understanding of her absence from the funeral.

"And finally," Elliot said, "you all know we lost one of the great small screen comediennes of all time in circumstances too tragic to belabor here." He folded his notes and leaned forward to the cameras. "But her passing has galvanized my resolve to keep her candle burning, too. Therefore, it is my privilege to announce that, as of this morning, UEN has picked up *Thanks for Sharing* for another season." The executive producer paused and dried his eyes. "I can't promise we'll be a better show without Bonnie Quinn. I don't even know yet what adjustments we'll have to make . . . retooling, recasting, obviously . . . that will be worked out between now and our press junket next week. But I do promise this: Bonnie Quinn battled to make *Thanks for Sharing* the top sitcom in a world of reality shows. She brought quality and comedy to her American constituency. And to her loyal family of viewers, I pledge this day to honor her spirit, to honor her life, to honor you, by producing more than a show—but her living legacy."

Elliot quit the podium and entered his offices past Monte Arnett, who held the tinted glass door open by its split hobbyhorse handle. Maybe her body was cold, but the sod wasn't tamped down yet. Then, with the amusement you survive on in this town, I thought, *at least he hadn't said Bonnie would have wanted it this way.*

But amusement is a luxury for the detached. My detachment was eroding under a parade of inconsistencies—for my money the greatest indicator of bullshit next to coincidences. Brick accosts me in an elevator with enough conspiracy gas about Bonnie Quinn's death to power a live chat room, then flip-flops at her planting. Bonnie Quinn was needle phobic, yet dies of an OD she gave herself—by injection. And then, Elliot Pratt, who hired me to find his AWOL star because there was no show without Bonnie, announces a new season of the show without Bonnie. None of these things alone makes any sort of case about anything. They don't even make one together. But as things mount up they gain momentum you can't ignore, even if you try.

All I wanted was a hot pastrami on an onion roll. Not exactly A-list on my runner's diet, but I was in the mood for guilty pleasure, and Jerry's Famous was the place to let the games begin. I got a sidewalk table for a view of the jacaranda showing lavender against the brown scrub and bland retail along Ventura Boulevard. The sandwich did not disappoint, and I did my part, too, matching just the right-sized bite of kosher pickle to chase the pastrami and brown mustard. What can I say, I'm a born chef.

Up the sidewalk, Dellroy Means stepped out the glass doors ahead of Chuck Rank and two other shooters I could get through my day without. I pulled my baseball cap low and hunkered down over my plate.

"Hey, Hardwick."

Chuck Rank. I should have known even a journeyman paparazzo would do a celebrity scan of patio diners in Studio City.

"Too cool to eat inside with us?"

"Air's better out here, Chuckie."

He didn't mention the nosebleed. I didn't either.

"Uh-huh. Just like Forest Lawn this morning, right? Not standing with your bros. Gotta sit with the congregation like you belonged."

The others ambled over, twirling minted toothpicks and sucking teeth.

"Guys. Check out the Hobby Horse houseman. Gets some inside work and his shit doesn't stink."

"Shut up, dickweed," Dellroy said, talking the way you talk to a guy who's used to being treated like shit and you know will take it. Probably the same reason Chuck didn't mention the nose. "Hardwick's no homer and you know it. Just because he's smart enough to get work doesn't make him a houseman, right?"

Dellroy shook my hand over the railing and Chuck Rank pawed through my French fries like it was OK. I checked out his fingernails and wrote off the rest of my lunch right there. A low hum made me reflex my hand to my hip, but it wasn't my BlackBerry, it was Chuck Rank's. He unholstered, and, as he squinted at the screen in the valley glare, I said, "Since when can you afford a BlackBerry?"

"You can bite me."

When he moved off to find shade, Dellroy shook his head.

"It's not exactly his."

"The Canuck's?"

"Himself."

Dellroy stared at the kid engrossed in his new e-leash. "Shit," he said. "We should fucking walk to Cheviot Hills."

"What's happening in Cheviot Hills?"

"Hey, that's good. Low-n-Inside pretending he doesn't know." Dellroy winked and rolled his toothpick between his thumb and forefinger. "Sitting out of doors, taking an easy lunch like the day's on your leash. You got your picture already, didn't you? Bet she even posed for you."

"Who would that be?"

"Oh, Hardwick. I am losing my deeply held respect for you as a role model."

I shrugged.

"Kimberly Duggan. She's replacing Bonnie Quinn on that sitcom you pretend to know everything about. Is this what happens when they let you inside the velvet rope? You go blind and deaf?"

Eventually Dell just snatched the BlackBerry out of Chuck's hands. He told him he could have it back when they got over the hill, and the foursome left me for their stakeout of Kimberly Duggan's home, a wholesome thought for Kimberly and her Westside neighbors. I declined Dellroy's generous invitation to stand for hours at a gated driveway with that crowd. Although I couldn't imagine what could be more fun.

"Who the fuck let you in here?"

"There was a door with your name on it. It said enter. The rest I pretty much figured out on my own." I smiled a disarming smile.

Rhonda York dialed some numbers and barked into her hands-free.

"I need a security guard. There's a trespasser bothering me."

Impervious to disarming smiles, she rose in a heave from her desk and made her way to the door, keeping her distance as if I were a cobra out of its basket.

"The door works the other way, too. See if you can figure that out."

"I'm here professionally. I was hoping we could conduct some business."

Leather creaked on leather as she crossed her arms and leaned back against the framed poster of Bonnie Quinn.

"What business?"

"I want to buy some flowers. To congratulate your new client on replacing your old one." I circled my hands in orbit around each other like a motivational speaker. "I think were coming close to synergistic elegance here."

"Get out."

"You have to admit, there is a certain efficiency to it all. I wish you were my manager."

The door opened and two pale grey uniforms filled it. I gestured no hassle and stepped to them.

"Just one thing, Rhonda. Exactly when did you sign Kimberly Duggan to replace Bonnie Quinn? Before or after she died?"

"Get him the fuck out. Now."

There's an ignominy to being bodily removed from an office building. Even if you say you don't care—even if you think you don't care—it's no fun getting the old heave-ho. The looks you get are simply not pleasant. Especially in the era of heightened security, there's a layer of alarm in the onlookers who were once merely curious or disdainful. I try to avoid ejection as much as possible, but with mixed results. It's the life, what are you going to do?

One security assist was enough for that day, so I resorted to some virtual sleuthing.

"Actually," began Elliot's assistant, employing the Hollywood assistant's red flag word for all mendacity, "Elliot is in conference and can't be disturbed."

Actually. It must be in the handbook somewhere. It always sounds like cover and always comes after they ask who's calling.

"Actually, Monte is at the network and can't be reached. Will he know what this is in regard to?"

"Actually, yes," I said, "Right after I tell him."

Petty, I know. The poor assistant was just doing his job. But I mess with them now because I can't after they take over the studios and they have someone else saying actually for them. I left messages and went back to the personal touch. Or, at least I tried to.

"I'm looking for Brick."

I stared at the tiny speaker in the lobby of Brick's apartment building in Boy's Town and waited.

"Who is this?"

"I'm looking for Brick."

"You said that already. Who are you?"

"Actually . . . I'm a friend of his from the show."

The tiny tin voice came back and vibrated the metal mailboxes next to the row of dirty white buttons.

"Brick's not here. I'm just apartment sitting for him."

"How long is he going to be gone?"

They should turn me loose at Gitmo. I'm a born interrogator.

"I don't know. He got a call to do a TV movie in Vancouver. Civil War or Revolution, same diff." A lame surfer dude chuckle. "Anyway, he booked, and all of a sudden, I'm dealing with all this."

"Well, I'm sure you're up to the challenge." Out of the country? Could be bullshit. I'd have Pinkman check. "Do you know how I can reach him up there?"

"He's not up here."

"I meant Canada."

"I don't know. You'll have to ask him."

"How can I do that?"

Another wait. I pictured some kid just out of high school theater arts flopping free at Brick's and trying not to screw this up, or it's back to the Y, or, worse, Tulsa.

"You could give me your number."

Ingenious. I left my number, same as I already had on Brick's voice mail, and with the same certainty it was an exercise.

"That's him there," I said, tapping one of the mug shots in the six-picture spread on Loot's desk.

"You sure?"

"Eat me, Loot, of course I'm sure. Why do you always ask me if I'm sure?"

Loot laughed and tilted back in his chair.

"Because I love to see you get so ripped when I do. And it's procedure. People get nervous when they witness a crime. Their eyes play tricks on their memories. Hate to have you ID the wrong perp and spoil the day for some poor guy."

"Save that for the Valley housewives, I'm sure they lap that up. We both know these other five guys are cops." I slid the shot of my man toward Loot with one finger. "So who's the Hawaiian?"

"Samoan, smart-ass." The detective opened a file and skim read. "Name's Manu Tulafono. We thought he skipped to the islands, but guess he's back." He ran a manicured finger down the page. "Played offensive linesman at Birmingham High in Van Nuys. Juvie sheet says his parents moved there from Compton to get him out of the gang environment, but he stayed close to the old hood and got busted on some aggravated assaults and a jacking before he graduated to a deuce in Kern County. He sliced up a guy running a chop shop outside Bakersfield."

"Quaint."

"Got early release from a youth work program as an apprentice carpenter on some movie shooting up there. Worked stagehand gigs here in LA till four years ago when he reconnected with some of his bangers and killed an old guy at a mini-mart in Inglewood." The policeman looked up at me.

"You sure there's no reason somebody was after you?"

"Just tell me why this gentleman was in my home and not doing his stretch for the mini-mart killing."

"Charges dropped. Insufficient evidence."

I held the mug shot and it all came back. His size, the hardness in his eyes, the smell of him, raw and gamey. And the look back before he jogged off. Like he enjoyed it. "Translation: Nobody would testify."

"Or could. I talked to the sarge in charge of this one. They were close to turning one of Mr. Tulafono's accomplices, a brother banger set for a long stretch for concealed weapons, some shit like that. Well, banger bro disappeared along with some other kid they think was driving for them that night."

"They skip?"

Loot leaned over the file to me.

"Never found the bodies. They did find two tongues nailed to their respective front doors."

He tossed two forensic photos across the desk at me. Nice.

"I'm telling you, man, you're president of the Fuckin' Lucky Club. Lucky you didn't corner this dude and leave your bungalow feet first in a bag."

"What's happening with that?"

I side-nodded to a folder at his elbow. It was the medical examiner's report on Bonnie Quinn.

"Hardhead, that's what you are, Hardwick. They got your daddy's name wrong at Ellis Island, that's what they did."

When he looked at the file I snuck the mug shot of the Samoan into my pocket. "Nothing new, otherwise I'd have told you."

"Hanging with the injection cause of death?"

I reached for the file and he gave my hand a little slap.

"Affirm. They bagged a hypodermic at the scene. Her prints, her deal."

"*A* hypodermic? Just one?" He nodded. "You don't think that's hinky? Any other works in the house? Her dressing room, her car, her purse?"

"The woman was a novice shooter. Newbies don't have a tool chest yet. In fact, it makes a case for the ME's finding, not knowing what she was messing with."

I looked at him in his suit and tie, fingers laced on the desktop beside the closed file.

"Loot?" I intoned it like a kindergarten teacher. "Is somebody voicing the company line?"

"Whatever you want to think."

"Did the chief just decide, who gives a shit about a drugged-out lunatic? Or is there still a little sand in his crack after the riff she did about the department on Imus?"

"Report's solid, Hardhead." Loot, amusing himself. "We're not in the witch hunt business. If I were you, I'd stop looking for conspirators on the grassy knoll and deal with reality. Like your new friend here."

Loot looked for Manu's mug shot on the blotter and shook his head when he figured out where it went.

"The guy's bad news. We're putting his face out there, but you keep your head on a swivel. And call if you see him. Don't take him on."

My gaze hung in the middle distance as I relived the tackle I threw on him. Hitting a bag of rocks wearing a T-shirt.

"Do you have a piece?"

"I don't need that kind of trouble, Loot."

"Looks to me like it found you."

# CHAPTER TWENTY-THREE

"Hi, this is Meddy. Leave a message after the beep and I'll get back to you."

"Hi, it's me. Saw you on TV today . . ." I paused and hated myself for calling like this if I wasn't sure what to say. "I just . . . wanted to wish you congratulations on the new show."

Numbskull. I said good-bye and pressed END, wishing my cell phone had rewind, too.

Why did I call her anyway? She had given me the sayonara speech. What more did I want, a restraining order? Time to tell my wishful thinking heart to let go.

Pinkman got in at the curb outside the *Hollywood Reporter*. I asked him to buckle up and he grumbled his usual about the government protecting him from himself and I gave back my usual about not wanting to tweeze bits of his toupee out of my windshield. Our transaction complete, he belted himself in and flipped open his dog-eared spiral pocket notebook.

"The movie your pal Brick is working is called *Dress Blue*. The *Reporter* has it down as some revisionist hooey about a woman disguising herself as a man to enlist as a soldier in the Civil War. Great, so now the dykes are calling the shots at the studios. Maybe I should be glad I'm retired."

"It happened a lot back then."

"Yeah, but when the town had any kind of class they kept it in the closet. They weren't putting it in your face."

"I mean the Civil War," I said. How do you tell Pinkman anything? Where do you start? "Lots of women joined up in drag to be near boyfriends and to get pay they couldn't get as, well, women then. Read some history."

He grunted and was off on his riff about how things had changed since the old days. The days of champagne cocktails at the Brown Derby, when studio starlets in white satin would linger at their cars at the premieres just to give the press boys a fighting chance, when guys like Pinkman played the game and loved it because it seemed like it was fair. Seeing him beside me in his brown suit, working the rim of his straw panama in his lap as he talked, I could see him in the day, licking a flashbulb before snapping it into its socket. I let him gas, and eventually he went back to his notes. I had long ago given up asking why he didn't get this stuff online. Hell, I could have found it online myself. But Pinkman was fast as I needed and the chance to see the fire of purpose back in one of the legendary warhorses made it worth the time and the complementary editorial.

There was nothing in his report that lit up my radar. Neither the production company nor the producers, director, or line producer had any connection to anyone I knew. And, most important, no connections to Bonnie Quinn's dysfunctional family tree.

"What were you looking for, anyway?" Pinkman asked.

"I don't know."

"Then you found it."

He swatted me with his hat, then after a mile or so, he asked, "OK, what's eating you?"

I had known him most of my life, which means he knows me, too.

"Ever feel some days that taking pictures like this is a shitty business?"

"Know what your father used to say? That he didn't take pictures, he gave them."

"Yeah. And for all his blue sky, what did it get him?"

We rode in silence.

"The studios didn't kill your dad. It was his pride that took him off that cliff."

We rode some more with that hanging there. Pinkman unbuckled as soon as I turned off La Brea onto his street of elbow-to-elbow pre-wars with shared driveways.

"I can type this up for you. You're going to want the phone numbers in Canada, right?"

"Sure."

"Fifty bucks" he said. "My time at the *Reporter* included."

He pocketed my money as if it was no big deal, and rode his bad hip to his front porch.

Sleep didn't come quickly that night, and when it did, it did not carry me through the maze of pop-up monsters of my dark hours. I don't blame Sleep. It's a tall order and I wasn't doing my part. I tried the little meditation thing I do sometimes to reboot frozen images on my brain screen: my father, legless from bourbon, punishing his darkroom with the Louisville Slugger; two dozen pairs of eyes watching me clean out my desk in the White House press room; the honey of them all, the corporal in Xuan Loc posing for a snap to send his fiancée when the NVA round hit the back of his head and his helmet landed over my camera. So long ago. Time heals, but the scars are ugly. Breathe, I said, just breathe. Trying to wave away the ghosts like cobwebs on basement stairs and make my descent.

But Bonnie Quinn had other plans. At 3:17 AM, according to the nightstand scoreboard, the woman turned her head to me from her living room death pose and made eye contact. A wordless stare. The green flies walked her lips and nostrils with full turf authority, yet she stared on, blinking only once to make sure I knew she was really looking.

A few hours later, sunrise. I lurked once again at the side window of her house in Larchmont, watching her death room fill with orange. I stood there waiting, as if its emptiness would sell me what I wanted to buy: That she was simply gone and it was done, move on.

"I'm not talking to reporters," said the woman's voice behind the door chain.

"I'm not a reporter," I said, which was mostly true.

"Damn press has been pestering the hell out of me. I just want to be left alone." Her voice was thick and raspy. I had awakened her, but I was on a mission, and you don't meet Bonnie Quinn's neighbors by ringing doorbells after they go to work.

"Like I said, I'm not a reporter."

A business card is a powerful tool, doubly so if it bears a color ID photo of you beside your name and your bogus company. My face stared out at VERONICA HENZEL with enough workaday passivity to lend authority to the notion that I was actually location coordinator for Metro-Wolf Productions.

"Sorry to be at your door so early," I said after the chain slid off.

The tedious part, as always, was the charade of going from room to room with the resident, shooting Polaroids destined for a trash can within the hour. I hmm'ed, scrawled notes, and even tape measured the fireplace width.

"What kind of movie is it?"

Veronica Henzel drew a steep drag on her first pink Sherman of the day and offered me the box. I waved it off and sipped the hazelnut coffee in the Hello, Kitty mug. I didn't answer, but turned pages in a file, which looked very official, considering they were merely Yahoo roadmaps I had downloaded for my trip to find Bonnie Quinn's trailer two weeks prior.

"Would you have a problem if we put in a new carpet?"

"I've heard about you guys." She pulled her robe together at the front without cause. "How you come in and repaint, rewallpaper, the works, just for one little scene. Is that true?"

"If it's in the budget. If I find your place compatible."

Another pull off the pink cigarette, and she talked the smoke out.

"What's the fee? Is it per day? This is a big movie, isn't it? It is if you're doing new carpet. What is it? Who's in it?" Hooked.

"Promise not to tell?"

She signaled an oath with the hand holding the cigarette.

"Steve Martin and Queen Latifah."

"I love them."

"A con sweet-talks herself into a lawyer's house."

"Didn't they make that already? *Bringing Down the House?*"

"Sequel." I leaned over the kitchen table. "*Raising High the Roof Beams: This Time It's Personal.*"

Veronica Henzel's eyes twinkled. Set.

"Just one question."

"Yes?" She froze in worry.

"Neighbors. How quiet is the neighborhood? We can't tolerate any interruptions in shooting."

"Very quiet. Very little traffic. Very quiet."

"What about this house next door?" I gestured through the kitchen window. "It's very close."

"Plenty quiet now." I gave a puzzled look. "Oh, my God, you don't know? That's the house where they found Bonnie Quinn, you know, the sitcom star? That's where she killed herself."

"There?"

Nodding now, talking through more smoke.

"Oh, honey, you should have seen it last week. Police, helicopters, reporters—damn reporters—but that's all over now. Quiet. Very quiet. The house is empty. And quiet."

"That must have been weird knowing she killed herself right next door. Did you hear the shot?"

"There wasn't any shot to hear. The cops said she OD'd."

"I hear she was sort of a druggie."

"A menace. I got to hate Friday nights. That was the one night a week she was there."

"A house like that, and only living there one night a week?"

"Went out to introduce myself once and she had such a mouth on her. I came back in the house and had nothing to do with her after."

"Looks like a nice big house."

"I have more square footage," she said, gripping the fantasy of Steve Martin in her kitchen.

"Big parties?"

"More like a love shack, if you catch my drift."

"Oh?"

Another pull on her robe and she turned to the window above the sink that gave on to Bonnie's Quinn's curtainless living room.

"I'm not a snoop, Mr. Hardwick."

"Veronica. Dish it up. It's not like I'm with the tabloids."

"She had this regular guy. I called him Mr. Friday Night 'cause he was over there every Friday night." Then she amended, "Well, most Friday nights. About three a month."

"Mr. Friday Night," I chuckled. "That's a good one."

"In fact, he's the one who woke me up last week. The night she died. Pounding on the door at midnight. Nobody answered. So what's he do? Lays on his horn. At midnight, the putzel."

"But wasn't the night she died Thursday?"

She thought, then nodded, so I pressed. "Mr. Friday Night was there on Thursday?"

She affirmed again and I decided if I was going to start pushing I would need camouflage.

"I love hearing this. I do all the location scouting but they never let me meet the stars." I scooted closer to her chair and dropped my voice to a whisper. "Mr. Friday Night. Was he famous? Was he a sitcom star, too?"

"Sorry to disappoint you."

"Oh . . ."

"At first I thought maybe he was. Looked from a distance sort of like that guy on *Seinfeld*."

"Not Kramer. Say it ain't so."

"No, the other one. Newman. You know, 'Hello . . . Newman.'"

"Hey, that's good."

So she repeated her Hello, Newman. I repeated my laugh and looked at the mug. Hello. . . Kitty.

"Did he go in that night? Newman, I mean."

"Nuh-uh. Drove off all pissed when she didn't answer the door. Guess she didn't answer 'cause she was dead."

"Or, maybe, had company. Perhaps Mr. Friday Night had competition, a Mr. Thursday Night, maybe?"

"Nuh-uh."

I noticed Veronica kept a pair of binoculars on the sill.

"The place was dark and I didn't hear anything over there till the coroner woke me up at three. The rest is all over the news."

Timeline alert: Loot said Rhonda York had discovered the body just after four in the morning. I looked at my watch, which mostly synchronized with her microwave clock and the wall clock in the dining room.

"It was right at three?"

"Two fifty-seven. The van door slammed, all sorts of lights go on, forget it, I'm not sleeping. So I went to my window—just to shut the drape. . . ."

"Sure."

". . . and there she is on the floor beside the bookcase. I thought she was alive. Drunk or something. But you don't think of someone sitting over there being dead. Then she tips over and the two guys in there, you know, the coroners, set her up again."

"How do you know they were coroners? Did it say so on the back of their jackets?"

I almost asked if they looked like Jack Klugman, but no.

"The gloves. The old guy, the one in charge, he had on rubber gloves. So did the big guy with him."

"I have an uncle in the coroner's office," I said. "Bright red hair, dye job now, but red. Maybe one of them was Uncle Freddy."

"I didn't see any red hair." Because I was making it up. "Didn't notice much about the big guy." Too bad. "And the old guy was silver. Slicked back. Looked sort of like that guy in the *Godfather*."

"Marlon Brando?"

"No, Fish. You know, that guy on *Fish* and *Barney Miller*?"

"Abe Vigoda?"

"Yeah, like him. He's funny. You should tell them to put Fish in your movie."

Veronica Henzel was probably not thrilled that I left the hideous hazelnut blend behind, but I did. On parting, I told her I had concerns about doorway width so she wouldn't get her location hopes up. After that, it was all I could do to keep from running from her front door to my car.

# CHAPTER TWENTY-FOUR

"This isn't on my schedule," said the old doctor. "You're lucky you caught me in."

Carmen Pizzarelli, MD, stubbed out a 100 in an ashtray full of bent filters.

"Don't know what to say, Doc. They just sent me right over here from casting."

I lied. BFD. Would the truth, that I had snuck on the lot wedged between the walls of a folded set being trucked to one of the sound-stages, aid my interview? I don't think so.

"What are you doing?"

"Unbuttoning my shirt. This is my cast physical, right?"

He started to laugh, and when he did, spilled a few butts out of the ashtray with his amber fingers.

"You keep your shirt on."

Not a hint of irony. He swallowed, trying to quell a squeeze in his chest. Then the cough came. Ragged and phlegmy, making him breathless and red in the face. At last he came around to me, steadying himself on the desk.

"I thought they were finished casting that show."

He lifted my eyebrow with a sandpaper thumb, looked into my eyes without really looking before letting go and doing the other.

"I sure hope not. They say I'm seven-of-thirteen as Kimberly Duggan's new office love interest."

"Tongue."

I gave an *ah,* but he turned away, and by the time I hit full volume I was counting lumps through the back of his golf shirt. He turned back to me with a battered stethoscope. He *hah-hah'd* the bell with spongy breath and polished it on his sleeve. More coughing as he ran it over the back of my shirt. He struggled for air and said, "Breathe."

Time for business.

"Things must be saner for you around here without her, may she rest in peace and all that. I mean, being Bonnie Quinn's studio doc . . . Do you get some kind of medal or something?" Pizzy thunked my back twice. "Crazy, am I right?"

"How's your BP?"

"I pushed up my sleeve and he clamped his fossil hand on it to stay me. Then I realized he wasn't stopping me, but supporting himself. He lassoed the stethoscope around the back of his neck and used his free hand to support his weight again as he palmed around the desk to his chair.

"BP?" he said.

"Good," I said.

He made a note, paused, tilting his head side to side as he picked a good number. "Were you surprised when she died, or did you see it coming?" He looked up at me from under a hedgerow of eyebrows. "Bonnie Quinn, I mean."

He closed the file he had started with the bogus sitcom actor's name I had given him. R. Honeycutt Burns. It was going to be either that or Stig. Just Stig.

"You can go."

But I didn't rise. I sat and watched the bony old doctor with the faint Italian accent toss my chart on a careless stack behind his desk. He wasn't going to be small-talked, so I decided to jam the little fucker.

"Was she still warm when you moved her, Doc?"

He rotated slowly in his chair. Wide eyes and sallow wrinkles on a lazy susan. We stared at each other a very long time. I broke the silence with another jab.

"Did her flesh have any heat, or had she already assumed room temperature?"

Drool was glistening on his veined lower lip.

"I, uh…" He cleared his throat and suppressed another coughing jag. "I don't know anything about . . ." Another ragged cough. He rose unsteadily. "Your exam is over."

I sat there.

Pens and swords can settle their own beef. Silence is mightier than a thunderclap. Dr. Pizzy lost color around his mouth and stole a quick look to his phone.

"You're not an actor."

"No, but I play one on television." When the old man started to tremble where he stood, I said, "Why don't you sit down, Doc?" And he did. "I know you were there with her. You were there a whole hour before—don't shake your head, someone saw you."

"Saw me? No. No!" His chest rattled and he cleared it. "Are you a cop? Because if you're not a cop you have to go. You have to go now."

"You and your pal were there with her at three in the morning."

"No."

"Your van was in her driveway."

"I don't own a van. You have to go."

"Do you own latex gloves? Because you were wearing latex gloves. Why were you wearing gloves, Doctor?"

The door shot open.

"How did you get in here?"

Monte. I twisted in my chair and there he stood, a mullet with a grin.

"We've got to start doing what they do down at the wharfs," he said. "You know, put those little metal dealies around the ropes so the rats can't get aboard?"

He strode in, more smiles than a Wal-Mart greeter, but I rose just the same, balancing weight on the balls of my feet. Ready to rumble. Oh, and I smiled back.

"Nice to see you, too."

"You lost?"

"No, just passing the time with Dr. Pizzy. What, do you have radar or something?"

"Something," Monte said. Then he made a sweeping gesture to the door. "If you're done . . ."

"Actually, I—"

"You're done. Time to scamper down your rope, Hardwick."

"Somebody saw your doctor with Bonnie Quinn the night she died."

"That's bullshit."

"An eyewitness," I said, more to Pizzy, who sat quietly rattled, a chihuahua afraid you'll find the piddle, "puts Dr. Feelgood there with the corpse an hour before the discovery of record."

Monte addressed his doctor for the first time with an offhanded, "Pizza Man, is this true?"

"Monte . . ." He suppressed a cough and said, "—No."

Satisfied, Monte gave me a what-are-you-thinking shrug.

"You were having some trouble keeping her from tipping over."

He huffed, cleared his throat, and said, "Maybe the body—"

Monte stepped between me and Pizzy. "We're done here, let's go."

"He was seen sitting the body up. Why? And why was there only one needle? Was that your syringe, Doctor?"

"No, no! You've got it wrong. What the hell did you know about her?"

"Pizzy," said Monte, smooth and take-charge in his way–past–cool bowling shirt, "easy. You don't have to talk to this guy."

"She was always out of control. She used to steal my prescription pads. Look. I have to keep them locked up now." He pulled on a drawer which refused to open. "See?"

"Pizzy. Relax, he's messing with you."

The door opened again and two uniforms from Empire came in. It struck me for the first time how they were always in pairs like nuns when Monte said, "So. How's this going to go?"

My last glimpse of Dr. Pizzy was on my way out. A back glance between two Empire Studios security shoulder patches. The doc was using both hands to steady the flame for his cigarette. I stopped at Monte's golf cart and the two goofs walked right into me. Both swore.

"Hey, Mont-ster?" I said.

"What."

He pulled Pizzy's door closed behind him and frisked paint chips off his palms, annoyed.

"Would it be too much trouble?" I pointed to his cart.

The production chief sighed the sigh of an annoyed parent and said, "Get in." Then, to the guards, "I'll take him. Why should you have all the fun?"

They were still having a big old laugh at my expense when I slid across to the driver's side and drove off. A chorus of "Hey," plus one useless "Get back here," and I was having a pretty good laugh myself. Two-ways must have been sizzling because, in the seconds it took me to reach Gate 4, a tan uniform bailed out of the guard shack to intercept me. I turned a hard right down an alley.

The lane took me between soundstages and ended in a T. I took the left and found myself humming straight for a security cart with my old pal, Sgt. Olson, at the wheel, all mirrored shades and blood lust. I hung a U-turn and chunked some tan stucco off the corner of Stage 6, which slowed me down enough for the sarge to ram me from behind. "Step out of the vehicle," he said.

I floored it.

Now, the Empire lot is not huge. In the industry it's what you'd call a boutique studio. But, as it turned out, a fellow can have a helluva car chase there if the car is a golf cart and he's hell-bent on staying upwind of the pepper spray. Olson was no slouch behind the wheel, but I had the Jessie Ventura of carts: no governor. There weren't any high jinks or auto-batics like in the movies. No driving over fire hydrants or through rolling racks of wardrobe, coming out dressed like Sitting Bull or Mata Hari. I did swerve around a fork lift pulling a flatbed of shrubs, but that was about as exotic as it got.

One right, then another, and I lost him. I made a clean turn— unfollowed, undetected—past the Hobby Horse offices, and the Hyster in front of Stage 2, where a team of painters was up high, rolling studio tan over Bonnie Quinn's face like Saddam's after the fall of Baghdad. Just ahead, seconds away, the Cahuenga Gate beckoned. Only one guard present, bent to a driver's window. Unless he had eyes in his ass cheeks, I could ditch Monte's cart, breeze behind him, and be whistling down the public sidewalk before he looked up from his clipboard. But then the rest of the posse arrived there. Good luck sneaking by them.

As I whirred past Stage 3, its elephant door was just rolling closed. I spun another u-ey, gauged the narrowing gap of the door, and gunned it. My fender nicked the jamb on the way through, but I cleared the door, then stood on the brake. Rubber sang a four note chord on the newly laid floor before I came to a sideways stop on the apron of the set. Behind me, the big door sealed reassuringly.

"Hardwick? What the hell are you doing?"

Meddy stepped into view about a yard from me. She was back-lit by about a million foot-candles from the set and I had to squint to see her. The back-light made her auburn hair aural. One of those Moses-POV-of-God things, or Redford's view of Glenn Close in *The Natural*. Another silhouette appeared beside her, stealing my halo moment.

"Monte didn't clear you to be here, did he?" said Elliot Pratt. Ever calm. Friendly, even. "I do think your services here are fulfilled, Hardwick. Aren't we done?"

I got out and stepped to a kinder angle for my eyes.

"I had another meeting on the lot, and thought I'd stop by."

I gave Meddy a hug she didn't ask for but didn't refuse. When we broke, Elliot lingered on me, then gave a nod to the second AD, who punched numbers on the stage phone. I walked past him to the anchor desk, a block of as-brick trimmed in cherry veneer. A three square yard image of Meddy filled the JumboTron behind it.

"Let me guess, your new set, Meds?"

"Tough to slip one past you." Was that a look of amusement, or was I projecting? "We're light testing for the pilot."

"Why a pilot? I thought this was a done deal."

"Elliot wants something to screen at the press junket next week." She made a grand gesture to her set. "Instant anchor."

"We missed NATPE by a couple of months," Elliot added, talking shop with me the way they keep mad bombers on the phone while they trace. "So our best shot to show the colors is when the legitimate press comes to town for our rollout party."

He put just enough sauce on *legitimate* to tweak me without being an obvious prick in front of Meddy. Pissing on trees, this one.

So I arced one back.

"You're keeping yourself mighty busy through your mourning period, aren't you, El?"

Meddy said my name. A plea to muzzle me, but I guess I just don't stress about being an obvious prick.

"You've got your pilot for this new daytime strip, you're recasting and retooling *Thanks for Sharing*, starting up your UEN production shop. . . . How can you do it, Elliot? Really. I want to know. How can you pump out a sitcom the day after your star is put in the ground?"

"Hey, in this business, you learn to compartmentalize." The boss suddenly became aware that work had stopped and the crew was eavesdropping. "Are we done here?" he said. Then he answered his own question. "We're done here."

"We're not done."

"Excuse me?"

Amused. Certainly unthreatened.

"Something stinks about Bonnie Quinn's death and you keep doing what you did when she was alive." Meddy said my name again, more urgently, but I continued. "I'm surprised you don't have sand in your hair from burying it so much."

"Come on, Hardwick, not this. Not here," Meddy said.

The AD called a five and the set began to clear out. I couldn't tell if Elliot cared about that or not. The three of us held our little spaces on the new linoleum. In my periphery, I became aware of uniforms. What's new.

"Ask your house doctor what he was doing at her place that night. Ask your house doctor why she had only one syringe to her name and it was the one that killed her. Ask yourself why someone so afraid of needles OD'd on one."

I could hear Monte's labored post-chase breath, envision a sweat-mooned Nat Nast on its way to the dry cleaners on expenses.

"Just like I want to ask how it was you were all set up to recast your Bonnie replacement. Seems awfully convenient to me, and I'm not even Bob Woodward."

"You've crossed the line. You don't stand on my stage and make implications like that." Elliot turned to the half dozen guards flanking Monte. "See him off the lot. Immediately and permanently." Then, so easily, "Meddy? Wardrobe, please?"

And Elliot left.

Meddy hung back long enough to give me The Nashua Look before she followed him. Two minutes later, I was pulling myself up out of the gutter on Cahuenga Boulevard.

# CHAPTER TWENTY-FIVE

I tried calling Meddy twice that afternoon. I got dumped to voice mail both times, but left only one message. Her caller ID would tell her the story. What was I going to say to the recording anyway?

I ran my thumb over Loot's speed dial button. By all that is right in the Good Citizen's Handbook, I was duty bound to fill him in on what I had learned from Bonnie Quinn's nosy neighbor. The Pizzy stuff. Mr. Friday Night. Body discovery timings that didn't jibe. Even the lousy hazelnut coffee. But know what? I get tired of getting told by cops to back off. A man has his limits and, frankly, Loot pissed me off. Dismissing me. Calling me Hardhead. Bullshit. I ran my thumb over the epoxy digit again, thinking about waiting. Waiting until I had an ironclad solve. I had information, but was he going to act on it, or just start the Hardhead routine again? Screw it. I'd get the solve first. Then, to ice his ass and teach him something about respect, I'd take the collar to Marr in Metro. Loot hates Marr in Metro. Hates the way he calls KFWB all the time with news leaks. That'd frost his balls to a pucker. Hardhead, my ass.

When I pulled into my driveway, I found Amanda St. Hillaire reading in the yard under the willow where she had been bowled over by the Samoan a few nights before. I eased to a stop and powered the window down, but she was too absorbed in her book to look up. I watched the old film star, bathed in the alpenglow, bare feet stirring the koi pond, reclaiming the serenity of that spot, calling it hers.

At last, she marked her place with her finger and turned to me, and I knew she had been aware of me all along.

"Jane Austen kicks booty." She brandished her *Pride and Prejudice* for good measure, adding, "Anna Quindlan's no slouch, either. In one three-page Forward, it's like being handed a good flashlight."

"Maybe I can borrow it when you're done."

"Sorry. I don't lend books."

She crossed to me, relishing the lawn under her bare feet.

"Your eye's looking better," I told her.

"The savage."

"If I find him, I'll beat him up."

"Do. The only language for a brute like that."

Then she crossed her arms tightly. Something was behind the small talk.

"Everything all right otherwise?" I asked.

"There's a bureaucratic snag with my trust," she said. "Nothing to concern us too much, just some sort of carelessness from bank staff. Someone new."

Her tone conjured visions of an apprentice "clark" in a starched collar and tails at a stand-up desk, botching things.

"If it's not inconvenient, Mr. Hardwick, may I have my rent to you two weeks late this month?"

Quicksand, I thought. I spend my life getting swallowed up wherever I step.

"No inconvenience at all, Miss St. Hillaire."

I smiled at the mock formality which was our play but also my way to shield the old star from more indignity. When hard times had forced her to sell this hills property, she offered it to me, her tenant, first, and

I bought it—on my sole condition that she stay in her own home and I keep to my cottage, which was more than adequate for my needs. Even though she had lived longer than either of us had thought after the deal, it was a fine arrangement for both of us. Now I carried a big second and her modest rent barely paid for the gardener I had just let go, but I was in no hurry to have things change. Besides, was I going to send one of Rudy's goons to collect?

"Then that is that," she said. "Much appreciated. May I cook you some supper?"

"All set, thanks." I indicated the white sacks with the shiny grease patina on the seat beside me. "Care to join me for some Poquito Mas?"

"Take-out Mexican?"

"It's great. It's Poquito Mas."

"My God, it's like warm cat food."

"Thanks."

"Bon appetit."

Meddy had left me an e-mail. Four down the list from the penis enlargers and the "XXX Sexy Housewives Right in Your Neighborhood!" Delete. Delete. Delete . . .

From Meddy's BlackBerry: "Got your v-mail. Swamped. Not a minute to talk. What was that about, this morning?"

From me: "Tell me about it. Elliot might as well just wear blinders. What's he afraid of, criminal negligence? This has a whiff of closed ranks and circled wagons. Maybe your Bonnie Quinn piece isn't finished, after all."

My phone rang two minutes after SEND.

"What is wrong with you?" First thing. No hello. "I heard about all the mayhem you brought to the lot before you crashed my set and insulted my boss. Now you want me to help you stir the pot?"

"I want you to pretend you're a reporter."

Meddy growled—an actual *grr*—then tapped her phone hard, twice, on something metallic.

"I want you to leave me out of this. No, wait, I also want you to listen to sense and stop this, this tear you are on. Jesus, you never change."

"Meddy, something's wrong here. I'm not on a tear. Inconsistencies and bits of evidence keep floating to the surface. Am I supposed to ignore them?"

"Evidence. What evidence?"

"Well . . . aside from the stuff I already pointed out—"

"Which both the police and I see as a nonstarter."

An Elliot term. Hated that in her mouth. Nothing to do but push on.

"I talked to an eyewitness this morning who saw Dr. Pizzy in her house."

"Yeah, you mentioned that to Elliot. I was there, remember? And Elliot says the doctor says 'No, sir.' Is that all you've got? Does your eyewitness even know Dr. Pizzy?"

"—No."

"How does he know it was Dr. Pizzy?"

"She."

"Fine, did she say Dr. Pizzarelli's name? Describe him? What?"

No way was I going to hang myself with the he-looked-like-Fish-on-*Barney-Miller* thread of conversation. As I searched for a less crackpot-friendly answer, she came back with, "What is it, Hardwick? What's got you fired up? Is it Elliot? Are you jealous on some unhealthy level that he and I are more than just colleagues? Is that it? Because you and I do not have a relationship. Especially not now."

"Help me out here. Exactly what's the Elliot thing about? What's he got?"

"Look at yourself. Everything."

Not the sort of help I was looking for, but I had to admit the lady made sense. "OK. Want to know what gets me about Elliot?"

"Please."

"I feel used."

"How?"

"Elliot Pratt hired me to find Bonnie Quinn and bring her back. I did. And now she's dead. I don't like that feeling."

"She was a ticking bomb. Sooner or later it was going to happen."

"But that's the problem. It wasn't sooner or later. It was on my watch. I was the falcon. I brought her back and she got dead. That weight's on me now."

"Well, Hardwick, you can personalize this all you want. That's what you do."

"Wait, I thought you said I detached. I'm getting mixed messages from you."

"The message is not mixed. The message, once again, is look at yourself. There's no evidence. And all you're doing is making everyone's life miserable while you play hammer and the world is your nail."

"This is a different song for you, Meds."

"What's that supposed to mean?"

"Seems to me you've bought-in like everybody else, after all. You've got the brass ring, your own show. And don't get me wrong, I under-stand. That's why they call it the devil's candy."

"I won't dignify that."

"And it could be blinding you to some possibilities too hard to face."

"Such as?"

"Elliot. He seems to be doing just fine now that his problem is dead."

"Oh, please."

"You might even say he's thriving."

"Oh, my God, listen to you. You know what, Hardwick? I should thank you. Thank you for erasing any bit of doubt I may have had about what has happened to you."

"And what happened to you along the way, Meddy?"

"Me?"

"I've spent years hoping the two of us could make another run at it. Now, I'm starting to wonder if I was dreaming of a different woman."

I thought I heard a little whimper before she hung up on me. Maybe I wasn't missing our arguments so much, after all.

By the time I got to my gourmet burrito, it was a doorstop. I considered the microwave, but didn't have the interest. I ate half of it, cold, right from my hands, then lobbed it into the sink where I knew it would harden by morning, but I didn't care. I stared at the version of myself I got back from the kitchen window when it was dark outside. Careful. Pity party brewing. I uncapped another Sierra Nevada and retreated to the living room for some reading to get me out of myself.

After I slid the novel from the envelope, I reread Bonnie Quinn's inscription about content and containers and seeking truth. A lesson in how to read Faulkner? A cry for help? A clue? Gibberish? I flipped open *A Fable* and started to read.

I gave Faulkner an honest shot, truly I did. Years ago, *Sound and the Fury* had made my head hurt from its curlicue structure and pretzeled time shifts, but damn, it's a masterpiece. All I got from *A Fable* that night was the headache without the buzz. OK, you'd never find me sharing the dais with Harold Bloom, but I read enough. I got the symbolism of the peaceful soldier and his twelve followers who spontaneously stopped fighting a war. Way to go, Faulk. Color me enlightened. I wrestled with another chapter and set it aside. Mental note to see what I could get on eBay for a slightly read first edition of *A Fable*, inscribed by a dead sitcom star.

How I wished I had not finished *Life on the Mississippi*. My head hit the pillow with the cheated regret that always blankets me at the end of a Twain story. It was past two, and when sleep took me it was a caress that let me fall slowly, luxuriating in reflections upon those currents and my hopes for my own photo book, which would bring the great river to the world at its gleaming ideal. I saw myself riding it, capturing the rainbow spray of a stern wheeler, walking its banks at Hannibal to shoot fisherboys, Toms and Hucks, barefoot in mud clods, angling for adventures and an afternoon's freedom.

But my ideal of a resting sun drizzling pink icing on a flat river suffocated at a bend where green water lapped against a turgid body. Face down, a bobber the color of a fish belly. Was it Huck's Pap? In my dream I poled it over. It spun a rotisserie turn, and Bonnie Quinn said to me, "I'm in a better place now. Hell." Her face disappeared in a froth of bubbles from her horsy laugh as she sank. I grabbed for her but pulled up Congressman Landry by the tie. His eyes were hooded and boozy, half cups of lids, a frog in the river. When I released him he didn't sink, but bobbed there, seeming beyond pain to the place it becomes rest and the pain becomes yours. I set course away from him, past the rising shoulders, elbows, arms and asses of the people I had ambushed. Streisand, Alec Baldwin, Tim Dash, Madonna, Iron Mike, Sean Penn, Diddy, John Cusack—John Cusack? I never shot you, I tried to say. He just *tsk*-ed me from behind a curtain of wet hair, the way he wore it in *Malkovich*. I fought the classic powerlessness of a dream: on the wrong river but could not turn. A hand reached up, alive, a silhouette breaking through a milky shelf of fog. I grabbed and it held me. A head rose up and spoke to me. It was a young woman I recognized, with black curls dripping on olive skin. Bonnie Quinn's dead daughter. "Nice job," she said. Then she released me and sank into the darkness. What was her name? They said it at the funeral. Shannon. Sleep came, but as I drifted to my fog, her face burned like a painting on black velvet from TJ.

The next morning I was a slug. A lazy stay-abed entertained by a streak of sun from the crack between my curtains that beamed a light sword across the bedroom. A sundial marking slow time. It bisected the dresser, lighting up my collection of revoked press credentials and then inched to the framed hug with Meddy in Saigon. When my phone rang, I kicked myself for not emptying my bladder.

"Mr. Hardwick?"

Sandy-throated. Caribbean.

"Yeah." I sat up and grabbed the notepad I keep on my nightstand. "Where are you calling from, Brick?" I asked as I wrote down the caller ID number.

"Never mind that, you. I am traveling, that's all anyone needs to know."

"Canada, right? Vancouver."

"—Uh, hey, forget that now." He spoke sharply, in stabs. "What are you doing about this? This has me jumping, mon. Tripping that I might be next."

"Brick, have you ever heard of the term grandiosity?"

"Shut your mouth. I did not risk my life calling you to listen to sass."

"How are you at risk?"

"You are blind, mon. Picture-mon with the eyes that do not see."

"Did someone threaten you?"

"If I am ever—" He started again in a lower voice. But very dry. And shaky. Genuine fear. "If I am ever discovered talking to you like this, I am so over."

I took the phone to the bathroom with me and pissed.

"Brick, stop the whining. Put up, or shut up."

"Are you—? That is so disgusting."

I finished peeing. "Lay them on the table, or hang up."

"Are you crazy? You won't hear the words from me. I don't even know all the words. Get them from the source." Sounded like sauce. I needed subtitles. "Her words is what will count. Get them from her, that's what you need. From Bonnie herself."

"Sure. I'll just have a séance. Invite the cops. They love that."

"Get it from her diary, mon. Do your fucking job."

"A diary?" Back at my pad, pencil ready, glad I had already pissed. "Don't fuck with me. Did you say she kept a diary?"

There was a phone click. Probably just static.

"I have to go."

"Brick. Did Bonnie Quinn leave a diary? Where is it? What does it say?"

"Jesus, Hardwick, she practically gave it to you on a platter. I thought you were so smart. You keep fucking around like this, you think I'm going to sit like some duck? No fucking way, mon. I'm going back to Kingston, that's what. There's places I can hide so that no man can make me the dead body next."

"I'm trying not to hear the grandiosity, Brick, but you're not helping me here."

"You think I have no reason to be shit scared? First Bonnie, now him?"

The phone grew slippery in my hand.

"Now who?"

"Ho, mon. You don't know?"

# CHAPTER TWENTY-SIX

They had found Dr. Pizzy's body floating in a Traveler's Express bathtub in Woodland Hills. Hotel security made the discovery after frantic pleadings from his wife, who was alarmed by what she called a strange voice mail from him which she came home to about nine o'clock. The doctor didn't answer her calls to his cell phone or his page, and he had not left a number with his service. His wife caller ID'd him to the hotel in Warner Center.

"The man was a doctor, he knew how to do it," said Loot, lifting the lid off his food court burger at the mall across from the hotel. He tossed the pickles onto my tray. "Love the pickles, can't stand them warm."

"How?" I said. "Pills, injection?"

"Polish street lamp."

He took a bite and I nodded. Novelist Jerzy Kosinski had done himself in years ago with a plastic bag over his head while immersed in a hot bath. The suffocation is said to be lazy and mild. More like going to sleep, not messy, and none of the ambiguity of missed bullets, broken falls, or premature garage openings. Mr. Kosinski's Polish heritage earned the bag-on-the-head method a cop's slang—a dark comedy touch the sly author might have appreciated.

"You must feel like King Shit on King Shit Day."

"Really?"

Come on, man. You were blowing your warning whistle, waving your arms, making your usual nuisance of yourself, and, for once, you were right."

I ate one of his soggy pickle chips. Slowly. Tasting the sour.

"Go on," I said.

"Shit, look at you, cool as the other side of the damn pillow. Gloat. Say 'I told you so,' something. You're pissing me off."

"Maybe soon as you tell me what you're talking about."

"Bonnie Quinn, asshole. You're going to make me say it, aren't you." He set his burger down and napkinned his mouth. "There was something more to the OD after all. Quite a bit more. Your thing about the lone needle, all that shit? Carmen Pizzarelli, MD, left a note before his swim." He waited for me to register, then said, "He killed her."

I heard my pulse whoosh in my ears. Took in a deep, control breath and let it out. "He said that?"

"Wrote that. Even better." Loot took another bite.

"What did he say? How, why?"

"I shouldn't be telling you all this, you know." Then he swallowed and said, "But we have our little relationship. You show me yours and I show you mine, right?"

I reflected on all the information I had withheld from him over the last twenty-four hours and smiled.

"Right."

"Plain and simple? The good doctor messed up. His star had a panic attack, he gave her a little something to calm her down, it turned out to be too big a dose, and interacted with whatever shelf of the pharmacy she already had floating in her system. Bad doctor, dead diva. Do I have to buy you a steak dinner now so you aren't shoving this in my face till the day I pension out?"

"Forensics is going to do his room, right?"

"Of course."

"Did you walk it yourself?"

"Yeah."

"Was everything, you know, 'consistent with'?"

"What the— I don't believe you."

"Did Pizzy leave a wake up call?"

"Jesus, here we go."

"Order room service, a newspaper for the morning?"

"The man left a note in his own handwriting. What more do you want?"

"Are you going to run prints on the plastic bag? The water taps?"

"Of course, but damn it, he left a note. A distraught confession to an accidental death he couldn't live with."

"Why do you suppose he gave her a sedative by injection this time? Had he ever done it before?"

"Why are you still grinding on this? You should be a smug ass, up on this tabletop doing an end-zone dance, spiking the ball in my face."

His two-way purred with something too low for me to make out, and after his relaxed 10-4, he started balling his lunch trash, pretending I wasn't there because he probably wished I wasn't. I decided to leap before he disappeared on me.

"Do you know anything about a diary?"

"What kind?"

"Just wondering if you guys inventoried some diary Bonnie Quinn might have left."

"Mm—no. Not that I'm aware of, why?"

Not really caring. Barely there as he tidied up, lamenting the day I saved his ass and he owed me these courtesies.

"One of my sources says she left one."

"Uh-huh." Fingernailing a sesame seed from his mouth to show his interest level. "Let me guess. Something that's going to blow this case wide open."

He laughed and sucked his teeth.

"Hey, Loot, come on. Don't I carry some cred after making the call about the needle?" He shrugged a small allowance. "And someone else close to her says she not only left a diary, but he's all shitless thinking he's next in the cooling drawer of the coroner's sub-zero."

Loot sat back and spoke to me in Friendly Loot tones.

"I'm going to try to say this so you don't just think I'm just some gatekeeper trying to shut you down."

"As you try to shut me down."

"Hey?"

"Sorry."

"I gave you respect for your lone needle theory, but that can't be license to poke around cases at will. Please try to understand, Hardwick, the choking volume of the conspiracy tips we get all the time in my area. Shit, I got mail yesterday on the Black Dahlia. And last week? A registered letter with sixteen pages, single-space, typed, on how and why Jayne Mansfield's decapitating car accident was orchestrated because she was Marilyn's body double at Kennedy orgies with the mob. But how can that be when I got a frantic call from a tipster saying he saw Marilyn alive and she's being held against her will in the Witness Protection Program? Now, I'm not putting you in that class . . ."

"Thank you."

". . . yet. But I've got to put my focus on police work on active cases, not your rejected *X-Files* pitches. You understand?" I just stared. "Good. Having said that, if there is a diary and you come across it or any other information that is material to this case, it is your legal duty to give it up to me or face prosecution."

"Of course," I said. "That's what relationships are all about."

Marr in Metro. Everything goes to Marr in Metro.

\* \* \*

I tried calling the production offices for the movie in Vancouver, but Brick had quit and left no forwarding information. I left another voice mail at his apartment and went for a run. What had he said? Something like, "She gave it to you on a platter, mon." All she gave me was a book. Breathless, chugging up Lookout Mountain, Bonnie Quinn's mantra about content as container hit my chest like a softball. I couldn't sprint home fast enough, and dodged cars crossing Laurel I was so caught up in the maybe. Back at my cottage, I forearmed aside a pile of the morning papers until I came across it, sitting right there on top of the fat envelope where she had written my name.

I sat down once more with the Faulkner novel she had given me the night she died. Delivered it to me personally and with a gravity I had dismissed without a blink.

### A Fable

The previous night, I had read it as literature, found it too dense, and set it aside. Now, I was looking at it as something more: Bonnie Quinn's diary.

A flip of the pages. No annotations. No secret writings or marginalia. I held random pages up to the desk lamp, uselessly, for invisible ink. I could lab test the book. Maybe I would. Probably not. My enthusiasm for this book hiding her diary irised down.

The inscription. If I could find a clue in it, I could feel like a criminology phenom instead of a confused paparazzo once-was.

> To Hardwick—
> A Fable reveals fact when content is container.
> Be smarter like your damn Tom Sawyer at the fence.
> Seek the truth. Go there.
> BQ

I spent the better part of the next two hours with an X-Acto knife and a magnifying glass painstakingly dismantling the book. Her content is the container thing brought to mind the convict I once knew who got his pot smuggled into the penitentiary in Florence, Arizona, stuffed inside the vinyl covers of family photo albums. So I sat hunched over my kitchen table, making my spinal incisions and peeling cloth binding from cardboard backings. In the end, I found no secret writing, no hidden notes, and accomplished little but the absolute devaluation of a three hundred dollar collector's first edition into thread, glue chips, and unbound pages.

My only conclusion was that my self image as a criminology phenom would have to be bolstered some other day.

# CHAPTER TWENTY-SEVEN

"**H**ardwick," said the voice on my phone. "It's me, Elliot."

"Oh, hey. Funny you should call. I was just thinking about you."

"Really?"

I answered earnestly, "Yeah, really."

The hobbyhorse split as the wrought iron gate swung open. I drove up the long driveway to Elliot Pratt's sprawling ranch home in the mountains above Malibu. The driveway was steep and cut back on itself, shoelacing the side of the hill before it plateaued at a wide gravel carport beneath the railroad tie stairs leading up to the house.

"Out there, that's where they used to shoot the *M\*A\*S\*H* exteriors," Elliot said, indicating the canyon to the east with its boulders pinking in the sunset.

He handed me a glass of white wine I knew would be oaky and perfect, and urged me to the west rail of his deck.

"And over here, I can sit and watch the whales migrating."

"Must be nice, lord of all you survey up here."

Either I was losing my sardonic touch or Elliot Pratt was not to be prickled. He let it go with a shrug and mounted the smooth riverstone steps to the wide terrace of velvet lawn above the deck. A man with both a terrace and a deck.

"You must have helicoptered the bulldozers in here to level this mountaintop."

"I did," he said as if stating the obvious. "Coastal Commission was its usual pain at every stage, too. So many environmental restrictions."

"So little time."

That one struck a nerve. His eyes flared, then he arrested himself from saying something he'd regret given he had an agenda of cordiality. But why?

Meddy stepped out through his French doors, draping a sweater over her bare shoulders against the Pacific dew point.

"Steaks are ready to toss on whenever you are," she said, looking a little too at home at Elliot Pratt's mountainfast replica of Will Rogers's ranch house.

The whole thing was testing my patience. I was trapped in one of those photo spreads you see in *Bon Appetit* or *Coastal Living* where scrubbed young comers have lawn parties for scrubbed young friends, only our civility and smiles ran about as deep as the glaze on the crème brûlée Meddy had whipped up in Elliot's $35K La Cornue oven.

We sat together around a patio table of imported ceramic. Elliot lifted his glass, and we raised ours.

"To all your dead employees," I suggested.

It was time to crack that burnt sugar crust and see what lay beneath. I heard the foot of Meddy's glass chink down on Italian tiles. I looked over at her and she turned from me, studying the squashed orange oblong of sun as it set. Even in the orange pink of magic hour, Elliot's face ashed. He set his wine down, too, and stared me. I get used to that.

"As long as you're going there, let me make my apology. You were right about Carmen Pizzarelli's participation in her death, after all. Sorry I flared on the set."

"You mean right before Monte had your rent-a-cops toss me into traffic?"

"I'm trying to reach out to you socially, Hardwick. I've made a big gesture, inviting you here to my home. Does that mean anything to you?"

"Why?"

"I'm asking because I wonder how you can come to my house and insult me like that."

"No, I mean, why are you reaching out to me socially? We both know I'm an asshole, so let's get to the real question. Why are we sitting on your mountain? I mean, if you want to dance with me, at least play some music."

He swirled the wine and looked back at me.

"OK. Fair enough."

Meddy turned back to us, willing to show her interest.

"I invited you here because I need your help."

"Again," I said and took my first sip of wine. Oaky and perfect.

"Before I say what it is, let me say up top that this is a business deal."

"Even better."

"There's a property I want to get the rights to. And for that I need possession of the source material."

"What about your business affairs goons?" He shook no. "Agents, lawyers?" He shook them off, too.

"This is an especially discrete matter."

When people used the d-word with me, it usually red-flagged the territory between shady and illegal.

"Do you want to hear more?"

"Your party."

"There's conversation that Bonnie Quinn left behind a diary," he said. "Do you know anything about that?"

For a poker face, my best trick is to pretend I'm a dog. On *Cheers* it was Coach's technique for acting dumb, and it's a beaut. I become a Labrador retriever, a chocolate in my mind's eye. Inquisitive, passive, guileless, revealing nothing. I cocked my head to the side a little and said, "No."

Elliot cocked his head in opposition to mine and said, "Huh."

But he wasn't as skilled at dumb. He had suspicion lurking. Very un-Labradorean. Coach would turn in his grave. I responded with silence, cocked my head to the other side and waited him out. Who's a good boy?

"Funny. I thought you'd know something about it."

"A diary? Nope."

He twirled his wine stem on the table again and regrouped.

"I'm willing to pay for it, you know." Meaningful eye contact now. "Lots."

"I wish I had it." No lie there. But he was not convinced, and pressed the point.

"It's very important to me, Hardwick. Even if you 'don't have it'," he said, with a wink to help me in case I was subtext-impaired. "I'd pay you a big fee to secure it. And deliver it to me, of course."

"Sounds like you think that diary of hers is pretty valuable. Or dangerous."

"Oh, come on. I have nothing to hide." I wanted to laugh, but stayed in Big Dog mode. "The value is obvious, isn't it?"

"You mean to sell, like to the tabloids?"

"Jesus, you can be one-track. There's major miniseries potential. An in-her-own-words docu-drama MOW would kill."

I gave the nod of the gullibly enlightened. "And your interest in scoring this diary is for a TV movie less than a week after her death. Is that sort of ghoulish, or just part of your famous ability to compartmentalize?"

Elliot jerked to his feet and shot his hands into his Tommy Bahamas. I guess I was frustrating the man—and on his very own mountain.

"Look. Somebody's going to make this mini if they get the diary. I want it to be me because I want it done right." He looked over to Meddy, the jury, for support. "Besides, I paid the price already just working with her." And then, to me, "Same deal as when you found her, in advance. Plus double on delivery. Are you interested, or not?"

"You're not even going to stay for a steak?"

Meddy leaned her forearms on the sill of my car window and actually smiled at me.

"No appetite." The air was laced with those ribeyes. I looked up at the finger of smoke rising from the terrace where Elliot was grilling. "Besides, I feel like the tolerated guest."

"Isn't that a step up for you?"

What I wanted to say was that I felt like a dick sitting there with the Meddy-Elliot vibe so strong it was all but making my hair rise at the ends. But I said, "You two probably have ample shop talk to talk. Besides, I guess I'm suddenly on assignment to abet him in covering his tracks."

"What must it be like to be so cynical?"

"Try it on. You might lose your appetite, too."

"I know you think I'm—"

"In denial."

"—not entirely objective, but even though he's a wheeler-dealer, I believe Elliot can be taken at face value."

"Oh, you mean like saying he wants his hot hands on Bonnie Quinn's diary so he can do the sainted lady justice?"

"Do you honestly believe he could have had anything to do with her death?"

"No. I think he could have killed her."

"And Dr. Pizzarelli's suicide note?"

"I'd rather see what Bonnie Quinn's last note was in her diary." The corners of her mouth showed a secret smile. "What?"

"You. Why am I trying? Go to it. Do whatever that bugle call in your head tells you to do." She stepped back from my car and I started the ignition. "Oh, and Hardwick?" She leaned back on the door. "Just so you know? Elliot was nowhere near Bonnie Quinn Thursday night. He was up in Santa Barbara."

"I suppose he has an unimpeachable alibi."

The confidence in her smile made my heart sink. Cinematic clips spooled of Meddy racing up the coast to Elliot at the San Ysidro Ranch after our upended dinner: Tattingers in the Banksia Cottage; the hot tub; the canopied bed; walks under the arbor where Jack and Jackie honeymooned. But her smile had a slyer angle.

"Depends. How unimpeachable is the CEO of Grove Broadcasting?"

Waiting for the damned hobbyhorse to part for me at the bottom gate, I looked up, hoping/not hoping to see Meddy join Elliot at the outdoor Viking. It was dark enough now that I couldn't see the smoke, just smell it. Longing or hunger spun in my belly. I tucked my advance into the glove box. Let Elliot pay me to nail his balls to the wall. I loved the elegance that he was funding my investigation of him. The gates opened and I drove off to buy my own damn steak.

# CHAPTER TWENTY-EIGHT

The next day, I centered Otis Grove in my viewfinder and snapped one off. Then another. I will say this, the man was downright photogenic. And not so hard to find, it turned out, standing there on the stern of his yacht in the Santa Barbara marina for the annual Blessing of the Fleet. From my position onshore, braced against the rail above the seawall, his head rose and fell in my lens. A balloon at Pong speed. His converted World War II mine sweeper was a gentle ride in the smooth roll of the little harbor. Money bought you stability, complete with an aft helipad.

But the billionaire CEO could humble himself. I panned down with him as he knelt on the deck before the bishop and received his blessing with head bowed. Rising, he offered the holy water to the prelate, who took the dipper and shook sanctified droplets onto the mixed flotilla of fishermen and pleasure boaters rafted in a semicircle below. The ritual took me back to Forest Lawn and a casket and the reason for my trip.

"Step off the gangway, sir. Now?"

The private security man with the clear plastic ear bud smiled. No goon. More like the affable college grads that keep order at Disneyland or outside Mormon temples. I retreated two steps onto the municipal dock and returned the smile.

"You'll be moving along, please," he said, affable, but certain.

"I'm off your gangway, see? Public property now."

Two more security guards, also in khakis and blazers, also more triathletes than Troglodytes, appeared from opposite ends of the dock and sauntered over to flank me. "How ya doing?" I said. Not expecting, or getting a response as they waited, smiling neutral smiles.

"Up to you, friend," said my man on the gangway. He turned and squinted at the sun kicking off the marina, then back to me. "Sure hate to get those expensive cameras all wet."

That gave me something to think about. My gear was slung in a sports backpack which did not say photo anything. He either knew who I was, or I had been observed. Respect and caution, I thought.

Just as I was formulating a face-saving exit line, one of the pair behind me gripped my shoulder. Now, most people have an instinct to pull away when grabbed, so he was not ready when I threw my weight back into him. A curse and a splash followed. I whirled to brace for the other two, but both had already cleared their service pieces, which they were two-handing in classic braces. I let my hands fall to my sides.

"What's going on here?"

There was no mistaking the voice. A gravel baritone with a hint of Southern patience. The security guy, my affable pal, did not take his eyes off me as he called up to his boss on deck.

"No problem here, Mr. Grove. Just someone who's about to leave."

Grove gave me a passing look, a glance at a minor curiosity, and started away, back to a stateroom lunch or a nap or maybe to buy another cable network. Or maybe all three.

"I'm not a trespasser. I'm a reporter and I just want to ask you a question, Mr. Grove." Hey, take the shot.

"Move along. That's plenty," said my man with the pistol, not smiling now.

"I'm investigating the murder of Bonnie Quinn."

Behind me, the wet detective boosted himself out of the drink. Up on his feet without even putting a single knee on the dock. The three moved closer to encourage my exit.

"Sandy."

"Mr. Grove?"

"Bring the man aboard."

My escorts led me around the bow to the far side of the yacht where an old salt who looked like he came with the boat was on his knees, sanding the wooden deck. "Wait here," said the wet one. He and affable Sandy opened a bulkhead door and disappeared inside with my backpack, leaving me with guard number three.

"I could have just opened that for inspection here," I said to him.

He showed his interest by crossing his arms and leaning a hip against the rail. I amused myself with the view of the Channel Islands. The deckhand took a break and stood beside me, stretching his back.

"Never-ending job, I guess, huh?"

"Hope so," he said. His smile was the first genuine one I'd seen on board.

"I had a sailboat once. Every time I'd finish varnishing, it was time to start over."

"Nature has its own plans, that's for sure," said the old man. He raised his wire bristle eyebrows in amusement. "Course, people have their own plans, too. I just put this finish down last week in time for the blessing and some blockhead does the cha-cha on it wet." He winked. "Makes me glad I'm on an hourly rate."

The bulkhead door opened and Sandy beckoned me inside. As the door closed, I could just make out the shish of the old man's sanding block and felt a tinge of jealousy for a craftsman's life where your mistakes could be sanded and stained over.

Twenty minutes later, I was sucking an ice cube from the bottom of a crystal iced tea glass in a room that was more like a den than a cabin. A brass ship's wall clock chimed a polite sequence of bells that made no sense to me. The subtle rocking of the yacht was making my eyelids droop. I yawned and forced myself a little taller in the leather armchair. Nothing like falling asleep on the job to kill your credibility as an investigative powerhouse.

The varnished wood door opened and Otis Grove, chairman of his own upstart broadcast empire, down-home and self-made, entered alone.

"Sorry to keep you waiting. Are you comfortable? Would you like more tea?" Grove was known for his personal charm. Whether it was innately Southern or just his caring way, he lived up to his reputation for making his fiercest business rivals seek his hand to shake even after he bloodied them in negotiations.

When he sat he said, "You're not exactly a reporter, it turns out, Mr. Hardwick." So explained my wait in the paneled comfort of the stateroom. He was checking me out.

"I'm more of a photojournalist. Different branch of the same tree."

"Or, weed, depending. Am I right?" He laughed to take the sting off it, yet point made. "But, I appreciate tenacity in any endeavor, and you have achieved some, er, status in your field, however dubious. So let's have our little interview and you can be on to more exciting things."

Odd, I thought, that he just didn't have his security boys show me off, but I brushed it aside to seize the moment.

"Fine with me, Mr. Grove. I just want to verify whether Elliot Pratt came here to see you last Thursday night."

"You said something curious before. That you were investigating the murder of Bonnie Quinn. You did say murder?"

"I did."

"And now you're asking me about the comings and goings of Elliot Pratt."

"I am."

"I should have you tossed for misrepresenting yourself to get aboard here. And for the brazen innuendo you're making about one of my most trusted colleagues and an old friend, to boot." He lounged back and crossed a leg. "But I made it where I am by listening, so go ahead."

He made sure I saw him check his watch, something I understood better than the wall chimes.

"First off, I did not misrepresent myself. I am investigating what I believe to be Bonnie Quinn's murder, whether anyone else suspects it or not. And, with all due respect, I made it where *I* am by nosing into things nobody else can—or will. And any inference about Elliot Pratt is yours. I'm just asking a question because I want to know the truth, and you strike me as a man who'll tell it. If you'd rather not talk, I'll thank you for the iced tea and find out some other way."

The CEO sat, staring at me, his hands at rest in his lap as he took my measure. Then he smiled.

"You're squandering your talent, Mr. Hardwick. I could use someone like you in sales."

"Gosh. My dream come true."

"You think that was an offer? You wouldn't last a day working for me. I just find you persuasive. At least enough to answer your question." He paused for effect. "Yes, Elliot and I met here in Santa Barbara Thursday evening over dinner."

"Just dinner? He didn't stay longer?"

"He stayed a lot longer."

"What time did he leave?"

"I don't remember the exact time. But he was here several hours into the night. We had a lot to talk about. You can imagine."

"I can't imagine him skipping the hundredth episode party when he hired me to find Bonnie Quinn so there would be a hundredth episode."

"He skipped the party so he could come up here and kick my can. Elliot did what a good executive should do: keep his new boss from doing something stupid like cancel a goldmine TV series." Otis poured me some unwanted iced tea, then one for himself, manners preventing him from simply pouring his own. "You see, I had made it a precondition that *Thanks for Sharing* go off the air, or no deal to buy Hobby Horse. If I wanted migraines from divas, I would have thrown in with Marcy Carsey or Tom Werner. They did it right. They have the expertise."

"So you're saying Bonnie Quinn was an obstacle to Elliot's big payday?"

"There's that innuendo again. I'm still not buying your murder premise, just so you know."

"But isn't that a motive for Elliot Pratt to 'get rid of the problem'?"

"Of course. But not the way you're thinking. Elliot's visit that night was to convince me the series could still be viable with a replacement star. He used Dick Wolf's casting changes on *Law & Order* as an example. I was persuaded. And it was cost effective. Achieving Episode One Hundred triggered an option on her contract." He read my surprise. "That's right. His problem child had no legal claim to continue. We wouldn't even need to buy her out. So I told him that I would pick up the show, but only if Bonnie Quinn was recast."

"Kimberly Duggan suits up."

A nod and a sip. "Look," he said, "I know all this has a tawdry aspect. None of us likes to see how the sausage gets made, and all that. And, I suppose it could look marginal in hindsight . . ."

"You mean now that she's dead?"

"This was a good deal, alive or dead. Now, I'd tell you to think twice before you waste anymore time barking up this tree, but I think we both know how much that advice would affect you."

"Thank you."

"Funny. You keep thinking I'm flattering you."

"No, I just appreciate the straight talk."

"I'm a realist. You don't graduate from the graveyard shift at a Jacksonville pulp factory to all this unless you are. My art is not in dealing the cards. It's in turning the hand into a winner."

"What would you do if this hand says I'm right?"

"That would take more that a paparazzo's hunch. That would take evidence."

"All the evidence is circumstantial."

"Then it's not evidence."

"She left a diary."

"A diary means nothing. Not unless there's something specific in it. Something that spells out something anyone would believe from a woman like that. What's it say?"

"I haven't seen it."

"Who has?"

"So far, she has."

"How do you know there is one?"

"I've been told."

"You're doing worse than wasting my time, you're wasting your own."

"Then somebody else is wasting his time, too. It's out there that she gave the diary to me and, the night she died, somebody ransacked my place looking for it."

"You're sure of that?"

"At first I chalked it up to a disgruntled business associate. But now, my math adds up to your trusted colleague hunting for the base he forgot to cover."

"Because Elliot's your convenient suspect?"

"Because Elliot offered to buy the diary from me when he thought I had it. Now he's hired me to find it for him and not involve the police."

Quickly, as if under the spell of a Vegas lounge hypnotist, Otis Grove closed his eyes and bowed his head. For a second, I thought he was napping. A narcoleptic thing. Maybe he was praying. Then, just as quickly, he looked up as if no time had passed and said, "I'm hiring you to find Bonnie Quinn's diary."

"Do I have a say in that?"

"There will be ten thousand dollars in cash waiting for you when you leave the yacht, an advance to cover your expenses and time. A balance of ninety thousand will come upon delivery of the diary to me."

"I accept."

"Say nothing of this to anyone, especially not Elliot. We have a close history that dates back to Harvard. I'm hiring you to find the truth, but if it turns out to be nothing, I don't want an old friendship spoiled because I was being prudent."

"And if it turns out otherwise?"

"If—that is to say, *if*—there is any conclusive incrimination of him in that diary, Elliot Pratt may be sly enough to skirt the law, but he will not have any financial relationship with me. In short, I'll see that he loses everything. I can be a practical man in a secular world, but I cannot turn a blind eye to the immoral or illegal. I am not afraid to follow His steps and cast the money changers out of the temple."

"Now I know why you didn't just have me tossed. You're wondering if there's something to this, too."

"Just find the truth, Mr. Hardwick. Then I'll deal with it."

# CHAPTER TWENTY-NINE

I t was just getting dark when tires slowed on my driveway. I turned off my lights and crept to the front door. Slid a three-iron out of the golf bag I kept there. Listening before I looked. Footsteps, then soft knocking. And then my name.

When I let her in, Meddy asked if I was trying out for the PGA tour.

"More like the Samoan Open." I sheathed the club in its Calloway bag and turned on a light. "You usually call first."

"There is no usually." Had me there.

"I also came by this morning."

"I was out of town."

"I know." Meaningfully. And then, "You think Otis Grove wouldn't tell Elliot you showed up?"

And Elliot told you, I thought. But knew better than to say it. Just as I didn't say Otis Grove had fronted me ten large to beat Elliot to the diary. I was in danger of becoming downright discrete.

Meddy sat on the couch without being asked. I took the chair at her knee.

"I brought something I thought you'd find enlightening," she said, and pulled a letter-sized manila envelope from her shoulder bag. "Elliot got this through Monte. A copy of Dr. Pizzarelli's dying declaration."

"That's a legal term. Is that what the police are calling it?"

"I don't know. Just read it. It says he not only took complete responsibility for her accidental overdose, but made a point of saying he acted alone—"

"'—as in all cases over the years of her drug abuse,'" I recited from memory, "'I was her hand of convenience. Elliot Pratt, especially, never knew what I was doing. I just thought I was being helpful.' Something like that?"

Meddy colored and she sat back against the cushions.

"Come on, Meds, you think Monte Arnett's sources are better than mine? I read it this morning at Roscoe's Chicken and Waffles with my man from the coroner's." I added a "Thanks, though," hoping to soften my assholity.

"You read this at breakfast, yet you still went to Santa Barbara to check Elliot's alibi?"

"Hey, you're actually starting to sound like a reporter."

"You're such an asshole."

"Don't change the subject."

She closed her eyes and drew a sigh, probably visualizing how good it would feel to slap me.

"Yes, I went to Santa Barbara. I went because that note is bogus."

"It was the old man's suicide note, for God's sake."

"An old man with terminal cancer and, maybe, two months to live." Her eyebrows raised on that one. "My guy at the ME says Dr. Pizzarelli was a walking corpse. He was much more descriptive than that, and, believe me, it didn't help the breakfast."

"Sounds to me like a good reason for Pizzy to clear his conscience."

"Sounds to me like Pizzy was taking dictation."

"It's finally happened. All these years in the tabloids and you've finally crossed over to certifiable conspiracy nut."

"I'm pointing to the facts as I see them."

"So do the Area-51 wonks in Times Square. Exactly how far are you from an aluminum foil hat?"

"Read the note again, Meddy. He spent more ink clearing Elliot than he did on his own wife . . . who, by the way, has suddenly paid off her mortgage and has hired a real estate broker to find her a villa in Tuscany."

"Insurance would cover that mortgage."

"Not for a suicide."

"Do you seriously believe the old man killed himself and left this note to clear Elliot in exchange for a buyout?"

"I don't know. Jeez, Meddy, I'm just taking a critical look here. Something I haven't seen you do since they started building you a set for your own show."

Meddy folded her arms across herself and chewed some lipstick. The little Y of a scar, that souvenir from Vietnam, showed on her brow, white against her rising pink. It wasn't the first time I missed our happier days: war.

"OK, smart-ass," she said. "I'll tell you what. First thing in the morning, we start to work this together. Shut up and listen before I hate myself for this decision and change my mind. I know you well enough to know you're not going to drop this until you play it out. I also think if we team up, we'll find her diary that much sooner and this can be done without you crashing around the china shop for God knows how long."

"I'm good with that."

"I'm not finished. We find the diary, it's done, agreed? This doesn't turn into one of your Grassy Knoll specials, some open-ended what-if investigation."

"Fine with me. I know when we find the diary we'll find the killer."

"No, when we find the diary we find the diary. Then we see what it says."

"Why do I think you want to do this, just so you can prove Elliot's clean?"

"As much as you want to prove someone else did it because you can't live with the fact that you led a vulnerable woman back to the life that was killing her?"

She set the envelope with Dr. Pizzy's note on the coffee table and left.

On a street of early-sixties tract houses and big-tire pickups in the flats of Reseda, Larry Bilkiss ran an unlicensed holistic supplements business out of his garage. A word-of-mouth enterprise like that was a natural step from some of the other things he used to sell there. Although he still dealt in cash, his new clientele was usually unarmed.

"Hardwick. Dude. Come on in and rest the load." Dealing with Larry was like hanging with a beach culture Moon Doggie, frozen in another decade. "Blend you a shake? Growing my own wheat grass now."

"Can't stay, Larry."

"That's cool." He moved a case of vitamins off a cracked Naugahide chair and dropped it on the floor beside a nursery flat of aloe vera plants. "Make a divot."

I sat.

"Business good?"

"Good enough. Day at a time." He hopped up on a carton of saw palmetto supplements and sucked something green from an eye dropper. "Colonic sales have picked up since the elections."

"It's an ill wind, as they say."

I waited for him to screw the eye dropper into a vial that said algae something. "Listen, I've got a gig for you, if you're free tomorrow. I was going to do it myself, but this project came up, working with a partner, and I can't break away."

A piece of me said I shouldn't farm out the job but another piece wanted to work with Meddy and guess which won. Besides, Larry was reliable and highly skilled.

"I don't do the cat burglar deal anymore, you know. Even though I'd do just about anything for you—man, you're like a brother—but I'm off the B&E and house creeps." He held up a Scout's honor hand. "Truly. Part of my twelve-step."

"Well, I do need you to get into a place, but the owner's dead and wanted me to find something she left me, so it's sort of with permission. A trailer in the desert near Anza-Borrego. Just get in and bring me all the stuff inside it."

"Everything?"

"Everything."

"Wouldn't it be easier for me to just bring you what you're looking for?"

"Won't know it until I see it. That piece of crap van out there still work?"

"The Van o' White? Dude."

"Excellent. Make a run to the desert in the morning, clear out the trailer, and I'll pick through it tomorrow night to see if what I'm looking for is there."

He said fine. When I paid him up front he hugged me and offered me a free colonic kit. I declined.

"Oh, Larry, by the way?" I said on his driveway, "the trailer has a padlock."

He beamed. "Who are you talking to?"

"Right."

Meddy, when she has something to prove, is a force of nature. When I showed up to meet her the next morning for breakfast at Du-Par's in the Valley, she was already established at the back booth with an open briefcase and a cell phone to her ear. She nodded for me to take the opposite side of the table as she *uh-huh*-ed into her Samsung and scribbled notes. It wasn't even seven AM and I was eating her dust, which was largely the idea.

"When it metastasizes like that and there's such bone degeneration, how long does the patient usually have to live?" Closing her eyes to listen, she wagged her head side-to-side in a way that would have been rude in person. "Of course you'd need more data, but speak generally. I won't quote you, Doctor."

I did an upside-down cheat off her notepad and could see Pizzarelli's name in her neat block letters at the top of the sheet near the spirals. The phone number underneath was a 212 area code.

When she hung up she made a brief note, and without looking up, said, "It's the number for Memorial-Sloan Kettering in Manhattan. You don't have to surf my notes, Hardwick." She looked up. "We *are* going to be a team on this, right?"

"Absolutely," I said. "Although, I feel like I just showed up late for the team meeting. In high school, Coach made me run bleachers in full pads and helmet for that."

"Relax. You know me. Early bird. Besides, I like to stay on New York time when I'm out here. Hate to sleep away phone ops while I could be working the East Coast."

While the waitress, a time-frozen Aunt Bea from the sixties, poured coffee, I asked Meddy, "So the early bird found a cancer specialist to back up the ME's prelim?"

"Two sources," she corrected. "Both agree he'd have been gone in six weeks, give or take." She took a file from her case and slid it to me. "My notes on Bonnie Quinn since her OD. These are her personal contacts I spoke with," she said, indicating a few names and phone numbers and notations in the Boston area.

Reading upside-down herself now, she continued, "Teachers, her priest pal . . . Next page is more professional. You already know, or know of, most of them: Her manager, Rhonda York, network and production people, guys she slept with, ax grinders, stalkers, disgruntled formers, personal assistants she went through like Murphy Brown on speed. . . ." She smiled, "Which is, I guess, kind of what she was."

"Welcome back," I said, smiling over the rim of my cup.

"Meaning?"

"Meaning for a reluctant bride, you seem mighty invested."

She shrugged. "Yeah? OK . . ."

"What kicked in? Was it my body slam to your objectivity, or does my capital-J Journalist smell an Emmy?"

Meddy scoffed. "Don't even. This is how I work a story, you know that."

"Uh-huh," I said. "In mere hours, you've not only covered most of my bases, you've got the double-confirm on Pizzy from the ME, and moved on to Bonnie's childhood acquaintances. All I've done is select a shirt."

"I wouldn't brag."

My ex continued the tour of her notes, and, as she spoke, her words fell to silent background, m.o.s., they call it in a movie, when the love song starts playing. Only no ballad here. Just Meddy, taking my challenge to her journalistic commitment and pounding it up my ass. Give that one to John Williams to score.

When she finished, she squared the pages and handed them to me. "Yours."

"I don't have anything to give *you*," I said, wishing I could click a big un-send on that sentence. "On paper, I mean."

While we ate, I gave her the oral history of my main moves so far. The cryptic stuff from Brick, the eyewitness details from Bonnie's nosy neighbor, the unclear meaning of the Faulkner book, and the ransacking of my apartment for which I did have a visual aid: the mug shot I stole of Manu. I showed it to her so she'd know the level we were playing on. She gave it frowning study.

"Do you have a hard link from this guy Manu to any of this?"

When I answered *no* she slid the picture back. I told her I had sent Vitamin Larry to one of Bonnie's hideouts to bring back her possessions. She didn't ask where it was and I didn't tell her.

"You have some sort of plan for the day?"

"I'd love to get into the business affairs files and see what jumps out about a few things," I said.

"Like?"

"Like, when exactly did Elliot cut the deal with Kimberly Duggan to replace our diva? I hear he had an option to replace her after Episode One Hundred."

"Who told you that?"

"Otis Grove, who said he was told that by Elliot."

"Then why check?"

"Why call Sloan Kettering?" Had her there, and she nodded. "Do you have a way to check the business affairs files without being detected?"

"You mean that I should not simply ask Elliot."

There it was. I chose my words with care. "I think we should agree not to share anything with Elliot we don't both agree to share with him."

She digested that and said, "Agreed."

"Now that we have our compact, I have one other piece to disclose. Otis Grove is expensing my diary hunt and doesn't want Elliot to know. Otis doesn't want to damage a friendship if it comes to nothing."

"You mean like suspicious wives who don't want their husbands ever to know they've hired a sleazy PI to tail them in case they're wrong?"

"Exactly. Except for the sleazy part."

"Sleazy like you getting double retainers sleazy?"

"It's all point of view. But if we're teaming up, you deserve to know about my retainer from Otis Grove."

"And what happens to the diary if we find it?"

I let my look say *don't make me say it.*

"It's academic. If the diary's a smoking gun, it won't matter," she said. "If it's not, Otis will just pass it to Elliot for his TV movie."

Waiting to pay at the cash register, Meddy said she'd work the business affairs inquiry. "And what are you going to do? Find someone else to piss off?"

"I'm going to say hello to someone."

"Hello?"

". . . Newman," I said in my best Seinfeld.

# CHAPTER THIRTY

It took me two passes around the block to find the worldwide headquarters of Whatev' Productions. Seems the worldwide HQ was in a second floor walkup above a tux shop in Studio City and one of the street numbers had been stolen. I found a parking spot under a eucalyptus on Whitsett, climbed around a pair of Goth holdovers in tragic black who were smoking on the painted stairs, and found the door I wanted. It was Masonite and the same color as the steps. When I knocked, the hollow thumps echoed down the linoleum breezeway. A toilet flush inside was followed by a musical "Coming, coming," and Earl Spandell opened up.

"Help you?" he said, taking a beat to remember me before his expression said he wondered what I was doing there.

"Hey, Earl. Mind if I come in?"

He frowned his wary frown, one of those rubber-faced looks I had seen him coach his son with on the *Thanks for Sharing* set.

"Sure thing," he said. "Pardon the mess. I was just getting a mailing out for the Jimbo Fan Club."

He moved some *Hustlers* and *Dark Nipples* off the couch and I sat down. I could smell his flush but I had, after all, dropped in unannounced. He squeezed his belly around the corner of his desk. It was a tight fit and he snagged the tail of his Hawaiian shirt on a stack of trading cards with his son's head shot on them. They cascaded to the brown shag and, from the looks of the place, they'd stay there a long time.

"It's a small office, but it's all I need to run the Jimbo stuff." Air sighed out of the chair when he flounced down. "I tried to write it into the boy's contract to have Hobby Horse pop for better digs, but business affairs called it bad precedent and claimed there was no room on the lot. He's up for renewal at the end of the season and I'll put it to them then. Trailer on the lot or we fucking walk."

I heard low whimpering through the wall he shared with the acupuncturist.

"They wouldn't have any kids watching that fucking show if it weren't for my Jimmy. See the letters we get? He indicated a slag heap of mismatched envelopes and post cards lining the wall like a geologist's slice of riverbank.

"Impressive," I said, wondering if I was talking too much.

"Fuckin-A. My kid knows what the kids like. The writers, what do they write for him? Drek. Fifty-year-old *Full House* retreads writing dialog for my ten year-old. So my kid ad-libs one night. Goes off the script and says, 'Whatev'.' Screams from the audience. Howls. Especially the kids. The writers stand there around the monitor like a daisy chain of shitheads, tapping the script with their pencils at the script supervisor. Then they hear the audience wet its pants and they start taking bows like they wrote it. Every week after, they had Jimbo say 'Whatev'.' Now it's like 'Dyno-mite' from Jimmie Walker. Or 'Kiss my grits' from . . . fuck it, who gives a shit. Anyway, my kid comes with the ad-lib, they act like they came up with this signature catchphrase, and I have to fight just to make sure my boy gets more than two lines in an episode when the bitch goddess starts cutting."

Talked out, he looked lost. Didn't know what to do with his hands.

"I'm a little curious about why you're here. You have some candids for sale from the set? Because I'm about to update the Web site. I can't pay you for them but I'll give you a credit for every shot I use."

"There are some things I want you to tell me about Bonnie Quinn."

"Hey, come on, the lady's dead." He made a sign of the cross. "If you're thinking I'm going to trash her for the tabloids, you've got another think coming. Let's have some respect."

"My editor at *Rumor Has It* says you've been his stringer for every Bonnie bash they wrote. Two hundred bucks a week just to keep your eyes open, three more if they print your stuff, so don't bullshit me about respect, Earl."

"That's not true and it can't be proved. Besides, I signed a gag thing with Hobby Horse. Think I'm going to mess with that settlement?"

"Five hundred thousand is what I heard. Your buyout for not suing after Bonnie Quinn lifted her skirt to pee on a script while your son was onstage. No panties, I understand."

"Yeah, well, you can call it hush money if you want."

"What do you call it?"

"Listen, the kid's mother was this close to yanking him off the show after that. My fucking wife. Clueless. She wants to adios him from fifteen Gs an episode and have him go to school like any other fucking kid. OK, so the settlement made it a little easier for her to swallow. Hey, I'm not so happy about the gash flash myself, but I think it was in his best interest to settle and stay on the show."

"A lot of people wouldn't see it the way you do."

"Thank you." Dolt. "It's not easy being a stage dad."

"Did banging Bonnie Quinn in Larchmont after every show help you cope?" Earl's lips pouted and a sheen glistened on his double chin. I wanted to say "Hello, Newman," but resisted.

"That's nuts. Get out."

He stood up. His Hawaiian shirt wet-stuck his back, making his love handles look like they had flowered mud flaps.

"What would you say if I had pictures?"

Earl Spandell's head turtled down.

"I see. That's why the visit." He sat again and ran a white tongue on dry lips. "How much do you want? How many you got? Let's end it here so it all stays here." Then, calculating, "The wife's got the half-a-mil tied up in a trust or some shit I can't touch, so if you're thinking large, forget it."

I shot the heel of my shoe against the lip of his desktop and jammed Earl in the tits. He cried out and toppled back in his chair. The back of his head whomped against the wall, forcing his chins down into his chest. He flailed his legs against the grey metal of the underdesk, frog kicks bonging the sides.

"You're chokin' me. What the hell was that for?"

I stood and reached over the desk, leaning on it to keep up the pressure. There was a milky line on his forearm where it was wedged in the top drawer. I reached in and pried a chrome plated .38 from his fingers. I held it up.

"What were you going to do with this?"

"I . . . keep that with my checkbook." Wet loofah cough. "I was going for my checkbook. You wanted money, right? Christ, get me up, I'm choking here."

He flailed again. Bong, bong—

"If I opened that drawer, would I find a checkbook, Earl?"

"Just help me up. Come on."

I slid the desk away from the wall and Earl sprung up in his seat, fanning spilled pencils and loose papers off his belly.

"I could have you arrested," he said.

"Is this permitted?" I held up his piece, grip-first.

He talked to his lap. "What do you want?"

"I want to know about Bonnie Quinn. I want to know things she might have told you."

"And you're not going to tell my wife?"

"Let's see how well you answer."

"All right, all right. Shit. So I was doing her. It started when she pissed in front of my kid. After, I mean."

"After the settlement?"

"No, before. I'm in Jimbo's dressing room that weekend boxing his shit to get out of there, and she comes in."

"Bonnie?"

"None other. So she comes in, she says, to apologize. Said the water show was for the writers and forgot the kid was there. She was living on the lot, you know. In her dressing room. Saw my car. I tell her there's nothing to say. Talk to my litigator. I go back to packing and she starts rubbing my shoulders. Crying. Says she's bipolar and screwed up that day and won't I forgive her. I turn around and she calls me Earl real close to my face. I mean, she was like this close, and she's pressing her boobs into me, and, well, one thing led to another and, well, we basically fucked right there on the floor."

I thought back to Hellhole Canyon the night I found her. How she took pot shots at me. Then cried. Then took off her shirt. I looked at Earl. Soft, pudgy, pasty, sweaty. In a loveless marriage and needy.

"Go on," I said.

"Not much more to it. We had this sort of regular thing show nights, mostly." Mr. Friday Night. "Mostly at her house."

"Mostly?"

"We fucked a coupla times at this regular place she kept at a hotel. But she said she didn't want to be seen with me in public. Like I cared. It was just a kick. You know. Sport fucking, she called it."

"Touching."

"Hey, it's not like she didn't get something out of it."

"And, meanwhile, your kid's still working the show with the woman who exposed herself to him. Was it worth it for the regular sex?"

"You make it sound cheesy. Fine. You don't know what we had."

"I know it got you to her house once a week. Including the night she died."

"So. She wasn't there, so I left."

"But she was there. She was just dead."

"No. She wasn't there."

"You mean she didn't answer the door."

"I mean she wasn't there. I went in. I looked. She wasn't there."

I tried to cover my shock. Earl was too into Earl to notice.

"My witness heard you pounding to get in."

"At first. I have a key."

"She gave you a key?"

"Once. I made a copy. We done?"

"Hang on. She ever talk about keeping a diary?"

"Oh, fuck—No. Is there one? I'll be in divorce court if my wife gets wind."

"As fascinating as your exploits would be, Earl, I'll bet Bonnie may have had some more volatile things going on in her life that she may have written down. No pillow talk about something like that?"

"No . . ."

"If I find out you're holding out on me, you won't be happy."

"I'm not. Trust me."

As a measure of my trust, I pocketed the bullets from his gun before I returned it to him. I was at the top of the stairs, heading out, when his door opened and his voice echoed down the hall.

"Hey. If there is a diary, how much would it be worth?"

"Maybe your life."

★　★　★

"You know I could get you deported for that," I said to Meddy, who pretty much ignored me as she dismantled her cheeseburger, stripping the meat of its essential companions. The crime of low-carb mania. "What camp does the pickle fall into, enemy or friendly?"

She draped her pickles on my open wrapper and told me to decide. I decided *friends close, enemies closer,* and tucked them under my bun without reservation. It was late for lunch, but when we celled each other looking for a mid-point to hook up and compare notes, a picnic table outside Carney's railroad car-burger stand was hard to resist.

"You know, you hear all the stories about horrible stage parents," Meddy said after she listened to My Morning with Earl Spandell, "but you're never quite prepared for how awful they can be."

"Tell me. I feel like I need HAZMAT to give me one of those decontamination showers."

"Jet sprayers?"

"And a wire brush."

We looked at each other for an instant and both began a laugh that finished with a held stare until she blushed and turned away. Then I hopped to my feet. Alert. Scanning traffic on Ventura Boulevard.

"Hardwick?"

By then I was over at the curb. She came over and stood beside me, following my eye-line as I squinted up the street through the crush of afternoon traffic. All I got was light blind from the sun kick off chrome and glass.

"Thought I saw the Samoan."

We walked back to our table.

"It was the night when he broke in, right?" she said, looking back toward the street. "Are you sure?"

"Not sure. But not so not sure." I glanced back again. Then shook it off.

Our food was cold but we ate it anyway. Meddy wanted to explore the stage dad.

"Crude Earl?"

"Mm," she said, sipping some Diet Pepsi through her straw. "If her body wasn't in the house, that means the time of death was wrong."

"Or she died somewhere else."

"What?" she said, "and drove herself home?"

"Pizzy. And the van."

"May I remind you Dr. Pizzarelli already copped to the accidental OD in writing?"

"Which, to my objective eye, only fuels suspicion of Elliot Pratt. He had the access, the stakes, and the resources to pull it off. Maybe in concert with the dead doctor himself."

"We only have Earl's say-so her body wasn't there."

"Why would he lie?"

"Let me play your little game."

"You wound me when you call it that."

"Devil's advocate, then. If—and that's the little game part—if Bonnie Quinn was indeed murdered, wouldn't Earl be your ideal suspect?"

Meddy's great at reading nonverbal cues, but I helped her out.

"Fuck, no," I said.

"Come on, it's all right there. The guy's cheating on his wife. A wife who holds his balls like this." She demonstrated. "He's got a high stakes clandestine affair going. Everything to lose if Bonnie Quinn exposes it."

"Why would she?"

"Who knows why she did anything? But my guess is Earl Spandell was not a keeper. She only prostituted herself to keep the kid on the show."

". . . And?"

"And then, that night, she sees Jimbo's dad take off his Hawaiian shirt one more time and says, 'Enough,' and it's 'Good-bye, Earl, and I'm telling your wife for good measure, you raunchy pig and—'What are you doing?"

"Hang on." I finished molding the foil wrapper from my lunch into a hat and handed it to her. "Put it on. It quiets those voices beaming down the kook theories."

"If it sounds like a stretch, it's only because I still don't buy your murder."

"Good, an open mind." She threw a French fry at me. "Look, Meddy, there are any number of people who had motives if you want to open it up. Deane Tacksdale, any of the writers, past or present, the security guard whose shoelaces she tied together . . . throw a dart at any name on your list from breakfast. But I just see Earl as too ham-fisted to finesse an OD and then cover his tracks so neatly. I'm still liking Elliot Pratt for it."

"Then you won't like this. Kimberly Duggan's deal was struck after the funeral, not before."

"Doesn't mean it couldn't have been negotiated before. A hand-shake deal shows premeditation on Elliot's part."

She handed my foil hat back across the table. "You need this more than I."

On our walk to the service road behind Carney's, we both saw it at the same time and stopped short. All the doors to my Xterra were open. There was a pile of glass chips under the driver's side window. Except for Meddy's car, the rest of the street was deserted. I approached it slowly, but knew it would be empty. I leaned in, saw the open glove box and the slashed seats. And I smelled him. Knockoff cologne mixed with— his odor. Something beyond sweat. Something fusty and wild. I scoped the perimeter. Trees, ditched shopping carts, a cinderblock wall with gang tags, a laughing threesome missing gimmes at the par-3 across the wash.

Meddy was staring at me when I turned back.

I had to ask, "Would you think I needed a foil hat if I said we aren't the only ones looking for Bonnie Quinn's diary?"

# CHAPTER THIRTY-ONE

I never would have bothered with the stupid police report if Meddy hadn't forced the issue. For my trouble, I got a long, blistering wait on a shadeless Valley sidewalk and a ration of 'tude from the responding officers. Loot was working the daily rock-star wife beating in Benedict Canyon, so a trio of geniuses from black and whites took my statement. They used the occasion to shit on my chosen field and suggest they haul in the entire AFTRA-SAG membership for a lineup of likelies with motives.

I showed them the mug shot of Manu, and when they recognized it as police property it didn't exactly push my level of respect into the red. The upshot was two hours down the crapper by the time Meddy parked us in her space at Empire Studios.

Welders were blowtorching the hobbyhorse off the front door to replace it with a brushed metal UEN handle. They paused to let us by. One advantage of Meddy's status there was that we got to breeze through the lobby and upstairs with a wave and an open smile from the receptionist.

"A lowlife paparazzo could get used to this," I said as we entered Elliot's office suite.

His assistant's desk was empty and an incoming call half-rang and dumped to voice mail.

"We should have called first," Meddy said.

"His car's here."

Then, from behind his office door, Elliot's most unElliot-like shout, "How could you presume to do this, you God damn stupid asshole!"

I smiled at Meddy. "I think he's in."

"This is bullshit, Elliot. Totally bullshit. Nice thank you, man!" hollered Monte from inside.

I made myself comfortable in the chair beside the door.

"Come on," said Meddy. "This isn't right. We should go."

"This isn't right. We should stay."

"Hello?" called Elliot from inside. "Is someone here?" The door opened and he stepped out. "Oh, Meddy, hi." His voice was chalky from adrenaline and the smile he wore for her stretched thin when he saw me. "How long have you been here?"

"Just . . ." said Meddy.

Elliot's assistant returned and reacted to Elliot's withering look.

"Bathroom," she said. "Well, sorry."

Monte emerged from Elliot's office and when he saw Meddy he gushed, "Hey, there's our franchise."

"Listen, if we're interrupting something. . ." said Meddy, letting it trail.

By now, Elliot had gathered his game and the face that went with it.

"Naw. The Mont-ster and I were just looking at some budgets for your show." Monte chewed a cuticle and looked away.

"Is there a problem?" she asked.

"Never. Right, Monte?"

Monte wore his smiley face, too, but you could feel the toxic burn.

"On rails, as always," he said.

I didn't buy a bit of the happy act and, as I wondered what we would have heard if we'd walked in two minutes sooner, I realized Monte was addressing me.

"I asked you a question."

"Monte," said Elliot. "Manners?"

"Why are you here? You don't have anymore business here."

I turned to Elliot and grinned. "Tell him, boss."

"Boss?"

Elliot had a caught look. "I, ah, hired Hardwick to help find the diary. It's like an extension of his prior services."

"Oh. OK, then." Monte sniffed twice sharply. I believe he was sulking.

"I was going to get around to filling you in. We did get a little side tracked."

"That darn budget," I said.

Monte shot back. "Hey, Sherlock. Do you expect to find it here?"

"We want to look in her dressing room," said Meddy.

Elliot turned sharply to her.

"I'm helping Hardwick out." She looked back and forth from me to Elliot. "Two heads and all that."

For a beat, Elliot looked as if he tasted yesterday's sushi but worked his charm. "No problem. Whatever you need, Monte will make it happen. Right, Monte?"

"That's the job description." Monte worked his jaw, chewing on the words he didn't say.

I knew pretty much what we'd see as soon as I smelled the fresh paint at the doorstep. The drumroll was there when Monte said it was unlocked and that we knew where it was. No escort, no protocol, no spin. I let Meddy push the door open and followed her in.

Bonnie Quinn's dressing room was as sanitized as a model home. The graffiti had been over-painted. Ecru, reported Meddy. All books and clutter were gone. The ratty cinderblock bookshelves had been replaced by clean, white modules from Ikea. The dismal old shag, which probably contained enough coke crumbs and pot seeds to fund a small cartel, was gone. In its place, a tan berber which pulled together the sandy hued love seat and arm chair. Harmony abounded in beige. No discordance here.

"My God," said Meddy from the pristine bedroom. "It's like we walked into an episode of *Extreme Makeover: Home Edition.*"

"Yeah. A conspiracy nut would think somebody wanted every trace of her gone." I phoned Elliot, who, of course, said he had no idea it had been cleaned out. He knew it was planned as the dressing room for Kimberly Duggan, but execution was Monte's area, and the Montster was one zealous guy, huh? Plausible deniability. Where would the powerful be without it?

Meddy dropped me at Professor Auto Glass where my window was being worked on. After my Trail Blazer, I figure I should get a frequent target's discount card. Or maybe just insurance.

"Feel like we accomplished anything today?" I said at her car door.

"Not a damn thing."

"Then we're right on track."

We sketched our plan for the morning, then I said, "I couldn't help noticing. Elliot seemed surprised you're working this with me."

"Because I didn't tell him."

She half smiled and held my look before she drove off.

"What's that on your ass, man?"

"Stuffing from my car seats. Somebody slashed them."

Vitamin Larry bent over and put his flashlight on me to inspect. "Looks like you've been in a pillow fight."

"Haven't had a chance to get them fixed."

"Amigo. It's why God invented duct tape."

The front end of Larry's van was a Smithsonian insect collection.

The engine was still hot and ticking from his run to the desert and back.

"Any problems getting in?"

"Cake. Sweet little Audi parked out there, too, so I took it upon myself to clean that out for you, also. That OK?"

"Larry, you're the best. And you got everything?"

"Everything not nailed down."

"It all fit in here?"

"Oh, most definitely. Check it out."

He swung open his rear doors and shined the light inside. The long interior was quite empty except for a boom box, a sleeping bag, and a pillow. When I asked what was in the big plastic trash bag, I could hear my own voice ring on metal in the hollow of the van. In it, Larry had assembled the loose items: toiletries, half a bag of pork rinds, fast food garbage, a paint can full of cigarette butts, spent wine bottles, malt liquor empties, her unloaded handgun, kitchen odds and ends, paper towels, a can opener. Nothing resembling a diary.

"I could have taken the VeeDub for this haul."

And he was right.

Late that night I Googled William Faulkner. I entered the key words from her inscription and let that cook but came up empty. By the third results page I even scored a few hits in Norwegian. Time to bail on that. But when I searched a simple "Faulkner Fable" I got a lick of excitement. On the Ole Miss Web page dedicated to him was a photograph and a caption: *To keep track of the complex plot in A Fable, Faulkner wrote outlines of the novel's seven days on the wall in his office at Rowan Oak.* The photograph was of his writing on the wall.

I opened my shots of Bonnie Quinn's dressing room, ruminating on content as the container and congratulating myself for hosing those rooms, especially now that Hobby Horse had turned them vanilla for Kimberly Duggan.

I studied every image of her walls, searching in the graffiti for the diary itself or a clue that would lead me to it, sort of the NC-17 version of "Where's Waldo?" Hours later, I finally drew the connection between William Faulkner and Bonnie Quinn: studying both made my eyes sting and my head ache.

As random as Bonnie Quinn seemed, she was too skilled a manipulator for me to believe the inscription and that book and the timing of its delivery were chance. But when I hit the pillow, it also crossed my mind that she was also manipulative enough to be having a good laugh at me from her dirt nap at Forest Lawn.

Rhonda York graced me with a turd-in-the-punchbowl grimace when I entered her office in Meddy's wake.

"Hey, what's this? You didn't tell me he was coming with you."

"We're doing a survey of how people react to unpleasant surprises," I said.

"Get the fuck out."

"Let's see . . . that would rate you a nine for 'highly engaged, but pitifully inarticulate.'"

Meddy jumped in. "Hardwick and I are working together. We need your help."

"Maybe I'd help you. Not this scumbag." She frowned as I took out my cell phone and dialed. "What are you doing?"

I confess to my totally unguilty pleasure at the melodrama that played out. I put a shush finger lightly to my lips and smiled. Then, to the phone I said, "Hello? Hi, it's Hardwick. I'm in her office right now."

"What's he doing?" she said to Meddy, who gave nothing.

"It's pretty much as I had anticipated," I said into the phone. Then I listened, nodded, even gave ol' Rhonda a wink. "Sure," again to the phone, "absolutely. Thanks." I hung up and relaxed in a guest chair.

"Who the hell do you think you are?"

The phone rang on her desk.

"That's for you, Rhonda. Isn't that your private line?"

Meddy sat in the other guest chair. Rhonda just stared at the ringing phone.

"Allow me," I said and reached across to hit the speaker phone. "Rhonda York's office."

"Rhonda York? Are you there, Ms. York?"

The baritone was unmistakable. Its honey-dipped Southern wrapping was at once soothing and authoritative.

"Yes, this is she." Rhonda sat, eyes glued to the perforations on the speaker.

"Ms. York, this is Otis Grove calling."

"Yes, I know."

She shifted in her chair. Leather on leather. The sound made me wonder if she'd lost control of her intestines.

"I want to congratulate you and your client, Kimberly Duggan, on her new role in our little series."

"Ah . . . thank you, Mr. Grove."

"Now then. I'm calling to solicit your cooperation with your visitor, Mr. Hardwick."

"But he's nothing but a—"

"Excuse me, but I can see you might benefit if I clarify the situation here," said the owner of the network. "We have our big press junket coming to Los Angeles, right?"

"Right."

"Oh, it's going to be one heck of a party. All those reporters and entertainment journalists from all the big outlets coming from all over the country and around the world to meet our producers and stars as we roll out our new programming. Nice catered bash at the beach to cap it off. . . . Kimberly Duggan will be there, too, correct?"

"Yes, sir, we're all very excited about it."

"Good." He paused. "Now. Mr. Hardwick is there to do a job for me. What you are going to do is cut loose with some major cooperation for him. Anything he wants. If I hear otherwise, Ms. York, your client will be there for the press party, all right, but not for the cast photo. She'll be serving canapés because I'll rip up her deal and not think twice. Are we clear?"

Rhonda York shifted again. Those animal skins can be so hot.

"Very clear, Mr. Grove."

"Then I'm glad we talked," he said. "Good-bye."

It fell to me to kill the speaker phone. The high-powered manager just sat in a daze.

# CHAPTER THIRTY-TWO

Following Rhonda York's PT Cruiser through Beverly Hills, Meddy took her hands off the wheel and air pumped her fists.

"I hate myself for this, but God damn, that was fun."

"Careful," I said. "It's a slippery slope from the ivory tower to the sewer."

"I've just gotten so used to doing everything straight up. I mean, you don't pull street tactics like that on senators and Nobel laureates."

"Yes, I do."

She steered to follow Rhonda from Little Santa Monica onto Wilshire.

"Wow, the look on Rhonda's face. I admit I feel sorry for her."

"That's your problem right there."

"She was humiliated. She's a human being."

"She's an asshole."

"Why, just because she wields power?"

"Not today, she doesn't. Take a look when she gets out at the bank. I believe you'll see some Rhonda tail between her legs."

"That's what it's all about for you, admit it."

"Here we go."

"It's your power issues," she said. "You see somebody in authority and you have to take 'em down."

"Are we back to Hardwick's a hammer and all the world's a nail?"

"God. I forgot about you and your memory."

"Peter, Paul, and Mary wanted to have a hammer. Had big plans what to do with it, too. Mornings, evenings, all over the land . . . the works. Did they have power issues?"

"Not like yours."

"Untrue."

"Is true. It played very well when I met you in Vietnam. It was all very cool and right-on then. But it's a little throwback now, don't you think?"

"How did we get from Rhonda York getting her ass handed to her to my perceived shortcomings?"

"Come on, you have to admit you're working something out. Elliot is just one example."

"Yes, in all likelihood, of a murderer."

"Just because someone is corporate or successful or rich does not automatically make him a villain."

"I never said it did."

"Your actions speak for you."

"I never make people do things, Meddy. I show them doing them. You don't want to be exposed as a hypocrite? Fine, don't act like one."

She stopped at the red light and tapped her French manicure on the steering wheel.

"I will, at least, give you credit for not accusing Elliot of purging her dressing room to find her diary."

"Are you kidding? He absolutely did. But he didn't find it. Otherwise, he'd have called us off the hunt." The horn honk startled her from a dark reflection. "Green light," I said.

Meddy looked up from the safe deposit box on the table. "Don't they usually seal these when the owner of the box dies?"

Rhonda York stole a glance at the closed door of our privacy cubicle at the bank and lowered her voice. "This box is in my name."

I leaned forward and whispered to the box, "Hello, Rhonda."

"Does he have to be in here?"

Meddy barely managed a straight face and began setting the contents of the box in neat piles on the table.

"What are you looking for, anyway?"

"Something that doesn't look like it's here," I said.

Eventually, we'd interrogate Rhonda about a diary, but Meddy, in an inspired moment of suspicion, suggested we keep our hostile pal in the dark. I was right there with her. Look first, ask later.

The contents of the box were spare: birth certificate, first communion holy card, some jewelry, a passport.

"This looks interesting." Meddy plucked out a cellophane bag of about a dozen prescription pills in various colors.

I took it and held it up. "Are these in your name, too, Rhonda?"

Meddy hid her laugh in the box as she repacked it.

The weeds were winning at the Quinn house in Larchmont. You could lose a small dog in the dandelions alone.

Rhonda sighed when she sorted through her key ring at the front door. Sighed the way she had at her bank. Sighed the way she had at the UPS Store where Bonnie had kept a P.O. box: "Insisted on a P.O. because of some crap about some Eudora Welty story. I don't ask, I just do," she said.

"Did," I clarified.

Sigh.

You never get used to being in the same room where someone just died. That seems like a given, but I have been in my fair share, with and without corpses, and I never managed the break of detachment that cop friends and coroner pals made. Reporters I knew had made the break, too, but Meddy wasn't one of them. She eased up to my elbow and stood close, and we silently took in the matted carpet where Bonnie Quinn's body had been found.

Heavy footfalls from the hall. Rhonda York tromped in and carelessly planted the sole of a Doc Martin on her actress client's final mark.

"I can't help you if I don't know what you're looking for."

"So much for the respectful interval," Meddy said.

"I just don't want my tit in a wringer with Otis Grove."

"Good."

I began opening cabinets in the empty bookcase. Meddy went behind the wet bar and did the same.

The manager sighed and leaned against the shelf to smoke. At one point during my search, I saw her flick an ash on the spot where she had found the body. Who knows? Just like her costar pissing on her grave, maybe Bonnie's legacy was irreverence.

Meddy and I entered the master bedroom together. She scrunched her nose when she saw the skeevy futon on the floor.

"Deluxe," she said. "Everything but the mint on the pillow."

"Whatever you do, try not to picture a big, fat, greasy stage dad with his fishbelly-white ass cheeks in the air, going at her like a pile driver."

"Thank you for that image." She socked my arm. "After this, I'll be checking into Canyon Ranch to detox."

Somehow it became my job to overturn the disgusting mattress to see what lay on the dark side. Except for an empty Cheetos bag and some condom foils, no joy.

"Now I know why the CSI crew wears coveralls and gloves," I said.

I figured Bonnie Quinn's house in Larchmont would be a bust from my walk-through two weeks before when I was searching for her instead of her diary. But I had to be thorough. And though it wasn't strictly my nature, I had to hope. But the returns came in, and my nature won.

Meddy gave it up, too. When I joined her in the kitchen to wash my hands after searching the garage, she opened a drawer and clawed up a handful of Chinese delivery condiments.

"Unless she kept a diary inside fortune cookies, I say we bail."

"The compulsive Meddy wants to read them, doesn't she?"

"But it would be so pointless."

"Like Lucy and Ethel eating all the strawberry preserves to find the lost ruby."

Meddy forced the fortune cookie drawer closed and it crunched, which made us both laugh. She rested a hip against the counter and crossed her arms.

"The police have already been through here, anyway."

"Doesn't matter. This house didn't mean enough to Bonnie Quinn to be a place she'd keep anything she cared about."

"Or anyone," Meddy added. She tossed me a towel for my hands.

"Want me to sing 'A House Is Not a Home'? Elvis Costello kills with the remake."

"I've heard you sing, Hardwick. Unless you've worked in a stint at Juilliard in the last ten years, I'll wait and iTune the Costello."

The manager came into the room, twirling her keys on her forefinger and catching them in her palm. Shink-Shink—

"Hear that, Meddy?" I cupped a hand to my ear. "I believe that's what social behaviorists call a nonverbal cue."

The sigh again. In her black leathers, Rhonda both looked and sounded like a tire losing air. I had the remarkable self-restraint to think it without saying it.

"It's fine, Rhonda," Meddy said. "We're wrapped up here."

"Good." Rhonda slung her purse.

"But we're not done," I said.

Rhonda dropped her purse on the floor. Another cue. "What else is there you could possibly want to look at?"

"Earl-the-stage-dad was a regular on the futon, I hear."

"So?"

"He told me that before they started coming here to profess their sweet nothings, she did him at a hotel."

"So?" This one came with an impatient shrug.

"So," I said, mimicking her, "Mr. Friday Night says Bonnie kept a spot there. I want to see it."

"Look. I've given you guys almost two days of my time. It's not like I don't have other things to do."

To my surprise and delight, Meddy beat me to it. She held up her cell phone and said, "We can make it so you aren't so busy, if you like."

Rhonda snapped her gum and glared at me. "She's fuckin' bad as you." Grabbed her purse. Stomped to the door. "Well, come on."

Meddy smiled at me and I *tsk*-ed at her. "Slippery slope, Meds. It's a slippery slope."

# CHAPTER THIRTY-THREE

The Huntsman's Den is a Rat Pack–generation holdout, thriving on a busy stretch of Ventura Boulevard across from a dry cleaner, a Petco, and a Starbucks. Really an upscale motor hotel, the Den has ponds, wandering mallards, gazebos, banquet facilities, and a bar somebody thought was a good idea to name The Sipping Duck. When I was a kid, I remember my dad pointing out Jack Lescoulie, the late *Today Show* cohost, in the coffee shop there. You can still walk the courtyard near the Patio Café and see the weathered faces of SAG workhorses from *The Wild, Wild West* or *The Rockford Files* meeting for their daily decafs after cardiac walks or visits to Human Resources.

That afternoon, there was true celebrity buzz at the Den. Meddy attracted whispers and stolen glances from the front desk as we waited in the lobby. When I got those kinds of looks, it was usually right before the night manager called the cops on me. A vacationer in shorts and a wife beater asked Meddy for an autograph. When the man also wanted a photo with her, she gave me a playful swat when I asked how to use one of these things. When I framed the picture, I took my time with it, wanting the look I was getting from Meddy to last and wishing it was my camera, not some drone's from Cedar Rapids. Rhonda York emerged from the hotel manager's office and held up a room key.

Meddy and I instinctively went to the elevator, but Rhoda motioned us on down the hall.

"Ground floor," she said. "Bonnie insisted on being near the pool."

"She was a swimmer?" Meddy asked.

"No. Too lazy to shower."

Rhonda stopped at a door and handed me her key.

"Look, I have a business to run. The room's all yours. Search it, sleep in it, fuck in it, run up a room service tab, raise sheep in it, I don't give a shit. But do your deal and be done. I'm closing my account here today."

"This is in your name, too?" asked Meddy.

"When I handled Bonnie, everything was in my name. Her credit cards, her banking, her loans, her car. She was a walking train wreck. I managed everything."

I couldn't resist. "Like the option that let them fire her after Episode One Hundred?"

"What are you talking about?"

It took Meddy and me about one second to radar each other. She nodded to me and took the lead.

"I hear she had an option in her contract that allowed the studio to release her without penalty after the hundredth show."

"I don't know who said that, but it's bullshit. What agent or manager would ever allow that in a deal?"

"Sometimes they get buried in the fine print. You know business affairs."

"Or new talent is desperate enough to mortgage the future," I added.

"Desperate? I'll tell you who was desperate. Elliot fucking Pratt was all over me to cut a new deal the day *Sharing* made the Nielsen top five."

"Why?" Meddy asked.

"Because we were a hit and Episode One Hundred sparked huge profit participation for Bonnie. Duh."

"Wait, " said Meddy. "Wouldn't Bonnie have had syndication points anyway?"

"Honey, there's points and there's points. The hundredth episode vested Bonnie Quinn as a fifty-fifty participant in Elliot's profits. The minute that show went to Episode one-oh-one, with or without Bonnie Quinn starring in it, Elliot would have had to give back most of his own points just to make her payday."

Meddy said, "That's a horrible deal."

"For Elliot." Rhonda grinned. It was the first time I'd ever seen her smile. "He made it in desperation when the network double developed and he needed Bonnie's casting to get the show on the air. Elliot was more worried about getting to episode one than one hundred. He figured he'd deal with it later, a high-class problem."

I hopped in on Meddy's behalf.

"Hold on. An excellent source of mine was told plainly that there was an option to terminate her after one hundred."

"Your source blows. Don't believe me? Otis Grove gave you access to my files. Come by the office, and I'll show you the contract. I gotta go."

I saw the pain take Meddy as the penny dropped for her about Elliot's lie to Otis. She leaned back against the wall, sifting through all the bad stuff.

"One more thing, Rhonda." Since we'd seen all the places she could show us, it was time for me to ask. "Did Bonnie mention anything to you about keeping a diary?"

Rhonda blanched. "Oh my God—A diary. She actually did it?"

"You know about a diary, then?"

"Last couple of years, whenever we got yelling at each other— which was, you know, part of the gig—she'd say someday she was going to write it all down and I'd be fucked-over royal."

"Did she?"

"Hell if I know." She got right in my face, suddenly manic and overwhelmed. All the implications blinking at once. "Is it in there, do you think? What are you going to do with it if you find it? Who else knows about it? I'll pay you for it. You can't let this out. If you find that diary, you have to let me know. We have a relationship, right?"

"Sure, Rhonda. Solid as ever. But relax. I'm sure you have nothing to hide."

I entered the suite behind Meddy and closed the door, leaving Rhonda York to manage her own private hell.

Bonnie's hotel room could have belonged to a bag lady with an allowance. Housekeeping had made the bed, cleaned, and excavated a path to vacuum, but the rest of the suite was a dumping ground. Years of clothes—dirty, clean, old, and new—were piled knee-high against all the walls and spilled out the open closets. Every flat surface, including the desk and tables and nightstands, were mounded with books, newspapers, pretzel bags, cracker boxes, loose cigarettes, candy wrappers, wine bottles, and twelve-packs. Same for the chairs and sofa. There was no place to sit except the bed. I looked for drug evidence, needles particularly, but saw none.

Meddy adhered to the door, shoulders hunched, slightly pale. It could have been repulsion at the room. I knew better.

"Elliot lied," she said, sounding hollow.

I nodded.

"Why would he do that?"

"I think the question is, why else?"

"I should know better than to ask you a rhetorical question."

"Not a lot of rhetorical going on here, Meds. The man hires me to track down Bonnie Quinn so he can shoot his hundredth episode and make his payday. Now, it turns out he takes a huge hit if the show continues beyond that because of the same Bonnie Quinn. Seems to me he only needed her for one episode. After that—"

She worried her lower lip under her teeth, mulling. "I need to confront Elliot about this."

"Love to hear what El has to say."

"We were so focused on Kimberly Duggan. I never thought to look at Bonnie's business affairs file. I . . . trusted him. Why would he go that far and lie?"

"Allow me to quote page one, paragraph one of the Investigative Journalist's Handbook: 'The cover-up is a hungry beast.'"

"Dr. Pizzarelli . . ." she said. Almost a question. Almost.

"So, you agree it's possible this could have been a murder?"

"I didn't say that. I'm saying I can no longer deny your suspicions just because they came from you."

"I'm getting all misty here."

"Don't," she said. Tossed her purse on the bed. "Let's see if we can find a diary in this haystack."

"One good thing."

"Yeah?"

"We can skip the shower. We know she never went in there."

"You know, Hardwick, I'd find this a whole lot more amusing if I weren't looking for the evidence that might send my boss to prison and kill my show."

"Two good things," I added. "You called Elliot your boss and not your friend." Or lover.

She paused and handed me a stack of magazines. "Get to work."

I began sorting mine as she sorted another stack. "Meddy?"

"Mm-hm?" Without looking up.

"Missed you."

I reached for another pile to sort through and caught her smiling at me.

Hours of searching turned up nothing. Shortly after we had turned the lights on at sundown Meddy called from the bedroom.

"Hey, check this out."

I found her on her knees pulling something from the bottom of the closet. A shoe box tied in a pink ribbon.

"This was jammed under a mountain of clothes on the floor."

We sat on the bed with the box between us.

"Do you want the honors?"

"Yours," I said. "You found it. I'd hate to man-spoil that pink ribbon."

"Not pink," she said. "It's champagne."

Meddy started to untie the pink, excuse me, champagne bow. I put a hand on hers to stop her.

"If it's old sneaks, they're yours. If it's drugs, we go halvsies on the cheddar we pull in at the crack house."

"Crack house, my ass. If that's what's in here, we're cruising Hollywood with it tonight. I drive and you sell from the back seat."

"I'll need a hat."

"Fine."

"And sunglasses."

"I believe it would be night."

"And sunglasses."

"Sunglasses, whatever."

Meddy took the lid off and we looked in. It was a shoebox filled with mail.

"Top letter is addressed to Bonnie," she said. "Return address is an S. Quinn."

"Her daughter."

"Shannon. The one who drowned."

I nodded. "Drove her car off the ferry at Balboa Island two years ago."

"My God, can you imagine?"

Flash back to Tahoe. Faces of pain. Wounds torn open at the scabs. I could imagine.

"Shannon," she said again. "She was the only *verboten* in the piece I shot for the hundredth show. The Hobby Horse media relations edict, 'Do not ask about the daughter.'"

"And you agreed to that?"

"Of course. Why not?"

"I don't know. Maybe because I thought you did news reporting for a living."

"Oh, yes, Hardwick. Lecture me on ethics." But she let it pass and riffed through the envelopes in the shoebox. "Every single one of these is from her daughter over the years."

I took the envelopes out and fanned them without opening them. There were, in all, about thirty letters and greeting cards. The more recent postmarks, the ones at the top, came from all over the country. The bulk, though, were on embossed Cranes sent from a boarding school in Brattleboro, Vermont.

Meddy turned the box over and a cocktail napkin fluttered out. She held it out for us both to see. I tried to ignore the fact that we were sitting on a bed and our shoulders were touching. The napkin was fancy. White paper with gold imprint in a staid font that said *Tory Club* under the interlocking initials *T* and *C*. Someone had written a phone number on it in ballpoint.

"The number's a man's handwriting, you think?"

"Not Bonnie's, I know that." I took the napkin and held it to one of the envelopes from Shannon. "Doesn't match her daughter's, either."

"What about the club?" she said.

"In Boston. I think it's one of those tony brownstones in the Back Bay. Need I tell you I'm not a member?"

When Meddy laughed, her upper arm shook, brushing against

mine. I didn't brush back, but she didn't pull away. My cell phone rang. It was Otis Grove. Meddy carefully replaced the letters in the shoebox as I talked.

"Kind of funny," I said, "hearing your voice on my phone."

"I get that a lot. People don't expect me to be a human being and place my own calls. But I do screen the incomings, as you can imagine. I just left a state dinner at the White House and I see Rhonda York has been desperate to reach me all evening. Before I let her off the tenterhooks, I thought I'd confirm with you that she was fully cooperative."

"Oh, Rhonda was cooperative, in an I'm-only-doing-this-because-I-have-a-gun-to-my-head kind of way. Thanks to you."

"Good, then. Any luck?"

"We learned something interesting about Bonnie Quinn's contract."

"Which is?"

"There was no option. Bonnie Quinn was locked into big profits for the new season, with or without her services. Your protégé Elliot lied to you."

Long pause. "I'll tell you something. It's a hard thing to work with friends." Ever the statesman, Otis Grove added, "Let's withhold judgment until after you find the diary. How's the search coming?"

"Early yet. We did the safe deposit, her house, all the usuals. Nothing. Meddy and I are finishing up a suite Bonnie kept at the Huntsman's Den. We found some letters from her daughter we'll take a look at when we can break away from all this charm and elegance, but I don't know that we have a diary just yet."

I lost concentration watching Meddy's strong fingers delicately retie the champagne pink bow on the shoebox.

"Are you calling it quits, then?"

"No, sir. Not unless the diary is in these letters."

"I salute your persistence. Keep me apprised. And good hunting, Mr. Hardwick."

# CHAPTER THIRTY-FOUR

I surrendered the room key and stepped out of the lobby where Meddy's Mercedes was idling in the carriage turn.

"This is why nobody carpools in LA."

"What do you mean?"

"Now you're stuck dropping me home in the canyon. Isn't that the opposite way for you?"

"I'm not going to Malibu, if that's what you mean. I can't deal with Elliot tonight."

The shoebox was on the passenger seat when I got in. I nestled it on the floor between my feet and buckled up.

"I thought you were sort of staying at Elliot's." Sort of in his bed.

She let out a hiss of air between her teeth and said, "To tell you the truth, I don't know where I am anymore."

She nosed the car to the hotel driveway and, as she waited for the procession of headlights to pass, I could sense the weight on her. She had grown quiet, taken herself inside by degrees since Rhonda pulled the rug on Elliot's lie.

"Are you hungry?" Throwing my question away. I'm such a punk.

"Starved." She turned to me from watching the traffic and broke into a smile. "Would a guy take a gal to dinner?"

"What are you hungry for?"

"A dark, quiet corner."

My go-to steakhouse in Woodland Hills is connected to a high-end shopping mall, which makes parking easy, but attracts enough impulse diners (aka atmosphere killers) to push the noise level. I asked for something secluded and they tucked us in a back booth.

The kitchen was working on our filets, the drinks were perfect, and we even managed to clink rims without spilling. For a guy who makes his living shooting action pictures under all conditions, I had to concentrate to steady my hand around my Jameson.

Meddy set down her calvados martini and lounged against the padded leather. "Mm. Feels good just to let down for a bit."

"Really? Because after dessert I was hoping we could search Bonnie Quinn's public storage unit."

"You'd better be kidding."

"I am. But I will check to see where else she might have had nests."

"Perhaps a cave in Afghanistan," she said and we laughed.

"I'm wanting a second look at Saddam's old spider hole. Nothing like a diva's personal diary to help a deposed strongman while away the days and weeks underground."

"Stop it." She was holding her martini glass like she was shipboard in a storm. "I almost shot calvados out my nose."

"Any chance to insult the French. Go ahead, pile on."

She set her drink down. "Let me ask. How much did it creep you out to be going through her things?"

I head-bobbed a sideways maybe yes, maybe no. "For me it wasn't the creeps, it was the frustration. Seems like every venue it was same search, same mess."

"There. That's my point. How empty her life seemed. She died sad and alone."

"True. I have to admit there's this feeling I have about this whole experience. It's worked on me from day one on some level I can't articulate."

"Or won't."

"What?" She shook her head.

I prodded. "Come on. Say it."

Meddy finished off her glass and leaned forward. "Isn't it obvious? Of course it works on you. It's the natural extension of what I told you—that you two were so alike."

"Let me see if I recall what you said—"

"Asshole." But with a smile this time.

"If memory serves, it was something about my anger. How the world's a nail and my life is Hammer Time."

"And this is where it leads. Isolation. Who wants to die alone?"

I thought about the nights. The long darks. Tossing. Listening to the coyotes on the hunt and living with myself until dawn. She slid her hand across the table and took mine.

"I'm only getting into this," she said softly, "because on some level I care about you, and I'd hate to see you self-destruct."

I was going to let her hold my hand all night, but she drew away when the waiter arrived with the next round.

"Oh, is there a special occasion?" he asked.

"We're together. That's special." I shrugged to Meddy. "Well, unusual."

"But no birthday or anniversary?" he asked. "I just saw the gift and was wondering."

The waiter indicated the shoebox tied in pink ribbon next to her purse. Meddy looked like she wanted to crawl under the table when I told him we were celebrating her expulsion from the convent and I asked for a bottle of Blue Nun to toast it.

When he left, she set the box between her silverware and announced, "I have one more sensitive topic."

"I'm ready."

"I don't think it's our place to read these letters."

"What?"

"It's been bothering me since the hotel. In fact, I wish you hadn't told Otis we had them. These were hers. Very personal."

"You're enunciating all the reasons we should read them."

"But her privacy."

"She's dead. They're both dead. And clearly these are among the few possessions Bonnie had that she took care of."

"But it's not her diary."

"We don't know that. And what if they could lead to her diary?"

"It feels like a violation."

"Even better. That's when you know you're in the zone."

One look at her told me I was holding a match that could light the fuse and blow this night of healing right out of the water.

"Tell you what," I said. "Can we at least decide not to decide until tomorrow? Clear our heads first?" I held up my new drink. "Or cloud them?"

"Agreed." Her cool fingers found my hand again. "Thank you."

And then a trapdoor popped open in me.

"I'm more sensitive about private letters than you might know." Meddy's eyes narrowed, not sure where I was going. I maybe I wasn't either. "I wrote you some over the years." Great, Hardwick, have another cocktail.

She pondered and said, "I never got any, honest."

"Because I never mailed them."

Our steaks arrived, sizzling in clarified butter, but neither of us touched them. We didn't acknowledge them. We just looked across them at each other, not breaking the thread of silence until the waiter got tired of standing there with his peppermill and moved on.

"What sort of letters?"

"Inadequate, mostly." I continued, in free fall without a chute. "About us. About what happened. At first that's what they were about, anyway. Then I quit trying to explain it all and wrote about how I missed you."

Out of nowhere, I choked up. Nothing girlie. Just cracked on *missed you* when the bottom fell out of my diaphragm.

"Where'd that come from?" I chuckled, fooling no one at that table.

Meddy took her napkin and dabbed something off my cheek.

"Anyway, I don't want you to think I was some kind of lunatic or stalker. OK, I do have the closet with the bulletin board of pictures of you—just kidding. Seriously, I didn't write every day or even every month. Just a couple of letters over the—"

"Don't," she said. "Don't back away. I want to hear this."

"Steak's getting cold."

"Tell me. Anything you wrote about."

I took a long drink. Water, this time. "I can put it in one sentence. I've written it often enough." I drew a steadying breath and said it. "My life has not been happy since Nashua."

Her eyes began to shimmer with candlelight and she looked away.

And then I asked, "Has yours?"

"I don't know if I'm ready for this conversation."

"You don't have to be. We're clearing some air. Let's see where it goes."

"So much has changed."

"Not everything."

"No. It's been in the atmosphere between us." The corners of her mouth twitched a little smile. "Today, especially."

"Magnetic."

She nodded, then picked up her fork and then put it right down. "It can't be. Look where we are in our lives. We're a sitcom."

"*Nobody Loves Hardwick.*"

Her cleansing laugh lightened things up but only a little.

"I'm serious, Hardwick. We're staring across a wide chasm. Look at what I do and look at what you do."

There's a Native American aphorism that goes something like, *When you come to a chasm, leap. It's not as far as you think.*

"What if I didn't do it anymore?"

"Get serious."

"I think about it now and again. More, lately. Especially lately."

"You'd never quit. You without your camera? Please. I think you need to get some food in your stomach."

"When have you ever known me not to do what I say?"

"Back then? Never. Back then."

"Meddy, I mean this."

"Maybe at this moment."

"What are you afraid of?"

"Tell me what you'd do. There's not a reputable paper or magazine that would hire you or buy from you."

"Don't you miss what we had?"

"And don't tell me you're going to do graduation photos and wedding portraits. Not until I've had a few more of these."

"Don't snow me. You felt the pull."

"You can't survive without the juice. Hell, you slept with a camera on the nightstand. Next to the police scanner."

"You still feel it. It was all over us today."

"The worst part? You love the work more than yourself. That's why you do so much damage."

"Sometimes I wonder if you're afraid if I quit the tabloids you'd lose your excuse to dismiss me."

"You loved the work more than . . ." She pulled herself short. "It was everything."

"I'd broom the slate. Take a new road."

"And do what?"

"There's a book proposal I want to make."

"To sell your ambush shots?"

"A coffee table book. I'm going to take a year on the Mississippi and shoot—"

"—The Twain book," she said, trailing important nostalgia behind it. I nodded. "You're actually going to do your Mark Twain project?"

"I don't know if I'll get an advance or anything. It's not exactly what I'm known for. But that's kind of the whole idea, isn't it? To do something else." She brought her elbows on the table, and steepled her forefingers against her lips. "Even if I don't end up with a publisher, so what? I'll give a year to the dream instead of just dreaming it."

"You're serious about this."

"I'm going to save up for a boat. Nothing big. Just enough for me and a sleeping bag while I float the Mississippi and shoot it north to south. There's also a stern-wheeler that'll let me shag along for a round trip. In the pilot house."

I was going to continue, but the transformation was slowly coming over her, and I let the silence do the work. She closed her eyes a beat and opened them, looking at me with a softness indelible.

"You talked about that book our first night on the river." I nodded. "In Vietnam." She settled back against the padded booth, fixing her gaze above my head, seeing through some decades.

"We were floating out there and I was scared as hell, so alone and nowhere, and you started in on Twain and the Mississippi and your voice was so . . . And you were . . . It was the middle of hell. But you made it feel like an adventure. Like I was reaching out over the edges of my life. I've thought about that night a lot, you know."

"I may have recollected it once or twice myself."

"Everything was pure then. Everything was clear. Everything was possible."

"Maybe it still is."

She looked me over slowly, thoughtfully. "Maybe it still is."

The Santa Ana winds were up when we stepped out of the restaurant. A plastic Subway bag cartwheeled past us and snagged on the cactus in the planter. No place in LA was clearer than the Valley when the desert winds were blowing.

"Check out Mt. Wilson," Meddy said. The red pulses of the TV towers seemed ten miles closer. "Is it me, or can you almost touch it?"

"Didn't you hear? They moved the mountain today. It was in the *Times*, so it must be true."

Meddy hooked a heel up behind her and kicked me in the butt.

"I guess I had that coming. Does that make us even?"

"Oh, Hardwick," she said with an evil grin, "there's not enough whoop-ass in both my feet to get you even."

I held out my hand, an invitation to escort. She hesitated only slightly, shifted the box of letters to her other arm, then, instead of taking my hand, laced her arm through mine and pulled herself against me.

We walked like that through the parking lot under the humming lights that cast no shadow. I didn't want it to be the calvados that tipped her weight a critical ounce against my forearm. I wanted it to be gravity, the force of our own possibilities that brought her hip to brush against mine every other step.

Alone now in the sea of cars, we stopped spontaneously. I turned to face her as she turned to me. The magnet was on. Until I caught a whiff of something and pulled away.

"What—?"

I put my forefinger to my lips and turned, craning upwind first, then all around the parking lot.

"What." she mouthed. Insistent. Not alarmed, but wanting in.

I dropped to the ground, palms on pavement, in the push-up position. When I looked under the cars on either side of us, I expected to see him. Thought I'd see Manu there, or part of him. A knee or a shoe carelessly exposed as he waited in a crouch. Or the iron head staring, dark eyes defiant and bold.

Not there.

On my feet again, I circled the immediate cars and then took a careful 360 of Meddy's. A shoe crunched gravel behind us. Meddy gasped. I whirled and was blinded by a flashlight.

"You folks looking for something?" Security guard.

I shielded my eyes from the damned beam and scanned the lot again, uselessly after his dose of Mag-Lite.

"Just her car," I said.

"This one here," said Meddy and she chirped the alarm. The guard snapped off his six-cell and urged us to buckle up and drive carefully before he continued his rounds.

"I thought I smelled him."

Meddy didn't need to ask who. And she didn't question. She sniffed the dry air herself and did a survey where we stood.

"Come on," she said. "Let's get you home."

I mourned our lost moment and got in.

# CHAPTER THIRTY-FIVE

Our drive was silent, contemplative for both of us. Twice on the Ventura Freeway I caught her looking over at me. Feeling like she was poised at the brink of saying something before she broke off.

I knew better—correction: knew Meddy better—than to force the issue more than I had already. *Let this play out*, I decided. If she comes back, wonderful. If not, heal and move on. Don't be living one of those pathetic piney-guy lives. As if I hadn't already had my head start.

I filled in our thick gaps of dead air with business. How the next day we would confront Elliot about his lie. How it really wouldn't hurt to see if Bonnie had a storage unit somewhere. How Meddy should inspect the Faulkner novel to see if her fresh eyes detected anything new.

In my driveway too soon. After she kissed my cheek and I opened my door to get out, the dome light illuminated the freeze-frame to which I tethered all hope. Her smile filled in where the words had failed us. It was a smile filled with meaning and history and reassurance all at once. She was about to speak again, but didn't. Instead, Meddy killed the engine and got out of the car.

First thing in the door we flew into each other. No debate, no decisions, no baggage. After a day charged with particles too raw and transient to speak of—slam. We tumbled onto the couch, both of us struggling to get closer, needing this. Needing to share more than mouths and breath. Clinging to each other's vulnerability and joy and hunger. I had the sense of us reforming, of our chaos struggling to order itself, pulling inward toward the core of the twister.

Later, in my bed, quiet, naked, enfolded in each other, I felt we were afloat. Meddy and I basked and drifted until a tear pooled on my chest. She lifted her head and looked at me.

"I never should have slept with him."

"You don't have to talk about this, Meddy."

She sniffed. Fingered dampness from her cheeks. "All my career, I always worked hard so I would always advance on merit. I believe that's how I got the show. But now that I've slept with him . . ."

"Let it go."

"I never thought I would, either. Sure, I felt the attraction, but I ignored it. Told myself I could just shoot my report, work around him. But Elliot's not that easy to ignore when he cares for you."

Even when he doesn't. I thought of the envelopes. The Leica. The charm.

"My big fear was that they'd say I got this job on my back. And now look." She sat up and plucked some tissues from the box. "That was the least of my worries. I feel so ashamed and stupid."

I sat up and hugged her and she sobbed into my shoulder. When she tissued her eyes, she looked at me again, pleading.

"Do you understand why I was so blind about Elliot? I'm not a kid reporter anymore. This felt like my last shot to get my own network show. You know the form for women like me. You settle for quiet desperation and ride an anchor desk in Albany or Pittsburgh or Fort Wayne right into retirement."

"I think you should let yourself off the hook for being human."

She incorporated that then pulled me down to lie with her, holding me tight. We dozed and I awoke to her getting dressed in the dark.

"You're not staying?"

"My stomach's in knots. I need some time with myself to do some sorting."

"You going to be OK?"

"Yeah. I just need to be alone."

"I understand. Can I come?"

That made her smile and she sat beside me on the edge of the bed. A dream reclaimed, stroking my brow.

"Where will you go?"

"I have a room at the Ritz in the Marina." She leaned down and kissed me. Tenderly. "Sleep. And, just so I don't send the wrong message, I'm glad we did this."

"Me, too."

"I could tell. Can I have a date for breakfast?"

"Sure. Where do you want me to meet you?"

She patted the bed. "Here."

After she left, I took out the Cakebread chardonnay. Off my budget, but I logged it in the week before when I blue skied Meddy coming over after our dinner at Arabesque. I set it on the counter beside a single wineglass.

I had bought an opener for the occasion, too. A sixty-dollar marvel called the Zappit corkscrew. A man spent sixty bucks on a corkscrew for two reasons: First, it shows taste, coolness. Second, guy gear.

This is one nifty piece of hardware. You squeeze the Zappit's handles together with one hand to vise-grip the bottleneck, jack the lever forward with your other hand to inject the screw into the cork, then jack it back, and—pthwap! Out comes the cork. The whole deal takes about three-point-two seconds and that cork rips out clean and crumbless. I have spent far more than sixty dollars for far less entertainment value.

I poured a gentleman's serving and held up the glass to swirl. In the perfectly slow sheeting of the wine inside the bell of the glass, blue light flickered. Closing one eye to focus, I watched the reflection of Amanda St. Hillaire's bedroom TV beam through my kitchen window, captured there as distant lightning in a glass of chardonnay.

What was this pattern of soft light from, I wondered. The rhythms were smooth pulses of blue, old movie rhythms for sure. Not the quick cuts of Woo or Tarantino. Amanda, my boarder in the main house, might well be watching herself, I thought. Swashbuckling against pirates as the ballsy virgin she played so often. Or valiantly leading a wounded cavalry officer on his lame horse through Monument Valley past the nation of feathered warriors.

I didn't pity her these endless nights of old movies. Amanda St. Hillaire's past was working for her in the present. Frozen in time, her ideal beauty in a story ideally realized never got old. Maybe it wasn't even the past for her. If it was her past, better to revel in one than be haunted by it. I raised my glass to the blue pulsing window in the dark house, said "Cheers, Miss St. Hillaire," and drank to her.

My cell phone rang. Meddy, by the caller ID. I kicked myself for opening the Cakebread alone. Maybe the night was not done.

"Got a late-night hankering to paw through Bonnie Quinn's storage unit, after all?" I said instead of hello.

No reply.

Call Ended, said the screen. Love those cellular dead zones. Even in LA. I got impatient and called her back.

Voice mail.

"Hi, it's me. Guess we're phone tagging. I'm up and I just opened some wine, if that gives you any ideas. Anyway . . . call or just show up." End. I tapped the nubby antenna on my chin. Took another slug of wine. Checked my watch. 1:37 AM. A minute can be very long. So I pushed callback.

Voice mail again. I hung up as soon as I landed there. Recorded the Cakebread, just in case.

Maybe she auto-dialed me by mistake. Or had something to tell me and changed her mind. Dread swept in. All the bad things that could happen to someone in LA played out like a flip book of random horrors. And then there's the not so random. I thought about him and the whiff I got in the parking lot that night.

1:38. *Merde.*

Then I played back Meddy's own words to me about how I let my imagination run wild. Didn't she say she wanted to be alone? She probably turned her phone off to avoid Elliot. I knew that game. I uncorked a pleasant but lesser wine, determined to both keep my hands busy and get full amortized value out of my sixty-buck Zappit. No sleep for me. Too alive. Too antsy.

I sat down with the Faulkner Bonnie had inscribed to me, now reassembled with clear strapping tape. What I really wanted to see were those letters from her daughter. But that would have to wait. The night Meddy was grappling with her moral identity was not the night to ask her to wink at it.

Meddy.

A little knot worked itself in my gut. What? Was it her call? Let it go. Was it the nagging suspicion we were at a dead end in the Bonnie investigation? Getting warmer. That I had prematurely committed myself to quitting for the Mark Twain book by voicing it to Meddy? Very warm.

On my knees in my hall closet. I cleared aside a plastic garbage bag of old running shoes perennially intended for Goodwill and made space to roll out the bottom drawer of the filing cabinet. The drawer was as I had left it last time and all the times before that. My navigational charts of the Mississippi River remained neatly tubed. Yellow Post-its rolled inside remembered my annotations. Photocopied articles on Hannibal and St. Louis and Cairo, Illinois, bunked in hanging files, dozing, waiting. Their Pendaflex hammocks rocked when I shut the drawer and walked away.

Too much swirling around. I polished off my wine and took a shower.

Under the stream came the biggest gut flutter. Meddy and I had made love, but was it passion, weakness, or the start of the next phase for us? I put my face to the spray and replayed our night for new meaning and promising frontiers.

The Santa Ana raged on. Bougainvillea thorns devil-scratched the bathroom window. A ghost moan harmonized under my eaves. The shower curtain flapped at the hem, making me think of those energy conservation cartoons that show all the leaks and cracks that rob your home of fuel efficiency.

But then the flapping became a billow. The vinyl fabric filled like a sail, reaching out, clinging to me, shoulder to knees. And then it sagged, empty of air.

I thought I heard my front door close.

# CHAPTER THIRTY-SIX

**M**eddy? She had no key.

The damned shower. I couldn't hear over the water. I turned it off and strained to catch every sound. Water beads plinked off me. The drain gurgled. The eaves howled. Was that a creaking floorboard? Maybe just the wind storm flexing the cottage. California construction.

Naked, dripping, I parted the curtain, tiptoed to the bathroom door, and eased it closed. Not all the way. I didn't want to make noise. And I wanted a small crack to listen. I worked my jaw to open my eardrums. Quieted my breathing which had become quick and shallow. Strained to hear over my own pulse. And the damned wind.

A quick appraisal of my options: Tiny room. One door. Frosted louvered glass window feasible to dismantle and escape, but not quickly, not quietly. No weapons. Maybe no need for weapons. Maybe I was scaring myself. Too much to drink, I thought. Dial that shit down. Just listen. Just think.

I slid the towels off the rack and pushed on one of the holders. It was killing my hand, but the spindle finally bent enough for me to pry the square chrome pipe out of the socket. Did I make too much noise? Leaning back to the door, fisting chrome. Listening hard. Ear to the crack.

When I caught his scent, the water chilled on my skin. My knees jellied and I felt my privates draw up. The bar in my hand grew heavy. I willed a better grip. I turned my head, looking for one more weapon to improvise. Maybe mace him with Glade.

Then came the explosion. Two hundred-plus pounds of Samoan defensive tackle body-slammed the door. The concussion ripped the room with thunder. When the wood smacked me, I blasted clean off my feet, flying backwards, airborne. My back hit the wall inside the shower across the room. I landed hard and loud on the back of my neck in the floor of the tub, clawing to free myself of the shower curtain that had swallowed me.

The door must have ricocheted closed because I heard it bang open again. Felt the Frankenstein's monster footfalls. My own feet were above me outside the tub, my legs draped over the rim. I kicked wildly, blindly, lost in the stupid wet vinyl. His forearms, or maybe it was his leg, swept aside my kicks with nonchalance. My ankle smacked porcelain and I cried out.

Manu laughed.

"Fuck you," I said.

Then choked for air when the sole of his shoe landed in my stomach. I held myself and moaned there in the bathtub. Heard him scoff again, and thought of the sound tennis players make on returns or weight lifters when they pump. Manu was having a workout.

I scrambled to get out of that tub, certain if I stayed he was going to stomp me to road kill. But his hands shot under my armpits and I was hoisted up and tossed on the john with enough force to knock the lid off the tank. I sat there, panting, fighting nausea, in a shower curtain toga, on the throne.

The Samoan said, "Fuck you?" mimicking me. "Fuck *you*, bruddah."

When I looked up at him, I had to squint. The bathroom overhead seemed cruelly bright. My eyes closed involuntarily. I tried to jimmy up my eyebrows to get a slit of vision.

"No you don't." He slapped me hard enough to jar my teeth. "Wake up, bruddah. We not done."

I put my head between my legs to slow the room down. At my feet lay the chrome pipe where I must have dropped it on the rug. Raising my head up to Manu, I mumbled and held his gaze to distract him while I toed the pipe closer.

"Pick it up," he said, "and I'll knock your fucking teeth down your throat with it."

I paused, calculating my chances. Then he cuffed me against my temple, throwing my head against the bathroom wall.

Blackness.

I was dreaming one of those feets-failing-me dreams. Got to go, can't move my legs to run. Got to fight, can't lift my arms to punch. Wake up. End this. It'll all be over. Just wake up. When I did, I couldn't move my legs. Couldn't move my arms. I heard sounds like a fight. Crashing, breaking glass. But no blows. Good, a dream.

I opened my eyes. Legs and arms duct-taped to a kitchen chair. Watching Manu paw shelves clear from my pantry. A grizzly got in my cabin. Nature's Fury on home video. He saw me awake over his shot putter's shoulder. Came to me.

"Hey, bruddah, you got to cooperate. Else you going to be in a world of pain." Then he raised his arm and I flinched which made him laugh. "Good," he said. "Man getting desensitized."

Desensitized. Moron. "If you're looking for money, it's under the sink. I keep five hundred in the Ruffy box. Take it and go. It's all you're going to find here."

"The Ruffy box, huh?"

• • •

I nodded my head to the sink. Just that little movement told me whatever healing had taken place in my shoulder was undone.

"Yeah, under there."

The big man opened the cabinet, pulled out the box and looked inside.

"Mm, Ruffy." He took out a soapy puck of steel wool and held it up, smiling. "Know what I like the Ruffy for?"

He locked my head under his armpit and vised it against his ribs with his bicep. I clamped, but his free hand pried at my mouth, parted my lips. I bit a finger. He punched my throat, and when I gasped, he shoved the Ruffy pad home and squeezed my jaw shut.

Steel wool scratched at my tongue and the roof of my mouth. My saliva released the detergent and ran soap to the back of my throat. I pushed to lean forward, fighting my own swallow reflex. My windpipe clinched. My stomach heaved. Manu stepped away and I spat the wad, coughing and gagging.

"You want to talk bullshit to me again, there's more. You want to talk more bullshit?"

I shook *no* and spat soap.

"This ain't no home invasion for cash, motherfucker." He pocketed the five hundred from the box. "Make it easy, bruddah. Tell me where it is."

A quick scenario played out in my head. Me, pretending not to know what he was talking about. Him, feeding me another mouthful of C-3PO's pubic hair.

"You mean the diary?" I said.

"Hey, there you go, dawg. We be done with this clean and easy, right?"

He ran the tap and gave me a glass of water. I rinsed and spat. Heaven.

"Thanks," I said. And then, "I don't have it."

Manu's face tightened like the skin on a fist. His forehead stretched to a gleam. He rolled his tongue and a drool bubble formed on the tip, then popped.

"You dead, fucker."

My head jerked back so fiercely when he grabbed me by the hair I expected a throat slash to end it all right then. Instead, he dragged me across the kitchen floor, one-handed, chair and all. Where the linoleum met carpet, the rear feet of the chair snagged and I toppled over with it, naked, duct-taped, cursing.

He left me there on my side with my cheek pressed into the nylon pile, watching helplessly as he ransacked everything. Manu at work. Back to finish the job. He yanked out drawers and upended them on the floor. Crash. Sift. Crash some more.

The side view was surreal. The view from a dropped video camera in combat. My neck was stiffening, and I had to get off that shoulder. I jerked the chair an inch and he turned. Scoffed. Like I was going anywhere. He pulled out another drawer and emptied it.

"I be back to your ass soon enough. You decide to help, you sing out. Then I'll make it quick for you, no shit." He moved on to the desk, not even looking back anymore as he talked. "But I find it on my own, I swear I'm gonna fuck you up."

I struggled the chair a few more inches around. From that spot, I could right my head a few inches off the Dutch tilt and see straight. He didn't seem to care. Dismissing me at that point. Knowing his power.

The center desk drawer stuck and when he jerked it the whole thing flew out. All its contents rained around the room. Paperclips hailed. Index cards fluttered. A pencil hit me in the face. But it wasn't a pencil at all.

It was my X-Acto knife.

My cutter was six inches from me. Half a foot from my mouth. I inched the chair closer. Manu didn't turn. If I could only work the clear plastic guard off the blade, I could . . . what? Ask him to please bend over and hold still while I slashed him with my mouth? But maybe I could cut the tape binding my arms to the chair.

One more lurch. Close. I extended my neck. Jutted my jaw. Reaching, reaching . . .

# CHAPTER THIRTY-SEVEN

"Hey." The Samoan sauntered over. "I need you, asshole."

Manu never saw the blade I almost got. He just grabbed my hair again like it was his business and pulled me up, righting the chair on four legs beside my computer.

"What you got on this thing?"

"Lots of stuff."

Manu slapped me.

"What do you want me to say? Jesus, it's my computer. Do the math. I keep all my shit on there."

"Any shit like a diary?"

"I don't have the diary."

"We'll see."

The bull sat at the keyboard. He tweaked the mouse and woke up the flat screen. Manu, the blunt instrument, the hulk, started to navigate my hard drive, opening folders, double-clicking files, and scrolling through docs nimbly, unabashed. Scratch a thug, find a geek. Welcome to Generation Xbox.

Skimming. Popping files like soda cans, sampling, moving on. He came to the draft of my Mark Twain book proposal and started to read.

"That's sort of personal."

He laughed again and said, "Bruddah, you strapped to a chair wiff your dick hangin' out. You don't got personal anymore."

The Samoan went back to surfing. I got sucked into a fresh spiral of fear and ice-cold sadness. I had been fighting it off, but it grew on its own from the seed of acceptance that I was indeed going to die there in that chair.

For what?

The how-did-I-get-here crank started to turn.

My last night was with Meddy, which warmed me, then ate my heart.

Manu found my photo archives. Of course, I kept backups on memory keys, CD-ROMs and a web storage vault I subscribe to. But thanks to hubris, sentimentality, and lax computer hygiene, there were a ton of images still nested there and he was all over them.

"One last time, foo'. I go easy on you if you tell me which one of these has the diary."

"They're pictures. There's no diary in there."

"So you say."

He clicked open my Congressman Landry file. Surfed a series of shots. Mostly, the rep on the stump. Shaking hands in a Franconia diner. Pumping a fist at a union rally. Wagging a finger at the Third Party Spoiler backstage at a presidential debate. Fucking his mistress in the hotel.

"Ho, now, what up here?"

I didn't have much time in there, but the shot was good. Good face, good light, good storytelling. Manu looked it over and over, turning his head all around.

"C'mon, man, no gash? You gonna shoot the ho, let's see the snapper."

Bored with the PG-13 view of the candidate's infidelity, he moved on to the next folder and a new slide show: Poolside on the rooftop of the SoHo House in Manhattan. Close on a stork-built nerd in bathing trunks, stretched out in a chaise longue. Nelson Pennette, the my-shit-don't-stink Pulitzer Prize—winning reporter who'd gotten me adiosed from the press bus, captured here at the chi chi club in the Meat Packing District. Significant, because Pulitzer Pennette claimed to be filing his from-the-scene series on Alabama's hurricane recovery from, of all places, Alabama.

I caught the lying sack of shit red-handed and red-faced, replete with zinc oxide nose coat. Dickhead even helped me fix the date of his subterfuge by reading the *Post*, holding up the front page like a hostage.

I struggled against my bonds. NG. I was wrapped tight. The armrests were bound to me as good as splints. My ankles ducted so tight my left foot had no feeling and my right had sparks in it. I tried to rest, make my joints small, so maybe I could Houdini out of them.

A right-wing cabinet member appeared on the monitor, fishing on the Chesapeake. No big deal, until my next shot, which included his fishing buddy, a Supreme Court justice. I had snapped these off just two weeks before the high court heard an appeal of a lawsuit against the very cabinet member baiting the justice's hook. What is it about politicians and scandals? With the Left it's always sex. With the Right, it's power. I didn't help my standing in the DC press with this Get, but I did show, if only to myself, I knew how to balance my targets.

Manu double-clicked the next folder. A metal rock slut handcuffed in an open ambulance, haggard and wasted, tits spilling out. It hit me. The Samoan was going through my files in chronological order. Banished from the Beltway, Hardwick hits Hollywood.

Next came the action star I captured at the lipo treatment center. For that Get, I wore whites and rode into the clinic in the back of an ambulance. The shots sold in a furious auction and cost the macho man his diet shake endorsement.

"Hey, she's funny." Manu, seeing my shot of Brett Butler at play, pretending to run over her *Grace Under Fire* writing staff in the McDonald's parking lot outside the Radford studios. The Samoan paused. "What was her name?"

Double-click. A deposed anchorman, rib-kicking Chuck Rank, outside the Zebra Club.

Double-click. A gay-bashing infielder cruising a male hooker in Boy's Town.

Double-click. The reality show talent judge checking into the Day's Inn with the hot diva finalist one week before her surprise victory.

The images on the monitor came faster. Manu raced through them, incurious. On a mission. Meanwhile, I experienced the ritual of the dying man. Every mouse click, every image, passed my life before my eyes. What I shot. What I felt. What I thought. Where I was.

Who I was.

I was a captive audience to the sum of my career. Each shot was one piece of a body of work comprising a life.

What had I done with mine?

What had I brought to the world? Ambush shots. Surveillance shots. Hand-in-the-cookie-jar shots.

Cheap shots.

Potshots.

Every picture told a story, none of them uplifting. All of them at the expense of the subject. The belief that they all had it coming was no solace to me strapped into that chair. It only made it worse.

Why?

These were good pictures. They exposed lies and indiscretions—even law-breaking, sometimes. That was my motivation. But stuck there watching The Hardwick Slide Show, the thread was unraveling on that mandate. Sure, I exposed the ugly truth (and better than any shooter I know) but was that really my motivation? Or was it just the effect?

Why had I done all this, then? All the nights sleeping in cars, peeing in empty milk cartons, climbing trees, ducking bouncers, taking punches, waiting, crawling, dangling out of helicopters, why?

I tried on my Gipper Goal: Rising to the challenge of the difficult shot. To get the impossible Get. The Nobody Does It Better mission statement. Might have worked for a 1970s James Bond, but it made an awfully hollow thump sitting there naked and bruised.

A Sean Penn, Alec Baldwin, Russell Crowe sequence flashed by. The parade of pissed off cinematic treasures. Snarling teeth and accusing fingers coming at my lens.

Next up: scornful looks from a TV shrink I captured smacking his wife in a parking lot.

Then, the shrink's wife, turning her wrath on me. Spitting at my camera even while her eyelid grew into a mouse.

To shut out the looks I was getting from everybody in my camera, I closed my eyes, only to see Meddy's face across the table. Hearing her say Bonnie Quinn and I were hammers, swinging out against the world. Hearing her ask me when I last took a picture that wasn't a payback. Feeling an ice pick in my soul when she said what I did was road rage with a camera.

"Here we go," said Manu.

I opened my eyes on Bonnie Quinn. The Samoan had come to her file and was viewing the long-lens shots I'd scored from her first rehab at Dawning Day in rural Connecticut. When I looked at the picture I had taken of her two days later playing drinking games at a beer bar at Grand Central I shivered. Bonnie had spotted me, and there was contact with my lens. Eye-to-eye as I looked at my monitor. What were the eyes saying? It wasn't hate. No. It was acceptance. Recognition. "Here I am," she seemed to be saying, "and there you are."

I found a lone shred of solace in the next sequence of pictures: the Lake Tahoe shots of Bonnie and her daughter. Hadn't Bonnie herself acknowledged my restraint in respecting her privacy? I had clicked off so many pictures of her and Shannon. And not one had been published. Until that night, no one else had even seen them.

Manu settled into his private screening. He studied each shot of the sitcom star and her estranged love child. Slowly. Carefully. Frame by frame trucked by of their sad and combative reunion, right up to the dust-cloud exit I captured when Shannon tore off in the Jetta. It was prologue. Within a year, that car would be her underwater tomb.

This went on for the better part of an hour. Manu was on the case, so he was painstaking in his review of every Bonnie Quinn shot I had. He paused at each image looking for some hidden message, or the diary itself. But he was coming to the end.

I closed my eyes again to hide from my legacy. When the show was over, Manu swiveled in the chair to face me.

"Where is it, motherfucker?"

I had answered him so many times already that I just shrugged and shook my head. He smacked me anyway. Lashed out with a prize fighter's kiss. The chair listed sideways, and he steadied it upright. I sucked back the rusty taste of my own blood. Comforting in an odd way. I was alive to bleed and it tasted better than the Ruffy.

I lost sight of him when he crossed behind me. He returned holding *A Fable*. His lips moved as he silently read the inscription from Bonnie to me. When he finished, he closed it.

"You holding out on me, hiding this under the sofa."

"I wasn't hiding it. You must have knocked it there when you—" I winced for the blow as he reared-up with the back of his hand. It never came. He just laughed.

"Shut up," he said, then flipped through pages.

"She didn't write this, though."

"No."

"Then who did?"

"William Faulkner."

"I can read, asshole. This book. Why she give it to you?"

"I don't know. "

"It's the diary, isn't it? Somewhere in here's the diary, ain't it?"

"No."

"Then why she give you this and no other?"

"I don't know."

Then, he closed the book and said, "Where's this Faulkner dude now?"

When I laughed, Manu jammed the corner of the book into my solar plexus and I wretched. Dry heaves doubled me up. When I was finished, he leaned his face to mine, and I got a dose of stank again.

"Don't fuck with me, bruddah. Why this book? Why this fucker?"

But I realized he was saying Faulkner.

"Get the idea, I don't know. Don't you think I'd tell you if I knew?"

He smiled. Bad sign. "Oh, you're gonna tell me, all right, homes. You're gonna tell me right now."

He left me for the kitchen. I craned to see him, but he was just out of view. But I could hear him pawing through the mess he'd made out there. Pawing for God knows what.

I spied my X-Acto knife across from the desk and started scooting. But on the rug, I was getting nowhere. Screw it, I decided. There was no way I was going to sit there waiting for him to find the Ruffy pads again. Figuring it would be my last shot at saving myself, I threw my weight to the right and rode the chair over as it toppled sidelong onto the floor.

The thud must have rocked the kitchen, but I didn't wait to find out. From where I'd landed the knife was almost in reach of my mouth. I jerked in the chair. Stretched my neck. Got it in my lips. It slipped out. Shit. Got it again. In my teeth this time.

The safety guard was still on the blade. I doubled myself over and dragged the tip across my thumbnail. No good. Tried again. Nope. On the third pass, my nail caught the guard and moved it. On the fourth, the blade was exposed.

Quickly now. I dragged the edge along the length of duct tape where it bound my wrist to the armrest. Again. And again. Perspiration draped my eyes, stinging them. I couldn't see how well the tape was cutting and didn't dare stop.

Another swipe of the blade.

Then another.

I could hear tape starting to part at the top of my cut. I repo'd the knife handle with my tongue and began to saw at the opening. Once, I stabbed myself in the wrist, but didn't stop sawing. Couldn't spare a second.

My jaws were numb from the strain. I bit hard, but lost hold. The knife fell to the floor. I flexed my jaws and reached out again with my mouth.

"Where you think you're going?"

Manu. I twisted to look. His club wrestler's body filled the doorway. He stood at ease, arms resting at his sides. But in one hand, he held something. What was it, a gun? No, not a gun. I squinted for a better look and my heart slammed into itself.

In his hand, Manu was holding my Zappit corkscrew.

"We gonna party now, motherfucker."

# CHAPTER THIRTY-EIGHT

I squirmed on the rug, stretching my neck, going for that cutter like a fumbled snap. Denied.

The Samoan yanked me upright again by the scalp. You bet I struggled. Struggled like crazy against the incision I'd started in the duct tape.

Manu stood over me and chuckled.

"Look atchew. You can fight all you want, dawg, you mine. Go ahead, fight. Scream. You so mine." He threw his head back and made a shrill yell, a wild war cry. When he finished he said, "Now you."

I hollered. I hollered a rebel yell that started in my feet and worked its way up, concentrating all its energy in one place: my right wrist. When I ran out of air, I still pulled. There was the sound of something tearing. Duct tape. When Manu looked down at it, he saw my fist on its way to his nose.

"God *damn*."

He brought his hand to his face, cupping himself. I threw another punch, a clumsy shot from my angle that hit ribs and glanced off. He brought his knee up and then down to pin my arm against my lap.

There was a red skim on his teeth when he snarled in a whisper, "OK, bruddah, moment of truth. Gonna give you two chances to give up that diary."

Then the man who had cut the tongues off murder witnesses and nailed them to porches raised his other hand.

He was holding my Zappit like a pistol.

"One chance."

He mimed shooting my right eye. Same for my left eye.

"Two chances, pop, pop."

His face took a tranquilizer. His own eyes went blank, staring at me the way Bonnie Quinn's had.

In the relative still of this awful moment, I tried to reason. Sounded as calm and assured as I could. Keeping any whiff of plea out of my voice.

"You don't need to do this, man. Don't you think I'd tell you if I knew?" He stared. "You can turn this around. Just go. You'll be in another state by the time I get out of this chair."

After a beat, he said, "OK," and for a spilt second I almost convinced myself he meant he'd let me go. But he ratcheted back the handle of the Zappit, setting the sharp coil back in its barrel, ready to plunge.

"One chance down."

The back of my chair groaned when he put his weight on my chest. I rocked my head side to side, anything not to give him a target with that thing. He vise gripped me between his forearm and his bicep again. I couldn't wag my head anymore, but he needed two hands to operate the corkscrew.

"Hold still."

"Like fuck."

I bucked and jerked my whole body. Gave that asshole some turbulence to deal with. But he put more weight on me, like a piano on my chest. I was pinned.

Up came the corkscrew. Up beside my head, the way a dentist raises his drill. On all of these gadgets there is a safety guard, a short metal rod, that juts out parallel to the screw coil. Just as I began to take heart that the little nod to consumer safety would prevent the mayhem he envisioned, he fit the blunt tip of the safety rod into the corner of my eye socket over the tear duct. The safety strut was now a monopod, giving him direct aim to my eyeball. My brain started firing off all the unhappy scenarios. The screw wouldn't extend far enough, so he'd have to force the rod into my eye, too. I was cooked.

I couldn't help myself. I looked up. The sharp point of the needle with three inches of black spiral locked and loaded in its precision-tooled channel was like staring down a missile silo. Which would be worse, I wondered, to close my eyes and let him puncture the lid, too, or watch it come and have that be the last thing I ever saw with that eye?

Manu banshee-hollered again. I braced for the plunge. Told myself to be a man. But the stab didn't come. Instead, he let it go and the whole Zappit fell over onto my face and dropped to my lap. He released my head and twisted off me, turning to look at something behind him.

"Mother *fuck*," he cried.

"Stand away," said the old lady.

I looked around Manu to find Amanda St. Hillaire in her bathrobe, holding her sword on him. She had opened a deep gash in his shoulder. Blood was dripping off his fingertips and staining the rug beside his shoe.

"I heard the screams, Mr. Hardwick, and I—Come no closer," she said when he shifted his weight.

Amanda, so grey and lined, was twenty again. Her eyes defiant, her chin thrust out, she dared him to make a move. But I knew this killer was probably seconds from feeding her her own sword.

Slowly, quietly, I got my hand on the Zappit. I made a fist around the handle, squeezing hard. Then, with all I could bring, I thrust forward, punching him in the back. I don't know if the safety rod or the screw punctured him, but he cried out, something in dialect, and whirled to me. As soon as he did, Amanda chopped at his leg, swinging for the bleachers. The sword tore through his pants into his thigh. The big man went down on one knee.

"Stab him, Amanda. Now. Don't chop, stab."

She struck a fencer's pose, elegantly curling her left arm behind her, and made a forward lunge at his chest. Manu's instincts were too good, and he was still alert. He swatted the flat of the saber aside with one arm, and shoved Amanda against an empty bookcase with the other.

There was an eerie beat of quiet before he struggled heavily to his feet. Blood trickled down his arm and, from where his pants were laid open at the thigh, a dark stain reached to his cuff. When he turned to face me, I had the sword in my hand.

Both my feet and one arm were still lashed to the chair, but I could hurt him and he knew it. When Amanda moaned and sat up on the floor, he took a step to her.

"Leave her alone," I said, which didn't stop him. "She's not in this."

"She in it now."

I calculated the odds of throwing the sword, maybe spearing him with it. He stopped in his tracks and cocked an ear. Then, he walked right past her. Limping, he trotted into the kitchen. I heard the back door open and bang against the wall.

Seconds later, I knew what Manu heard: the low engine roar distinct to police cars. Then the sizzle of tires on asphalt. Car doors opening. Multiple brakes squeaking. Squelches and flatline voices from a scanner. Red and blue lights strobed through the windows. And footsteps. Lots of running footsteps.

I didn't wait.

"In here," I yelled. "It's all clear, he ran out back to the canyon. Come on in."

Cops appeared in every doorway I had. Guns drawn. Tense for anything. I dropped the sword.

"Help the lady," I said.

I described the Samoan. Gave his name. Told them which way he left. The copter searchlight was already working the thick chaparral of the canyon, but I knew they'd never find him.

Amanda must have gotten my bedspread because she covered me with it while they cut me from the chair. I thanked her for calling the police and for her courage. "You're still hell with that sword, you know, Miss St. Hillaire?"

"So now I have your confidence. Moments ago you were ordering me to stab with a saber." She turned to the uniforms, certain they would share her sense of umbrage. "Stab. With a saber?"

I scanned the debris of my house, desperate for my phone, feeling every bit the earthquake victim. One of the cops came up with it. I punched redial and explained to Amanda.

"He might be after Meddy next. I've got to—"

Voice mail.

"Meddy, it's me. The Samoan was just here. Bad stuff. Whenever you get this call. Don't come back here, not yet. And just to be on the safe side, if you're in the hotel call security and don't open your door for—"

I closed the phone and lost balance. Someone, one of the cops, steadied me.

"Get him a chair," he said.

Back in that chair. Feeble. Wasted by a sick certainty. A Brady Bunch grouping of faces floating before me, asking if I was OK, telling me EMS is pulling up now. I heard the siren, I think.

Amanda St. Hillaire, who saved my life that night, knelt before me and asked, "What is it?"

My eyes fell to the floor. To the place where her saber had laid open Manu's trousers pocket. Resting among two of the hundred dollar bills from my Ruffy cache lay a blood-stained, champagne pink ribbon.

# CHAPTER THIRTY-NINE

Loot was waiting for me outside the ER when I got there in the black and white. Whether it was experience or compassion or both, he didn't make me wait for the headline. He was still opening the door of the patrol car for me when he came with it. "She's in bad shape, but she's alive."

"How bad?" I asked in a voice I barely recognized.

"She's still in surgery. Let's see when she comes out."

He turned away to lead me to the door; the quick back he showed me said more than the face he was hiding.

The next few hours were a blur I'll be sorting out in my nightmares. I do remember attaching myself to Loot like a pilot fish. Following him into the ER. Passing gurneys and wheelchairs of moaners and stoics. Hearing a nurse telling us Meddy's surgery was still going on and saying that cut on my cheek needed closing. Letting a kid doc stitch my face while Loot leaned against the poster of the human skeleton, hands in pockets, filling me in on what happened to Meddy.

A 911 caller saw a Mercedes get rear-ended on Lincoln Boulevard in Santa Monica about 1:30. Recognized Meddy from TV when she got out to inspect her bumper, then watched her speed away when the "big Hawaiian dude" who hit her got out of his pickup. The pickup's hot pursuit is what prompted the witness to call 911. That would have been around when Meddy tried to call me and got cut off.

By the time the Sheriff's chopper spotted a car nose-down in Ballona Creek near the Marina, Meddy had long before been beaten and abandoned. Her attacker was miles away in Laurel Canyon, forcing my front door.

Ten points to Loot for self-restraint. The cop in him wanted to hand me my ass for thrashing around the Bonnie Quinn deal after he told me to lay off. I could taste it. But the lieutenant knew what I'd been through and was still enduring, so he made his point with silent disapproval. If things improved, then he'd drop the anvil.

He let me join the circle in the hallway when the surgeon who wore Meddy's blood on his scrubs briefed the detectives on her condition. They were listing her critical and the next twenty-four hours would be crucial. They successfully mended her internal injuries but there was trauma to her cerebral cortex which had put her in a coma. At no point was she conscious or coherent. She had said nothing, mumbled nothing. With the coma, no way for an interview or statement, so don't bother to ask.

A fidgety sergeant who snapped his chewing gum wanted to know if she'd been sexually assaulted and I felt an arm drape my shoulders. Loot's. The doctor said no, adding it was his belief the worst of her injuries weren't associated with the car crash. There was blunt trauma to the back of her head that was more consistent with being hit from behind, perhaps while running or lying on the ground.

"I'll leave it to your experts to reconstruct the crash," the surgeon said. "But I'd be surprised if she was even conscious when that car went over the embankment."

Another kindness from Loot: he got me into ICU. Estranged Former Lover doesn't legally qualify as kin, so, thanks to him, I got five tortured minutes to watch science help her breathe and circulate bagged nutrients in the dusky room before we were both asked to leave.

I felt like the living dead and Loot tried to convince me there was no use waiting at the hospital. He called over some uniforms to drive me home, but I waved them off.

"Even if there's nothing I can do, I can't bring myself to bail. Not in the first hours." I gave him a look of emphasis. "You know."

He did. These hours were Meddy's fatal window and to press the point with me would mean one of us would have to say that out loud and neither of us would tempt that sort of karma.

"Obviously, the guy was tailing you two. We'll have to get your formal statement later," he told me, "but we know who we're looking for, and we are going to get that sonofabitch."

"And then you get the sonofabitch who sent the sonofabitch, right?"

"If we can establish he was sent in the first place, count on it."

"Loot, come on. Manu told me himself he was after Bonnie Quinn's diary. What more do you need?"

"Something like a name. And proof would be good. Courts are funny that way."

"Elliot Pratt has done everything but propose marriage to me to find that diary. He's so fucking paranoid that I've already got it and I'll give it to somebody else he sent Mongo after both of us."

"Prove it."

"Jesus, look what happened tonight. How can you not see somebody's taking some mighty desperate measures to grab a smoking gun? And who has the most to lose? And why?"

"We'll get the Samoan. Then we'll know why."

"Can you look me in the eye and say Bonnie Quinn wasn't murdered? Even now?"

"My gut? I'm with you. But you know I need more. This is LA, not Guantanamo. But hear this." Loot swaggered inside his designer suit and got some street in his voice. "Man goes after Meredith Benson like that, I'm going to bring the party to him. Hard."

"Loot?"

"Yeah?"

"Man went after me, too."

He paused and smiled the slightest smile. "Oh, right. Now I'm good and mad." And then he left me to go outside and deal with the night beat reporters who were gathering.

I shared the waiting room with a snoring nun and the television. There was no remote control, so it was Ron Popeil and his miracle carving knives until I cashed out. I fought to stay awake, but by the time Ron's uncle (or was it his cousin in that chef's hat?) demonstrated the thin turkey slices falling off the bone "like butter," I had joined the snoring nun.

The TV sound was off and the sister was gone when I woke up, but I found a holy card on the cushion beside me. St. Jude. It said on the back, *Answering prayers for the impossible.* Twenty-four hours a day or you don't pay, I thought. Nice, Hardwick. Way to say thanks to the Big Man for sending Amanda in with the sword.

My throat clenched when I looked up at the muted TV and saw Meddy's file photo keyed behind the morning anchor. I stood up to read the fine print underneath, praying I wouldn't see two dates separated by a hyphen. It said *critical condition.* I fanned the air with the holy card then pocketed it.

What was this? Something else in that pocket. I pulled it out. The cocktail napkin from the shoebox. I had stuffed it in my khakis at the Huntsman's Den after Meddy tied the bow on the letters. I folded the napkin and put it in my wallet.

"Mr. Hardwick?"

The voice filled the room. Warm, deep, enveloping. I turned to the doorway. Not exactly St. Jude, but perhaps someone on speaking terms. Otis Grove stepped toward me, incongruous in his tuxedo. His face a basset hound's worth of worry and sleeplessness. "This is all just horrible," he said, shaking my hand in both of his. "One horrible thing following another. Sit, please." As we settled in, he continued. "Iå got the news on my jet flying back from D.C. The doctors briefed me en route. They tell me she is still in a very bad way."

I nodded.

"You and Meredith have a special bond?"

"We have . . . history."

He nodded. "Which is why I want to assure you that whatever Meredith needs, she shall have it. The best specialists, anywhere in the world. We'll fly them in, or I will fly her there."

"That's very generous. I only hope . . .You know."

"We all hope. Some of us pray." He hung his head and squinted his eyes for what seemed like a very long time, then looked up as if he had merely blinked. "This nasty business seems to know no end."

"Try living it."

"Pardon my manners. How are you feeling?"

"Been better."

I watched him play with one of the loose ends of his dangling bow tie, noting he was a man who tied his own. Of course.

"The police said it was that, what, Samoan you told me about?" I nodded again. "Little solace knowing you were right about him. Did he get the diary from you?"

"I don't have it to get."

"And what about the letters you found. Did you learn anything from them?"

"I haven't read them."

"Really," he said with no attempt to mask his skepticism. "With your fanatical curiosity? You mean to tell me you had that shoebox of letters and didn't take a peek at just one of them?"

Otis Grove fixed me with a look, a Spaghetti Western stare-down. All we needed was the harmonica and the whip crack.

"Meddy didn't think we should, so I never got a chance to read them," I said, and shifted gears. "I notice Elliot Pratt is not on sick watch with you."

"It looks bad for Elliot, but don't run away with the bit in your mouth."

"Too late."

"I'm a believer in people, but eventually they disappoint you in some fashion, hopefully small." He looked up from his shoes. "We are all quite human."

"Your man lied to you."

"I've reflected on that. Elliot's lie may have been a white one in his zeal to save the show. Maybe he figured once he had my OK there would be some other way to relieve himself of his Bonnie Quinn encumbrance."

"I know one way."

Otis Grove stood. "There comes a time to let things go, Mr. Hardwick."

"This isn't one of them."

I might have sounded more convincing if I hadn't moaned when I hauled myself up to face him.

"I disagree."

So. The old mentor was going to circle the corporate wagons around his protégé after all.

"I thought you wanted me to find the truth, no matter what."

"I meant no matter what the truth was. Not no matter who got hurt in the process. There have been too many deaths."

"Murders. And Elliot Pratt is hip deep."

He hooked his forefinger and rested it on his upper lip. Reflective. A wealthy man cloaked in the weight of a Shakespearean patriarch.

"In my life, Mr. Hardwick, I have a path I walk, or try to. Now, I know you are not a religious man, so I won't try to minister to you. But regardless of your good motive, isn't there any part of you that sees the destruction you have sewn?"

First Meddy, now him. This was like a time-release intervention.

"Even if you don't," he continued, "I do. I feel that by engaging you I have visited harm to innocents. This can stop. It all needs to stop. After your ordeal, you, of all people should know that."

"I've had better nights."

"I'll still pay you. Your full fee as if you had found a diary."

"Mr. Grove, you know me well enough to know the fee's not my concern." I side nodded to ICU. "Especially not now."

"Of course not." He waved his hand as if clearing the board of the pawns. "Continue, then. Carefully, please. Would you like protection? I have excellent security."

"Yes. And good swimmers, too."

The billionaire shook my hand in both of his again and held on, gently.

"I'll pray you change your mind."

He let go and strode out.

# CHAPTER FORTY

**M**aybe I was too fried to drive, but after I passed on Loot's offer to hitch an LAPD ride home, he had my car dropped at the hospital and there I was behind the wheel, rodeo sore and squinting into the glare of the 405 morning rush from the Marina. Hardwick, the effing Energizer Bunny. I keep going and going and—

Horns. I swerved back into my lane in a forest of middle fingers. One of the drivers, a mid-level drone with a joke set of hair plugs, asserted his manhood by swerving his Saab back at me before he chucked me the bone.

I jerked over and pulled an inch from his Swedish engineered ass, giving him the full horn treatment. Fuckwad. How fun would it be to watch his pencil dick shrink when I pulled beside him and he got a good look at me? But when I checked my rearview for the lane switch, I got a good look at myself. That was enough.

I laid off my horn and pulled over, hyperventilating, in the break-down lane. If ever there was an aptly named space. I forearm-slammed the passenger seat and sunk into my headrest to quiet the storm. Maybe I was there ten minutes, fifteen, who knows? But my heart slowed, my breathing evened out, and I decided bean counters in Saabs weren't the problem.

Elliot Pratt's office stonewalled me. First call, his assistant actually said, "Actually, he wasn't available." Second call, she fed me voice mail. If you think you're being dodged, press 2 or hold for an operator. I contemplated a swing to his dude ranch above the sea, but I had lit up the radar and he would either be hunkered behind his overwrought iron or long gone by the time I got there.

I checked my watch. Just after nine. I smiled and threw myself in gear, busting north to Wilshire. This time, I didn't mind the horns or the fingers. In fact, I waved.

Simple advice for assholes who don't like to be found by assholes like me: Break up those habits. Nine-thirty on a weekday morning, and there he was. Monte Arnett, gut-to-tablecloth for his expense account breakfast at the W in Westwood.

The hostess didn't seem to care that I looked like I'd jumped from a moving freight car. I waved off her menus and made for his table. His usual. In the corner, cheeks-deep in red leather where he could survey all the moguls and starter moguls who had adopted the W. Monte didn't see me coming. He was too focused on his guest, Bonnie Quinn's former head writer.

A waiter placed a fresh Bloody Mary down in front of Zack. When the waiter removed the empty and left, I was in his place.

"Nothing kicks off a workday at the comedy factory like a couple of cocktails, eh, fellas?"

Monte craned for the hostess. Zack just goofed. Picked up his drink and played his tiny red straw like he was Kenny G but wishing he was Conan O.

"Uh, this is a private meeting, Hardwick." Monte, so full of false hope.

"You bet it is," I said.

Zack half rose in his chair. "No, sit, Zack. Hardwick's leaving."

"Zack-meister. The trades said you ankled out of conscience."

"I quit, all right. For about five minutes. Monte held a gun to my wallet." Zack sure enjoyed his own jokes. "Anyway, we're doing notes." He indicated the pair of *Thanks for Sharing* scripts on the table. "Retooling, post-bitch."

"This what you do, Mont-ster? Your franchise anchorwoman's in a coma, and you sit down to table drafts and eggs Benedict like it's just another day in paradise?"

"That's a shitty thing to say, man. Even from you. We are all shocked and saddened by what happened to Meredith. It's a tragedy."

"You make her sound like a victim of random violence. She was fucking cowboyed."

I slammed my hand down and bounced silverware. Do I need to say that all conversation at surrounding tables that hadn't already done so ground to a halt? I didn't care, and that bothered the Mont-ster more than anything. He side-glanced the other power brunchers.

"Zack. Later."

"'Scuse me," said the writer as he ankled out of fear.

"Why don't you sit?" he said in a library whisper. Role modeling tone for me. "You look like you had a helluva night yourself. Sit?"

I did. Funny, but nobody tried to give me a menu.

"That looks like a bad cut."

"It's nothing." I touched the gauze on my cheek, which was still numb. "I'm not the one in the coma."

"She'll make it. She's a fighter."

"Sure, if it's a fair one. You ever cross paths with a big Samoan?" I tossed the mug shot to him. "Name's Manu."

"Why would I know this guy?"

"I don't know. He works crew. Or maybe Sally Struthers shamed you into sponsoring him for just fifty cents a day."

"Get this the fuck off my breakfast." He flipped the picture back to me.

"Not like you're defensive or anything."

"I'm not defens—Jesus, Hardwick, you roll in here looking like you just got voted off the island and you're looking for a dog to kick. How did I get so lucky?"

"Because whenever something starts to smell bad about this, I look up and there you are on the edge of the circle. Bonnie Quinn, Dr. Pizzy. . . . But I'm asking about the Samoan because since you do all the below the line hiring and firing, I'd be stupid not to."

"Can we move on, or do you want to blame me for global warming while you're at it?"

It was all I could do not to scald his face with his latte and smash the blisters with my boot heel. But a cooler head prevailed. This time. I counted three and chose a slyer angle.

"You're going to get rhino-boned, you know that, don't you?"

Monte's brows pinched a vertical crease above his nose. "What do you mean by that?"

Defensive, or dumb? Or just playing dumb?

I picked up Zack's abandoned Bloody Mary and took a long pull. "It's so obvious. Are you going to make me say it? How Elliot has you do all the heavy lifting and he takes the bows."

The production coordinator waved a dismissive hand. "Shit. That's the job-D, man."

"Yeah, but how far does it go?"

"For me? I breathe this job, you know that."

I leaned closer, and spoke like the friend I wasn't.

"It's like this. You cover for the man professionally. Sets get built, shows get made, episodes get delivered on time, budgets get met or fudged, problems get addressed or made to disappear quietly. . . . Sure. All in the D."

"I just said that."

"But when you cover for him outside the job, maybe the line blurs between the professional and the personal, and the areas get a little more 'grey.'"

I actually made air quotes around the color.

"Yeah?" he said with no affect. Monte. Soldier all the way. Giving up nothing in service to his boss. So I tried to drive the wedge.

"You can play the solidarity brother all you want, Monte. But I know what I see. Like that dustup you and El were having the other night when Meddy and I walked in on you."

"That's just how we work. You never heard how old couples bicker? That's us. He got hot over the budget is all."

"Come on, what was it, Monte? Why was Elliot so rattled? You call him on the Dr. Pizzy suicide?" Wishing I had saved my air quotes for that.

"You keep fishing, Hardwick, but I ain't bitin'." He sipped his latte and didn't like the way it tasted.

"I know you're wired to make your boss look good. But you've got to know guys like Elliot don't share. Not credit and especially not blame. When this thing blows up—and it will—do you think Elliot Pratt's going to raise his hand and say 'My bad'? Or is he going to look for some big ol' shoulders to take the weight?"

"This a game of divide and conquer? You think I'm too dense to see what you're working?"

Too easy. I made another three-count to let the urge to answer evaporate. "No, I'm just giving you the heads-up courtesy so you won't be the fall guy."

"Don't you worry about me."

"Whatever you say. But your shot at saving your own ass by not covering Elliot's may be a limited-time offer. I wouldn't wait until it expires."

"You crack me up, you know that, Hardwick?"

"How so?"

"Look at you." He pointed to my bandaged cheek. "Whatever you were into, look what you brought down on yourself. And look what you brought down on Meddy. Lecture me again about sharing the weight."

Then he laughed.

Thunder cracked in my head. A tree getting split in the backyard. I bolted up, double-fisting my side of the tablecloth. The fat fuck didn't know what to try to grab first. It was comical to watch him try to push back hollandaise and herbed potatoes and tomato juice and espresso and a vase of tulips all rolling at him at once.

"Use The Force, Monte," I whispered. "Use The Force."

He gave up, and his Nat Nast Blues Tour shirt became a canvas painted by his breakfast. As he looked at me in disbelief, I walked away, replaying his dig about me bringing this on Meddy. The only thing that kept me from taking his head off was I knew he was right.

The ICU nurse knew who I was when I called. She sounded unhurried and treated me with some welcome warmth. Whether that was her caring way or because Loot had cleared me for access, I was grateful for the kindness. I would have been more grateful to hear that Meddy was sitting up eating broth amid some miraculous recovery, but her status had not changed. *Maybe that was cause enough for celebration,* I thought when the nurse hung up, and I nosed onto Sunset Boulevard.

That's when I spotted the tail.

# CHAPTER FORTY-ONE

By survival habit, I drive in my mirrors as much as my windshield. But I was especially vigilant that morning. Part of my Ruffy-free diet program.

The Mustang was new and muscular. Graphite. Low to the ground with custom rims. Pent up. It caught my eye when it busted the red eastbound at Stone Canyon to keep me on a leash through Beverly Hills. The windows were shaded to match the car, but I made out two men. The driver was dark-skinned, the passenger white.

The driver knew enough about what he was doing to hold me at his preferred distance. When I fell back to try to make out faces, he did, too. When I punched it, he kept pace. So far, his game. I was careful not to be blatant. No sense tipping I was onto them yet. Shaking a tail is one part experience, one part balls, and one part leap of faith. You play the traffic on the fly and never, never mow down innocent folks. See? I have a code.

Crescent Heights was coming up fast. For me, a left off Sunset would take me home up Laurel. On open roads, I could lose that Mustang in the winding canyons. But it was one tight lane each way. A single ounce of traffic and I'd be stopped dead. No escape without a llama.

A rapid 180 ahead: driveways, buses, traffic, pedestrians, signals, flashing walk signs, a beer delivery truck making a left. Fast mirror check. I suicide-spun my wheel. Screeched right, crossing two lanes. Trailing blue tire smoke. My cut was perfect. Right across the Metro bus loading riders at the curb. I hit the strip mall driveway fast. The bounce jammed my head on the roof liner. I struggled for control, got it, and made a beeline across the empty lot to the exit driveway feeding back to Crescent Heights. I skidded to a stop to see where my tail was.

The MTA bus was just clearing the driveway. The Mustang broke through its exhaust. Coming on. It took the same bounce I did. Settled, and bore down on me.

I waited, waited. . . .

The Coors truck I had pinged waiting in the left bay on Sunset made its turn and lumbered my way. As the driver ground through the low gears, I mirror checked the Mustang. Ripping closer. The truck: short yards and closing.

I pounded horn. Floored it. Shot across the truck's front bumper. Close enough to lick the headlight. I fishtailed onto Crescent Heights. The startled trucker hit the brakes, blocking the Mustang in the driveway. I gunned it to the corner and hauled down Sunset.

There was still no sign of the chase car when I rolled up to Fairfax, a few blocks east. I ignored the red light, threaded the needle between an oncoming gardener's pickup and a Bentley (LA), and hooked a left up Fairfax. At Selma, I cut another sharp left into the neighborhood of prewar residentials wedged between spearmint-green stucco apartments. Still no pursuit.

I had cruised a big circle that would dump me back out onto Laurel, which was fine, just not so soon. I passed a house with an overgrown hedge and an empty drive. Slammed the brakes. Popped into reverse and backed deep into the driveway. I sat there, hidden from the street, making a mental note to pay my car insurance.

A screen door wheezed and clacked shut. In my side mirror, an old fossil in madras jackass shorts and a KHJ Boss Radio tee was bending to see who I was and what I was doing in his driveway. He had a relic Eighties cordless with one of those big aerials and was calling the police while a teenage boy in desert cammies brought him a pump action Riot-20.

Back out on Selma Avenue, idling. I considered finding another blind to hunker down in, but I was too irritable. The only sleep I'd had was on the hospital couch. And do I need to mention I'd also been tortured and abused and felt every bit of it? Balls I'd wait. I slapped it in drive.

A few blocks up from Sunset, past the turn to Mt. Olympus, there's a little spur that forks off to the right and parallels the rise of Laurel Canyon for about a half mile before it merges back onto the main road. It's for canyon locals to circumvent the commuter molasses, and I am righteously disdainful of the passholes who take it as a shortcut to network pitches or run-throughs in the Valley.

Strictly as precaution, I became a passhole. The dirt bank dotted by trees and occasional wild shrubs between little Laurel and big Laurel provided good cover as I crept my way up the canyon. And when I saw what was ahead of me as I approached the merge, who felt like the smartest passhole in the world?

Where the roads rejoin, the gray Mustang purred in the Laurel Canyon Market parking lot. It was tucked behind a delivery van, positioned for surveillance on the big road. The fuckers had lost me, but they knew where to wait. This meant I had to deal.

I pulled off on the shoulder twenty yards behind them and got out with my homage to Jack Nicholson: a nine-iron persuader I keep on the floor of the back seat. Traffic was at a crawl up to the merge. I found cover walking behind a Range Rover with an ICM parking sticker. To the agent, I must have looked like I had the worst lie in golf.

When the Rover edged even with the rear of the market, I jogged in a low crouch behind the Mustang and knelt on one knee at the bumper. I gophered up for a fast look, but the back window was blacked out same as the sides.

Feeling every bit like the dog who had caught the car he was chasing and didn't know what to do with it, I looked at the nine-iron in my hand. I decided in my next quiet moment to revisit my stance against carrying firearms. There were two of them, one of me, and, unless they were carrying sand wedges, I was probably outgunned.

Options: I could drive back down the canyon and just disappear—until they found me again. Or I could let the air out of a tire so they couldn't follow—until they found me again. Notice a theme developing? I sniffed the air for Manu, but all I got was tailpipe. I thought of my night. I thought of Meddy. And then, I didn't think.

I duckwalked to the driver's door. Put my right hand on the handle and, with my left, whipped up the head of that Titleist. The window shattered into pebbles. A slot machine payout of safety glass rained down. Startled shouts inside the car.

Up on the balls of my feet, yanking that door handle. Choking up on the iron for close work in the front seat. I stayed behind the driver so he had to twist to get me. Knew he'd be unbelted if he was on the hunt. Grabbed him in a choke hold with my free arm. He clawed at my forearm using both hands, meaning no gun to deal with from this one.

I ripped him from the car and dropped him face down on the pavement. Got my knee in his spine. Pulled his head back by the hair as I pinned him, fucking with his skills. I checked the ground for a spilled gun, saw none, then looked up to check on his partner. He was coming slow around the back of the car, holding an army issue forty-five.

"Shit," I observed.

"Hardwick?"

"Pinkman?"

"Dammit all, Hardwick, let go. You're killing my neck." I released the man on the ground. Dellroy Means rolled over on his back, panting. "Mother fuck."

"Pinkman. Think you can put that thing up before you shoot somebody?"

"Right. Sorry."

The old man engaged the safety and tucked the weapon into his William Frawley waistband. He made a ceremony of fluffing his suit coat to conceal it, but the brown plaid was plenty camouflage.

Dellroy stuck out a hand for a boost. "Little help?"

He didn't get it. "Tell me what the hell you geniuses are doing, Lojacking me like this."

"'Lojacking.' Shit, I told you, Pink. We should know better than to do his ass a favor."

"A favor?"

Pinkman nodded. Dellroy sat himself up. "Aw, man . . . My new car. Hardwick, that car's under three hundred miles and look what you did to my window."

"What kind of favor?"

Pinkman said, "When we heard about Meddy and then what happened to you, we thought you could use a little coverage."

"Do you know how loud I had to yell at the insurance company to get me that car?" Dellroy, still pissed.

"Jesus, you two. Do you see what happened? What almost happened? What the fuck were you thinking?"

Dellroy plucked gravel out of his elbow. "You're welcome."

I looked over the pair. An old widower who loaded up his Korean War sidearm and had to be picked up for his mission in a carpool. And Dellroy Means, the struggling ex-CPA. Seeing them chastened by defeat made me soften.

"It's not that I don't appreciate the gesture, but did you guys ever think it might be a sound idea to ask me first?"

"Oh, we thought about it."

"We did."

"But we could never picture you saying you needed help."

"Pinkman's right. You are one stubborn and prideful dickhead," said Dellroy as I hoisted him to his feet. "So we took it on ourselves to watch your back."

I smiled. "Good job, men."

Minutes later, in my driveway, I braked in front of Amanda's house and waved the Mustang up. Dellroy pulled beside me and I told them to wait in my cottage.

"Is the door open?" Pinkman asked.

"Permanently. Until I can call a locksmith."

A policewoman answered Amanda's door. Gotta love Loot. He cleared the OT for the old actress to have company for the day under the category of protection. Both would do her good. The uniform told me Amanda was fine but was still sleeping it all off. I kicked myself for not thinking of covering this base myself and made up my mind the starlet who saved my life would have care, meals, and a captive audience to watch her old movies with her for as long as she needed.

Back in my cottage, Pinkman and Dellroy stood ankle deep in the wreckage of the living room, staring at me saucer-eyed. In daylight, my place had lost the surreal menace of the previous night. It was merely a FEMA disaster zone the morning after the force five hurricane. I threaded my way over to them through my life's debris, thinking all that was missing was the back-slap from the president before he got back on Marine One to rack up more photo ops.

The three of us stood there, glazed and speechless.

Finally, I said, "Sorry for not tidying up."

"Is that blood?" said Dellroy.

"Yeah. Rug's shot."

"No, I meant there at the wall. Near the dent in the plaster."

"Think so. Not sure whose."

"How's the star doing?" Pinkman wanted to know. I filled him in, but he kept on it. "She's going to be OK, though, right?"

"Pretty sure. Tell you what, though. You still have the number of that visiting nurse service?"

"The one I had for my Esther during chemo?"

"They were good."

"I thought I gave you that number once. What was that for?"

I had hired the private nurse for Amanda when she had her hip done, but that favor was my little secret. I even had the nurse tell her it came with her insurance. I dodged Pinkman's question and gestured at the desk.

"The number's somewhere in all this mess. I want someone to sit with Amanda for a few days after the police bail."

"The number's in my book at home, but I could look it up. Where's your Yellow Pages?"

Dellroy let out a cackle. "'Where's your Yellow Pages,' the man asks. Pinkie, try in the fireplace with the fine china and the DVDs."

I didn't have enough juice left in the tank to dissuade my self-deputized posse from babysitting me. I figured I owed Dellroy the satisfaction after exploding his car window like that, anyway. So I said OK, as long as Pinkman promised to keep his army souvenir tucked in.

One more Meddy check at intensive care with Nurse Ruiz (no change), and I made a drunk's stagger to bed, still wearing clothes, shoes, cell phone, the works. When my head hit the pillow, the barbed wire wrapping my brain poked the back of my eyes. Maybe I moaned. If I did, I wasn't around to hear it.

It was the bacon that roused me. The aroma of so many campfires and lazy Sundays wafted in and found me, beckoning with a smoky finger. I drifted on the scent. Then my heart klonged. I bolted up. How long had I been out? It couldn't be morning. My watch said seven—PM.

"What do you two think you're doing?" I said from the hallway.

"Hey, Pinkman, look who's up now that the work's all done."

My cottage, my FEMA site, was the after picture in one of those tearjerker reality shows. In the eight-and-change hours I'd been down, Dellroy and Pinkman had transformed it into a miracle of order. The only things left to me were the blood stains and the broken furniture.

"We had to sort of guess where everything went," Pinkman said when we sat down to his BLTs and coffee. "As many times as you've had me over here, I couldn't remember your exact layout."

"Pinkman. I've never had you over here."

"My point," said the old man. Toasting me with his mug, the shit. "So if you can't find something—"

"—then fuck yourself, you antisocial hermit," said Dellroy.

They both thought that was pretty rich, and, as they slapped fives and snorted, I looked around the room again, then at these two yahoos who'd taken it on themselves to step up to the plate for me.

"Uh-oh, check him out. Hardwick's vibin' the *feng shui*." Dellroy laughed again and tore into his sandwich.

"I don't know what to say, you guys, except I feel weird about you doing all this for me."

Pinkman said, "It's not a sign of weakness to accept help."

"It's not that."

Dellroy weighed in. "I know. Feels weird, sort of like you don't deserve it weird?"

"No. It's, well . . . The thing that makes this so hard is, now that you've done this, I'm going to feel extra-special bad when one of you needs a favor. Because you dicks are on your own." My turn to laugh. "*Feng shui* that."

We took shots at each other like that through the meal. Macho ass-holes eschewing direct affection. So, instead, we do for each other.

I let it be said with a simple thank you, eye-to-eye. And in it, they knew what I knew. I would have their backs. Wherever, whenever. Some things in life are elegant like that. But you voice it, you ruin it.

I hit my limit, though, walking to my car. They followed me like a Woody Allen chain gang. I stopped in the middle of the lawn.

"Guys. I'm going to the hospital for visiting hours. I don't need bodyguards."

Dellroy shook his head. "Don't be a fool. What if he comes at you again? What you gonna do then?"

"Worry about you two getting the snot kicked out of you. Or worse, getting shot by Pinkman doing a fast draw. Now that would piss me off. If you want to be useful, hang here and keep an eye on Amanda's house."

"I've been thinking about her," said Pinkman, a little too loud. Dellroy and I traded looks, wondering where this was going. "If she needs a nurse, that's one thing. But if it's some heat, in case Island Izzy wants some revenge, I think she'll be better off with me than some RN."

Dellroy turned away so Pinkman couldn't see his amusement. We both drew the same *Sunset Boulevard* picture of the old widower pro-tecting his silver screen damsel. Dellroy couldn't hold back, though.

"You got some heat for the starlet, Pinkman?"

"Shut up. It makes perfect sense. If Hardwick's kicking me loose, why not cover her for a few days in case the Samoan wants payback? Besides, I can be a hop and a skip from his cottage."

"Hot dog. Like neighbors," I said.

But it wasn't the worst idea. I wanted Amanda to feel secure. And I knew she would love a captive companion to guide through her old films day and night.

# CHAPTER FORTY-TWO

An hour later, I dropped Dellroy Means at LAX for the red-eye, but he didn't go quietly. Maybe that's something to like about him.

"You're not giving me crap to work with, Hardwick."

I tapped the photocopy on his lap of the cocktail napkin from Bonnie Quinn's shoebox. "You've got as much as I do right there. Dazzle me."

"Shit . . ." He snorted, amused, and looked at the traffic. "You haven't even told me what you want."

"Whatever you find out, that's what. Was she there and when? What she was doing there? By my calculation this isn't the sort of club where you do stand-up unless you're William F. Buckley."

"Hey, hey, not so close." Dellroy nodded toward the Ryder truck in front of us. "I said you could drive me to the airport in my car, not depreciate it further."

"When you get back from Boston, it will be good as new."

"Speak up. I can't hear you over all the wind blowing in my broken window."

"Bite me."

"Funny man. Now, listen to me. I want you to take this to the Ford dealership. Don't you cut corners replacing my glass at one of your Pacoima chop shops."

"Can you make out that phone number? I pushed the tone when I made the copy."

"Darkened it up, just like OJ on the magazine cover."

"Just tell me if you can read it."

"The 617 number here? Relax yourself."

"I get it as a disconnect. See if you can find out who had it before."

"How'm I supposed to do that?"

"You packed your old CPA suit, right? Put it on. Feel the inspiration."

"Feel the nausea." He turned to me, grinning. "Truth? I'm kind of pumped."

"Liking the honest detective work?"

"Fuck that. I'm flying first class. Room at the Lenox. Luxury rent-a-car."

"Full size," I said. "You bump up, it's your nickel."

"Twelve years on that ass bite CPA gig and they never let me travel like this. Send me in for an audit, it was always No-Name Air and Bedbug Inn."

I pulled his Mustang over to the white curb. "Don't thank me, thank Otis Grove. Or Elliot Pratt. They don't know it, but it's their money."

"Hardwick, you are showing us all how it's done." He shook my hand. "You should go to Boston yourself."

"I would, except . . . you know."

"I'm saying prayers for her, man."

"Do."


Visiting hours were still on at the hospital. I sat silent vigil with Meddy, trying amid the clicking and beeping and whooshing of her lifelines to explain myself. To her. To myself. As if I was going to untangle that knotted basket of Christmas tree lights in the ten minutes they gave me in there.

I fended off the urge to speak to her. Too much like soap opera treacle or chick flick melodrama. What would I say, anyway? I'm sorry for getting you into this? I was. I'm sorry we split? I was. I'd trade places in a second? I would.

The ventilator kept its rhythm. The beeps held their count. What if I did talk to her, what would I say? *We came so close, Meds. Get through this. I'd do anything for us to be together again.* I didn't say it but came close. I knew her well enough to know her response. *Show me,* she'd say. Meddy was never one for chick flick melodrama, either.

I stopped at the nurses's station and found Pilar Ruiz writing a new patient's name on the white board. When I introduced myself, she smiled and thrust a slender hand across the counter. She vibed experience. In it for what she could give. Smile lines at the corners of her eyes. She waved off my thanks for the care she was giving Meddy and for answering my relentless calls. She asked how I was feeling.

All I could muster was a shrug and a half look to Meddy's window behind me. "How do you think she's doing?"

"Her best," said the nurse. "So we must do ours, too, right?"

"I have a feeling you are."

"Call me often. To make sure I am."

Even angels get a meal break. Pilar Ruiz was enjoying hers when I arrived back at ICU first thing the next morning. Maybe it was the low ceiling of sky cloaking the west side, but I swear her absence dimmed the whole floor.

Meddy looked smaller to me. Her vitals were constant, but there was a settlement I sensed and didn't like. When I asked the shift nurse how she was doing, she said I would have to ask the doctor for that kind of information, and I resolved to bring Nurse Ruiz some flowers when she got back.

I camped there the whole day. Between ten-minute stints in Meddy's room, which Pilar Ruiz allowed me to stretch to twenty by pretending not to notice, I roughed myself up under a blanket of guilt for drawing Meddy into the whole mess in the first place. Otis Grove may have hit it dead on: being right wasn't worth the body count.

In the waiting area, I tried to watch one of the afternoon judge shows on the ceiling TV until somebody's family came in and formed a prayer circle by the window. Try to concentrate during all that on a divorcee seeking justice from the two-timing boyfriend-landlord who stole her parakeet. When Dellroy called from Boston, I ducked into the men's room for a break and an illicit cell phone call.

"I'm missing some prime photo ops, Hardwick. That UEN rollout is ducks in a barrel. Did you see *Rough Cut*? See the stars they're trotting out for the press junket?"

"Dellroy, you're supposed to be hitting the bricks. I didn't send you there to sit in the hotel and watch TV." Dellroy's laugh was infectious, even over the phone and I found myself smiling. "What?"

"You need to ice down that mode of yours H-man, else you'll have me suspect you are hiding some closet colonialism on your person."

"And why would you suspect that?"

"By acting like you sent some shiftless brother man on an expense-paid trip and alls he can do is order up room cervix fo' cocktails and punnani while he watch de TV."

"Nothing closet about it. That's exactly what I suspect."

His shock laugh got us both going.

Then he said, "Hey, tell me this. What time you got?" When I told him five PM he said, "Check it out, Hardwick. Three-hour time difference. I've put in a day's work back here already."

He told me how he went straight from Logan to the Back Bay to hit the Tory Club before it opened.

"There's all sorts of ways to go at this shit. There's the front door, there's the back door. There's the upstairs, there's the downstairs. I got there peon early and knocked on the service entrance at the public alley. This envoy knows how to hook up."

"Gee, Dellroy, should I take notes or just wait until you publish your handbook?"

"You done? Because I have more of your work to do when I finish with your abuse."

"Go, caller."

"I sat for coffee with this old waiter who has been working at that club since before the ivy started climbing the brick. You should see the brother, white starch jacket, tuxedo pants, the works. I asked Mr. James about Bonnie Quinn being there ever, and he said *once* and remembered that night very well."

I started to pace. "Did she do her stand-up?"

"You ready for this? She was a waitress. An hourly they brought in from a catering company."

"That means it wasn't recent."

I stopped pacing and pictured another trail with frost forming.

"Try twenty years ago."

"And he's certain it was Bonnie Quinn?"

"Oh, yes. He said she was very street for a white girl. Living in the projects would account for that. He called her a 'hottie,' and said that girl was undoing her top blouse buttons before she served and hitting on everything in pants."

"Sounds like a match. Did Mr. James remember her because she got famous?"

"He remembers her because she blew a guy in the walk-in freezer."

"Yeah, I guess you wouldn't forget that."

"Especially if the guy in the freezer was you."

"Well, good for Mr. James," I said. "Big questions left, though. Like what was this event and who was there?"

Dellroy was a stud. Between his laptop WiFi and called-in favors from old accounting colleagues, he had already pulled up some annual reports from the Tory Club. It was basically a loose charitable affiliation of wealthy intellectuals who liked to gather over wine and brie once a month and play think tank. He read off the names of the board members. I recognized a handful because they were banking and software titans and one was an author. None connected me to Bonnie Quinn.

"Good research but it doesn't move the needle, pardon the expression. Any chance your new pal Mr. James remembers who else was there that night besides his frozen dessert?"

"No. He said all those evenings blend when you get to be his age. But he checked the guest sign-in books, you know, like at weddings? He found the book but those pages were missing. He says it's the way they store the old books. They get moldy and break apart."

"And what do you think about that, Dellroy?"

"Same thing I did whenever I went in for an audit and some of the ledger was missing. Or the hard drive accidentally got erased."

"Or the cat ate it."

"Oh, hey, now, that happens. You have to know cats."

"If it turns up, fax it to me, OK?"

"Done."

"And Dell? Thanks."

"Not finished yet. I still need to nail down that phone number from the napkin, remember?"

"Well, what the hell you been doing?"

"Not much. Freedom Trail, evening at Pops, high tea at the Four Seasons . . . I'm working a contact at the phone company. She is all over that number. She not only loves the challenge, this girl is wetting her pants over the Hollywood murder mystery."

"Look at you, Dellroy, out of that cubicle, learning to clang the brass."

"You think?"

"About time."

"Kind of fun."

"Maybe you should buy her dinner if she comes through."

"Already part of the package. Let's just say this won't be the only phone number I get."

"Nice to see you have your eye on the ball, man."

"See? There you go again with the compliments. I may just have to reassess my relationship with you, H-man."

"I find it disturbing you think we even have one."

A team of doctors took over Meddy's room for a series of exams so I broke for dinner. There was a Daily Grill nearby and I ate at the counter surfing the two TV sets above the bar. What was it about my day that was all about watching the tube with my head tilted back?

Both TVs mounted above the premium vodkas were tuned to the syndicated entertainment strips and Otis Grove was Big Brothering each. United Entertainment Network was suddenly a corporation with a face. Just as Bill Gates fronted Microsoft, the human brand for UEN was Otis Grove. Since the day he bought the network, it was impossible to escape the avuncular CEO on the covers of the trades, the top glossy newsmags, the financial weeklies, and in the electronic media.

To my left, *Taking Hollywood*'s reporter was filing from opening day of the UEN rollout, the affiliates meetings at the Wiltern Theater. The size of the venue told the story. This was a network in desperate need of a bigger station base.

When video cut to Otis Grove waving from the stage, holding up Elliot Pratt's hand, both of them beaming like they were accepting party nominations, I stopped chewing and tongued a burger wad into my napkin. When Otis took the rostrum alone, the closed captioning on the bar TV scrolled out his standard message: "We begin small like all great movements. Challenged by our goals but bolstered by our mission to rise above the media sewer." [APPLAUSE, CHEERS] "As the leader of your UEN, it is my mission to prove that a TV network can prosper on programming that is smart, entertaining, relevant—and suitable for the entire family." Behind him, Elliot nodded, affirming it all.

During the cutaway to his ovation from member station suits, I looked over to *Rough Cut* on the other TV. *RC* gave short coverage to Mr. Grove's actual speech—too much talking head. Instead, they showed their Tom Cruise-clone reporter bonita fishing in a muscle shirt with Otis from his yacht. They talked for the camera about his humble beginnings working swing shift at a pulp mill: "The same principle applied then as it does now," the CEO said in the closed caption. "You start with the same raw material as anybody and do something good with it. That goes for making paper at minimum wage or making television." Obligatory cut to the nodding reporter in his Prada sunglasses, then back to Otis as text scrolled: "My foreman used to call to me when I was stirring a vat. He'd yell, 'Do good work, Otis.' And I'd call back, 'I will.' And he'd say, 'The job is for pay, but the work is for Him.'"

Video: Otis netting the reporter's thrashing tuna. Video: Otis holding Elliot's hand high onstage at that morning's kickoff.

Me, wondering which hand smelled fishier to God's broadcaster.

Although I didn't talk to Meddy, I thought if my voice seeped through the mystery of the coma and coupled her to the living world what was the harm? In the snippets of time I was allowed in her room, I read aloud from the book Bonnie Quinn had given me, using a gift from the dead to break through to the living.

*A Fable* was thick stuff, still challenging me even after my primer from Professor Quinn. I soldiered on, however, hoping if my voice didn't comfort Meddy she would at least have a good laugh at my struggle. Maybe I would look up and see her propped on an elbow doing just that. No such luck when I glanced up.

Returning to the book, I found my eyes stinging, blurring words as I stammered through them: *". . . something ineradicable still remained, as the unfrocked priest or the repentant murderer, even though unfrocked at the heart and reformed at the heart carries forever about him like a catalyst the indelible effluvium of the old condition . . ."*

I closed my eyes, then the book.

My cell phone hummed. The caller ID flashed LOOT. I slid out to the empty waiting area near the *no cell phones* sign.

"You at the hospital?"

"As we speak."

"How is she?"

"Same."

"I never made this call, OK?"

"Should I hang up?"

"No, you should listen up. Monte Arnett swore out an assault complaint against you for your magic trick with the table cloth at his breakfast meeting yesterday. And Elliot Pratt's attorney is pressing me for a special detail to keep you from further harassing him. They don't want you messing with them during their junket, and, frankly, with every entertainment reporter in the country in town this week on my watch, I don't either."

"They're just pissed I'm flipping over rocks, and they don't like the sunlight. Both of them should have their heads on a pole next to the ice sculpture at their fucking beach party. Except Monte has his so far up Elliot's ass, you'd have to slant drill just to get at it."

"All right, look, I did the courtesy. You want to posture, that's you're deal. Just know this: There's going to be a warrant for your arrest now because of the Monte complaint. I can only do so much, Hardhead. Now, I won't hassle you at the hospital, but if any of our finest see you, they're going to take you in for real."

Over the years, I have been threatened, arrested, detained, searched, and handcuffed countless times, but Loot's call got to me. Even more than a delousing I got once in a Puerto Vallarta jail and all the dignity that implies.

What rattled me was my justice sense. And my diary futility. And my self-recrimination.

I needed to nail that diary so I could nail whoever hurt Meddy.

I just wasn't smart enough this time.

# CHAPTER FORTY-THREE

Visiting hours were over but Nurse Ruiz let me in to see her once more without a mention of the clock or the rules. I returned the courtesy by not overstaying my time. After ten minutes in the scientifically controlled environment, watching Meddy's chest rise and fall, searching her placid features for something to cling to, stumbling through half-remembered prayers from my Baltimore Catechism, I kissed her dry hand and left.

Pilar Ruiz was putting on a sweater and going over charts with another nurse. She excused herself and came to me, holding life itself in her smile.

"You can't go home," I said. "She's not all better yet."

The nurse laughed. "Then tomorrow if I do better, maybe she will, too."

The elevator delivered me to the hospital lobby while I tried to keep Nurse Ruiz's faint glow of comfort from dying too fast. I held my breath through the gauntlet of smokers outside the door, including one poor guy in a wheelchair and jammies holding onto his IV tree with one hand, a menthol filter long with the other.

I squeezed by an orderly who was hunched over his food cart blocking half the exit. Midway down the access ramp, I wondered *what orderly brings a food cart outside?* I kept walking, but gave a back glance. The kid was still stooped over his wagon like he was looking for something but he had pivoted, keeping his back to me.

My radar lit up. The food cart. The kid. The stooping. The Skechers—on an orderly?

He stole a peek over his shoulder, and I made him. Chuck Rank. I hooked back up the ramp toward him, puzzling what the lowest of low-end shooters was doing at that hospital when I answered my own question. My expression must have given me up. Soon as I light-bulbed, the shitwipe dropped his small-world smile and shoved his cart down the ramp.

Behind me, down the incline, an old relic with a back hump and a walker did the math on gravity, velocity, and the food cart.

"Whoa, Nellie," he said.

Chuck was on the move, but I lagged to spare the old man. I caught the cart and stole a sourdough roll to wedge the wheel. I was out of silver bullets to leave behind.

Rank was a dough-bellied slug. Thank God. Even with my adrenalin kick I was too sore to make a heroic sprint. He called "Help!" and "Mugger!" between asthmatic gasps. Pitiful. I took him down on the hospital lawn with a tackle to the back of his knees.

"I'll sue you, Hardwick. Hit me and I'll sue your ass."

He wasn't threatening as much as pleading. Crying. He pulled up all fetal and covered his face with both palms.

I stood up, straddling him. "The camera, Chuck. Give it up."

"I don't have any camera."

"The camera. Now."

"Don't you touch me, or I'll have my lawyer all over your a— acchhh."

I rested the sole of my hiking boot on the side of his head. Just let it sit there, persuading. I wished I had stepped in dog shit first.

"Ow. You can't do th—aaaah."

"Hey, Chuck. Ever see Letterman explode a melon?"

I pressed waffled Vibram on his ear.

"'Kay-okay, you can have the camera. Just don't hurt me, 'kay?"

My answer was a finger snap. He fumbled under his stolen scrubs and handed up a Cybershot that was probably stolen, too.

The LCD screen booted to Meddy in ICU. White noise filled my ears. Surf pounded louder with each shot:

Meddy, full length.

Meddy, waist up.

Meddy, head shot.

Meddy, extreme close-up.

Meddy, bruised.

Meddy, swollen.

Meddy, comatose.

Meddy, at her most vulnerable.

The photography was shit. Drive-by crap. Tilted. In every image I could see the ghost of Chuck's camera reflecting back in the nurse's observation window. But he'd gotten her. The slimeball had tagged her seven times.

The ocean in my head calmed. Scary calm.

"Get up."

I lifted my foot off his head and he cockroached backwards on all fours until he had enough distance from me to stand.

"C'mon, Hardwick, you know the rules. It's no rules."

"Run."

I said it so softly I thought he hadn't heard me.

"It's the job, dude. Like Armantrout said. Fair game's fair game." He added a Canadian "eh?" and, when I didn't unlock, he inched back a step. "I don't like the way you're looking at me, man."

"Run. Now."

His eyes twitched to the camera, then back to me. Urine ran down the crotch of his scrubs. He spun and huffed across the lawn toward the parking lot. I fantasized how a soft-nose from Pinkman's cannon would drop Chuckie like a musk ox, then he was swallowed by the night. He reappeared under the lights of the parking lot and stopped.

Distance gave him courage.

"That's my property, you cock."

"Whatever you say."

I ejected his CF card of Meddy's shots and pocketed it. The Sony had fine heft. It arced beautifully across the night sky when I Hail Mary'd it. Chuck Rank dodged, otherwise I would have beaned him. Instead, his camera exploded on the asphalt.

Letterman would have been proud.

When I turned, a lone woman was standing at the top of the hospital steps watching. The backlight from the lobby put her form in silhouette like a dashboard Virgin Mary.

"What was that about?" Pilar Ruiz asked when I walked over.

"Paparazzo." I held up the memory chip. "He got Meddy."

The security guard arrived at Meddy's door in no time. Nurse Ruiz moved a chair over for him to use and handed him a cup of coffee. She took off her sweater.

"You go home and sleep, Mr. Hardwick. I'm going to stay a while to make sure the head of security is briefed."

Where do people like this come from, I wondered. What is the gene that hatches the angels among us?

"That's, well . . . extraordinarily kind."

"Thank you," was all she said. Simple. Honest. No parades, please. But then she continued. "I used to work across town at a bigger hospital before I decided the commute from the beach was insanity. Anyway, we cared for a lot of celebrities there."

Cedars, I guessed.

"I saw it all. Fake florists making deliveries with cameras, private medical records stolen or photocopied, even a hidden microphone, which I disposed of in a bedpan."

Something lassoed my gut. You have to know I had heard all the stories like these. Worse ones, in fact. Even knew some of the prick bastard sociopaths who pulled those stunts for two hundred bucks. But my disdain had always been in the abstract. I always shook my head and moved on the way you pass highway carnage. Now it had a face and a heart. Maybe I should have given Chuck his beating. Teach him something about going full-Dark Side with the Canuck.

"There is no way a patient in my care is ever going to suffer that violation."

I nodded. "No, I don't think so."

"What I always wonder, though," said the nurse, "is how can a person stoop to that work?"

Sometime in the middle of the night, my cottage door opened and I jumped. "When did you get back?"

Pinkman and his army forty-five.

"Not now, Pink."

I didn't look at him. Just kept my eyes on my monitor. Driven. Clicking. Opening. Deleting. Clicking. Opening. Deleting.

"And where's your car?"

I had beelined home from the hospital, but parked off-road on Willow Glen, down the canyon from my house. Loot's heads-up about the warrant fed my paranoia so, like a fugitive, I hiked the deer path through the ravine to my back door. Lyme disease was not on my list of concerns that night.

"You ought to at least have a light on in here."

"Go back over with the old lady."

"What are you working on?"

Pinkman sidled up behind my desk chair.

"Hardwick? Are you erasing all those pictures?"

I was. Clicking. Opening. Deleting.

"Hey, don't. That's a keeper. Big time celebrity chef coming at you with the cleaver like that? Tell me you have copies."

"Used to."

"What the hell are you doing?"

I stopped, swiveled, and lasered him.

"I need to be alone."

Pinkman would never piss his pants, but he saw the same something in my eyes Chuck Rank had seen hours before and backed away, too. When I heard the door slam I went back to work. Call it a mission. Or a purge. The Meddy ICU shots had gone first. Soon as I hit the chair. I couldn't bear to look at them again, so I formatted the sucker. Gone.

That was the start.

After that, I destroyed everything on my Web storage. Same for the backup media.

Then I rode my hard drive, same as Manu had twenty-four hours prior. Finishing what he started, how weird was that?

But Manu had clicked and opened. I was deleting.

Yeah, I could have just done a gang delete and nuked 'em all. Nuked 'em with extreme prejudice. But the monsters in the darkness demanded sacrifice. One shot at a time. See it. Feel it. Zap it.

Gone.

Feeling the pain of every vulgar intrusion I had made. Cutting at the cancer. Washing away the sins.

Lake Tahoe froze my hand on the mouse. I pulled away.

What?

Galena Forest. Bonnie Quinn. Shannon Quinn. Mother and daughter. On this very monitor the night before, this sequence was my candle against the gloom. Now it didn't feel that way. Not after Chuck Rank. Because I was no better than Chuck. Sure, I had made a choice to embargo these shots but it was still a stalk. Still an invasion. My decision to spike came later. Up to then, I had still been the hunter and they the prey. Their trophy heads were on my monitor in megapixels to prove it.

Losing resolve. Keep going. Delete, you asshole. Out, damned spot. No.

Why was I stuck on this?

My pictures were talking to me, but I couldn't make out the message. So I stopped.

I made a slide show of the Bonnie-Shannon snaps and sat back to watch it sequence by. What story was I telling back then? New thought: What story were these two telling me now through my lens?

I paused on their driveway argument because when Shannon turned her back on her mother, I got good eyes on both. Studying the two women, mother and daughter, they seemed so different. Bonnie, blue-eyed, Irish, and freckled. Short-waisted, square, and tomboy-ish, even with the personally verified implants. Shannon, to whom she had given birth, was her opposite: tawny-skinned and olive smooth. A lithe, statuesque model's body in the making. But they shared one thing, a temper. Shannon's dark eyes seared into her mother.

I stared—What?

Something tore loose and floated out in front of me. A feeling in search of words. A clumsy instinct crying out to become a thought. I let my eyes haze over. Just sat there like that, bathing myself in a fog, getting out of the way, respecting the connections the subconscious makes between experience and input.

Connections, yes. Always look for connections. I quieted all the noise of detail and tried to see what primary glue was holding me to Bonnie Quinn.

I saw anger.

And I saw Faulkner.

I got up and circled the room, walking off nervous energy as new thoughts ponged. A serpentine line of dominoes was lying out, begging to cascade.

But there was a gap. Too wide a gap.

I needed something to connect, but couldn't get there, couldn't bridge it.

Stop stalling. Clean house. Stoke the bonfires, said the archbishop. On with the purge.

Scrolling through my remaining pictures, I serial deleted every image in the Bonnie Quinn file as I came to it. One shot, then another. Gone. Playing Pac Man with my career until there was only one snap remaining. One last image in a lurid portfolio. A split second before pulling the trigger on it I stopped.

Because what I saw stole my breath.

Could it be?

Not conclusive. Zooming in. Too big. Off-center. Settle down. Do it right. Fingers weak and twitchy. Center there. Zoom 25 percent. Hm. Pixilated. Blurry. But promising. Very promising. I had to sit on my excitement because it wanted to get up and dance.

What next? I knew exactly what Meddy would say. *Don't go rogue, call Loot.* Loot would say *don't be an asshole, call Loot.* I picked up my phone. And pocketed it. Grabbed my keys and crept out of my own home to duck Loot.

# CHAPTER FORTY-FOUR

I hit ninety without even noticing. My speed was in the envelope for these roads except I got distracted by the missed call beep on my cell phone and when I looked down to thumb the menus, I nearly rolled my SUV over on a curve. Cliché death. No, thanks. I corrected the skid through a hairy patch of shoulder gravel and, as soon as rubber bit pavement again, I goosed it to ninety-five but with both hands on the wheel.

Cellular service was crap out there and I went from no bars to no service, so forget even retrieving the message. Later, I would learn it was from Dellroy, who had a name to go with that old phone number. If I had gotten his message, it would have spared me a lot of trouble, but that's the way it falls sometimes, and you can't look back or play what-if.

The call I wanted was from Otis Grove. In my voice mail I had told him that I finally had a handle on Bonnie Quinn's diary. I was sort of annoyed not to get a callback. Maybe he was too wrapped up in his press junket. Or maybe he meant it when he told me to beg off the search. Otis Grove was a man of bankable words.

Even though he had promised to pay me anyway, I didn't care. Out of my car in Hellhole Canyon, standing under the desert sun on the very spot where an AWOL diva had put a bullet in the dirt at my feet, I allowed myself the hubris that these things are never about the money for me.

I approached Bonnie Quinn's trailer. My man Vitamin Larry had cleaned it out just days before, but the entry was already a nest of tumbleweeds and spiderwebs. Dry winds had blown a drift of sand on the folding steps and, reading the footprints there, the only recent visitors had been kangaroo rats.

The door was padlocked. For an aloe vera peddler Larry was still a pro cat burglar, leaving things exactly the way he found them. With slightly less finesse, I busted the thing open in three swings of my sledgehammer. The crack of metal on metal echoed up the steep walls of the canyon but I wasn't worried about attracting attention. The place defined the middle of nowhere. If a door gets bashed in the desert, and there's no one there to hear it, and all that.

The interior was hot and stale and dark. Bonnie had left the generator to run dry and there you had it. I flipped the wall switch anyway. Dead, what else. I fumbled toward the sun-bleed at the rim of a window shade and yanked it open.

Shocking hot light filled the camper, bouncing off fresh white walls—the ones I guessed I had waited outside for Bonnie to finish whitewashing the night I surprised her. "You caught me in the middle of something. Ten minutes, tops," she had said. Back to my car for the True Value sack and the spray bottle of Wall-Eze paint remover. The guy in the paint department said as long as it was latex it would wipe off and leave what was underneath. Time to find out.

I sprayed the middle of a wall and did what the directions said. Waited sixty seconds. It was the same wall I had zoomed on my home computer that morning. The same wall I had captured over Bonnie Quinn's shoulder the night I blinded her with my camera flash to get her gun. My digital zoom into that slice of trailer door had captured a fuzzy suggestion of the columns Faulkner had written on his study walls. I grabbed the sponge. Itching to see what she had painted over. Gave the solvent-wet paint a swipe.

> *was so full of arrogance and coldness about my situation. God's truth, it led me to my first attempt to flee the searing agony of it all with narcotics. I wasn't born a user. Getting used made me a user. And I*

Son of a bitch, content was the container. Bonnie Quinn's diary was the goddam trailer itself.

# CHAPTER FORTY-FIVE

The camper was William Faulkner's study writ large. And, just like the walls of Rowan Oak, these walls told a story, but in the same careful, loopy whorls that she had inscribed to me in the book, her key.

I moved to the far left wall and spritzed from the upper left corner near the ceiling halfway down the wall. Waited and wiped. Sure enough, this is where it began under a title and byline in bold Sharpie.

### NOT A FABLE
#### by Bonnie Quinn

It must have been a hundred degrees in there and I swear I shivered. I rubbed the gooseflesh on my forearms and began to read.

> *I don't care how fucked up you think I am. Whoever you are, you'd better read this and pay attention because every word I put down I swear is true and it may be the only thing left of me when I am gone.*
>
> *Oh, yeah. I am straight as I write this because for once I don't want the additives to buffer the God damned pain I cannot bear*

*but need to feel so I can access the truth of my story with all its
ugliness clearly captured.*

*How ugly is it? You tell me when you get there. Everybody says
I am some fucking drama queen. Well, read on and see if you don't
disagree with that and conclude that I have had all the REAL
LIFE DRAMA any one person not trying to win a washer-dryer
on "Queen for a Day" should ever have to endure and still wake
up every morning and decide that, OK, maybe I will do one more
lousy day on this mean little planet.*

I stopped there and wondered if I was not reading a diary at all but
a suicide note. And what would that mean about how she died? My
head started flooding with doubts and self-reproach. A blast of wind
rocked the trailer like a threatening sea and the door slammed with a
shot.

When I propped it open with my sledgehammer, I looked out on
the cove of sand and ocotillo and cactus boxed by high walls of rock
and pictured Bonnie Quinn doing the same thing, clinging to the
solitude she escaped her star's life for. Coming way out here, desperate
to get her story down. The loneliness of the place must have pumped
all her monsters, making them bigger and scarier the way a long night
makes a simple fever feel like Death's advance man.

The trailer rocked again on its crude stack of cinderblocks as the
wind picked up some weeds and swirled them in a mini-tornado
before dying out. A lizard, a nice, fat one with no tail, moved in fits
and starts on one of the canyon rocks then broke through old spiderwebs into a dark crack between two boulders. Break's over. I went
inside, too.

Mindful of her inscription, I became Tom Sawyer on rewind at the
white fence. I sprayed and wiped away the whitewash a section at a
time, reading each segment as the solvent worked its magic on the

next one. Just like Faulkner, she had written in columns, top-to-bottom. But she went ceiling-to-floor, left-to-right on every wall there was to write on. Her text continued into the sleeping compartment and even the tiny head.

When I was done reading, I came out for air. I flopped down on the bottom step and hung my head between my knees. It was like an oven in there, but what made my head throb wasn't the stifling atmosphere in that box but the diary on its walls.

Bonnie Quinn had not written a suicide note, after all. Nor had she written her life story. With unexpected discipline and clarity of detail she had chronicled a lucid record of the shocking and soul damaging events that led her to fear for her life.

I read it and understood more about her than I ever thought I could. And all that I then understood had me fighting my own panic because I was not only certain that Bonnie Quinn had been killed, I knew why.

And I knew who killed her.

My mouth went gauze dry. I had no spit to swallow. My fingertips lost grip when I opened my cell phone and wished for bars. No service.

I needed to drive to Borrego Springs. I needed to call Loot.

But first, I went back inside to photograph the walls. Just as I set the white balance and framed, light flickered on the galley cabinet. A shimmer like sun-glint off a mirror. Or chrome. I moved to the doorway and flattened against the wall behind the doorframe and peeked out.

A white Hummer was idling on the dirt track, blocking the exit to the cove. It just sat there, maybe seventy-five yards away in the opening between the rock walls, purring. Its AC kicked on and the motor voxed up. Otherwise, it sat. There was no movement anywhere else. The wind had died. The air had stilled.

I turtled my head out for a perimeter check. Nobody in sight. I pulled back in and weighed options. That box was a bad place to be stuck. With the Hummer blocking the exit, the only other way out was to billy goat the cliffs. I chose a rear-facing window to kick through when the Humvee door popped and I watched the driver get out.

Manu didn't make a move. He just stood there beside the ride with his hands loose at his sides. Not in a hurry. Not advancing. Like he was a movie poster for a new urban exploitation flick in his fresh basketball shoes, baggy jeans and a 310 Motorsport tee under an unzipped metallic jacket. The bulge on his hip was no cell phone.

Run for it. Why not? The Samoan had a wounded leg, and I could try for high ground before he got close enough to have a say. What I really wanted was that fucker with my bare hands for what he did to Meddy, but I probably wouldn't close half the distance to him before he emptied that gun into me.

Moving window to window, I surveyed the canyon wall for a path with the most cover. I heard the other car door open. Out of the passenger side stepped Monte Arnett. As the two men began to approach, I hustled out of the trailer and put my SUV between us.

Monte called out, "Hey, where are you going, Hardwick? Relax."

I backed slowly toward the hitch end of the trailer, figuring I could at least break for cover behind it while I made my sprint for the rocks. Monte said something to Manu, who unholstered his pistol and fanned out to work a flank.

"Stay there. I just want to talk to you."

Monte was thirty yards away now, close enough to see his forehead sweat. Manu was edging up to my right, holding the Glock-20 at his side, pointed down.

"Oh, sure thing," I said and stopped. "Are you here to make a citizen's arrest for spoiling your breakfast meeting?"

I deked a step toward Monte then cut a sharp left for the front of the camper. I sprinted all of two steps when Manu fired and the sand exploded where I would have been on my third. I froze.

"Much better," said Monte. "Now turn around. That's the idea."

He stopped a few feet away, just out of my reach. Manu got closer but stayed outside my periphery.

"The chauffeur's new, Monte. Did he come with the car as standard equipment, or is he part of the optional gangsta wannabe package?"

Manu's punch came without warning and dropped me to my knees. At first, I thought he had pistol whipped me behind the ear, but when I shook off the meteor shower, I realized he had bare knuckled me with his left. I totally rethought that whole tearing-at-him-with-my-bare-hands scenario right then.

Monte said, "Little advice, Hardwick? Not your day to be a smart-ass."

"Word, bruddah," from Manu. "No old bitch with a sword to do your fighting for you this time."

"That's right, you prefer to fight women who are unarmed."

The left again. Damn, I even saw him start out. But he was boxer quick, and I couldn't duck it. My face hit the dirt, and I tasted blood. Monte told the Samoan to pat me down, and I spat sand while I got frisked. When he was finished, Manu said, "Cool."

A walkie talkie squawked. I rolled over and looked up at Monte keying the mic on his two-way.

"Site secured," was all he said.

When the flat "Ten-four" came back, Monte pocketed his radio. The cove fell into the dead quiet of the desert where the sand pulls everything in. A breeze stirred and rested. The Hummer AC tweaked down. The two men flanked me, relaxed and waiting.

The helicopter burst up over the top of the canyon wall in an aerobatic maneuver I last saw in combat. Its sudden cresting was startling, powerful, and intimidating. The roar of its engine and the pockatta of the blades filled the cove with noise and blowing dust.

We shielded our faces with forearms and palms as the pilot gentled the Bell Jet Ranger a foot off the ground, then rotated on an axis to deliver the passenger door to face us before he touched down. I wanted to say that I knew for whom the Bell Ranger tolled, but I wasn't up for another left.

Otis Grove opened his own door and strode to us at full height under the spinning rotors. He was a big man who knew all the tolerances. He was still walking toward us when he said to Monte, "Does he have to be down in the dirt like that?"

"Seems fitting," Monte said, then regretted it.

Otis snapped, "You stop that." Then the CEO extended his hand and gave me a boost up. He scorched the Mont-ster with a warning look and said, "Let's not debase ourselves any more than necessary, understood?"

Monte mumbled something and looked down.

"You don't look too surprised to see me, Mr. Hardwick."

"Not after what I read, no."

He studied me a beat as he had so often and nodded slowly.

"Then you've answered my question." He looked at the trailer then back at me. "You found the diary."

"That's right."

"In there?"

"Hard to miss."

"Excuse me," he said and disappeared into the trailer.

Manners to a fault. Even when the transaction involves a captive and, likely, gunplay.

"Nice guy," I said to Monte.

As usual, he was too dense to know irony from insult. He side-nodded toward the trailer, and Manu moved away to stand near the door. I could see he was gimping the leg Amanda had slashed, but his face remained an Easter Island statue, too cool to let it show.

Monte said, "You sure gave us a run today. We actually lost you for a minute last night after the hospital when you ditched into the brush behind your house. I almost thought you made us and were trying to shake our asses."

"Is this the nervous small talk before the hired muscle puts me down?"

"Fine. You want to be a dick? Fine."

He turned and watched the trailer door.

"I should have guessed Manu was on your leash the first time he crashed my cottage. You remember that, Monte? The night you forced me to go to Bonnie Quinn's fake wake up at the Sheraton to collect my pay?"

"Hey, I tried to get this job done without you getting hurt. You left the party early. I can only do so much."

"Wanna bet?" I gestured to Manu and the copter and the camper and the whole sorry mess. "Wake up, amigo. Look around. Look where the next stop is for this train. Two people dead. One in a coma. Meddy, for chrissakes."

"I feel just awful about her. I really do."

"Then stop this insanity."

"Ship's sailed there, bucko."

"Jeez, you honestly believe this is done?" I drilled my finger into my chest. "You think I'm the end of it? Listen to me. When this shits the bed who do you think's taking the weight? It's like I said at breakfast, guys like these survive on the backs of guys like us."

"That's when you thought I was covering Elliot's ass. Fuck Elliot. All these years, treating me like the family pet? I ask for a title bump, maybe even a partnership? He laughs. Laughs." Monte windmilled his arm in the air, King Kong sweeping away planes. "Fuck Elliot, man."

He smiled, feeling his own power. "That night? When the shit hit the proverbial and everyone panicked? I stepped up to the plate, man. I threw in with Otis. And when this little service I'm doing for Mr. Grove is wrapped, Elliot Pratt is going to be kissing my rosy red heinie."

Before I could ask what had hit the proverbial, Otis Grove emerged from the trailer. The billionaire CEO and new head of an up-and-coming broadcast empire took three rocky steps down the folding stairs and vomited.

# CHAPTER FORTY-SIX

**W**hen a powerful man shows vulnerability it makes the tribe feel downright awkward. Monte started out toward Otis, then retreated. Manu suddenly became a birdwatcher. I did not turn away. I stared, and as I did, remembered naively telling him Meddy and I had found those letters. Recalled him asking me in the ER if I had read them—even knew they were in a shoebox when I hadn't told him that detail. Then trying to call me off the job because the hidden truth was he had gotten the letters he wanted. Letters with Meddy's blood on them. Yeah, I watched Otis Grove wretch because it might have been the only satisfaction I'd come out of that mess with.

When he was done he waved off Manu's assistance and wandered on unsure legs to me, wiping bile from his mouth with a mono-grammed handkerchief.

"I take it you read the diary," I said.

He closed his eyes, fighting nausea or ignoring me or both. When he finally spoke, he sounded small. Sedated.

"How can a woman of such evil and Godlessness presume to judge morality like that?" His head shot back, and he barked out a single laugh, a flash of the madman. "Morality. Her." He retreated inside himself again, embarrassed for the outburst. "Even you must have been surprised by that, Mr. Hardwick."

What was this about? I wondered. Was he hoping for some sort of exoneration-slash-validation from me? A never-you-mind capped by a jaunty two-finger salute before he had me killed for what I knew? Bullshit.

"Yeah, I was very surprised. I thought I was going to read a smoking gun of all the abuses employed by Elliot Pratt and his posse just to get a show made. Stuff better left quiet about power and a weak woman's weaknesses. Sex, drugs, sex and drugs. Insanity. More drugs. But none of that was in there."

"No."

"What surprised me, Mr. Grove, is that it was all about you."

"Yes, but it's all nonsense, isn't it? Who would ever believe her garbage?"

"You believe it," I said.

As a hard coldness shaped his face, I wondered if I had just blown the out he was looking for to spare my life. I doubt it. Regardless of my spin, I was then, and would always be, a loose end. The thing I knew about Otis Grove is that he didn't abide loose ends, just as the thing he knew about me was that I could never just walk away and leave this alone.

"Don't presume to tell me what I believe. My position is she made it up."

"A little DNA test could settle that score."

"Oh, there won't be any DNA tests."

"No, I guess not. Wouldn't help your standing on the family values stage if it was confirmed that you fathered Bonnie Quinn's daughter out of wedlock."

"The fornicator seduced me."

I pointed to the trailer. "According to her diary, you raped her."

"And you believe the whore."

"She makes it sound pretty convincing. Girl from the projects waiting tables at the Tory Club twenty years ago, some millionaire gives her his phone number, invites her to dinner the next night—"

"It was weakness. A businessman's indiscretion. I was on an extended trip away from home. Who knew it would become more?"

"Bonnie Quinn sure didn't. You held a broken wine glass to her throat in your hotel room when she wouldn't give it up. Want to read along?"

Otis Grove backhanded my face. It was the glancing slap of the non-fighter, so I took it. Manu raised up his gun in case I didn't.

"I'm sorry, but this is all very raw for me. You don't know what a constant drain this has been over the years. When her bastard was born, I made a substantial settlement to the whore in exchange for her discretion." Hush money, I resisted saying. "In addition to her settlement, there was a large trust fund for the, ah, girl. But the constant threat of exposure, that was the overwhelming burden."

"Bonnie Quinn threatened you? Blackmail?"

"Well, no. It's not so simple. The mere existence of the girl and the volatility of the whore were toxic elements, unexploded bombs."

"The dirty little secret with a mouth of its own."

"Mouths."

"You've lost me."

"The girl, too."

"Your daughter?"

"The bastard, yes."

Otis used the word so casually it lost charge. To him it was just a noun. A way to make the personal impersonal.

"One of the settlement terms was that the girl should never know about me. The harlot broke the promise a few years ago, I'm sure during one of her drug binges."

Images QuickTimed in my head: my shots of a latte skinned beauty on an emotional, explosive visit to her mom at Lake Tahoe.

"The girl came straight to me when she found out."

"She wanted to meet her father?"

"She wanted money. I ended up giving her some. Then some more after that. It was all going to alcohol and drugs, I checked. The apple doesn't fall far from the tree."

"I guess her death was sort of a solution to a problem, right?"

"I had absolutely nothing to do with that girl's drowning. When she drove off that ferry she was already half dead from Vicodin and vodka. Trust me, I got a copy of the coroner's report. It could have been an accident. It could have been suicide. But I had absolutely no part."

"Must be nice to have such a clear conscience."

"Do you honestly believe I have a clear conscience, Mr. Hardwick?"

I looked at him. One of the most powerful men in the country, broken, vulnerable, aging before my eyes. So steeped in his own anguish he would pour himself out to me in some hope of assuaging the new guilt he was about to bear when I, too, ceased to be a problem.

"I am a sinner," he said. "That night in Boston twenty years ago I sinned against God, my dear wife, my children and myself. I prayed for forgiveness, told myself to be humble, rendered restitution, and vowed to avoid the occasion of such sin again. But I committed an even greater sin last month, Mr. Hardwick, and for that I have trumped Satan's power from the former trespass.

"My sin is the sin of pride. My pride weakened me when I knew I should resist buying the broadcast network. My pride made me feel invincible. It told me not to worry about the whore. I would banish her show. I would pay her money to go away rich and I would proceed with my mission."

"So. How did all that work out?" I asked.

"Hey," said Monte, "Show some fucking respect."

Otis Grove held up a staying palm. Like he was blessing the fleet.

"It's all right, Monte, it's all right." Then, he turned back to me. "Your smart mouth would offend me if it weren't so true. My pride blinded me and brought fatal consequences."

"You killed Bonnie Quinn, then."

Monte chimed in again. "You don't have to answer his questions, Mr. Grove."

"I know that. But Mr. Hardwick has worked rather hard to figure all this out." And then, "You almost got it right, too, except you were chasing Elliot. Understandable, but incorrect."

"You expect me to believe Elliot Pratt is clean?"

"Elliot Pratt looks the other way. It's a remarkable talent that has kept him free of the uglier aspects of all this. But I don't know if any of us standing here is clean. Including you."

"Here's where we differ. I didn't murder Bonnie Quinn."

"Nor did I."

"Not personally, maybe."

I directed my gaze to Monte as a suggestion. Monte shook no. Next, I looked across the dirt at Manu, who was starting to show signs of overheating inside all that urbanwear.

"I vote for bachelor number three."

"Then you'd be wrong," said Otis. "That man didn't come on the scene until after, when some damage control was necessary."

"When word got out she left a diary?"

"And you became so persistent."

"Flattered. Who killed her?"

"I'll tell you what happened, and Monte's going to back me up. Come here, son." As Monte swaggered into our little circle, Otis continued.

"While you all were at the wrap party, Elliot was in Santa Barbara with me as I told you, pitching me to save the show with Kimberly Duggan instead of Bonnie Quinn." He nodded to Monte, who cleared his throat.

"OK, so down at the studio, she was in her dressing room wiping the cake icing off her tits—"

"Monte," said Otis.

"Sorry. Anyway, Rhonda, her dumb-fuck manager, lets it slip that this is her last show. Who knows why? Kimberly Duggan was her client, too, and maybe after all these years putting up with the cooz she wanted to be the one to slip the knife in, who knows her agenda. Anyway, Bonnie fucking freaks. Chases me in her car, cuts me off at the gate like a fucking carjacker, ranting about how she's going to blow the fucking lid off everything and demands to see Otis Grove, or else. I had no clue what she was freaking about but I called Mr. Grove."

"And I told Monte to use one of the helicopters to bring her to Santa Barbara to see if I could calm things down."

"Offer her money," I said.

"Right."

"So how can Elliot not be involved if she met you two up there?"

"Elliot was already on his way back to Malibu. In fact, I specifically instructed Monte not to tell him about any of this."

Monte stood a little taller.

"No wonder you wanted this diary before Elliot. He doesn't know, does he?"

"Elliot is still not aware of my, ah, relationship with that harlot. If it came to pass that I needed him to know, fine. Otherwise, why open the circle?"

"Only so many body bags, right?"

"That put me in charge," said Monte. "But the bitch refuses to get in the chopper without Dr. Pizzy along. She pulled that before. Pizzy was sort of her security blanket. So the doc belts in with us for Santa Barbara."

"We met on my yacht," said Grove, moving Monte's heroic narrative along. "The situation went from bad to worse."

"You should have seen her, Hardwick. Take the most over-the-top freak-out and you're not even close."

"She called me every name imaginable, then ran on deck and climbed up in the rigging like some crazy monkey, shouting across the harbor that I raped her and killed her daughter and was trying to kill her next." He blinked as if still seeing it, then came back. "When we coaxed her down, she slipped and tumbled onto the deck."

The autopsy. Traces of varnish. They thought she was a sniffer. And that explained the new surface the deckhand was laying down.

"Then she grabbed me. She spit in my face and beat my chest, saying she was not going to be silent anymore."

"She definitely threatened him." Monte, with a firm nod. "And she got some licks in, too. I put a bear hug on her to restrain her. But she kept yelling. Saying she was calling the FCC. Going public with the media."

"The woman was wildly out of control."

"Sounds to me like the woman knew exactly what she was doing."

I had to say it. What the hell.

"I feared for her own safety," said the billionaire, steeped in rationale. "I asked Dr. Pizzarelli if he could do anything. You know, give her something to sedate her."

A silence hung there. Nobody needed to explain to me what happened next and nobody really wanted to.

"It was an accident," said the thin voice that choked out of Otis Grove.

"Pizzy fucked up." Leave it to Monte to put a fine point on it. "He was old. Half blind. You see the Coke bottles he wore? See him shake?"

Monte quaked his arms before him like a cartoon.

"She died right there. I didn't know what to do."

I raised a schoolboy hand.

"You mean like call the police?"

"I suggested that."

"And I said no fucking way. Told Mr. Grove this was an accidental OD that was going to happen somewhere else."

"And everyone would have lived happily ever after, except I smelled bullshit."

"Anywhere along the timeline I can see any number of mistakes," said Grove.

He had moved off his vulnerability onto the more familiar turf of executive decision. Bad news for me.

"But the single greatest misjudgment can be traced to Elliot Pratt for hiring you to find that woman in the first place. He didn't take proper measure of you. The very character aspect that drove you to succeed at that task made you a natural liability in letting go afterward."

And then, Otis Grove did the most chilling thing he could. He looked at his watch.

"I'm late for my own press party."

Manu crossed over from his post at the camper door. The helicopter jets ascended to a whine. Blades cranked to a blur.

"How do you know I didn't photograph the inside of that trailer? Upload it from my cell phone?" He wasn't buying, but this was my shot. "How do you know there's not another copy floating around somewhere else?"

"I have enough lawyers, Mr. Hardwick, to know that filth would never stand up in court."

"What about the public? What about the FCC?"

Sand and wind kicked from the chopper. He had to shout to Manu.

"You know what to do."

Monte insinuated himself into the grouping and said, "Don't worry. I'm on it."

Otis gave him a placating smile, then fixed himself back on the Samoan.

"And when you're done, burn the trash."

Then he crossed to his helicopter without bothering to look back.

# CHAPTER FORTY-SEVEN

**M**anu held his gun on me while Monte loaded cans of gasoline into Bonnie Quinn's trailer. Monte Arnett was not accustomed to doing his own lifting but the Samoan refused to give up his gun for the chore so the Mont-ster huffed the red jugs from the Hummer.

Watching him load those canisters took me back to childhood when we would get to our vacation cabin at Arrowhead and find our beds filled with rice. While we were away, field mice would get into the pantry and carry it upstairs a grain at a time where they would hide it, a secret treasure between our sheets. But my dad put out poison. And know what? The mice did the same thing with those blue pellets. Carried them upstairs to bed. They didn't know the difference between food and what would kill them. That's sort of how I felt after my fool's errand to hand over to Otis Grove the smoking gun, his exoneration.

"Inside, Hardwick."

Gas fumes drifted out the door. Monte was at the bottom of the steps, stuffing a rag down the neck of one of the smaller jugs. I didn't budge.

"We can load you in dead."

Manu smiled and took off his sunglasses.

Every minute was another minute, so I climbed the three steps slowly. Outside the door, I paused and took in the sun, the sky, the canyon, wishing I could honestly feel that it was a far, far better thing.

"Hey, Kahuna. You bring a lighter?"

The Samoan sucked his teeth. Monte shook his head and mounted the steps, fishing a Bic out of his pocket. He backed me into the doorway and said, "Sorry about this. Really."

"Is that what you said to the old man?"

Stalling. Rapid scan of the camper. Looking for anything to use as a weapon. Or a way out.

"Dr. Pizzy took the deal for the sake of his family. He died at peace. The old guy was relieved."

"Touching. You should take your act to nursing homes. Decrease the surplus popu—"

Manu fired and a wad of Monte's shoulder hit the doorframe. He dropped the gas can on his foot. We both yelled. I was astonished not to be hit.

Monte's arm hung limp and a continent of blood grew around the hole in his shirt. He hooked his good arm around my neck for support and called out, "The fuck you doing? You're not supposed to shoot me."

Manu, too calm, said, "The fuck I'm not."

I jerked Monte down not out of any love for him but in a reflex to preserve a life. We hit the floor as the next shot exploded the hanging lamp right behind where he had been standing.

Forget the slow motion stories you hear. Everything happened fast. The trailer rocked from Manu's weight on the steps. I grabbed the nearest gas jug and lobbed it, blind, out the door. A shot fired as I heard the metal can hit him. I stayed low and stretched over Monte to pull the door closed. To reach the handle, I had to expose myself in the doorway. Nano-flash of Manu. Flat on his back, gas can beside him, struggling upright.

My sledgehammer still wedged the door open. Damn. I kicked it outside and yanked the handle in. But the door hit Monte's ankle and bounced open. I reached for the handle again. Manu was on his knees, gun coming up.

"Your foot, your fucking foot."

Monte was out or dead, I couldn't tell. He was slumped on his side and his head rested in a pool of blood on the linoleum. I hauled in his leg with one hand, pulled the door with the other, threw the inside bolt, and flung myself down against the side wall.

Four bullets punctured the door in a tight pattern. They all missed me, but Monte whimpered and new blood streamed down his scalp across his face.

I scoped the window above the dinette. One kick and make a scramble out the back. Manu fired another shot right through the wall, just above the floor. Then another, closer to me. I leaped up on the galley stove and flattened there. Sunlight lasered through the bullet holes below me as he patiently stitched the trailer front to back in even cadence.

A pause. A click. Was it a dry fire? Maybe it was a jam. Or a reload. How many rounds did a Glock-20 take? Fourteen? Fifteen?

I jumped down. Snatched Monte's Bic off the floor. Torched the rag from the gallon jug. Threw the bolt. Kicked the door. Met Manu's eyes. Looking up from loading a new clip.

I threw so hard I slipped on Monte's blood and went down. The Samoan tried to deflect the can but when it hit his forearm the flaming wick popped out and landed on his jacket followed by a slosh of gasoline.

Whoomph. Tiki torch.

He dropped and rolled on the flames. I sprinted at him and kicked at the gun. Even on fire, his grip held. He kicked at me while he rolled. I circled outside his reach then charged in to kick him again. The Glock flew from his hand and clattered into the shadows of the crawl space underneath the trailer.

I choked. Gasoline and smoke from Manu's jacket closed my throat. I stepped upwind and bent at the waist, heaving for air. When my smoke-stung eyes cleared, Manu was on his feet. He flung his smoldering jacket at me and lunged. I backpedaled, but his shoulder chucked my hip, and we both went down.

When he pulled himself to all fours I punched his thigh. He screamed and fell, clutching both hands to the spot where Amanda had slashed him with her saber. I sprang up and kicked the spot again. His covering hand took the force of the blow, but he yelled again so I kicked again. He reached for my foot and missed. My next kick struck hard. Blood darkened the thigh of his jeans.

But he was a born fighter, one of those men whose pain jump-starts hidden reserves. Before I could land another blow, he vaulted up and threw a shoulder block that carried me backward across desert real estate. I walloped my back into the trailer hard enough to rock it on its cinderblock supports.

Manu wasn't the only one with reserves, though. I fought for my life, true. But I also fought the monster who put Meddy in a coma. When he rose up to face me, I butted my forehead into his nose and heard it crunch. I grabbed his shoulders and hammered my knee into his wounded thigh again and again, and when he bent over in pain, I shot my other knee into his broken nose. He dropped down but his iron hands sunk into my shirtfront, and he threw me over in some sort of martial arts move that sent me grabbing sky, upside-down. I thumped down and moaned.

Manu stayed on the ground. He stretched to his full length sideways and logrolled underneath the trailer. He was going for the gun.

I made a headfirst dive and got a hand on his ankle. He kicked free.

I lurched again for a pant leg, shoelaces, anything, but he scrambled into the shadows in a desperate move on all fours.

Suicide to chase him. He was mere feet from the loaded Glock. By the time I caught him, it would be in his hands. Running away across an acre of open desert offered the same shitty odds. I threw myself at the trailer steps, clawing at sand and rock on hands and knees. The Samoan made a lunge, face in the dirt, and got a hand on the pistol. But my move put his feet to me. He had to curl around to get his shot.

I gripped the sledgehammer. He saw me heft it and scoffed. As he bucked around to take aim, I flung my hammer, sidearmed, with all the anger, vengeance, and goddam hope I could bring.

It landed sweet. The steel head smacked into the single tower of cinderblocks holding up the front end of the trailer. The impact shot the middle block clean out of the stack.

Manu saw what I had done but was helpless. He barely had time to lock disbelieving eyes with me and raise his hands above him in a reflexive act of futility as Bonnie Quinn's two-and-a-half-ton diary crashed down on him.

# CHAPTER FORTY-EIGHT

I leaned on the horn and never let up. The tunnel at the end of Interstate 10 spit me out on the incline leading down to Pacific Coast Highway hauling ass, hoping the damn horn would keep me from picking up a surfer or an au pair on my front grille.

Santa Monica was in the gloaming. Across the bay, the magic-hour tones bathing Malibu and Pacific Palisades bled out to purple-gray. Time to juice the high beams and add the emergency flashers to the mix. I must have been quite the spectacle of sound and light when I blasted through the divider of plastic tubes that is supposed to keep jackasses like me from cutting across the Coast Highway.

The big parking lot north of Santa Monica Pier was coned-off, too. Closed for a private function, according to the sign. Those cones flattened like beer cans as I sped past a cluster of uninvited paparazzi and breasted the driveway at boulevard speed. I clipped the side mirror off one of the unlucky limos parked in the waiting line. I mumbled an insincere apology and floored it toward the beach.

Valet attendants fled ahead of me. A pair of security guards lurched forward into my headlights then retreated. I had done exactly what I wanted and caught them all flatfooted.

Ahead near the beach, where Cirque du Soleil usually pitched its tent, gas torches and Chinese lanterns flickered through a picket line of potted cypress. Party guests milled, photo flashes strobed, and the hot spot from a minicam light shone under the huge UEN Rollout Week banner. I gunned it.

My ancient disdain for the Hummer fell away when I mowed a path through the cypress barrier and those potted trees scattered like bowling pins. Ahead of me, actors and reporters at the UEN press party scattered across the pavement onto the beach, scampering for their lives amid dropped cocktails and flying satay. I stood on the brake and pounded the horn in bursts with the heel of my hand. My tires slid on a veneer of sand. The Hummer fishtailed, but I wrestled enough control not to kill anybody as I bounded off the asphalt and beached myself inches from broadsiding the UEN satellite uplink truck. The video technician inside looked out at me with wide eyes and a mouth that formed a perfect O.

When I popped the door and my feet hit sand, dazed celebrities and entertainment press gingerly made *Dawn of the Dead* appearances from behind ice sculptures and buffet tables. They approached slowly, with not unreasonable wariness. A few of the reporters said my name to each other, but I was already past them, trudging up the beach to where the brightest light was shining.

A *Close Encounters* glow spilled out of a three-sided interview set, which was constructed on a riser and backdropped by the circulating neon of the pier's fun zone. Entertainment reporters, cued up for their five-minute allotments on the set, made a hole when I approached. I'd like to think it was respect, but my wild look and scorched bloody clothing might have had something to do with it. They parted to reveal a mosaic of plasma-screens clustered together proclaiming, *UEN: Quality at Last.* Underneath the monitors, Otis Grove looked up at me over the Interviewer-Babe's shoulder as if one of his midnight ghosts had broken free of his sleep to make a cocktail hour service call.

He rose unsteadily from his director's chair and stared at me through a haze of disbelief. He opened his mouth but it quivered closed, speechless. He looked at the director, cleared his throat sharply, and told her, "Cut."

Footsteps and walkie talkie chatter behind me. I didn't turn. I kept focus on my favorite CEO. Someone kicked my feet apart while someone else pushed my chest down on the utility table and zip-corded my wrists behind my back. After the pat down they stood me up. I didn't resist. I didn't have to. I had already accomplished what I went there to do.

I knew it from the growing commotion down the beach. Knew it as the flashes strobed with more frequency near the Hummer. Knew it from the urgent calls of reporters to their crews. Knew it from the silhouettes of camera operators huffing across sand to meet them.

But mostly, I knew it from the look on Otis Grove's face as he peered over my shoulder and down the beach at the entertainment press corps gathering around the white Hummer that crashed his party and, behind it, in tow, Bonnie Quinn's trailer.

His day got worse. Elliot Pratt strode up spitting Grove's name like a curse. As he entered the pool of light rimming the interview set, Elliot's cheeks were mottled crimson. "What the hell is this I hear about sending your goon to shoot Monte and Hardwick?"

Otis Grove vapor locked. He side-glanced all the reporters—all the witnesses. "That's crazy talk. Come on. Let's go someplace private."

He tried to put an arm on him to steer him away. Elliot swatted it aside hard enough to draw gasps and make his Frampton Comes Alive curls slinky up and down. "Answer my question. You tried to kill them?"

"Sounds to me like this tabloid fella's been filling your ear. You going to take his word on anything?"

"I haven't talked to Mr. Pratt," I said.

"Well, I don't know who else could have told you such nonsense."

"I did."

Heads turned. A woman muttered an *ohmygod*. Otis Grove clutched the camera ped for support as Monte Arnett limped through the crowd and into the light. His arm was slung in my belt and his head was wrapped in a turban of blood-caked truck stop gauze. Two security guards propped him up.

"What was I, Otis? One more annoying witness?"

The CEO turned to go, just wanted out, but the camera and the lights and the reporters and crews were in his way.

"I'm telling it all, Otis. Bonnie Quinn, Dr. Pizzy—"

"Shut up, you idiot."

"—Everything."

"I suggest you hold your tongue until we can talk privately. For your own sake."

"Hell, you don't think they'd give me immunity? And if they don't, I don't care. I'm coming after your ass."

Monte's knees buckled and the Interviewer-Babe raced her chair over in time for him to sit.

"You're fucking toast, Otis," Monte slurred with his chin on his chest.

The man was Mont-ster tough. Even got pissed at my offer to drop him at the ER on the way. All he wanted to do was blow this open with me at the party. How could I say no?

Elliot was quaking with rage. He pointed a finger at Otis.

"You killed Bonnie?"

"No."

"And Dr. Pizzy?"

"Elliot, use your head."

"Hate to pile on," I said, "but who do you think called out the hired goon when I told him Meddy and I found a box of Bonnie's letters?"

"Meddy, too?"

I still don't know whether Elliot was truly piecing things together or putting on a public face of outrage to cover his weeks of denial, but exit polling favors the latter. Elliot Pratt was an instinctive survivor, and my gut said he was exploiting his forum, creating distance.

"What kind of monster are you?"

Yep, Elliot. Found your sound bite.

Otis's own survival instincts were a little tardy, but finally went to work.

"I have nothing to say about any of this."

"Looks like you don't have to," I said, then pointed to where the press swarmed the trailer in the sand—press Otis himself had invited.

Photo strobes and minicam spots radiated out the camper windows and turned the bullet holes into a constellation. Otis stared at that scene a long time, it seemed to me. Perhaps an eternity for him. When he turned back to me, his eyes were moist and his voice came from far away.

"What have you done?"

"My job. You hired me to deliver Bonnie Quinn's diary. Here it is." Then I pointed to the heavens and said, "Remember, Otis, the job is for pay, but the work is for Him."

Otis Grove sagged into his chair and put his face down in his hands. It was the last I saw of him as sirens approached and security led me away.

# CHAPTER FORTY-NINE

My boat was tied off to a snag on the downriver tip of Turtle Island. It was a nasty log, a half-submerged devil's claw waiting to rip gunwales in the night. My afternoon shirt was drying on one of the branches and was still as wet as when I had hung it there and put on the fresh one, which I had also sweat through.

August in Missouri. The most oppressive humidity I had experienced since Khe Sanh, when I swore I was done with the tropics for good. Thunderhead castles built up to the west, wrapping Hannibal in champagne cotton candy. I planted my tripod in the muck, framed for the panorama I wanted, and waited for late summer's light to ratchet down to sunset while I blasted *My Old School* on my headset.

I had been working the banks and sandbars upriver for almost a week, shooting barge traffic and wildlife and sunrises that would make you cry. I wouldn't say that I had found the soul of my book. Not yet. Just a slew of promising images that my gut told me would lead somewhere good if I stayed out of my own way and didn't push it.

If I could stand the mosquitoes and didn't tear my skin off to escape the humidity, I might do all right.

I ditched the Steely Dan and listened to the evening grow. A nature stakeout this time. In the slow descent into night, I reflected on LA and how easy it had been to pack a duffel and leave. How I had resisted the brief tug I felt to visit the grave. Rituals for the famous dead among us run the gamut from state funerals to quiet ceremonies to having their ashes shot out of a cannon like Dr. Hunter S. Thompson. All Bonnie Quinn got was pissed on by an angry costar before the graveside brawl. For me, it would have been mawkish to stand there at that headstone pretending respect. Better to acknowledge her tragic journey and whatever vindication was due after a flame-out life by moving on with my own.

The available light neared perfect. And no jet contrails to spoil the fun like the day before. I rechecked the viewfinder. Splendid. The sky mirrored itself on water so taut it seemed I could dance from there to the darkening banks of Riverview Park. Seconds passed. Oranges joined pinks and gradually scarlet and plum tinted the far trees.

But just as I clicked my first picture, something broke the surface of the water. Ripples fractured the shiny dance floor into granita. The rounded shape bobbed toward me. Meddy's head swam closer and I got a pang from my old ghost-dreams of the river presenting its claimed souls.

This was no dream, though, and I squeezed off another shot. As she found shallower water, she rolled over to backstroke, and her wet face pointed heavenward and all the light the sunset offered put her brow, her nose, her lips, and her breasts aglow, and, as I shuttered the best shot of the hundreds I had taken that week, I thought once again of Mr. Twain, who said that the difference between a miracle and a fact is exactly the difference between a mermaid and a seal.

The miracle of my life swam out of frame, grabbed the side of the boat, and hoisted herself on deck. Meddy sat on the edge and breathed heavily.

"Aw, hell. Did I spoil your shot?"

"Nope. Just all the ones to come after."

"Flattery will get you laid, you know."

I slapped my forehead.

"Flattery—All this time I thought it was self-involvement. You're in deep trouble now, gorgeous."

She laughed and kicked a footful of Mississippi at me.

Later, when I had squared away the ashes from the barbecue and cleaned the galley after our steaks, I brought a bottle of Cakebread from the cooler and two glasses to the bow. Meddy had her back to me and stared into the night.

"You feeling OK?"

"Sure. Great."

"You did a lot today. You sure you shouldn't lay off tomorrow?"

"Hardwick, the doctors told me I'm not going to break. If you really want to know, it feels good to push it. I can feel my old strength coming back."

"I'll consider myself warned."

We toasted and sipped. Music drifted across the water. Not the banjos or ragtime piano of another era but hip-hop as two boys raced by in a Boston Whaler with fishing poles and illegal beer.

"Huck and Tom, the Sequel," I said.

We rocked in stillness until she turned abruptly.

"I'm scared about what's next."

"Then don't rush a decision. Didn't your agent say all the offers would wait till you were back? Take your time. Hell, maybe Elliot Pratt will even be out of Chapter 11 by the time you're ready."

"I'm not stressing over which network, I'm worried this can't last. I'm worried you're only doing this because you thought I was going to die and not because it's what you really want." She paused, then said, "And I'm worried you aren't really done with . . . you know, all that."

"We'll have to find out, then, won't we?"

"Hardwick."

I reminded her of the Hotel Bel Air during her recuperation. Of how we stumbled on Tim Dash poolside very much with the wife of his director. And how I walked on, pretending not to notice. And how easy it was to do that now that I had made my choice.

"And how crazy it drove him to be ignored?" Meddy added.

"There are benefits, you see?"

"I'm serious. When you say you're done, I don't doubt you think you mean it."

"You think it's in the blood."

She swayed side to side and said, "Well . . ."

I watched a stick float by. It suddenly accelerated into the current and got carried away into the channel.

"I'm a little worried, too," I said, staying focused on the water, but feeling her eyes on me. The stick disappeared into the darkness, and I said, "I'm thinking about your own pull. What it must be like, going from riding in cramped little vans with dishes on their roofs to standing on the set of your very own show."

"That show never happened."

"That's even more seductive, coming so close."

"What are you implying?"

"That the reporter job you are made for might not be enough anymore." I turned to face her. "Meds, I saw how you bought in."

She studied me so long that I honestly wondered if she was going to say *Screw it,* and start swimming for St. Louis right there. But then she cradled my face in her palms and drew me to her and we kissed deeply. The rumble made us part. Twenty miles distant, on the far side of Hannibal, Missouri, lightning forked, brightening the sky as it had for us once on a river half a world away.

As we had then, we lay down on the deck, clinging fast to each other amid the booms and flashes, invisible to our fears, feeling only each other and the river flowing beneath us.